I0599004

WORMHOLES
A NOVEL

WORMHOLES

A NOVEL

Dennis Meredith

Glyphus

Copyrighted Material

Wormholes: A Novel

Copyright © 2013 by Dennis Meredith. All Rights Reserved.

No part of this publication may be reproduced, stored in a retrieval system or transmitted, in any form or by any means—electronic, mechanical, photocopying, recording or otherwise—without prior written permission from the publisher, except for the inclusion of brief quotations in a review.

The characters and events portrayed in this book are fictitious. Any resemblance to people living or dead is strictly coincidental and not intended by the author.

For information about this title or to order other books and/or electronic media, contact the publisher:

Glyphus, L.L.C.

4159 Summit Rd., Purlear, NC 28665

www.glyphus.com

editor@glyphus.com

Library of Congress Control Number: 2012950608

ISBN: 978-1-939118-00-4

Printed in the United States of America

Cover and Interior design: 1106 Design

To Ryan

CHAPTER I

"Ed? *Ed!*" The husband opened his eyes and squinted up at his wife. "We're going to the store," she announced. She stood over him with the sun at her back, her curly hair highlighted like a frizzy halo, so he couldn't fathom the expression on her shadowed face. The commanding edge in her voice, however, told him what was coming next. "Now you remember the barbecue's tomorrow, so if you don't mow the lawn today it won't get done in time for all the grass to dry—"

"Okay, sweetie."

"—and I don't want everybody tramping wet grass through the house."

"Absolutely, dear." He strove to prove his commitment by making a dramatic effort to rise from the chaise, achieving a sitting position on its side. The cool breeze swirling beneath the trees felt good on his face. He looked beyond her out into the large sunny lawn where it was hot. The lawnmower still sat there in grass-stained patience where he had trundled it earlier that morning.

"Okay, then," she said with the curt exasperation of a woman at the top of her daily energy curve, whose husband was indolently wallowing around at the bottom of his.

A soft, small form barreled lovingly into him, wrapping its arms around his neck, and he laughed and fell back onto the chaise. The little girl sat up imperiously on his chest, her sweet, big dark eyes staring seriously into his.

"Daddy, you got to mow the lawn. Mommy says."

He laughed again and looked up at his wife, still silhouetted against the sun.

"*My* daughter," she declared with mock haughtiness. He knew her shadowed face showed a smile of womanly triumph at their daughter's sassiness. She gathered the giggling girl into her arms, kissing her loudly on the neck and padded off through the tall grass to corral her older brother from the yard next door.

Ed laid there in lizardlike repose, hearing the garage door open with a whine. There was a pause. He tensed slightly. The car started and backed out, the door rattled shut, and the sound of the car faded. Home free! After a few vague plans wafted through his heat-soaked brain, one cool image crystallized itself. A beer.

He heaved himself to a sitting position, felt around in the grass with one foot to find his comfortably ratty deck shoes, slipped his feet in and stood, letting a full-fledged plan slowly accrete around the concept of a beer, like a pearl around a grain of sand. It was near noon. Hottest part of the day. She'd be back in an hour, maybe two. The sun would have begun to go down beyond the tall oaks in the Matthews' back yard. He would have plenty of time for a leisurely beer or three. Then maybe a nap.

He went into the quiet house, pulled a cold can of Coors from the refrigerator and relished the fizzy whoosh when he opened it. He took a healthy sip of the cold, malty liquid to help him face the return trip. He shuffled back outside and cagily estimated where the shade of his own more modest stand of trees would be in an hour. He moved the chaise to ensure that he would be safely situated in shade the entire period of her absence. He kicked off his shoes and curled his toes in the lush grass, congratulating himself for having fertilized it well that spring. Finally, he eased himself back down onto the creaking chaise, scratched an itch that he couldn't scratch in polite company, felt around on the grass beside him for the *Sports Illustrated* and placed it on his chest, closing his eyes.

Enough activity for a while. He lay there trying for perfect, blissful immobility, save for an occasional smooth move of his arm, raising the beer to his lips.

Zen, he thought as the cold liquid tingled his mouth and washed down his throat. Perfect Coors Zen. He blanked his mind. He would send all the bad stuff into Coors Zenland. He sent away into Zenland that damned memo from his boss about excess inventory. Away went the screw-up that Shipping made Friday on the Baker order. Away went the business trip to St. Louis next week. His mind thus cleared, he made significant progress on the beer and hazily considered getting another. But the breeze played over his body and he began to doze.

In his dim torpor, at first he thought the annoying sound was the guy down the street starting up that damned chainsaw. The noise was kind of a chainsaw sound, but deeper, with more . . . rumbling. He sleepily lifted his head as the sound grew louder and cocked his ears one way then the other, the better to pinpoint the direction. The muffled sound originated toward the yard. A lawnmower? Nope, his Lawn Boy stood silent.

With a gut-wrenching roar, the sound erupted into the open, sending him leaping with a loud, startled curse off the chaise. He glimpsed a movement out of the corner of his eye, turning to see one of the big trees in the Matthews' yard—one of the *really* big ones—jerk over violently at an angle. Its massive branches quivered as if being shaken by an unseen giant hand, and it slumped several feet into the ground. The grinding, sucking noise rose to a deafening level, like being thrust inside a jet engine.

Unthinkingly curious, he took a few steps toward the massive, shuddering tree—the worst mistake of his life. The tree sucked down into the earth like a celery stalk chewed away into an unseen hungry mouth. For an instant, the vibrating tips of the topmost branches slashed back and forth before disappearing. The earth around the vanished tree began to collapse away, opening a great spreading maw of a crack. The smooth green fabric of the lawn slumped and tore, falling away in tattered chunks. The widening gorge revealed the hidden earth beneath, like a deep slash in the skin exposes raw flesh. The gaping hole ripped its way up to the lawnmower sitting in the grass like innocent prey, and the lawnmower too was sucked away. The devouring of the machine produced a brief shriek of tearing metal above the subterranean roar.

With a chest-clutching horror he had never known, he realized that the rift was eating its way toward *him* at the speed of a running man, so he became one. He turned and hurdled the chaise, sprinting barefoot toward his house and, he hoped, safety. He leaped onto the back deck and glanced over his shoulder to see the gorge yawning into a great dark malignant cavity, widening to devour his yard and part of the neighbor's. Panting with fear, he slammed the door and backed through the kitchen, watching through the screen the crater's hellish approach. Jesus, dear Jesus, it seemed like some predator coming for him!

The phone! He yanked the receiver from its cradle, checked for the dial tone and punched in 911. He gathered his wits, took a deep breath, prepared his speech. But it rang only once, then went dead.

A crunching, grinding roar enveloped him, a sound of pulverizing concrete mixed with the explosive crack of snapping foundation timbers, and his whole house dropped with a massive thud, tilting toward the inexorably approaching, invisible monster. The abrupt slanting of the floor made him slip and fall, and he scrambled desperately up its treacherous slickness toward the dining room.

"OH GOD! OH HELP ME!" he screamed, grabbing the door jamb and hauling himself through the doorway. The oak china hutch tilted and crashed to the floor with the lethal tinkle of shattering glass. It slammed into him with a ponderous inanimate determination, smashing one hand on the jamb, crushing the bones like matchsticks. He screamed in agony, desperately tore the shredded bleeding hand from the trap, and clawed his way over the top of the hutch, cowering behind its bulk. The kitchen imploded with tortured sounds of tearing metal, splintering wood and cracking ceramic tiles, all ripped away into a darkness he could not fathom. Sobbing with gut-wrenching fear, cowering on the floor, he felt the house shake to its very foundation in its death throes. He heard the snakelike hiss of a ruptured gas pipe and smelled the sickening stench of natural gas filling the house and his lungs.

He screamed a final scream as the dining room walls collapsed over him, as moist earth smothered him in darkness.

CHAPTER 2

Firemen, rescue workers, policemen, reporters, TV crews, and neighbors crowded around the crater . . . or sinkhole . . . or earthquake fault . . . or whatever it was. They stood and speculated, still trying to figure out the frightening chasm that had devoured a chunk of quiet residential neighborhood, an entire house, and a man some of them knew. Taking care to stay behind the yellow police tape and away from the edge, they stretched and peered down into the gaping pit as if intense scrutiny would compel the hole to give up its secrets. The crater slashed seventy-five yards through the well-tended suburban lawns. Because the low sun shone palely through the trees, its depths remained hidden in shadow, making it even more ominous. Only the periodic flash of camera strobes or the glare of video lights lit the hole. Everybody, it seemed, was taking pictures. The Internet was already rich with video and images of the pit.

An occasional car horn blast, a revved motorcycle, and other street sounds reached the crowd, but the unfathomable hole in their neighborhood and their lives riveted their attention. All day their numbers had grown, attracted by television news reports. The police held the crowd well back, except for the neighbors who lived nearby and asserted their property rights to examine the hole.

The rescue chief stood solidly scowling into its depths, his large tanned arms folded over a pronounced stomach. It wasn't the hole that had provoked his anger. The hole was a freak of nature to be dealt with. And it wasn't the crowds. From beneath his battered, yellow hardhat, he glowered at the idle equipment and people poised to mount a rescue effort. A full complement of ladders, ropes, climbing gear, stretchers, emergency technicians . . . all just waiting. The fire chief had ordered him to hold, damnit!

An insistent rising sound of honking made him turn away from the hole to see a battered Range Rover jump the curb, bull its way through a line of policemen and speed across the front lawn stopping smack up against the police tape.

A young woman leaped out and ducked lithely beneath the tape. She ignored the shouts of the cops, striding briskly toward the hole. She peered down into its blackness from beneath the bill of a baseball cap that said "Schist Happens." Her light brown ponytail jutted impertinently out the back hole of the hat, above the adjustment strap. She wore a sleeveless work shirt, slightly baggy khaki shorts and sturdy hiking boots with rumpled white socks. She stood with her hands on her hips, her feet apart, her sturdy tanned legs braced.

The rescue chief strode toward her, a freshened anger raising the veins in his neck. But he reined himself in at the last instant, remembering the public relations class he'd had to take.

"Honey, what the hell do you think you're doing? You just get on back there. You might fall in. I'm the rescue chief here and—"

"What's the situation?" She turned to the scowling middle-aged man, her gaze intent from beneath the cap bill. He took note of the attractive, oval, apple-cheeked face, the full lips, the slightly bent nose and the light blue-gray eyes. She was certainly an athletically attractive young woman, but he had other things to deal with.

"Look, honey, I'm going to have the cops take you out of here."

"I asked what's the situation?"

"The situation is, honey, that my boss says we got to wait for some damned geologist from the university to tell us it's stable and we can go down and start a rescue operation. That's what the damned situation is. Now get on back."

"I'm the 'damned geologist,' chief."

The rescue chief blinked. He decided to hide his embarrassment with bluster. "Fine . . . well, honey—"

"And my name's not honey. Dacey Livingstone. Now, tell me what's known."

Dacey turned back to examine the crater, as the rescue chief managed to switch gears and relate what information had been gathered about the hole and how it got there. Dacey nodded as he talked, intently examining the crater with a geologist's eye.

She'd seen plenty of cave-ins, impact craters, sinkholes, and other gashes in the earth's surface. But this hole somehow seemed different. Its darkness seemed to harbor a special sense of dread. She took a deep breath and began to let the rocks, the soil and the vegetation tell her what they knew.

She saw evidence of sudden, unrelenting violence here. For some of its circumference, the thick grass hid the violence, slumped over the lip, obscuring the edge. But along large stretches, the topmost layer of sheared-away raw earth revealed raggedly torn grass roots, as if great hands had clawed viciously at the soil. Farther down, the crater walls showed layers of tortured soil and dark tan clays. The apparent depth was about thirty feet to a rubble-strewn floor.

The crater floor was especially striking, showing what could be a roof. Ignoring the rescue chief's recitation, and deep in thought, she walked back to her SUV, passing the impatient rescue workers, whose stares she also ignored. As she returned with an iPad, a siren's keening warble rose in the distance. She turned briefly back to the rescue chief.

"You mind explaining what I'm doing to those cops there? They started chasing me on the freeway. I didn't have time to stop and explain."

The rescue chief started to protest, but she was gone, striding away along the hole, stopping occasionally to peer in or to crouch down to poke at the soil. Finally, she rose and began to peck at the iPad, staring intently at its screen.

With a muttered curse, the rescue chief turned to meet two uniformed cops angrily exiting their squad car, its lights still splashing color across the dusky landscape. Dacey heard cursing as they colorfully described a hundred-mile-an-hour chase. But she was intent on the iPad.

The chief returned to her side, his annoyance replaced with curiosity. She held up the screen for him to see. It showed a flashing dot marking their position amidst a three dimensional map of the underlying rock strata.

"There's no obvious reason for this hole," she announced. "I positioned it with the GPS and accessed the Oklahoma Geological Survey data on the area. There's nothing down there but solid strata. No quake faults, no mines, no caverns . . . solid." Before the chief could launch into a lecture on the dangers of police chases, she strode off to get the best view of the crater bottom.

She saw most of the roof of a house wedged amidst the rubble. Some of the edges had been ripped away, leaving shredded shingles and plywood, but the gray-shingled peak jutted up as if it were perfectly normal for that dwelling promontory to lie in a deep hole in the earth.

From behind the police tape came a voice quavering with anguish. "Miss? Miss? Are you the geologist? Can you do something?"

Dacey turned to see a young woman with short curly hair, tears staining her puffy face, with two children clinging to her side. A little boy, perhaps seven, stood staring up at Dacey through dark frightened eyes. But it was the little girl, maybe four, who riveted her attention. The child clung to her mother with small hands, her round little face forlorn, still not truly understanding what had happened. Dacey had managed to keep a cool professionalism until she saw the little girl. She felt a tightening in her chest, which she quickly replaced with a growing anger that these kinds of disasters had to visit themselves on innocent people. The anger, in turn, hardened into determination. She ducked under the police tape and took off her cap.

"Did you live here?" she asked the woman gently.

"My husband. He's down there. You have to . . ." The woman's voice choked. A middle-aged lady moved to comfort her.

"I am so very sorry." Dacey took the woman's hand, then reached down to stroke the soft brown hair and delicate cheek of the little girl. She took a deep breath. "I'll certainly do everything I can to find him." Then, as gently as she could, she questioned the mother about any earth tremors, any ground subsidence, anything unusual that had happened in the back yard over the previous weeks. The woman pulled herself together enough to answer, relieved that she could be of some help.

After a moment, Dacey felt the impatient presence of the rescue chief once more looming behind her. She reassured the mother once more and turned back to him.

"Any change in the hole since you arrived?"

The rescue chief decided to postpone once again his lecture about the cop chase. He'd have his chance to give this nervy young woman some hell.

"Well, an EMT who was first on the scene said he thought he saw that roof shift a little once. But he couldn't really tell for sure. So, you got enough information? Can we get started now?" Dacey walked back to the hole, scanning its sides.

"Not you. Me. I've got to do some more examination before I let anybody down there."

"So, what are you going to do?"

"Well, I'm gonna get harnessed up and let myself down in there and see what we've got." She strode briskly away toward her Range Rover.

"Look, I don't care—" began the rescue chief, but she was gone.

She reached the Range Rover and opened the back, hauling out a long bright blue coiled rope, a scarred yellow miner's helmet, fitted with a light and video camera, and a black climbing harness from which hung a jangling array of tools and bags.

"Damnit, this is my case and you're not going into that hole, you hear?"

Dacey ignored him, taking off her cap and deftly stepping into the leg loops of the climbing harness. She belted it firmly around her waist, tightening the loops around her thighs. She pulled on leather-palmed climbing gloves, efficiently twisted her ponytail into a tight rope atop her head and jammed on the helmet, fastening its strap beneath her chin.

"Do you hear me?" The rescue chief moved around in front of her, considering whether to call up a couple of the men to restrain her.

She clicked the helmet light on. "Am I lit?" she asked the rescue chief.

He nodded in spite of himself. "Yeah, sure, but I'm not going to let you down there without a partner," he announced with authoritative finality.

But Dacey had already attached the rope to the Range Rover's front winch.

She reached up and switched on the camera, fiddling with the iPad to bring up the video image on the screen. She handed the iPad to the rescue chief, who found himself looking at his own image. "Okay, you'll see what I see," she said. "Just flick the switch to let me down, and when I tell you, flick it the other way to hoist me up."

"That's it!" growled the rescue chief, with a wave of his hand that brought two burly rescue workers to his side. "You don't hear what I'm saying, so I'm—"

"Do you hear what I'm saying?" She glanced at the two confused rescue workers and pointed up at the rescue chief. Her blue-gray eyes flashed and her jaw tightened. With a sharp yank, she tied off the blue rappelling rope on her harness and pitched the coil down into the darkening chasm. "Your chief asked me to check out this hole and he didn't say I had to answer to you. You talk to the chief. You tell him that poor lady's husband . . . those children's daddy . . . could still be alive down there, and I'm not waiting on one of your guys to figure out how to put on a harness. And if you do send these guys down there without me checking it out first, and you got an unstable soil structure, and it collapses, you're gonna be digging more bodies out!"

Before the apoplectic rescue chief could answer, she slipped over the side, the tools and carabiners on her belt clanking. The rope tightened and cut into the turf on the crater lip.

She signaled the rescue chief to start the winch, and it whined to life, lowering her into the hole. She examined the layers as she went. Now she was in her element. Now she could bring into play her almost instinctive understanding of rocks and soil. She still saw in her mind's eye the little girl's somber, innocent face. She dug her fingers into the wall and pulled out chunks of soil and crumbled them, letting the bits fall away. She pulled a small geologist's pick from her belt, prying out rocks and turning them over in her hand before pitching them away, too.

"Ya got good compacted clay soil here," she called up to the rescue chief, whom she couldn't see over the rim. "It'll keep the sides stable." Finally she had descended out of the waning sunlight and into the shadows of the crater's bottom. The winch had reached its limit, so she pushed off from the crater wall, swinging out and paying out the rope.

She stepped lightly onto the ripped edge of the roof, testing it with her foot. Satisfied with its solidity, she let out the rope, walking across the roof, feeling with her boots for weak spots.

She stopped and surveyed the side of the hole, looking for unstable areas. She sensed the sudden violence that had produced this hole, felt a dread here. It was so raw, so fresh; not the slow geological violence that thrust mountains up from the earth's crust. Not even the ponderous, rumbling violence of an earthquake or a volcano. This was sudden, ferocious, somehow more powerful than any geological processes. This was not natural.

She remembered the woman and her children, and sadly realized that amidst this violence, the husband and father could not possibly have survived. But if force of will could save him, she would have that force of will. She also resolved that she would learn what had happened here.

She continued paying out the rope to give herself room to maneuver across the roof and tied off the rappelling knot so it wouldn't slip. She crouched on the rough shingled surface, putting her ear against it. She called "Hello?" loudly several times and listened intently for a response. She pounded on the roof with her geologist's pick and listened again. The reverberations of the roof gave her information about what was beneath, but it was confusing. The sound was too hollow to have dirt beneath it. She looked up and shook her head somberly. The few faces that poked over the crater's rim watched her solemnly. Only the murmur of conversations filtered down to her.

She raised her pick and took a wide swing, embedding it into the roof with a dull thunk. She pried up shingles and worked her way through the splintered underlayment, producing a small hole. With several more blows and pryings, she widened the hole, until at last she could peer in, shining a flashlight. An unsettling darkness swallowed the light. She looked up again and was about to shake her head to the people above.

The roof lurched crazily, sending her sliding down almost to its edge, scraping her knees on the asphalt shingles. She recovered and stood up tense and still on the tilting roof. Her heart began to pound, her senses became razor-sharp. She took two steps as if walking on eggs. The roof slumped again, with a creaking, scraping sound, cocking itself into an angle that transformed it into a deadly vertical slide into oblivion. Dacey saved herself by leaping forward and just hooking her pick over the roof's peak. She strained to pull herself up to reach over it to the other side. She heard the rescue chief shout for ropes to be thrown down. One rope fell wide of the roof to the left, and before another could be thrown, the roof plummeted away with the splintering crack of tearing wood and shingles, carrying her down with it.

She rode the roof down, plunging into the darkness, then grunted painfully as her rope zinged to a lifesaving tautness. A viciously battering cascade of soil and rocks pummeled her, the choking dirt forcing its way into her eyes and mouth. She hung almost upside down, struggling to right herself, praying that the rope and harness would hold. Blinded and suffocating, she spat out the moldy-tasting dirt, grabbed the rope and curled into a blinded ball, swaying back and forth in the blackness, enduring the bombardment. Large rocks careened off the helmet and others struck her legs, leaving red welts. One small boulder glancing off her hip launched her into a slow spin.

But even under the hammering deluge of earth and rock, she remained keenly aware that no sound had yet arisen from the roof's impact. Then she heard it, a distant booming crash reverberating up from the utter darkness signaling the chamber's immense depth.

She clamped her jaw, the grit crunching between her teeth and hung on for her life as the rain of rocks dwindled to a trickle, then stopped, except for stray pebbles and occasional light spatterings of soil on her helmet.

She unfolded and coughed raspily, spat and cleared her eyes with the backs of her gloves. She pushed panic down deep, stowed it away as useless. Down to business. She checked herself. Scrapes, bruises and some blood running down her leg, but she was basically okay. She could see nothing of the dark chamber by the waning light that filtered from the large hole above. She toggled the switch on the helmet light. It had been smashed. But the camera was still intact. Still swaying precariously back and forth over the unfathomable abyss, her legs dangling, she dug into a pouch and came out with a small flashlight, shining it up the rope to check whether the lifeline had been damaged. She saw a couple of abrasions. She had to get out quickly before the rope began to unravel. She examined her harness and found it basically sound.

"Okay, you're still alive," she whispered to herself reassuringly. "Still kickin', babe." She jerked and twisted at the end of the rope to rotate, so she could shine the light around her. She could barely make out dark distant earthen walls in the huge cavern. But this was no time to explore. Later. This crater held many secrets. She brushed more dirt from her eyes, coughed again, bringing up more grit and peered upward at the light.

"SAY, CHIEF!" she bellowed. "YOU WANNA START THAT WINCH AND PULL ME UP?"

•   •   •

The Tennessee state cop eased the patrol car through the darkened parking lot of the rest area. Over the past month, there had been two robberies and a rape in these isolated rest stops along Route 40 between Knoxville and Nashville. He and his partner figured that some sick itinerant son-of-a-bitch had decided to attack a few people before moving on to another state. Not on their damned shift, though.

Traffic was sparse on the nearby freeway at three a.m. An occasional truck roared past, its red running lights outlining the large silver boxy form, its headlights pushing an island of brightness ahead of it in the enveloping gloom. A few cars whizzed past, too, probably carrying sleeping passengers and all too often, a nodding driver.

The cop stopped the car at the restroom building and nodded to his partner, who understood his message from five years of working together.

"Yeah, Leo, I know. It's my turn," he said tiredly, pulling himself from the car and trudging through the warm, humid night, through the fluttering moths madly circling the lights outside, and entered the men's room. He walked along checking the stalls. He came out and went over to the women's side of the red brick structure. He rapped on the metal door with his nightstick. The metallic clunking brought no response.

"State police. Anybody in there?" No response. He repeated, then ducked in and checked the room out. He emerged, stopped and got a drink from the water fountain and walked back toward the car. He nodded to a bleary-eyed trudging couple who'd just gotten out of a Honda, as they split up to head for the restrooms. He paused before he got into the car, peering away down the parking lot into a shadowy area between the street lamps.

He leaned down to the car's window. "Leo, that van down there. There's nobody out here for it to belong to."

"Yeah, Johnny-boy. That's true," said Leo scanning the area. "You stay out. Go around, come up from the front. I'll block it."

Leo eased the patrol car down the lot and right up behind the dented old blue van. Johnny circled out into the grass, coming up in front, standing on the slight rise beyond the parking lot and peering through the darkened windshield. Leo keyed the plate into the car's computer, but since it was a Massachusetts plate, he didn't expect information on wants or warrants back soon.

Leo got out, his eyes riveted on the van. He was a beefy man, but he moved smoothly and quickly when his adrenaline was up, and it was up now. He drew his Glock 9mm pistol, a signal for his partner to do the same. No sense taking a chance. Aiming the Glock upward, Leo moved up to the van, took out his nightstick in his left hand and banged on the side, moving out of the line of fire of the back doors. Johnny would warn him if the front doors opened.

"State police. Please come out slowly and keep your hands in sight." After a long moment, the old van creaked and shifted on its springs from somebody moving inside. He banged again harder, the thunking sound rising above the roar of a passing truck.

"Just a minute," came a muffled reply, and the handle on the back door moved. The door swung open with a rusty scrape and a head stuck out.

Leo always looked at the eyes first. The eyes told you whether the subject had in mind to cooperate or to go for a gun. But these eyes that squinted at the light were fathomless—like onyx marbles. The distant street lights cast shadows on the face. The man had long, unruly, curly dark hair and a dark beard and moustache. He pulled himself out of the back of the van and stood peering at Leo. He had a slim, taut-muscled body and the long arms were very white. He wore a t-shirt that was wrinkled from having been slept in, faded blue jeans and old white socks with toes flapping loose. No tattoos, prison or professional. No visible scars.

"Sir, do you know it's against the law to camp at a highway rest stop?"

"No, sorry. I was tired," the man mumbled blearily. "Thought I'd rest an hour." He rubbed his eyes and focused them on the officer. "Why do you have your gun out?"

"Just move away from the van. Let me see your driver's license." Leo kept his gun aimed skyward. The man obeyed and Leo saw Johnny's flashlight click on as he began to inspect the van through the windows.

"Where are you headed, sir?" Leo holstered his pistol and studied the license. It was Massachusetts. The name was Gerald Meier. Photo matched the face. He thought he'd known a sneak thief named Gerald Meier once.

"I'm going to Oklahoma."

"Where in Oklahoma?"

"Gillard."

"You got family there?"

"No, business."

"What business?"

"Uh . . . it's too complicated to explain." The man was awake now and a slight edge of indignation crept into his voice. Leo sensed that there was something very much more with this fellow than even his practiced eye could discern. But he couldn't figure out what.

"Try me."

"Look, I don't have to tell you my business, do I?"

"You better if you don't want to find yourself in a lockup back in Knoxville while we check you out. We've had some robberies go down in this area."

"I'm . . ." The man paused and looked at Leo, sizing him up. "I'm looking for a job. I just finished one in construction up north. I heard there was an opening from my brother-in-law. I'm meeting him there."

Leo's experience told him the explanation was being concocted on the spot. There were too many subtle hesitations.

"Lemme see your hands." The man offered his hands. They were smooth, no calluses. "Pretty good hands for a construction worker."

"I wear gloves. I do electrical work."

"Right. Anybody else in your van? Mind if we look?" Leo was still on the fence about this guy's story, still trying to decide whether he believed this long-haired hippie-looking guy.

There was another pause. "Nobody in there. Uh, go ahead."

Leo nodded to Johnny, who held his gun aloft, slid open the side and peered inside, rummaging around. Meantime, Leo stepped to the police cruiser, keeping the man in sight and radioing in Gerald Meier's name. He returned.

"Gillard, eh? Ever been in Oklahoma, Mr. Meier?"

"Probably. I guess maybe passing through." They waited while Johnny finished searching the van. The police radio crackled and emitted a message for him. He reached into the car and spoke into the microphone. The dispatcher told him no wants, no warrants on the guy or the vehicle. Leo still didn't like it.

"Piles of books and several computers in here," reported Johnny. "Lots of electronics I can't figure out. It's kind of a mess. He sleeps in there, looks like. This was taped on the dashboard." He handed Leo a Google News printout. The story was about a sinkhole in Gillard, Oklahoma, that had swallowed a house. The article included a picture of a young woman in climbing gear who'd gone into the hole. A very attractive long-haired young woman in shorts. Leo held the printout up to the man, who stiffened almost imperceptibly.

"You interested in this, Gerald? You interested in sinkholes? Or are you interested in pretty girls?"

"Officer, look. I'm sorry I stayed too long here. I'm not doing anything. Just let me go on my way." The black eyes stared at him now in a smoldering anger, but the emotion was carefully controlled. The man reached out his hand for the clipping. Leo hesitated. Damn, he didn't like this at all. But he handed the man the clipping.

"All right. You go on now, Mr. Meier. But don't camp in rest areas. There's lots of motels along the highway."

"Thank you." But the man said it with such flat intonation that the actual meaning might have been far more inflammatory.

The two cops got into the car and Leo slowly backed it out of the way. The man cranked the van's engine, which after some churning finally roared to clattering life. He backed the van out and proceeded with almost insolent slowness down the parking area and onto the freeway.

Leo looked at Johnny and shrugged. "Hell, wasn't a thing I could do."

Johnny nodded. "Think we ought to call the Gillard cops? Tell them about this guy and the clipping?"

"We'd look like idiots." Leo held up a pretend telephone receiver to his ear. "Hello, officer, we stopped a guy here who clips newspapers. And he sleeps at highway rest stops. Shoot to kill." He chuckled wryly, but his face quickly became serious as he accelerated the patrol car onto the freeway and into the night. "Well, maybe there's something we could do . . ."

CHAPTER 3

"Let it down," Dacey instructed, waving her hand and watching the crane operator shove the lever forward. The steel mesh basket began to descend with a slight lurch and sway into the crater. She held onto the edge of the basket, staying in her corner to balance the three rescue workers lodged into the other three. From her vantage point, she did a full-circle scan of the craggy earthen walls, searching for signs of more collapses. It had taken a day to rig the crane with extra-long cable and move it into place, and she worried that the sides of the hole might have dried and become crumbly. But as the basket sank from the sunlight and the crowd of onlookers into the dank musty gloom of the cavern beneath the crater, she saw no evidence of further erosion. The last face she saw in the crowd was the drawn face of Anita, the man's wife. She stood with her hands clasped in front of her, hoping for a miracle. The children were not there. Anita said they had been sent to their grandmother's. The little boy, Brad, cried a lot. And the little girl, Jenny, had been having nightmares.

Dacey promised herself she would find their daddy if he was there. This time they would see everything. One of the rescue workers switched on a floodlight, powered through a black electrical cable snaking down from the surface. The brilliant glare of the light revealed an enormous, ragged chamber that matched the sides of the hole, looking as if it had been ripped from the inside of the earth. Dacey directed the light to various quarters of the crater wall, recording the scenes on her helmet video camera for later study. She began to mentally chart the cavern's shape. How could it possibly have been formed? Not by running water; not by the collapse of a mine. Water table was high here, but the chamber seemed to have a long undulating topography, roughly the shape of one of those ripply kid's balloons. Water would have made a smooth straight chamber.

While the chamber had broken the surface at the crater, it was generally horizontal, stretching away on either side. And below? She took another floodlight, carefully leaned over in the wobbly basket and flicked it on, shining it down. The house roof was there, lodged at the bottom. Now they were suspended, swaying slightly, fifty feet above it.

As they settled down upon it, with some scraping and creaking, she motioned for quiet. Amidst the immense, shadowy silence, she could hear the faint sound of trickling water. That, together with the damp earthy smell told her that water might somehow be involved in this cavern's formation. They clamped the two floodlights to the basket, and the lights swayed and shook with each movement of the people, casting shifting shadows on the walls.

Dacey attached herself to a rope via a climbing harness and heaved herself over the swaying basket's rail and onto the roof, which had been collapsed by its plunge into a flat expanse of splintered rafters. The rescue chief, now more respectful, had instructed rescue workers to do whatever she said, and they were happy to comply. They realized that these depths were her domain, not theirs.

Shining a large flashlight across the crumpled roof, she carefully let out the rope, gingerly walking on the shingles, which shifted and crackled under even her light weight. She looked back at the other three in the basket, shrugged and proceeded to stomp and finally jump up and down on the roof. In places it was springy, but it held.

"Feels solid," she said. "It'll hold me anyway. Probably okay. Stay harnessed, though." Her voice was attenuated by the vastness of the chamber, absorbed by the craggy earthen walls.

The lead rescue worker, a wiry middle-aged man named Lonnie, spoke into his two-way radio to the crane operator, hooked himself up and hopped over the railing, letting out his rope and walking across the roof, also carrying a large flashlight. They both played their lights about the gray-brown cavern walls, checking for possible sources of collapse. It looked like they were safe for now, she concluded. She shined the light down the chamber lengthwise in either direction, noticing that the gloomy ends of the passage seemed to narrow significantly. Frustrated, she wrinkled her brow and adjusted her helmet. There might be answers there, if only she knew what geological questions to ask. The others followed, one proceeding to rip a larger hole in the roof with a crowbar.

"Dacey? We got a real problem here," said Lonnie, peering into the hole.

Dacey carefully walked over beside them. "What's that?"

"We got no house." Lonnie rubbed the gray stubble on his face. Meanwhile, a worker carrying a large prybar had stepped to the edge of the roof and probed the solid earth that surrounded it. He nodded in agreement. He took up the rescue group's video camera and began taping the results of their explorations.

"None?" Dacey crouched onto her knees and explored the hole in the roof. Sure enough, there was almost no debris beneath the roof, at least not enough to constitute anything resembling a full-sized suburban house. Just dirt and rock. Loose dirt and rock, but solid, she judged by the dull chunking sound it made when the men poked at it with a crowbar.

"Looks like all that's down here is this roof. Could something like quicksand have swallowed up the house?"

Dacey squinted her puzzled squint and sat down on the roof, her forearms on her knees. A distant rumble emanated from one end of the chamber. "Well, there's a phenomenon known as liquefaction. In earthquakes, the shaking can make water-soaked soil act like quicksand. It'll sink houses a little ways, but I don't think it'll suck one down all the way. I'm still waiting for the seismic records for this area from the earthquake center in Golden, but I'm sure this was no earthquake." She was silent for a moment, then stood up resolutely, breathing in the cool, dank air.

"Down there," she said, pointing in the direction of the rumble. "I bet there's something down there that might tell us something." The rescue workers hesitated and she understood their reluctance. "Look, there's no need for you guys to go down there. I'm the geologist—"

"Yeah, but you're a—"

"You were gonna say 'a damned good geologist,' right?"

Lonnie chuckled. "Yeah, sure. What do you want us to do?"

"Let's tie together a couple of ropes. I'm gonna walk out over the bottom of this cavern to that narrow part and go in. I'll holler if I'm in trouble. Haul me in quick."

The men rigged the ropes and tied her harness firmly to the end. They braced themselves against the rafters in the largest undamaged part of the roof. Dacey checked her helmet camera to make sure it was transmitting, and stepped off the roof. She stumbled slightly in the spongy uneven earth, but recovered and began to slog forward.

Her heart beat faster as it always did when she descended into the depths of the earth. And more generally, she was always jazzed when there was an adventure to be had, and this one was a doozy. A healthy fear squirmed in her gut, and she found herself trembling slightly, but she was spurred by the prospect of some new geological discovery. The people in the department called her Rockhound for good reason.

For the first two hundred feet, the floodlights from the basket were sufficient light, but the gloom farther on made her switch on her helmet lamp. The trickling sound was louder here, and the passageway did begin to narrow. She made sure to aim her helmet camera at the sides, to record their structure. The passageway became distinctly cylindrical and the sides smoother, angling slightly downward. As she walked, she noticed that the passage had shrunk to about six feet in diameter. Smaller and smoother. What did it mean?

"You okay?" she heard faintly behind her.

"Yeah, peachy," she shouted back. The passage grew still smaller. The trickling was louder. Now the passage was about the size of a storm culvert, like a tunnel. She sat down and peered into the tunnel, slowly scanning her head left to right so the camera could capture the scene. She stopped, noticing that farther down the tunnel a chunk of granite lodged in the wall that looked like it had been worn away or chipped. She sat down, tightened her helmet strap, and scooted down into the narrowing tunnel feet first on her bottom. She was just able to sit up in the small tunnel.

She reached the rock and examined it closer. It was glass-smooth, like the polished granite on the side of a building. She screwed up her face in puzzlement. This was a strange rock she *had* to have. She pulled out her geologist's pick and chopped carefully around the rock. It was bigger than she had thought, about the size of a shoebox and wedged hard in the wall. She continued to chop the hard earth, reaching around the rock with her fingers to pry it out. She yanked hard at the same time that she realized her fingers were wet.

"DAMN!" she yelled. The rock had plugged a hole into an underground stream bed! The slippery rock fell heavily into her lap, and she was inundated by a gush of cold muddy water. She kicked back with her feet, but the downsloping bottom of the tunnel had immediately become a water slide and she skittered down into the flow. She tried to dig in her heels, but the mud wasn't deep enough and she began to slip. She fell onto her back, the cold muddy water gushing into her nose and mouth. She slid farther downward, the wet suffocating muck collapsing in on her. The rope remained slack as she slid. The men were still feeding rope as she went. They thought she was still okay. The meaning of the distant rush of water hadn't registered with them yet. She shouted, but the sound was a stifled wet gurgle in the rushing mud and water, which was filling the little tunnel.

She slid downward, coughing and gasping for air, faster and faster, realizing that the camera was now out of range of the iPad. She had to do something! She could let go of the rock, but using her arms wouldn't help. They weren't strong enough. She spread her legs and tried to jam them against the tunnel sides. But they continued to slither along. The tunnel was so slick! She couldn't get a breath in the thickening, foaming mud. It rose over her head. She was drowning. She was gathering speed. Still the rope trailed slackly. Soon she would be buried. They could never pull her out.

The toe of her left boot caught on a rock wedged in the tunnel wall and she skewed sideways and jammed herself in the tunnel, the mud and water rushing over her, oozing over her. She held herself there with all the muscle she could muster, tightened her stomach muscles and with a deep grunt forced her body upward. If only there was air above. She felt her face break the surface. She spat the mud from her mouth and shouted. It was not articulate, just a hoarse bellow, but she hoped it conveyed her danger.

The rope jerked taut! She felt herself being hauled against the slimy pitch-black current upstream. The cold sludge flowed and gurgled around her and she struggled to breathe and hold tight onto the rock and reach up to grasp the helmet camera.

Abruptly she was pulled beyond where the stream had broken through. She allowed herself to be dragged over the damp earth and into the floodlights.

"Okay, okay," she waved weakly, staggering to her feet, still clutching her cargo, covered with mud. She spat again and tried to clear her eyes with the back of her wrist. She felt strong hands under her shoulders bearing her toward the basket. She shivered as the cold air of the cavern washed over her wet body.

"You alright?" It was Lonnie.

She nodded and coughed hoarsely, bringing up an earthen taste.

"Let's get her out of here," he said to the men. They crawled into the basket and Lonnie instructed the crane operator over the radio. The basket jerked upward swinging back and forth across the floor of the cave. After switching off the camera and stowing the rock, Dacey untied herself and leaned panting and coughing on the rail, watching the vast, dark chamber fall away beneath her. She shook her head. She still couldn't figure the damned thing out.

The crowd standing at a safe distance around the crater saw the disconcerting sight of the basket rising into the sunlight carrying three relatively clean rescue workers and one thoroughly mud-covered, bedraggled woman geologist. The crane's gears ground slightly as it swung the basket clear of the hole and set it down on what was once a quiet suburban lawn. Dacey waved away any help, as well as requests for television interviews, crawling laboriously out of the basket, still clutching almost obsessively the rock and the helmet camera. Anita stood before her, face drawn, eyes wide with fear. Dacey shook her head.

"I'm sorry," she said hoarsely. "I'm truly sorry. He just wasn't down there." Anita slumped and a friend took her around the waist.

"Thank you for what you've done. Thanks so much." She touched Dacey's muddy shoulder.

"Well, it wasn't enough. I'm going to figure this thing out, I promise you."

Anita thanked Dacey again, mumbling something about hoping she was all right, and was helped away. Dacey found a garden hose, turned it on and washed down the rock, oblivious to the mud covering her and the crowd of reporters shouting questions at her. The rock had been sliced smooth on one side. As smooth as if eons of water had worn it away. But the edges were as sharp as if cut by a saw. She detached the helmet video camera and gently washed it, finding it battered but intact. She'd pull the memory card out under more pristine conditions.

Then she stood and took off her helmet, leaving an incongruous dome of relatively clean hair crowning her mud-covered face and body. She turned the hose on herself, scrubbing off the mud from her face, arms and body. She flooded her shirt and shorts with water, squeezing as much as possible from their fabric. Then she squirted and scrubbed off her legs, until the tan emerged from beneath the mud. She removed her boots and socks and washed her feet. She picked up the boots, socks, rock and camera and carried them to her Range Rover parked at the curb, stowing them inside, removing dry clothes and locking it.

Among the crowd, watching her steadily, was a slim man with long curly hair and a scraggly beard and moustache, who wore a white t-shirt and faded jeans.

She gratefully accepted an offer from a kindly neighbor woman to shower at her house. As she took her shower and washed her hair in the bathroom with flowered wallpaper and a tasseled shower curtain and fancy soaps, she decided that it was better than the stock tanks or mountain rivers she usually bathed in on field trips. She emerged from the house in cutoff jeans and white t-shirt, still barefoot because she hadn't brought extra shoes. She was ready to give a few television interviews:

No, she told the interviewers, she still wasn't sure what had caused the cave-in, but she'd be working with engineers from the state to figure it out. Yes, it was scary down there. Yes, it was a terrible tragedy. She excused herself as quickly as she could.

After a debriefing with the rescue workers and the rescue chief, who now called her Dr. Livingstone, she climbed tiredly into the Range Rover and drove it slowly through the police line and the crowd of tourists. She pulled out onto the boulevard that led into the well-tended middle-class housing development whose streets were now clogged with sightseeing traffic. It was forty-five minutes to her townhouse in Norman and she relished the time to relax. She accelerated onto Route 40, which would take her across the flat prairie landscape into Oklahoma City, and from there south to Norman. Traffic was light. Maybe everybody was still back at the crater. She smiled tiredly, wriggled her bare feet and thought about the crater and the cavern beneath. She glanced in the rear view mirror. A blue van was following her.

She decided to pick up dinner at a Wendy's drive-through and left the freeway when she saw a Wendy's sign. She bought a double burger, fries, and some chili, and maneuvered the Range Rover back onto the freeway. As she neared the exit for Highway 35, she noticed a blue van behind her. The same blue van. She munched a fry reflectively and veered onto 35 south into Norman. She exited the freeway and wound through the city streets, taking a more circuitous route to her townhouse than usual. It was late, getting dark. She could barely see the blue van, but it was there, following her. She munched another fry, becoming a bit more concerned. A TV crew? A fan? Or maybe . . . She remembered the phone call that morning.

She turned into the short driveway of her townhouse and pulled herself out, looking around. She didn't see the van. She took the Wendy's bag and went around to the back of the Range Rover, opening the tailgate and reaching in to pull out the camera and the rock. She was aware of somebody behind her. She whirled to see a bearded man in a t-shirt. He stepped toward her, reaching out.

She stepped back, whirled and with an expert karate side-kick, plunged her bare foot deep into his abdomen, leaving a dirty footprint on his t-shirt. He grunted in surprise, his mouth flying open and his dark eyes wide. He bent over double and she stepped toward him, grabbing his hand bending it straight behind him, twisting his wrist and driving him to his knees. He yelped in pain, but she twisted harder and shoved her foot onto his back, slamming him down onto his stomach. The concrete knocked the breath out of him and he offered no resistance, but she didn't take any chances. She wrenched his arm behind him, set down the Wendy's bag and reached up to her head, yanking a long white plastic strap from her ponytail, letting her damp hair cascade around her face. She kneeled on his back, grabbing his other hand and twisting it around behind him, making him grunt in pain. She wrapped the plastic around his wrists and threaded it through a built-in fastener and yanked it tight. Another grunt.

She was tempted to jump up and throw up her hands like she'd seen rodeo calf ropers do. But instead, she sat hard on his back, picked up the Wendy's bag and took out a fry, popping it into her mouth.

"Got a call yesterday from a cop in Tennessee," she informed the man as she chewed. "Said he couldn't do anything official, but told me they met this weird guy who had my picture. Guy had a beard and was wearing a white t-shirt and jeans, just like you. Look, I've had enough crap today. The cops'll take it from here. Just remember this the next time you pick on a defenseless woman!"

The man groaned.

CHAPTER 4

"**D**acey?" said the little-boy voice. "Why come you sittin' on that man?" Little Sammy had pedalled up on his G.I. Joe camouflage-painted Big Wheel and sat there, his fine, blond baby hair askew, his cowboy boots planted solidly on the concrete.

"Because he's a bad man, honey."

"No I'm not," wheezed the man, beginning to recover from the blow to the stomach.

Dacey ignored him. "Tell your mom to call the police. Go get your mom now, sweetie." Sammy was three and had learned all about police on Sesame Street, so he clattered away toward his house, a boy on a mission.

"Calling the police isn't a good idea." The man's voice was stronger, but it was muffled from being stuck flat on his stomach under a one hundred thirty-pound load.

"Why not?"

"Because I could charge you with assault and battery."

Dacey stood up and looked down at him, his hands trussed behind his back, a faint footprint on his shirt. "You came at me."

"I was going to help you carry your stuff."

"*Sure* you were, pal. You didn't say anything. You just came at me." She finished the last French fry and set the bag in the back of her Range Rover.

He paused to breathe and to gather his words. "I'm sorry. I'm not very communicative sometimes. Can I get up?"

"Nope. You might be a smooth talker. I know about smooth talkers." She spied a bulge in his back pocket and bent down to fish out his wallet. She flipped through the cards.

Sammy's mother ran out of her townhouse holding a nine-millimeter pistol. Hurrying toward Dacey, she shouted, "Are you okay? I'll call the police!"

Dacey looked up from the wallet. "Just hold a bit, Nance. Let me see what we've got here." Nancy, a slim, dark-haired woman of thirty-two stood, feet wide in an expert marksman's stance in flip-flops, baggy blue shorts, and a man's shirt, holding the pistol with both hands, pointed in the general direction of the man.

"Says here on your license you're Gerald Meier from Cambridge, Massachusetts."

"Right. Keep looking."

Dacey held up an identification card. "It says you're with the Harvard-Smithsonian Center for Astrophysics."

"Yes. I'm an astrophysicist. A theoretical astrophysicist."

Dacey hmphed sarcastically. "That's the only kind, isn't it? Like, you could do experiments with stars, eh?"

Gerald took the comment to mean his identity was accepted and he could roll over. He shook his hair back from his face and stared up at Dacey with dark, questioning eyes. Nancy backed up and looked dubiously at Dacey, who gestured that the movement was allowed.

"Why don't you let me explain? Take these off."

"Not quite yet, but we'll get you a bit more comfortable." Dacey nodded at Nancy, who stuffed the pistol in the waistband of her shorts and helped hoist Gerald to his feet. Dacey yanked at the cuff, checking that his hands were still bound firmly behind him.

"What are these things?" Gerald twisted to try to see his hands.

"Plastic zip tie. Makes a good handcuff. I keep a few pair handy in case of people like you. Girl can't be too careful."

"Hmm," said Nancy, eyeing the cuffs. "Could I borrow some for Sammy?" Dacey laughed as the two women helped Gerald over to the steps leading to Dacey's townhouse and sat him down on the second step.

"Can we talk privately?" the man asked.

Dacey considered the request. "Nance, I think we're okay here," she said. "Go make sure Sammy's not up to something. I'll holler if I need you." Nancy offered the pistol, but Dacey declined, so she walked away, still eyeing Gerald suspiciously. The man shook his hair out of his eyes and breathed deeply.

"Look, let me give you a number to call. It's Norm Mankiewitz, the chair of my department. His home number. He'll vouch for me." Dacey paused, then nodded as Gerald recited a number. She stood up, looking suspiciously down at him.

"Well, I guess you won't get into mischief with your hands tied behind you." She pulled a cell phone from her pocket, unlocked her door and went into her townhouse, leaving the door open so she could watch him. Gerald shifted himself to get more comfortable, leaning against the wrought-iron railing on the steps. He heard the murmur of Dacey's conversation, as she apparently had reached Mankiewitz. He looked around. It was a nice street, a nice townhouse. A middle-aged woman walked by with a small white dog on a leash. She eyed him suspiciously. He couldn't conceal that his hands were tied behind him, so he tried to look nonchalant, stretching his legs out and crossing his ankles. He managed a smile and a nod, but she didn't return the smile, shaking her head in a way that said she expected as much from the young woman who lived in that townhouse. After about ten minutes and two more head-shaking neighbors, she returned with two cans of beer.

"He says you're not a psychopath. He says you're a pretty nice guy, actually, although you're quiet and kind of spacey. He didn't say spacey. He said absentminded. He said you're a genius. He also said nobody knew where you'd gone and he was glad I'd found you. He wants you to call him." Dacey kept to herself her own observation that Gerald was a pretty good-looking fellow.

"Well, I guess all that's true. Will you cut me loose?"

Dacey considered the idea. "Yeah . . . provisionally. I want to hear a satisfactory explanation. If it's not, I yell for Nancy and she brings her gun." Gerald nodded and Dacey drew a small Swiss Army knife from her pocket and sliced through the strap. She set the open knife down on the porch. Gerald rubbed his wrists to erase the welts. He accepted a beer from her, opened it and took a deep swallow. His stomach still hurt badly, but the beer helped.

"Look, I'm sorry," she said, fetching the Wendy's bag from the back of the Range Rover. "Maybe I overreacted a bit. But you sort of moved in without warning. A girl can get a little freaked." He said nothing, so she unwrapped the hamburger and sliced it in two, offering him half. He took it and nodded in thanks. She sat on the top step, and he twisted sideways on the bottom step, resuming the position leaning against the wrought-iron railing, and looking up at her curiously. She was not like the women he usually encountered in academe. They didn't usually kick one in the gut. He actually admired the act, even though it would leave him sore for some time.

She extended her legs and worked her feet around to stretch her leg muscles. "I'll be sore from all the stuff today, including that kick." She took a bite of hamburger, and when she had swallowed it, asked, "So, if you're not a criminal, why'd that cop call me about you?"

"Misunderstanding. I don't come across to people very well, sometimes." He took a bite of his own half.

"I'll say you don't. Okay, let's start over, like we never had our little rumble. What do you want?"

"Help with a puzzle." He took another bite of his hamburger and a sip of beer. His stomach was slightly queasy, but it was empty. The hamburger would help him recover.

"What kind of puzzle? Astrophysics? I don't know anything about astrophysics. I'm a geologist."

"Well, actually I don't know for sure what the puzzle is. Maybe geology. Maybe unnatural. Maybe some astrophysics."

"You're sounding weird, Gerald," Dacey warned.

"Sorry. Look, I should explain that, because I'm a theoretician, I just think about things. Why they happen. I can't explain it, but I kind of sense how theories should fit together. I see concepts, visualize them. I'm sorry, I just can't—"

"—articulate very well," she finished his sentence. "It's okay, I'm kinda followin' you. I took a course in the psychology of science. Einstein was like that. And there's Stephen Hawking. Almost intuitive."

"Yes, intuitive. Anyway, about six months ago . . . well, more like a year . . . I became aware of lots of strange things happening. I would read in the papers or see on TV about some strange things."

"Like what?"

"I've got it all on my laptop in the van. I'll get it in a minute. You'll see what I mean." He was so intent on his subject, he forgot his hamburger. His gaze grew distant. "Anyway, the only way I can classify them so far is they involve things appearing and disappearing."

"Appearing and disappearing? That's it? That's your big scientific theory? Boy, I'm even more sure than ever why I like rocks."

"I know it sounds—"

"Stupid?"

"—vague. But a lot of theories start out vague."

"Appearing and disappearing," Dacey said again reflectively, taking a sip of beer. "Like that house. That's why you had that article with my picture. The cops told me." Gerald nodded. She shrugged. She was interested. "Okay, let me see your stuff." After all, she was totally stumped by the mystery of the disappearing house. And there was the unexplained cavern. But mostly, she remembered Anita. And she remembered the woman's daughter, little Jenny, and her confused, fearful look, not understanding where her father had gone.

Gerald rose and walked, slightly bent over with his sore stomach, around the corner and out of sight. She felt even sorrier for having kicked him. He seemed okay, she thought as she finished the half hamburger and started on the chili, rummaging around for the plastic spoon in the bag. The chili was lukewarm, but still tasty. She was halfway through the bowl and almost done with her beer when he drove up in the van and disappeared from the driver's seat into the back. From the rocking and squeaking that emanated from the van, she could tell he was rummaging around. He appeared out the back door with his laptop. A can followed him, rolling along in the gutter. He retrieved it and pitched it into the back and shut the door, trying twice before the latch held.

She had turned on the porch light as dusk rose, and sat down on the steps just as he reached her and perched beside her, opening the laptop and launching a database program. He brought up an image of a multitude of stars, with a bright streak cutting through the middle.

"This is really what got me started. They were doing a sky survey at Palomar, taking photos with this wide-field telescope. They got this shot of this really bright object out in space. Brighter than an asteroid, even brighter than a little sun. It was moving against the background of stars, so they knew it was in our solar system." He clicked to the next picture of what looked to be about the same star field. "Then a couple of hours later, they did another exposure of the same star field. Bang! It's gone! Disappeared!" He clicked back and forth between the two photos, showing how the streak has vanished.

"Maybe it just zoomed out of the area."

"They could tell how fast it was going from the streak. Really damned fast. But they allowed for that."

"It might've exploded."

"Maybe, but there was no flash. Disappeared," he said portentously. "Anyway, I don't like things like that . . . things that don't fit. It means that something's wrong with a theory. So, I started going through astronomy data from planetary probes. And I found more objects in space that appeared or disappeared. It was tough, because they were mostly in raw data. None of the astronomers would publish them, because they all thought something was wrong with their instruments." He brought up the next photo, a swirling mass of red, orange and yellow color with a large, dark splotch in the middle. "This did get published. It's a closeup of Jupiter taken about a year ago. There's this big anomaly in the atmosphere that showed up one week and was gone the next."

"Anomaly?"

"Well, they did measurements. The atmosphere seemed to be swirling inward to a point. Like a whirlpool. But that's all they could figure out."

"So, what's all that stuff up there got to do with us earth people?"

"Well, after Jupiter, I started looking in the newspapers, searching online news services. I don't know why. Just a hunch." He brought up a news story on the screen. "Few months ago, there was this gas cloud that killed a big reindeer herd in the Arctic circle. Something *appeared* just out of nowhere." He clicked through the database and brought up another news story. "These climbers in the Caucasus mountains went on an expedition to climb this mountain and found the topography had changed. A whole big chunk of mountain had eroded. Or *disappeared*."

"And now that house."

"Yeah, that house." His eyes were bright now. He'd forgotten the injury, forgotten the welts on his wrists, forgotten his half-eaten hamburger. "And there are explosions and eruptions and—"

"Whoa, pal!" She stood up, edging toward the door. "This is all getting too weird. I agreed to listen, but this is just too tall a story. What do you expect me to believe here?"

He stood up, too, but knew enough to back away instead of approaching her. "I don't expect you to believe anything now. I don't believe anything. I've just got this—"

"Obsession. That's what they call it."

"Well, all right. But I left Cambridge to go find out about these things. I've just got this . . . this obsession. All I want now is to find out what you know about this crater. Just let me look at your data."

"Yeah, my data," she said. "About all I'll have is data. I've got no funds to continue this. The university won't give me the kind of help to mount a major exploration of that cavern . . . to do isotopic analyses . . . seismic profiling . . ."

"See? See? That's where I can help you."

"Yeah, like you've got the money?" She glanced at his ratty van, with its crumpled fender and peeling paint.

"No, of course not. But there's a foundation that supports me. It funds research that's kind of speculative . . . you know, at the edge."

"Like Bigfoot and UFOs?"

"Well, I don't know about that, but I heard about it and put in an application, and they're paying for me to do this stuff."

"What's the name?"

Gerald took a crumpled card out of his pocket and handed it to her. The card read "Deus Foundation" and had a New York address and phone number.

"Deus, like the Latin for God? They religious?"

"Well, I don't think so. I think they meant the name to mean, like, the ultimate. The search for the ultimate."

Dacey knew there were dozens of odd little foundations around, and that they tended to support research that wasn't yet well-established enough to get money from the big government agencies. She stretched out her legs, wriggled her toes, looked at the card and thought a minute.

"And what'll you do?"

"I'll tell them your research fits in with mine. That might help when you put in a grant application. All they can do is say no."

Dacey gave a what-the-hell shrug and put the card in her jeans pocket. "Well, maybe if this'll get me any closer to figuring out that damned hole. But I've got to think about this. You go away now. Just go get in your little van and go sleep somewhere. Call me tomorrow. I'll let you know whether I've decided to work with you or run you off."

He backed away, smiling slightly beneath his beard. "Fine. That's all I ask." He turned and got into his van, cranked its recalcitrant engine to clattering life and drove away, leaving a slight pall of smoke over the quiet street. She waited until he was gone and retrieved the rock and the video camera from the Range Rover.

"Well?" she heard behind her. It was Nancy, the pistol still in her waistband. "I watched out the window. Was he a mugger or what?"

"He was a 'what.' Kind of a nut. Or maybe a genius."

"Or a nutty genius."

Dacey nodded, thanked Nancy for the firepower support and carried her valuable evidence into the townhouse.

CHAPTER 5

obert Langdon Balch, the second youngest-ever Senior Associate Vice President at the San Francisco investment firm Darien, Bowles and Gladstone Ltd., twiddled his Mont Blanc pen impatiently as he flipped through the corporate report. He glanced up again at the digital clock on his desk—the one he positioned in his line of sight across the walnut desk, so he could surreptitiously watch the time when he had visitors. Indeed, it did show seven o'clock. A seven and two zeroes. He'd been ready since the clock showed six-five-zero. *Really* ready. The corporate stock prospectus bored him, and he flipped the last page over and pitched the thick blue booklet in his to-be-filed box for the secretary. The company was a dog. No glamour. No glitz. It mass-produced some kind of electronic sensors for industrial boilers. Not an exotic biotech firm; not a balls-out aggressive software firm. Not the kind of company he could profitably pitch to his investor clients.

He decided to pass time playing with his computer. He shouldn't need to keep on working. The clock glowed with seven-zero-five now, past time for everybody to be gone. Time for things to start happening. He pressed a few keys to check his computerized schedule. Yes, indeed, he had scheduled the appointment from seven o'clock to eight. It was a blacked-out listing on the computer network, so the other executives who looked at his schedule couldn't see the purpose; just that the hour was blocked out. Seven until eight, then he would go home for dinner.

Bored with the computer, he swiveled his big leather chair to look out the large window at San Francisco spread out below in a vibrant clutter. The city's lights were coming on in the slightly hazy dusk, and the buses and cars were rolling up and down the hills on their way to wherever. He caught sight of a cable car slowly making for Nob Hill. He looked over to the other buildings, to the windows about level with his twenty-third-floor office. They were almost all empty. He reminded himself that he had a good office, third one down from the president's corner suite. Last year, his office had been fifth from the corner and hadn't had room for the sofa and easy chair that he'd had the designer select. Before that, he'd worked on a lower floor in one of those cubicles. He congratulated himself again on his progress.

He became bored with the view and picked up the phone and punched in her number. It began to ring. She would tell him if everybody had left. It was probably that damned Huston holding things up. Huston sat in his little office with no room for a sofa until all hours reading all the fine print on the goddamned IPO prospectuses to find out whether some pissant little stock might make a little surge when it went public. Huston was a damned sardine fisherman. Looking for lots of sardines to make a damned sandwich.

Finally, she answered in a cool, efficient, but very feminine voice.

"Anybody around?" he asked.

"Well, Carl's still in his office. He's about to leave."

"When he does, you'll come in?"

"If I have time."

"It's on my calendar. Don't be late." With an impatient flick of his wrist, he snapped the receiver back onto its cradle and leaned back in his chair to watch more lights come on in the city, peering to his right to see the bobbing gleam of the boats plying the slate gray waters just off Fisherman's Wharf. His clock's numerals now glowed with seven-*one-eight*. Eighteen minutes late! He turned on the desk lamp, which cast a nice soft kind of glow over the office, without spoiling the view of the city lights. He watched the view for a moment.

The door opened and the New Accounts Officer came in. She wore a conservative burgundy skirt with a matching jacket over a silk blouse. Her medium blonde hair was done up in a twirly bun with a bow that matched the skirt. She always dressed well. She also wore high heels, which accented the shape of her slim calves. Most women wore more comfortable low heels, which he thought looked dowdy. She approached his desk and the line-of-sight clock read seven-two-zero. Plenty of time.

"You wanted to see me?" She smiled, the smooth skin around her green eyes crinkling. Her straight, white teeth contrasted with the nice red of her carefully applied lipstick.

"Everybody gone?"

"Yes. You wanted me?"

"Yeah. Something's come up." He pushed back the chair and stood, adjusting his Countess Mara tie and straightening his vest. Below the vest his shirt tail hung down like stage curtains, and below that extended only his bare white legs decorated with sparse black hairs. His interest in her was becoming rapidly evident, peeking cyclopean and bald from between the shirt-tail curtains like an old nearsighted actor.

He leered, bright-eyed and smooth-jawed and raised his eyebrows. She gasped and brought her manicured hand to her open mouth and backed toward the door, wide-eyed. He came out from behind the desk in his stocking feet and advanced toward her, the bald actor leading the way.

"God, what are you doing?"

"I want you!" He continued his advance.

"Are you nuts?"

"I know you want me."

"Well, not here!"

"We've done it here."

"Well, . . . not now. God, there's people . . ."

"Fuck 'em. No, actually . . . fuck you."

"God, you are terrible!" She laughed, showing the white perfect teeth and slammed the door, leaning back against it, her smile becoming vixenish. As her hands fumbled behind her to lock the door, he had already begun working on her clothes. She immediately returned the favor. In a lustful confusion of unbuttoning, unzipping, unsnapping, disrobing, they quickly reached a deliciously disheveled state of undress that offered adequate access for the evening's performance.

They writhed together around the room in the soft light from the desk lamp and the vast twinkling city. She pulled him down onto the sofa and they began diligently working toward their mutual delight.

A thundering whoosh erupted into the room, shaking them to their very bones. All went dark and she screamed, but the sound was lost in the gale that followed, as papers leaped off the desk like a flock of startled birds and streamed toward them. They were assaulted by flying objects—the desk lamp, the desk clock and even the computer—all part of a vicious, shadowy attack, trailing severed, whipping electrical cords. The tumbling objects didn't hit them, but passed overhead in the darkness, vanishing with a clattering, ripping sound into some unseen netherworld. Amidst the howling wind that tore at their skin, his massive walnut desk, shifted and tipped, thudding onto its side. It bounced once, then jerked its ponderous way along the carpet toward them, silhouetted in the city glow.

They both howled in terror, as the breath sucked from their lungs, searing pain stabbed behind their eyeballs and their skin seemed insufficient to contain their flesh which throbbed and bloated in an attempt to escape their bodies.

She felt him lighten and lift away from her, and he flailed at her, reaching to grasp arms, hands, fingers, but was too late. A dull sucking thwop and the room was quiet—except for the strange, now-louder roar of the city. The brief lull was broken by the rise of his breathless moaning.

Whimpering, she rolled off the sofa in the darkness, eyes ripe with tears, entire body aching, crawling and feeling her way along the thick carpet around the massive desk to the base of the wall and up to the light switch. She stood and pressed the switch, the sudden glare of utterly white fluorescent lights making her squint. Some of the lights were shattered, dark; others flickered crazily, but others shone balefully down on the ruined office. She brushed the hanging hair from her face and turned to search for him. As her gaze swept the room on its urgent mission, it abruptly stopped, riveted by a sight so utterly bizarre that even his pitiful groaning made her ignore him to stare at his window.

A perfectly round hole in the floor-to-ceiling glass let in the sounds of the city, as well as a cold breeze that chilled her skin.

Another groan from him suddenly spurred her search again, as the groan gathered strength and became a howl. With a stunned gasp, she spied him, or certain parts of him, directly across the room from the window. His head shook back and forth and began to spit curses and his arms flailed weakly, then more vigorously as indignation grew within him. His body was stuffed ass-first into a spot roughly chest-high on the wall. Immediately below his head, his legs and feet, one socked and one bare foot, kicked and struggled ridiculously. She approached him awestruck, her fine jaw slack, her eyes wide. She grew more alarmed at the sight of a thin smear of blood on the wall from a scratch on his back.

His indignation and outrage erupted. He spewed a stream of all the fricative-rich curse words at his disposal, spitting them in random order in an unrelenting steady tirade. As his wits caught up with his invective, the epithets crystallized into a series of interrogative conjectures.

"What the fuck is this? Is this a fucking joke? Is this . . ." he paused to pant. ". . . Was it Catherine? Did that goddamned bitch set a bomb? Yeah! Or maybe it was the ventilation system! Yeah! Fucking ventilation system got fucked up!"

She approached, waving her hands in delicate ineffectual confusion about how to help him. But as she considered strategies, she riveted her attention on only one of his spat-out theories.

"Your wife? Your wife, Catherine, did this?"

"Pull me out! I'm stuck! My ass! Cops'll be here! Pull! Now, god-damnit!" He kicked and flailed mightily, eyes afire with a blend of anger and fear.

She looked back toward the door, and down at herself, remembering with a start that she was largely naked. She wavered between helping him and finding her clothes. She found her blouse on the floor and slipped it on. Fortunately, her skirt had been spared the mysterious fate of the desk accessories by being caught in an eddy. It was by the desk, and she hurriedly slipped it on and returned to snatch at his arms and feet, trying her best to obtain a firm hold to haul him out.

A pounding on the door and the alarmed, muffled voice of Carl Huston spurred their efforts. She yanked hard at his foot and he budged slightly, but yelped in protest. She stopped abruptly, wisps of hair hanging in her face, lipstick smeared, eyes wild. She took her lower lip reflectively between her teeth. This moment would be the only chance for her to truly command his attention for some time to come.

"Bob, I want you to know that if your wife did this, we're through!"

CHAPTER 6

"**O**kay, now tell me why the hell we're here? This is just a damn hole in a damn window. Straighten me out, Ralph." San Francisco Police crime scene and ballistics expert, Jimmy Cameron, perched on the edge of the overturned desk and looked blearily around the destroyed office, rubbing his eyes with his fingertips and scratching his stubbly beard. The lean black man didn't like being hauled out of a warm bed in the middle of the night.

Cameron didn't get an immediate answer. His fellow expert, Ralph Gaston, stood at the window, his brow furrowed, his rimless glasses slipping down his nose, closely examining the large, smooth round hole in the glass. He had a long thin face with a straight aquiline nose and an intense, quiet way about him. Cameron had once told him that when he was studying something like he was now, he looked like one of those hunting dogs pointing a covey of quail—his body tense with concentration, dark eyes riveted on the quarry. Cameron declared that on such occasions he even thought he'd seen Gaston's small ponytail rise a little bit, like the tail of a pointer.

"Well, Jimmy we're ballistics experts, right?" Gaston finally said, his gaze still fixed on the glass.

"That's the sign on my door, yeah."

"And ballistics experts study things that explode and make a hole?"

"Yeah, when it's daylight preferably."

"So, we've got some kind of explosion and we've got a hole. What more do you want?"

"Just seems to me that there wasn't any gunfire. That's just a damned hole that somebody knocked in a building." He shook his head in final surrender. "Damn, man—" he grumbled.

"Also, the lieutenant said to. Now check the other hole over there."

Resigned, Cameron hauled himself up and went to the other wall which showed a hole that looked the same size. Gaston knew his partner's griping was more to poke a little at him. It was their kind of friendly sport. Jimmy Cameron knew his partner hated disorder. He hated anything that didn't fit with the scheme of things. And these large, smooth holes didn't fit with the scheme of things.

Gaston watched Cameron examine the hole in the wall with a feigned indifference, his sleepy eyes performing a routine scan. Cameron put his hands on his hips, hmphing.

"Damn, this hole here just sliced right through this plaque thing. Man, sliced it right on through."

"Yeah, this is strange all right," said Gaston, joining him to view the hole in the wall, which had neatly severed a corner from a metal-on-wood plaque from the San Francisco chapter of the Society of Investment Professionals honoring Robert Balch. The award was for "*something* of the Year," the *something* part of the award's name having been sliced off by the hole. "And another thing," continued Gaston. "I don't see any debris."

Cameron examined the floor under the wall. "Yeah, if this was the entry, shoulda been some kind of stuff on the floor. Or if it came through the window, some glass."

A faint scraping noise emanated from the hole in the wall. Both men stepped around the large leather couch and peered in. They could see nothing at first. Then a chunk of material was yanked from the hole on the other side, and they saw the jowly face of the police sergeant looking back at them.

"This damned thing goes all the way into this office," said the cop. "And damned if it don't keep goin'!"

They both strode past the patrolman assigned to guard the office and found their way through the hallway to the next room, where a photocopier stood beside large metal racks holding sealed reams of copy paper. Sure enough, the hole had come through the wall, and even burrowed cleanly through the paper reams and out the other side. The small room was awash with paper, which also clogged the hole in the opposite wall. Gaston instructed three patrolmen to help them trace the path of the hole through the building, removing debris that had apparently been sucked into the hole.

Soon, they returned to the original office and were peering through the hole in the wall. Now it showed—except for some bits of material the patrolmen couldn't remove—a distant dark circle that appeared to lead to the outside.

"Jesus," whispered Cameron excitedly. "All the damn way through the building! Okay, that's ballistics!"

"Let's get some angles. Let's get some sizes. And let's shoot the scene." Gaston had backed up to the middle of the room and was staring at one hole, then another, lost in thought.

"Yeah, sure, Ralph. You stand there and think, I'll go and get the tools. I got to get the tools. The black man got to get the tools, because the white boy, he got to think. The Twinkie can't get the damn tools."

Ralph smiled slightly. It was an old joke between them.

"'Yup. That's about it," he said and went back to his thinking.

Cameron left the room and in the outer offices opened their cases full of equipment. Actually, he always got the tools, because Ralph never could remember to bring everything. Ralph was always too involved in reconstructing what had happened. But then Ralph always packed the tools when they were done, because the methodical criminalist put everything back right, so Cameron could find it again. They'd been a good team all these years.

The patrolman watched as Cameron opened the cases to reveal the orderly set of tools and camera equipment. He began to select measuring tapes, string, a protractor and three-D still and video cameras.

"This is screwy, huh?" asked the large red-haired cop.

"Yeah," said Cameron as he checked the camera. "Looks like we got an all-nighter here."

"Never saw anything like this at home." The patrolman leaned his beefy shoulder against the door frame.

"Where's home?" Cameron wasn't really interested, but he sensed an opportunity coming along. He began laying out more tools from another case.

"Just moved from Mississippi," continued the burly cop. "Never saw this kinda thing. San Francisco. Jesus. Screwy stuff. Screwy people. Like, I never saw so many gays." Cameron grunted. The cop took Cameron's response as a sign that the conversation could continue. He leaned over confidentially. "That guy, for instance . . ." He waved his hand at the direction of Gaston, who was reaching into the hole in the wall. ". . . I hear he's gay. That true?"

"Just don't bend over around him, you'll be okay."

The cop chuckled nervously. He wasn't sure whether it was a joke or not. "You guys partners?"

"Yeah. Nine years."

The cop raised his eyebrows, realizing that he might have made a mistake in raising the question.

"Uh . . . you . . . uh . . . friends?"

"Sure, but not real close in *that* way. I'm married."

The cop breathed a subtle sigh of relief.

"My wife's name's Phil." Cameron paused in his work and looked at the cop straight-faced, to see the cop's reaction.

"Oh . . ." The cop's ruddy face reddened slightly ". . . well, that's fine, too."

"Look, as soon as we're finished here, we want to interview the people who were in the building." Cameron finished gathering his tools and went back into the office. Gaston was withdrawing his arm from the hole.

"I can feel metal back in there," he said. "It's sheared clean, too. And there's traces of blood on the top here. We'll have to call the blood guys."

Without a word of discussion, the two hefted the desk onto its bottom and laid out their tools. The best, and also most frustrating, team of investigators in the police department was on the job.

Gaston began to measure the sizes of the holes using a tape measure, while Cameron shot video and still images of the room and closeups of the holes.

"You were talking to the officer?" asked Gaston, running a string between the holes.

"Yeah. He asked if you were gay."

"And you told him?"

"Sure. Said you were a Twinkie." Cameron paused in his photography and grinned the broadest grin of the night, showing white teeth amidst the rich caramel face and black whiskers. Gaston knew what the grin meant.

"And I suppose you told him you were married? And then you told him your wife's name was Phil?"

"Yup. He asked."

"But you didn't tell him Phil's full name is Phyllis, and that she's a lovely lady, and that you have two great kids."

"He didn't ask."

Gaston couldn't help smiling himself. Cameron loved his little jokes. "Jimmy, one of these days you're going to play your head games on the wrong person."

"Hasn't happened yet." Cameron arched his eyebrows, pleased with himself. They bent to their work. Over the next two hours, they tracked the path of the hole wherever it led—through offices, storage rooms, elevator shafts and stairwells, finally reaching the other side of the building. They ran string, took angles, measured diameters, took video and photos and chemical samples, and sawed off samples of wallboard and metal at the holes' edge.

Finally, they'd reached the far end of the building, peering out the last hole that penetrated a steel girder and the modern angular skyscraper's granite stone facing. Their view was of an early morning San Francisco Bay and its famous bridge. As they breathed in the cool air and watched the dawn begin to break, they decided it was time to talk to the only two people who had witnessed the event.

Soon, Bob Balch and Anna Mercer were sitting on the same office couch that had supported their lovemaking the night before. However, this time, they sat as far apart as possible. Balch wore a white shirt with a suit coat and pants and black shoes, his ankles revealing only one sock for his two feet. Mercer wore a maroon skirt and an overcoat she'd found in one of the offices. She clutched it tight around her.

The rising noise of morning traffic spilled through the hole, but Balch and Mercer avoided looking at it, as if it were evidence against them of some crime.

The large cop stood uncomfortably at the door. He knew Gaston and Cameron were supposed to wait for the lieutenant. But hell, he was just a beat cop. It wasn't his business.

"We told our story to the first cops already," said Balch, waving his manicured hand at Gaston. "There was just this big damn explosion. That's all I know."

"And what happened to your clothes?" asked Gaston.

Anna Mercer shifted uncomfortably, held her knees tightly together and looked nervously at Balch. But she said nothing.

"Well, like we told the first cops, they got messed up, so we took them off," said Balch.

"How about your pants?" asked Cameron.

"They didn't get messed up."

"So, you had them on the whole time?"

"Yeah . . . sure."

Cameron reached down behind the couch and held up a pair of men's black bikini briefs. "Real amazing, I'd say. The explosion must've blown off your cute little shorts without even taking your pants. Just real amazin'."

Balch tried to stammer out an answer and Anna Mercer blushed and clutched the coat tighter around her neck with both hands.

"Look," she said. "I'll admit. We weren't exactly . . . well . . . engaged in a business meeting. He thinks maybe his—"

"Shut up, Anna," spat the man. "We don't know anything about this thing."

"*You* shut up, pal," said Cameron, jutting his face forward for emphasis. He nodded at Mercer to continue.

"Like I told you earlier. He thinks his wife did it."

"I don't have to take this shit!" Balch leaned forward to go, grimacing as he pulled himself off the couch. Gaston picked up on the cue.

"Are you hurt?"

Balch shook his head emphatically, but Gaston's antenna had gotten the signal. He asked Balch to take off his suit jacket, and after a moment of indecision, Balch did so, revealing a crease of dried blood staining the white shirt across his back.

"Look, I just tripped," said Balch.

"My butt," offered Cameron. "You're not cooperating with us. We're taking you downtown."

"Okay, don't do that. I just figured if I was taken to the hospital, my wife would find out."

Gaston and Cameron zeroed in on Balch, and for the next hour learned the real story of what had happened, including being sucked into the hole. Mercer mimed how she had yanked at Balch until he had popped out. Taking careful notes, Gaston managed to fill in other important details of the whooshing explosion and the decompression they had experienced.

There was a noise at the door, and they all looked up to see a skinny, slightly stooped man in his late fifties with short, thinning grey hair. Lieutenant Buddy Barnes' stained suit looked as old as he did, but what distinguished Barnes this day was an angry scowl that incorporated every wrinkle in his small face. Standing beside him, the burly cop showed a mixture of tension at the lieutenant's appearance and relief that he would not be the object of wrath.

Barnes said nothing, but flipped his head, indicating that the two criminalists were to come outside the room. Without waiting, he stalked away down the hall to an empty conference room. Gaston and Cameron followed him in and he whirled around, his jaw clenched.

"What the fuck were you two clowns doing?" he shouted, advancing to within inches of their faces. "You've done the same thing I fuckin' told you not to do before! You're the goddamned lab boys! I'm the god-damned officer in charge! I'll interview the goddamned witnesses! You got that?" He looked back and forth from face to face. Gaston looked back at him calmly, and Cameron seemed fully ready to enjoy what he knew would happen next. Gaston spoke first.

"We needed details you would have—"

"I'll get the goddamned witness details, and you'll just gather infor-mation, do you hear me?" He reined himself in. He was smart enough to realize that this case might hinge on lab results. And he knew Gaston and Cameron were untouchable for the moment. They'd solved a lot of high-profile cases. But there would come a time when they would be vulnerable. "Just tell me what you got."

Unperturbed, Gaston sorted through his notes and Cameron opened his notebook with the measurements.

"Hole's the same size all the way through. Exactly 38 centimeters," said Cameron. "Also at the same angle, a couple of degrees from horizontal. It's all one hole made by a single . . . uh . . . well, we don't know what." He went on to detail the measurements. Then Gaston outlined what they had to do back at the lab—mainly chemical analyses for explosive residue and microscopic studies of the surfaces to detect marks that would indicate the kind of projectile.

"So what the fuck do I tell the media? The cameras are ass-deep downstairs wanting to come up."

"Tell them we don't know."

"Goddamnit, Gaston, give me your best guess. I'm not gonna stand there with my thumb up my ass!"

Gaston and Cameron looked at each other. "Tell them it may be an unexploded projectile of some kind," said Cameron. "We don't have the projectile."

"No evidence of terrorists?"

"Nope," said Cameron.

"I'll say act of God," said Barnes. "Maybe a meteor or frozen crap from an airplane. Okay?" The lieutenant could see by the two criminalists' faces that it wasn't okay. But he didn't care. He yawned, indicating that he felt confident he'd exerted his control over the two. "Okay, do the samples, file a report and turn over the whole mess to . . . hell, I dunno . . . to the FBI and the insurance company. Yeah. Act-of-God kinda thing."

"Barnes, wait a minute." Gaston held up his notes. "Those explanations just won't fly. We've got something really strange here. We've got something really unexplained. This could be a new kind of weapon, like a cannon, or maybe some laser beam."

The lieutenant sighed, as if he were about to explain something to a moron. "Look, Gaston, nobody was hurt. We got no evidence of foul play. We just got a building that has a hole in it. We've got a couple of dozen open murder cases to deal with. Just file a fucking report, will you?"

The lieutenant left to do his own interviews of the man and woman. Gaston quietly gathered his notes and they walked back into the office, passing Balch and Mercer, who followed Barnes to a private office.

This was something different. Gaston almost tasted his need to investigate this case further.

"That was one lucky man. That Balch guy," said Cameron enthusiastically to hide his sense of foreboding. He began to busily wind up the string and gather their tools, signaling, he hoped, their final departure.

"How's that?" Gaston said distractedly, as he continued to stare at the two holes in the office wall.

"Well if the hole had been larger, the guy would be sucked all the way through. Or if it had been smaller and the suction larger, he'd have been squeezed like toothpaste."

"I'm sure he figures this was his lucky day."

"What do you think, then? Meteor? Airplane crap like the lieutenant said? Or some terrorist with a big cannon? Or maybe a secret laser beam? Like maybe from that Livermore Lab. They do fusion stuff with big lasers. There wasn't any debris. Maybe it got burned up. Yeah."

"Or maybe sucked out. Maybe. What we do next is follow the trajectory. Let's see where this hole goes."

"Where it goes?" Cameron looked dubiously at Gaston, following him into the outer office with his arms full of cameras and tools, a piece of string trailing behind him. "What the hell does that mean?"

"We might find something interesting at the impact point."

"C'mon, man, what impact point? Let's just do like the lieutenant says and give this to the Bureau. We're not required to go beyond the scene. Let the insurance guys handle it. Then we can watch them jack around with it. We got no reason to go on with this thing, Ralph."

"I've got an idea I want to try first." Gaston took out his wallet and thumbed through a sheaf of cards and slips of paper. He took out a card and scrutinized it for a moment. Then he picked up the phone receiver.

"Don't you pick up that phone," Cameron ordered, as he began piling up tools and camera equipment for Gaston to load into the cases. "I see that damned stubborn look in your eyes. Like in that other case. It's just been a month since the last time . . . the dead guy . . . you know what the hell I'm talkin' about."

But Ralph Gaston was punching in the number.

"You pick up that fucking phone, you're not ever comin' to my house again!"

Ralph smiled and set the card on the desk, listening to the phone ring at the other end. The card read "Deus Foundation" and gave a New York address and phone number.

•　•　•

"Patrick, I'll give you just ten more minutes, then you just have to go to bed." Patrick's mother stood at the door from the kitchen, peering into the darkened back yard, barely able to make out her son.

"Mom, you should come look," came back the voice from the darkness. "This is radical!" His mother had used the long version of his name, but she hadn't really hollered it, so he knew he still had some time.

"I'm sure it is." She closed the screen door, smiling. Patrick had fallen in love with his new telescope. She hoped the enthusiasm lasted. It got him outside and she liked it better than video games.

"Mom! I'm not kiddin'! Come look! There's a cloud on the moon! Get Dad!" Patrick closed one eye and peered once more into the Celestron telescope at the great, bleak expanse of the half moon spread out before him. He could see the vast maria, or flat plains, and the violently produced punctuation marks of the immense craters. And across one of the maria was a wispy cloud of what looked like mist or steam. It must have been huge. He'd planned to look at the moon just to calibrate the new telescope and then on to the planets. But he'd seen this fog thing.

"The moon doesn't have an atmosphere," a deep voice behind him said. "It's probably just a cloud in front of the telescope. Let me look." Patrick backed away and let his father peer into the eyepiece. After a few adjustments of the eyepiece, his father settled in and looked for a long time. First casually, then more intently. "Hmm," he said. "You may have something here, pal." Patrick itched to get back to the telescope, but his father wouldn't relinquish it, so he looked up at the moon to see what he could see with the unaided eye.

Finally, his father stood back and Patrick peered once more at the strange sight. It was still there, floating above the surface, seeming to emanate from a single spot. "I'm gonna send out a message. See if anybody else has looked at it!" He left the telescope to his father and ran into the house. Within a minute, he'd logged into his Twitter account. He laboriously pecked out a query about whether anybody else had seen the cloud on the moon. He knew he might be ridiculed. Nobody looked at the moon. Nothing important happened on the moon.

CHAPTER 7

"Isn't he ready yet?" Cameron shivered and clasped his arms around himself to ward off the cold, damp wind swirling over the darkened platform. Skinny ballistics experts weren't supposed to find themselves standing atop a thirty-story tower of the San Francisco Bay Bridge in the middle of the night. "Damn, I thought we were gonna get this thing over quick."

Dacey stood beside him, somewhat warmer in her climbing suit, and together they peered out over the glittering San Francisco cityscape. She had to admit it was probably the most incredible view she'd ever had of a city. The streaming lights of the cars on the busy streets, the colorful neon of Chinatown, the faint gleam of the windows on the skyscrapers, the shimmering reflections of the city from the bay waters, the halo of light the city cast into the night sky. It was well worth the cold.

Ralph Gaston and Gerald Meier ignored the weather, busy conferring with the warmly jacketed bridge maintenance supervisor who had brought them up the small creaking elevator inside the steel tower. He'd been only too happy to help them in their quest. He loved his bridge and was deeply concerned that something violent had been done to it.

Dacey was surprisingly calm, considering she was about to climb over the side of this steel tower and be lowered down its face like a spider down a wall. Cameron continued to gripe about the cold. He was a funny guy and they'd hit it off the minute they'd met.

But what *was* she doing here?

It had been two weeks since she had gone down into the crater in Oklahoma, since she had hog-tied Gerald. Two weeks since she woke up the following morning to find Gerald sleeping in his van out front, probably because he couldn't spring for a motel. She'd taken him in, fed him breakfast, then taken him to the university to show him her data. He reminded her of Bobby Lister in high school, the quiet, nerdy kid in calculus. Lister had helped her ace the course and she'd taken him under her wing as a friend.

And it had been two days since Gerald called her up out of the blue to tell her he'd found something in San Francisco that reminded him of the Gillard crater. A hole through an office building. Sitting at her desk, running her fingers over the glass-smooth piece of granite from the cavern, she'd scoffed at first. "Come on, Gerald, a hole in an office building?"

But he'd sent a seismogram—a trace of the ground motion in San Francisco that day—and that had convinced her something strange was up. Whatever made the hole in San Francisco had burrowed underground. And it had left the same characteristic jagged up-and-down lines on the seismogram as had the event that made the Gillard hole. She'd gotten the Gillard trace from the National Earthquake Information Center in Golden, Colorado. Neither of the traces were earthquakes, or an underground explosion. Damnit, they looked like some giant gopher rooting around, grinding through the earth, south to north.

So it was seismic squiggles on a computer screen that brought her to this high, cold bridge tower . . . and the fact that she had applied for a grant from the Deus Foundation, and it couldn't hurt her chances to cooperate with an existing grantee! But she also knew that deep down it was also the haunting agonized faces of Anita Lafferty and the kids, especially Jenny. This phenomenon had torn a hole in their lives. She couldn't fix it, but she could damned well find out what it was!

"Maybe he's still lining it up," said Gaston coming up to stand beside them, concentrating on the tall, graceful Bank of America building that jutted above the skyscrapers around it. As a ballistics expert, he was always calculating trajectories, and he couldn't fathom how a projectile that had pierced a building would travel all the way to the bridge. But they had seen evidence of an impact through their binoculars.

"Call him," demanded Cameron.

"I just did."

"Call him again. He's probably screwing around with the gadget and we're up here freezing."

"Then it would slow him down. We'd be up here longer."

"Shit." Cameron jogged around the platform, stopping to look at the winch that had been bolted on the city side of the platform. He shook his head and kept jogging.

Gerald came up to stand beside Dacey, and she looked over at him with more than a little interest. His bearded face was dramatically lit by the city glow, his dark curls shining. He turned to her, his gaze intent with concern.

"You okay with this?"

"Piece of cake, Gerald. I've climbed down rock faces taller than this. And it's a motorized winch. Piece of cake."

"Well, you saw the crater in Gillard. You saw the hole in the building. You can tell us a lot, maybe."

Dacey could tell he was trying to convince himself as much as her. He was worried about her. That was sweet.

Gerald looked up at the three-quarter moon, shining steadily.

"Lot of strange things going on. You hear about the cloud on the moon?"

"The one the kid found? The gas vent? Hasn't everybody? You think that's one of your mysterious 'appearances'?"

But before he could answer an intense green laser beam pierced the night, emanating from the distant building and striking the bridge tower somewhere below them.

"There!" Gaston smiled, but he didn't have to point. The glittering beam seemed almost a shaft of solid matter, for it did not spread, but maintained its tight columnar shape. It seemed to declare its own identity in the darkness, to assert its presence as a power that was alien to everyday routine.

"Man, this is gonna be all over the news tomorrow," said Cameron. "Barnes is gonna be pissed as hell we kept on with this investigation." He paused and with great relish concluded, "Well, fuck 'im!"

"Wow!" said the bridge supervisor, his sunburned, wrinkled face breaking into a broad grin. "That sure is somethin' all right. A laser, eh?"

"Yeah, an argon laser," said Gaston, leaning over as far as he could to see where the beam struck the tower. My friend uses it in his laser light shows, but he said he'd use it to help me trace this trajectory."

"You were right, Ralph," said Cameron. "The path does end on this tower. And looks like the thing would've hit the tower. Good sightin'."

But Gaston had already moved off, following Dacey and Gerald. Dacey was strapping herself into the bridgeworker's harness that had lain in a pile in the middle of the platform.

"Y'know, you coulda taken a picture of the tower, like through a telephoto lens," said the supervisor as he helped Dacey buckle the leather harness firmly around her chest and under her legs.

"Then we wouldn't have the trajectory," said Gaston. "I want to know how much this projectile dropped over this distance. If Dacey can find a dent, she can measure how far it is below the beam. Then, we can figure out the mass of the projectile. Maybe even trace fragments."

Dacey liked Ralph Gaston, too, even though the quiet man was very different than her in personality. Neither of them would let this mystery rest until they had figured it out.

As Gerald checked out the buckles and straps that held Dacey into the harness—with almost obsessive care—Gaston flipped open his cell phone and punched in a number. After a moment, there was an answer. "Elton, it looks good. Yeah. You sure you're sighted right down the middle of the holes? Yeah. Okay, I'll call. Bye." He slipped the phone into his belt pouch.

Cameron had been inspecting the winch, and he stepped over to Dacey and also began to assiduously check the straps, buckles and clasps of the harness, as well as the bag of tools on Dacey's belt.

"Guys, guys, it's all right," Dacey waved her hands at them and strapped on her trusty battered helmet. "You're like a bunch of mother hens."

Despite her protests Cameron continued his examination, yanking hard on the heavy metal shackle to which the cable would attach.

"I could go," said Gaston.

"I wouldn't let him go," explained Cameron. "I just didn't trust him. I figured because of him being a fairy and all, he'd think he could fly."

Gaston's elaborate sigh at his friend's teasing brought smiles that helped ease the tension, as Dacey moved to the edge of the platform and the technician snapped the steel cable onto the harness.

"We use this harness, this cable, for painting and inspection all the time. It'll hold about five hundred pounds."

"I'll remember that when I'm hanging by it," said Dacey. She donned a headset the supervisor gave her and they tested the intercom link. Then Dacey swung out over the dizzying precipice, bracing her feet on the edge of the platform. Below her, the huge support cables of the bridge arched downward to the bridge deck, where miniature cars and trucks flowed in a steady stream across the bridge. Dacey realized she was panting and had clenched her hands around the cable in front of her. The fact that she wasn't rappelling down good old rock made her edgy. This was cold, unfriendly steel and below her, a highway and cars. She willed herself to relax, to put her confidence in the cable. The very, very thick steel cable.

"Ready?" she heard in her ear. It was Gaston, speaking into his own microphone. "Cameron says you don't have to do this. He could do it."

"Then he can do it." There was pause.

"He says, 'Hell, no.' He was just being polite."

She smiled. "Then lower away." The workman flipped a switch and the winch whined to life lowering her inch by inch down the side of the massive tower. She fended off the cold gray-painted steel face with her hands as she went, rivet by rivet, down the side. She twisted and looked down. The laser beam splashed its green color against the tower far below and to the right of her. She'd have to swing back and forth to reach the spot. As she'd done so many times before on a rock face, she began to walk herself to the left across the face of the tower, swinging back to the right, to see how far she could get.

"What are you doin'?" she heard Gaston in her ear.

"I'm going to have to swing over to line myself up. I'm just testing."

"Well, you're scaring Jimmy."

"So *damned* sorry," she laughed. After another thirty feet, she had lowered to about the level of the laser beam. She ordered a halt and twisted to look back at the building. It was a remarkable sight, the intense green light streaming from the distant building. Many of the lights in the building were on, as the tenants had stayed late to watch the experiment. She turned back to the vast steel wall before her.

"Okay, I'm going to start at the level of the beam, then work down until I find an impact mark." She began to walk herself to the left, swooping back to the right. Walking left, swooping right . . . left . . . right, until she began to build up enough momentum to swing herself over to the laser beam. One last bounding stride to the left and she knew she had enough momentum. She swung wide right and into the laser beam and was astonished to see flash past her eyes a hole as large and perfect as the one through the building.

"Jesus!" she huffed as she swung back left.

"Jesus, what?" asked Gaston.

"There's a hole here, too. Same level as the beam."

"Wow!"

Dacey pushed left with her legs and hands to give herself enough momentum to swing wide right once again. Sure enough, she swooped into the green brilliance and the hole was there. Whatever had made these holes was unaffected by gravity!

Suddenly, the laser beam was overwhelmed by a white glaring light and a powerful thudding sound behind her. A news helicopter had drifted in to hover between her and the beam. She waved the helicopter away. The cameraman leaning out of the helicopter waved back. She waved again. She heard the faint pop of gunfire from above him. The helicopter swooped away and the laser beam returned.

Dacey pushed out and looked upward, although she knew she wouldn't be able to see anything. "What was that? Did you shoot at them?"

"Jimmy brought a gun. He says it was just blanks. I made him put it away."

"Well, hell, it worked!" Dacey resumed the swinging. Sweat trickled down her forehead from the exertion. She swung up to the hole and grabbed for it. An excruciating pain shot through her fingers and she yelled and grabbed her hand and allowed her swing to dissipate. The two slices had cut right through her gloves and to her fingers. They were the width of the tower steel's thickness, and they bled profusely, like being cut by a razor. She rummaged in her tool bag and pulled out a cloth, wrapping her fingers tightly. Through the pain, a realization: the hole was sliced as cleanly as the sliced-off rock that rested on her office desk!

"What happened?" asked Cameron.

"The edges are sharp," she said, not wanting to worry Gerald more. She set her jaw and resumed the swing. Using the bloody cloth as a cushion, she grabbed the edge of the hole again, careful not to draw her hand along the edge. She could see that the ultrasharp edges were fraying the cloth, but she was determined to see this hole up close. She hauled herself up even with the hole.

The cut edge of the inch-thick steel plate gleamed in the laser light like polished metal. Holding onto the hole, she carefully stuck her leg through, hooked it gingerly into the hole and leaned out so her helmet camera would get a good shot of it. She could feel the extreme sharpness of the edges through her thick climbing suit pants. She couldn't stay like this long. She grabbed the hole and brought the helmet camera in for closeup shots. She also fished out a tape measure, payed it out and held it up against the hole. Diameter of 38 centimeters. Same as in the building, if she remembered Gaston's briefing correctly. She reported the measurement to Gaston.

Finally, she hauled herself up as best she could to peer through the hole, leaning over sideways in the harness. Her eyes came into line with the hole. Her head blocked part of the laser beam, but she could see that the hole passed all the way through the tower. Beyond, she could see the shimmering waters of San Francisco Bay. That's where whatever-it-was had gone into the ground, making the seismic trace. Maybe the next phase of this search would be underwater. If she got the Deus Foundation grant. She took more pictures. This was getting weirder and weirder.

"Pull me up," she said tersely into the microphone. "We've got a lot of thinking to do."

CHAPTER 8

Dinner on the supertanker was mock turtle soup, Caesar salad, veal marsala, asparagus with hollandaise, a potato soufflé the chef had invented on the last voyage, and peach melba for dessert. The drink was an excellent sparkling water.

With a final sip from the crystal goblet, the captain stood and nodded contentedly to the officers, who were preparing to adjourn to the wardroom for after-dinner sodas, and the nightly card game, and later a movie. They didn't ask him to join. He had clamped his pipe between his teeth. They knew it was a sign he would spend the next hour strolling the vast deck in the darkness, breathing the cool sea air and thinking about whatever it was he needed to think about.

At that moment he was thinking of his pipe. He would have dearly loved to light it. He admitted he was simply torturing himself. But given that the supertanker Castile carried four million barrels of thick Venezuelan crude in its cavernous steel tanks, there was the usual rule that it was a no-smoking ship, and even though he was the captain, he was not about to break that rule. He thought of the pipe as a reminder that in two weeks they would be docked at Fos-sur-Mer. The chief officer and the pumpman would do their duty, and he could leave the tanker to the experienced men and go ashore to meet his wife and smoke his pipe.

He was a small, spare man, with sharp Mediterranean features, thinning dark hair, and intense, dark eyes. But the crew swore that he grew much larger when he became angry, which was seldom. When a seaman did well, he offered as reward a half-smile. Together with the twinkle in his eyes, it was a sufficient communication of approval for any of his longtime crew.

And so he was happy tonight. Four days to the Strait of Gibraltar, good seas, and only the single significant valve problem, which would be fixed long before they reached the sea dock.

He climbed the stairs to the bridge deck, entering the darkened control room with its long row of monitors, indicator lights, buttons and switches. The radiance from the computer screens was more than sufficient to overwhelm the faint starshine outside. And there was not much of a moon to contribute its light. He sauntered along the row of instruments. At each station, the mate on duty tensed slightly, prepared to report verbally if necessary the status of his watch. But the captain merely nodded at each and glanced at the screen to glean the information himself.

Although the captain had begun his career before the age of computer controls, he had taken great care to learn them.

He completed his control room inspection and stepped out the door into the night. He descended to the main deck, walking around to the catwalk. Under the single tall deck light amidship, the catwalk stretched down the center of the great ship for most of its thousand-yard length. He loved this walk, along the very spine of this gigantic moving island that he oversaw. But he didn't admit it. He insisted that this was a nightly inspection trip. He started along the catwalk, his hand now and then brushing the cool rail with his fingertips to mark the rhythm of his walk. The only sounds were the faint metallic thunk of his shoes on the steel grating, underlain by the delicate distant whisper of the breeze. The gigantic screw that drove the supertanker was held deep underwater by the weight of its cargo. And the bow, his objective, was almost a quarter-mile ahead. That destination represented the only real contact he had with the ocean on this immense vessel. He loved to lean over the bow in the darkness and watch the ocean being relentlessly cleaved into a curling, hissing froth by the advance of the ship's bulbous prow.

He reached the midship deck light suspended high on a pole and proceeded beyond toward the darkness of the bow. The first mate knew to briefly extinguish the bow lamp for him when no other ships were on radar. And since the broad windows in the looming superstructure behind him were heavily curtained, the darkness on deck was profound, and to some, frightening.

Peering out at the ocean, he was just able to make out the faint white frosting of foam on the occasional breaker. He didn't like perfectly calm seas. He liked seas that had some character, some intricate interweaving of waves that offered a challenge to a mariner's sea sense.

He looked downward occasionally as he walked, scanning the familiar labyrinth of pipes and valves below the catwalk that allowed the great mass of ebony liquid to be transferred and managed. He knew every component of that system, and when the offending malfunctioning valve passed beneath, he gave it an especially reproachful look.

He stopped in the darkest part of the catwalk and looked up at the stars. Only the brightest ones shone through the faint haze that marked the nearness of the African continent, even though they were a hundred miles at sea. This region was the nursery for hurricanes that would begin as mere storms in the warm ocean, drawing strength and power to slam against the East coast of the U.S. He always gave this part of the Atlantic the proper respect. Again, he looked out across the dark sea stretching away to the horizon. He remembered his beginnings as a seventeen-year-old seaman on an ocean-going tug. He had been close to the sea then, learning the infinity of its fluid moods. Now he commanded this floating island that rode apart from the sea's governance, a law unto itself.

His reverie quickly faded, though, eroded by a growing realization that the water had grown strangely visible. He stared hard at the sea. Yes, he was sure. It had begun to glow with a faint greenish phosphorescence that he could only barely discern. This was new. This was unsettling. He watched for a while to make sure it was not some trick played by the night on his middle-aged eyes. Or maybe it was like the faint bioluminescence called the white sea he'd seen many times in the Arabian Sea. No. Indeed, there *was* a new, an unusual, source of light somewhere below the surface. He decided the glow was strongest to port, clenched his pipe between his teeth and strode briskly along the catwalk to a portside ramp and hurried along it toward the railing. Around him the glow rose to suffuse the ship in a half-light that he had never seen before, giving the familiar steel clutter an eerily ghostly aspect. He reached the railing and leaned over, peering into the water.

Despite the surface chop from the ship's wake, he could make out the glow deep in the water. It had brightened, revealing the immense depth of the deep green ocean beneath the ship.

He inhaled deeply, his nostrils filling with a salty aroma marking heated seawater. He felt steam rising against his face, moistening it.

The ocean erupted. Huge boiling fumaroles burst to the surface, launching curling clouds of salty vapor high into the air. The light deep below intensified into a yellowish glare that overcame even the ocean's light-absorbing abilities. He scanned the horizon. Far out beyond the ship, he could see the usual smooth progress of the waves suddenly overcome by the boiling. He looked over the side once more and was met with a scalding geyser of water. He staggered back, his face and hands stinging from the heat. A heart-pumping fear rose within him, but was promptly suppressed by his discipline, by the weight of responsibility.

He turned and ran back to the main catwalk and on to the aft superstructure, pounding up the metal stairs to the bridge deck and into the wheelhouse. He found the watch crew desperate for his presence. Their questions piled one upon the other.

"What is it?"

"What's that light?"

"You seen that before, cap'n?"

He waved them off. Before any speculation could be done, he had to know the status of his ship and its now-ominous cargo. The chief officer's strained face, lit by the glow of the computer screen and the growing light from outside, told there was a problem.

"Temperature's rising," he said quietly, frowning at the screen as if a stern expression would set things right. But as they watched, the numbers on the screen inexorably advanced.

"Core up?"

"Not yet, but peripheral's up. What think?"

"Jesus. Undersea explosion of some kind. Maybe a volcano." The captain turned to the first mate, a sandy-haired young man, who stood ready to do just about anything the captain asked. The mate was tense with the certain knowledge of the consequences of a rising temperature in the tanks. "Ernesto, get up on the monkey island. Take a radio; tell me what you see." The mate grabbed a portable radio and hurried out. The captain scanned his gaze back and forth across the row of computer screens. He motioned to the radioman. "Start sending out a full description of this . . . event. Put Ernesto on speaker. Tell whoever you raise that best we can figure it's an undersea volcano. Get this out."

"S.O.S., captain?"

"Not yet. Don't know the fix we're in yet." But, in fact, he did as he watched the tank temperatures continue to rise. He'd never seen anything like this. He also knew that the middle of the Atlantic crustal plate was no place for a volcano. Nuclear submarine explosion? Possible. He looked out the window. The glow from the ocean bathed the ship in an undulating liquid light that approached daylight. Ernesto's voice came over the loudspeaker from the monkey island, the ship's topmost deck.

"Cap'n, it's boilin' all around. The steam's rising and great spurts of water goin' up."

"How far?"

"Mile around maybe."

"Anyplace we can make for, to get out of this?"

There was a pause, filled by a crackle over the speaker. The captain held his breath.

"Starboard," came the answer. "I can see maybe reg'lar seas forty degrees starboard!"

"Okay, good work." The captain turned calmly to the helmsman, who looked back at him with frightened twenty-year-old eyes. "Starboard forty, full ahead." But the captain knew it was a meaningless act. A supertanker took miles to make any maneuver. But it was something to do.

"Jesus!" said Ernesto over the speaker. "Cap'n, I wish you'd come up. I just can't figure—"

But the captain was already out the door, taking the stairs two at a time. He felt wet tropical heat billow around him as he reached the monkey island and stood among the antennas and the radar dish whirling overhead, peering out.

The ocean had transformed into a glowing, boiling cauldron for a mile around, and the gargantuan tanker was a mere toy floating trapped in its midst. The rising light from below had caused the sky to withdraw into an unfathomable blackness. They seemed to be situated near the middle of the seething eruptions. He looked down on the deck, suddenly aware of the oily smell from the heating cargo that was rising from vents.

"Transmit s.o.s.," he said quietly, and the first mate relayed the message through his radio.

A new sound rose. The fiery hissing roar of a giant blowtorch. The unmistakable smoky tang of melting metal. A blindingly intense light growing portside.

"God, captain! God! We—"

But his voice was drowned out by the deafening explosion that ripped the heart from the ship and unleashed a dark, glistening wave of oil onto the boiling ocean.

With the banshee shriek of tearing steel plate, the immense vessel began to rip itself in half. The oil burst into flame between the separating halves, giving birth to a monstrous cloud of carbon-dark smoke and a roiling orange-red fire reaching into the sky.

The captain staggered back as the deck listed crazily, but he recovered and pulled himself to the railing. Ernesto leaped down the stairs and away. The captain looked down in horror as the crew scurried for their lives below, wrestling life rafts to the side and over into the demented fiery sea. His whole being reached out in grief to these men, these doomed men whom he had loved. He sobbed as they slid desperately down swinging ropes into the boats to be enveloped by the roiling flames or die screaming in the seething ocean.

He stood desperately clutching the railing, watching the main deck become awash in burning oil and steaming water. As the swirling maelstrom rose toward him, boiling and crackling, the shattered stern of the tanker tilted back to face the inky sky. Oil streamed from the jagged wound and the heavy superstructure weighted the stern, driving it down into the flaming waters.

But the captain refused to release the railing, as if his unyielding grip would somehow pull the ship back together and lift it from this hellish death. He held on even when the fireball burst forth, the storm of flame that marked the explosion of the largest tanks. His body was buffeted by a hurricane of wind that rushed in to feed the fireball, which rolled upward for a mile, carrying flaming oil, smoke and a fine mist of black vapor. The captain suffered only a brief searing agony as the flames charred his skin into shriveling cooked flesh before the burning surface rose to cover him.

And then he was gone.

CHAPTER 9

"THIS JUST DOESN'T HAPPEN! THIS JUST BLOODY GOD-DAMNED WELL DOESN'T HAPPEN!" Gordon Haggerty bellowed into his headset microphone over the helicopter engine's roar. The red-haired, bull-necked Vice President for Transportation Operations glared in the direction of his fellow passenger Philippe Togani, a wiry dark-haired Frenchman, who agreed with a solemn nod of his head. Togani, the company's best structural engineer, knew that it didn't happen, too. Haggerty peered once more out the helicopter window at the tragic scene passing slowly below. Scattered on the choppy gray-green ocean, periodically brightened by shafts of traveling sunlight peeking between thick puffy clouds, were the pitiably meager remnants of what had once been a 350,000-ton supertanker. A few scattered bodies in orange lifejackets bobbed among oil-stained boxes, chunks of plastic, unidentifiable clumps of debris, empty lifejackets and life rafts, one fully inflated. All of the remains were surrounded by a black layer of oil that lay in great dark amoeboid patches on the ocean, riding the gentle waves up and down.

The gleaming white Seahawk helicopter with the Shell Oil logo on its side hovered over the stricken area like some grieving angel offering last rites on the tragedy. Haggerty was bone-tired from the overnight flight from London to Tenerife, and the run out to the site in the helicopter. But for the moment the anger had banished all traces of fatigue.

"Am I right, Philippe?" he asked in his rolling Scottish brogue. "We've got a young ship . . . maybe five years old. We've got a fine captain, an experienced crew, a good sea . . ." he paused. Below them, the crew of the rust-stained Argentinean freighter that was first on the scene was pulling an orange-lifejacketed body from the sea. He continued ". . . deep water, full load. This just damned well doesn't happen!"

"Well, it did, Gordon. Something went very wrong," came a voice in his headset. He twisted around to glare at Brendan Cooper, a sandy-haired young man, who looked back at him with his characteristic straightforward gaze. Cooper was a man of medium height, medium build. At first glance, people didn't take him for one of the world's leading oceanographers. But he was animated by a breezy confidence, even brashness.

At this particular moment, Haggerty hated the disrespectful little son-of-a-bitch, but he knew that Cooper's disrespect was what made him valuable as an independent consultant in these matters. The insurance companies, the media and his superiors would trust whatever the Woods Hole oceanographer concluded about this disaster.

"Well, it's your goddamned business to figure out why," said Haggerty. "This is no Gulf of Mexico. We were doing everything right, as far as we know. You know that. It was terrorism! Had to be!"

"We'll see," said Cooper simply and went back to surveying the wreckage out the back window. With the practiced air of one used to scanning the ocean for insight, he searched the debris-strewn ocean for clues. He made notes in a battered notebook with the insignia of the Woods Hole Oceanographic Institution. He was making decisions as he watched the tragedy slide by below, watching the freighter gathering bodies. He was figuring out what help he would need on this one. He knew he could do whatever he wanted. That was always the deal when an oil company brought him in as a consultant.

"What about the slick?" shouted Haggerty. Cooper turned his attention to the huge shimmering dark stains on the ocean below. He tapped his pen on the notebook, calling up in his mind what he knew of wind, currents and geography in the area.

"Just my first estimate, mind you," he said. "You'll have to consult with your containment group. But I don't think the Canaries are in danger. I think maybe in a week it will end up in Morocco. And I think it'll be well-weathered by then. Maybe thick tar. They've got time to get the equipment out there, to develop a cleanup plan."

Togani's voice in the headphones: "You know, Gordon, there's still the question of whether the gas-inerting system failed."

The structural engineer was right. That was a vexing question. Like any modern supertanker, the Castile had a system to pump cooled engine exhaust gases into the oil tanks. The gases displaced air, preventing explosions that had ripped supertankers apart in the past. But Haggerty had a good answer.

"True, but even if the inerting system did fail, explosions like that are really only a problem with empty tanks, right?" Togani nodded in agreement. Haggerty twisted around to Cooper. "Say that, Cooper. Make sure you say that to the press when they ask."

"Gordon, I'm not saying anything till I'm ready. Turn your high-paid flacks loose on it for now. Better still, have your president be a stand-up guy for a change."

Cooper could tell he'd gotten to Haggerty from the knot of tensed muscles that rose in the back of Haggerty's neck. He grinned, showing white teeth amidst the tanned, thin face. Some people avoided Cooper because of his tart tongue. Other people enjoyed the spice of his personality, appreciated the fact that Cooper was always up front with his opinions. Cooper always believed in the virtue of the fresh breeze of honesty. He also believed that just the right amount of needling yielded useful information in most situations.

But enough bear-baiting. He had work to do. He issued an instruction to the pilot and the co-pilot over his headset. "Ready the winch. I'm going down to the deck."

Haggerty shook his head vigorously. "Well, only if I go," shouted Haggerty over the noise. "I damned well want to see what happened."

"No," said Cooper. "I don't want it said that I had any company people looking over my shoulder. And you'd be a distraction."

"I'm not a fucking distraction! I'm your fucking employer!"

"Then fire me, Gordon. Look, Lloyd's is going to be all over me with questions tomorrow, and I'd better be ready with answers that I can vouch for as untainted."

Haggerty's gathering anger evaporated. He could picture the row of stiff, formal Lloyd's of London agents sitting across from him in their richly appointed conference room, looking for the slightest opportunity to avoid paying the insurance claim. He could put up a much better argument if Cooper could say he did his investigation without any participation from the oil company.

Haggerty muttered instructions to the pilot and co-pilot to go ahead with the drop.

"Video the whole area," Cooper told the co-pilot. "I'll call you with further instructions." He picked up a hand-held radio and clipped it snugly to his belt. He was already dressed for a drop, in khaki work shirt and pants, an inflatable life vest and rubber-soled work shoes.

He donned sunglasses and waited impatiently until the co-pilot slid open the helicopter's large door and readied the sling. He grabbed the cable, slipped into the sling and swung fearlessly out the door, as the co-pilot flicked the switch activating the electric winch to let out the steel cable. The punishing wash from the helicopter blades whipped at Cooper's clothes, and he squinted his eyes and peered down. The pilot had brought the helicopter in to hover over the freighter's bow deck. When the freighter crew saw what was happening, several took up stations below to receive him. He twisted slowly as he descended, using the opportunity to scan the area around the ship from a new angle. The deck pitched up with a swell, making him land with a thump. He quickly extricated himself from the sling and strode down the deck to meet the captain.

After exchanging greetings in Spanish, the short, round-faced captain showed Cooper through the maze of battered crates and deck equipment to the ladder leading to the large wooden lifeboat from which rescue operations were taking place. Cooper lowered himself nimbly down the ladder and found himself standing amidst a scene he never ever wished to have witnessed. In the bobbing boat were two bodies that had just been brought in. He steeled himself to keep from vomiting at the overwhelmingly putrid odor of rotting, burned flesh mixed with the suffocating stench of oil that would stay with him the rest of his life. He stood for a moment recovering his composure, reminding himself of his mission. Even he was not ready for this grisly business. The shirtless, sweating crewmen wore bandannas over their mouths, and one of them held up a cloth to Cooper, who gratefully took it and tied it tightly on. It reduced the smell only slightly. The men were preparing to load the bodies into a cargo net to be hoisted aboard, but Cooper waved for them to stop. He turned one over. It was but a charred remnant of a human being, the life vest burned away, the flesh black. Cooper stood up and willed himself once again to keep from vomiting. God, but it was hot! Unnaturally hot. He filed away the piece of information, even as he recovered from the shocking sight. The other body was burned as badly. He waved the crewmen to take the bodies away and spent some time staring out at the sea to recover.

The crewmen finished unloading the bodies and cast off. Cooper pointed toward the life raft he'd seen bobbing several hundred yards from the ship. The flat crack of rifle fire sounded from the ship. Cooper peered toward the sound's source, and saw the captain standing beside a crewman with a rifle and pointing seaward. He peered in the direction indicated and saw a shark thrashing in a pink spreading cloud of its own blood. Another fin swerved and headed for the wounded creature slamming into it, creating a boiling foam of tearing flesh. They had to hurry with their gruesome harvest.

Cooper fought to avoid being overcome by the oil fumes as the lifeboat approached the rubber raft, in which lay a lifejacketed body, slumped on the bottom. A crewman grabbed the handhold on the raft and secured it to the stern. Keeping an eye on the nearest shark fin, Cooper made his way down the pitching boat to the stern and leaned down, hauling on the line until the raft was fast against the side of the boat. He leaned over and grabbed the body by the shoulder of the life vest, rolling it on its back. The face was the dead white color of a fish belly and bloated. There was no charring. He picked up the hand. It, too, was white and grossly swollen, with some fingernails torn off. The man had not burned to death. He appeared to have boiled to death! Cooper braced his hand against the slick gunwales of the boat, preparing to stand, but he slipped and almost fell into the water, his hand plunging into the oil-covered ocean up to his elbow. He felt a crewman grab his shirt to haul him up. But he waved with his free hand to be let go. He left his arm hanging in the heaving ocean. The ocean was warm! No, by God, it was as hot as a bloody bath!

He stood up and stared at the ocean in disbelief. The Gulf Stream wasn't anywhere near here, and even if it were, the warm tropical water it carried was nowhere near this hot. The heat became a highly significant piece of data.

He queried the seamen in Spanish and they answered that they had smelled the heated water and the oil for an hour before they sighted the debris and the bodies. He peered at the helicopter, which was making a low video-recording run over the ocean. The video file would be transmitted via satellite to the company headquarters that night. He took out the radio and clicked it on, pulling the bandanna down from his mouth.

"Cooper here. Gordon, you copy?" There was a click, and Haggerty's voice came back clearly in the affirmative.

"What's the situation with your data-gathering?" asked Cooper.

"The HMS Greeley will arrive in a couple of hours to take over the investigation. Our team is on board, and we'll have a survey report on the slick within three hours."

"Fine. Now, Gordon, we've got something here that I've never seen before. Some bodies were burned, but one that should be alive in a raft looks to have been scalded, boiled."

"My God, really?"

"Yes. And the water is incredibly warm here. I'm going to stay and take temperature measurements and chemical samples. I'll want infrared satellite data from the National Weather Service. I know they monitor ocean temperatures. We'll want to know the extent of this anomaly. And get me seismic records." Cooper stared down at the body, which was awash in a shallow pool of seawater in the bottom of the raft. He thought a moment. "Oh, and tell him that I know the Navy still runs its SOSUS hydrophone system in this area. Even if they deny it, tell them I damned well want the records from the last twenty-four hours. Your Los Angeles organization can put pressure on, if necessary." He added, "Gordon, I want to see that wreck when Philippe does."

"Aye, of course. I've called Bradley in the exploration division. I've told him to cut loose that new ship of his from the North Sea . . . the Acorn. I want an ROV down on the wreck within a week."

"And I'll want a manned unit. Get me Deep Flight. And I want you to locate and fetch another guy I know. An astrophysicist."

"What the hell do I need an astrophysicist for?"

"Gordon, this is really screwy. A lot of things don't fit. I want somebody who has no preconceived notions . . . who understands a lot of physics. Y'know, like when they got that Nobelist Richard Feynman to be on the committee for the Space Shuttle Challenger explosion."

"I suppose I'll have to pay for this astrophysicist."

"Well, yeah, if he remembers to bill you. He sometimes forgets."

"Is he a smart-ass like you?"

Cooper looked up at the huge helicopter hovering over the ocean a quarter-mile away. He could almost see Haggerty's glower.

"Nope, but he sees things in a way nobody else does. He's smarter than me. His name's Gerald Meier." Cooper signed off, clicked off the radio and slipped it onto his belt, still staring down at the body. Another rifle shot from the ship interrupted his private mourning for the seaman he'd never known, the one who, without even speaking, had told him of the horror that had happened here.

* * *

Dacey ran her hand absentmindedly over the glass-smooth surface of the rock from the cavern, as she sat at her desk and studied the seismograms once more. For two weeks she'd pondered the mystery, leaving it and coming back, as if she might sneak up on some unsuspecting insight and pounce. She leaned back in her comfortable desk chair in her well-appointed office in the geology building. Geology at Oklahoma Tech was very highly prized and well-supported, given the state's dependence on oil. So, the building was a handsome concrete-and-glass structure with carpeted halls, offices outfitted with the best oak furniture, and walls decorated with handsome framed images of geological strata and formations. Dacey had taken care to decorate her own office to suit the quality, with some beautiful geodes, a chunk of iron pyrite, some large malachite crystals, and a small collection of framed antique geological maps.

Today, she was especially glad she'd made it a nice office; and that she'd spent two hours the day before cleaning up piles of papers, books, rock samples, and assorted tools.

Today, she would get a site visit from the representative of the Deus Foundation. He'd probably inspect the research labs, talk to the department chairman, and critique her research plan. And then she would know whether she'd gotten the grant.

She felt a bit out of place sitting in the neat office, dressed in nice beige linen pants and a blue cotton blouse with puffy sleeves, low heels and her silver Indian-feather earrings. Her hair was done up in an efficient, businesslike bun, although stray blondish wisps kept escaping to hang down at her neck.

The graduate students who had come by to consult on their research had noticed the changes. Especially that she wasn't dressed in her usual jeans and t-shirt with a flannel work shirt. She'd always had problems dressing like an associate professor, however that was supposed to be.

She remembered the newspaper photo one of the students had taped on her door, and arched an eyebrow and made a worried face. Maybe she should take it down. Maybe the guy from the foundation wouldn't think it professional. After all, it showed her covered in mud, rising out of the cavern in the basket with the rescue workers. The handwritten caption was, "Guess which one is the geologist?" Beneath it, somebody else had added, "Our den mudder."

To hell with it, she shrugged. That's who she was. She went back to her study of the seismograms, fiddling with her left earring as she examined the jagged up-and-down scrawls on the laptop screen. Side by side were the traces from the Gillard collapse and the San Francisco event. Her conclusions were still unshakeable. These weren't earthquakes. No way. An earthquake typically produced two sharp spikes of ground motion, one right after another. When an earthquake fault ruptured, it sent out shear waves and pressure waves—those that shook the earth back and forth, and those that shoved it forward and backward. One kind of wave always traveled faster, arrived before the other, making two separate spikes the signature of the earthquake. And an underground explosion would show up as a two-spiked pulse, something like an earthquake.

But these traces! Just steady jiggling and shaking. Again she thought of some huge animal rooting around.

Still no closer to capturing an elusive insight, her mind wandered. What had become of Gerald Meier? After her adventure hanging over the side of the bridge tower, they'd all gone to the San Francisco police department laboratories to work up the data. Then they'd had a late dinner at a fish place on the wharf. Gerald had dropped her at her hotel, stuffed his worn spiral notebooks into his blue van and taken off, promising to call her the next day. But he hadn't.

She found herself worrying about him, and wondering why she worried. Maybe because he was different from her usual friends—beer-drinking jock-intellectuals, who built bridges, or who tore them down, or who looked for oil or minerals in Godforsaken places.

Typical of that group was her last boyfriend, Kenneth, the civil engineer. He was the second since her divorce. He was the Iron Man contestant who ran six miles at lunch and wandered the apartment at night like a caged animal. He'd not gotten tenure, though, and had moved out West and gone to work for a mining company. They decided a couple of months ago that neither of them was committed enough that she could be expected to pull up stakes and go with him. She wasn't sure she could ever follow a man anywhere after what she'd been through. Since then, she'd had occasional dates, fending off all of them. Well, not fending off one—the visiting geologist with the incredible smile whom she'd briefly made a fool of herself over. Her spirit was feeling the weight of the past when she was aware of somebody standing at the door.

A very tall, very large man in his late fifties stood there in a slightly too-small blue suit, whose coat couldn't quite close around his round belly. The prominent paunch strained at the buttons of his shirt and rested heavily over his belt. His jowly face, which spilled over his collar, was flushed from exertion, with the faintest sheen of perspiration. He didn't notice the photo of a mud-covered Dacey.

"Dacey Livingstone?" He breathed raspily, hefting a large case at his side.

"Yes?" She paused. Could this be the Deus representative? Somehow, she pictured a more dapper man; a fastidious, well-dressed gent who looked like the grants officer for an exclusive private foundation. "Lawrence Platt?"

"Yes. May I come in?"

She stood and shook hands, his large, meaty mitt enveloping hers. She asked if she could get him anything to drink, and he requested a glass of water. She left him sitting in her guest chair to get a glass and water from the department office. As she did the chore, she reviewed what she knew about the Deus Foundation.

Very little, it turned out. The university fundraisers told her it wasn't listed in their reference books of foundations. They did a Google search for media mentions and found a few stories about research projects the foundation funded in physics, philosophy, medicine. But they assured her the lack of information wasn't too unusual. There were dozens, probably hundreds of little foundations out there, set up with bequests from individuals, or with private money from some rich businessmen.

These foundations were often "unconventional," the fundraisers had told her. Sometimes eccentric in what they funded. But they also were willing to write out checks based on a good idea, even if it was unproven. And they didn't require the volumes of applications and the incredibly stringent reviews that government grants demanded. But even so, the two-page application and four-page research description she'd done for the Deus grant seemed incredibly perfunctory.

She found a nice glass and filled it with water from the cooler. She decided that, no doubt, Platt would more than compensate for the short form with a lengthy grilling and inspections.

She returned to find Platt sitting quietly, his bulk filling her guest chair, holding a slim folder on his lap. He accepted the water gratefully and downed half of it in one drink.

"Now," he said fishing glasses from his coat pocket, opening the folder and peering at its contents. "We've looked over your application and it looks fine. Here's our standard agreement. Fairly simple." He handed her a single sheet of paper and waited for her to read it. Basically, it said that she would periodically report her findings to the foundation and would agree to work with other foundation grantees on projects of mutual interest. And it gave all patent rights to her and the university.

There were no accounting requirements, no reporting, no requirement to even acknowledge the foundation.

"This is it?"

"Yes. Would you sign it?"

"Uh, sure." She scribbled her signature on the paper and handed it back. The university lawyers normally wanted to go over such contracts with a fine tooth comb. But this one sure didn't need a lawyer to protect the university's rights. The university had all the rights, anyway.

"Fine, well . . ." Platt heaved himself out of his chair and handed her an envelope. "We're pleased to have you as a grantee." He reached out his large hand and she shook it, and turned and left.

She stood there a moment unbelieving, looking at the envelope. That was it! No grilling, no lab inspections? No seminar to describe her plans? No interviews with deans or department chairmen? No lawyers? She opened the envelope and pulled out a check. Her eyes widened in even greater disbelief.

It was made out to her personally, not to the university. And it was for $180,237.00! A hundred thousand dollars more than she'd asked for!

CHAPTER 10

The scoreboard clock ticked off with inexorable authority the closing five minutes of the football game, and the crowd cheered in its collective teenaged soprano voice for the Tigers of Melville, Missouri. The cheers were especially deafening, because the team had made it to the five yard line, and were about to score a game-tying touchdown against the conference-leading Porter City Yellow Jackets.

But the lanky teenagers at the other end of the verdant green field leaned with calculated cool against the chain link fence. Out of the full glare of the tall lights, they practiced their indifference. They presented to the world a sharp contrast to the bright-eyed bouncy cheerleaders and the striving athletes dueling over an inflated pigbladder at the other end of the field.

Displaying multiple earrings, nose rings, tattered sneakers, funky-sculptured hair and a matching ultrahip attitude, they had labeled themselves the Zoners. They made it a resolute point to occupy at each game the deserted grassy area beyond the end zone opposite to wherever the action was. That is, if they could predict the flow of play, which required careful attention to the game without seeming to pay attention.

But they were satisfactorily out of the action now, so they practiced air-guitar, capered about, and performed adolescent boy-girl play that involved teasing, touching, and occasional voluptuous girl-boy embrace.

Suddenly, the area was enveloped by an eardrum-tearing shriek that seemed to rip open the black sky, south to north. The entire crowd simultaneously clasped its hands to its ears and gasped in distress, except those whose hearing had been sufficiently deadened by rock music.

Ironically, when the sound struck, one Zoner member in baggy shorts and black high-tops had just twanged off a silent chord from his imaginary guitar. He stared at his remarkable hand in foggy amazement for a moment, then realized that he was not the cause of the noise from the heavens.

The game stopped as everyone searched the offending sky, but it remained silent, coal-black and anonymous beyond the lights. The players milled about on the field, and the crowd chattered about the possibility that the sound blast came from an airplane, a missile, or even a UFO. But the mysterious sound had died and seemed to result in nothing more phenomenal, so the play resumed. The third down began and the crowd quickly restored its full concentration on the players.

But the real celebrity from the night's events would belong to the motley Zoners. As they arranged themselves along the fence for the final minutes of indifferent loitering, an object plummeted silently from the dark sky. It flashed into the bright lights of the field, bounced once on the thick turf beyond the ten-yard line and came to rest. A long-haired boy in a tie-dyed t-shirt and knee-torn jeans first spied the object, narrowing his eyes in puzzled concentration, since it was too far away to be instantly recognizable. He nudged his five-earringed comrade, who also brought his attention to bear on the identity of the object.

"Man, is that a hand?" asked Tie-dye.

"Like, an arm, too, maybe!" exclaimed Five-earrings.

"Dummy arm, man. Somebody threw a dummy arm on the field."

"Looks real."

They dared each other to run out and fetch the arm, foreseeing great fun with the fake appendage. It was concluded that, since Tie-dye had seen the object first, he was under primary obligation. So he let himself through the gate at the end of the field and to the raucous cheers of the other Zoners, sprinted raggedly under the goal posts to the one yard line, the five, the ten and beyond. He reached down to pick up the arm. Then he stopped, looked closer, straightened up and stood staring, shocked out of his cool.

"C'mon, man, bring it back!" shouted Five-earrings.

The boy merely shook his head in frightened puzzlement and continued to stare. By this time, he had attracted the attention of the referees at the other end of the field, who yelled and waved at him to get off. He looked at them, pointed down, shrugged, and stood there, not knowing what else to do. Finally, two angry referees began the laborious slog down the field, their bellies shaking. They arrived puffing and aggravated, berating the boy, who jabbed his finger down at the arm.

"Damn," observed the line judge, looking down.

"Yeah," agreed the umpire.

Lying on the green turf was a grayish pink arm, with the hand partially closed, the fingers pointing up. But it was more than just an arm. It had been severed from the body of its owner beyond the shoulder joint, including a section of collarbone and chest muscle. The severed appendage wore the remains of a white short-sleeved shirt, which was stained with blood. Clots of dried blood covered the broad stump, but the appendage had been largely exsanguinated, hence its grayish color.

The referees angrily accused the boy of a ghoulish prank, but he shrugged his shoulders and insisted upon his innocence. Other Zoners quickly came to his rescue, running onto the field, pointing skyward and asserting the truth of the event. The two referees with capped heads and striped shirts stood stolidly amidst the Zoners, and after initial skepticism, abandoned their initial theory that a cadaver had been scavenged and the limb put there as a joke.

"Aw, man, gross!" said one of the Zoners, reaching down to touch the arm. One of the referees slapped his hand away. Reminded of their oversight duties, the referees pushed the Zoners back away from the grisly object, as if to give it air. By this time, the football players had abandoned any thought of their game and had sprinted down the field for a look, so an outer circle of green and yellow helmets surrounded the inner core of long hair, with the two white caps in the center.

Pushing their way through the crowd came two sheriff's deputies, who next assumed responsibility. They covered the arm with a towel and waved for a stretcher, which was all the deputies could think to do. Two emergency technicians joined the growing crowd. One undraped the object and examined it, declaring that it had been recently severed. However, since it had fallen onto the field, this was not a crime scene, so he ruled that the object could be safely removed.

He donned rubber gloves, knelt and lifted the rigid, severed appendage onto the stretcher. He covered it with a red emergency blanket and he and his partner carried the stretcher to their waiting emergency van, which roared away, siren blazing, lights flashing.

The referees stood and looked with puzzlement at each other amidst the dispersing crowd, then walked away and huddled alone. There was some gesturing among them and a few raised voices. After a long while, the head umpire returned and with a decisive tweet of his whistle, announced that since there was only five minutes to play, the game would be finished. The players clapped their hands heartily and sprinted bulkily down the field to the line of scrimmage. The cheerleaders tentatively began a cheer, quickly gathered confidence and rose to full girlish throat. A continuing low chatter among the crowd indicated that gossip about the event still occupied their collective mind. But they began to cheer nevertheless and the Tiger Band struck up a fight song.

The Zoners retired back behind the chain link fence and wondered at the weirdness of it all and how the dumb game could possibly go on after what had happened.

And the Tigers scored on two carries, finally winning by a field goal when they subsequently recovered an on-side kick to the Yellow Jackets.

CHAPTER 11

Gerald had driven all night to make it to Columbia, Missouri, the next day, but he had to see the arm. He had to talk to the man who was to autopsy it. It was something that had inexplicably "appeared," and was thus of great interest. He drove the van slowly through the neat grid of streets, following the instructions periodically announced by the GPS receiver suction-cupped to his windshield. Taped to his dashboard was a printout of an Associated Press article describing how an arm had fallen from the sky in Melville, Missouri.

He took a corner particularly fast, and cans clattered about in the back of the van. It was time to do a housecleaning, but he didn't know where he would find a steep hill in this flat area of the Midwest. He knew that if he accelerated up a steep hill and maybe let the van roll back down and hit the brakes a few times all the cans and much of the other trash would shift to the back. So, he could just open the rear door and sweep it into a garbage can—after, of course, sifting through it to make sure he wasn't throwing away any valuable data or printouts.

Maybe he'd get the van tuned up, too. Or whatever was needed to quiet the uncharacteristic engine noise. He also needed to put more air in the air mattress.

He knew his wandering was weird. But when the compulsion came, he knew he had to leave his research at the Center and go wherever was necessary to gather data. At first, the compulsion had been a mere tickling at the edge of his conscious, a feeling that things were happening out there beyond his little office that just weren't quite right. He knew from experience not to dismiss such tickles. In the past, even while he was working on the most difficult theoretical problem—for example, the mathematics of accretion disks around black holes—his unconscious was always taking in information, processing it, deciding whether it was significant. His unconscious had caused the tiny uneasiness that had exploded into this year-long journey of data-gathering.

He'd found all these anomalies to be really significant. They were beyond usual physics and they were concrete. Not like UFOs or Bigfoot, where the physical evidence was not quite there, not really something that a scientist could gather and analyze.

But nobody had put them together. They were just separate, strange phenomena, reported with passing interest by the media, but which so far only he had believed were connected . . . somehow.

So, he had left his job, his research, his family, his girlfriend. Fortunately, Lisa had already begun to pursue other interests. She didn't seem to like being called his girlfriend, which was one sign, and she'd taken to going home at night, sometimes early, leaving him searching through news sites on the computer.

The other scientists at the Center for Astrophysics had been tolerant. They had seen such instances before, when one of their physicists veered off onto a strange tangent. Sometimes it proved incredibly important, sometimes a quirky dead-end.

Either way, they had all judged his explorations peculiar, but he was certain his compulsion wasn't as mystical as it seemed on the surface—especially when he kept encountering other people who were puzzling over a weird phenomenon they had encountered. He would gather as much information as he could from them, connect them with the Deus Foundation, and move to another mystery. Someday soon, he knew a theory would crystallize itself out of all these multifarious happenings.

He returned from his reverie. There it was. The GPS's last instruction had brought him to an anonymous, windowless, tan brick building with an ambulance entrance and a sign that said Boone County Morgue. He found a parking place, grabbed a new spiral-bound notebook and pushed through the front door. The guard at the front had his name and gave him a visitor's tag, directing him to the basement examining room.

As he pressed a big black button that took the aging elevator down, he became aware of the strong smell of formalin and a disconcerting organic odor that he took to be the smell of cold, dead bodies. He found George Voigt sitting in a small, cramped office, shuffling papers about, peering down at them through rimless bifocals.

"Ah, yes, Mr. Meier. From the foundation. I did get the call from Massachusetts, from my colleague there. You're interested in the arm." George Voigt was a spare, small man in his late seventies, with a bald head encircled by wispy white hair. He was affable, easygoing, but Gerald's contacts had told him that "Curious George" Voigt as he was known, was a legend in Missouri and, indeed, among pathologists. He was expert and he was thorough. His counterpart in Suffolk County, Massachusetts, had told Gerald that Voigt was famous for snooping incessantly around crime scenes and deeply annoying some police, especially when he proved innocent one of their prime suspects.

Voigt offered him coffee, tea or lemonade, but Gerald declined, given that he was about to see a part of a dead body. Voigt then buttoned his clean, starched lab coat, picked up a gray notebook and led Gerald into the aging, but meticulously clean, white-tiled examining room. Two stainless steel autopsy tables occupied the room's center, and one wall was covered with stainless steel doors with refrigerated containers for bodies.

"I thought at first that maybe I should wait for the rest of this gentleman to turn up," said Voigt, opening one of the steel doors and sliding out the body-sized tray that held only a small cloth-draped object. "But the police said they needed as much information as they could get PDQ, so I examined it. Most strange, Mr. Meier. Indeed, this is most strange."

He undraped the object, and Gerald found himself staring at a grayish, lifeless arm that looked almost like a clever fake. The stubby-fingered hand was upturned and the fingers were curled into the kind of grip one might use to hold a violin bow. The fingertips were stained with ink. The bloodied stump was sliced clean through. Very cleanly through, even such that the bloodstained white shirt looked as if it had been sliced with a razor.

"Are you okay?" Voigt asked solicitously, and Gerald nodded. He was so fascinated with the arm, he forgot to be queasy.

"Well, let's see now," said Voigt opening his notebook. "Subject is a left arm and hand belonging to a white adult male . . ." he began describing in detail the hand, the arm, the few distinguishing birthmarks and scars, the amount of muscle and fat, the status of the nail beds, and the multitude of other factors that constituted a thorough autopsy. He went on for a few minutes, saving the most interesting part for last. "The arm is severed from the body above the shoulder joint, cutting through the clavicle and scapula and the pectoralis major muscle, and . . ." He paused and smiled at Gerald significantly over his glasses. ". . . the severing incision is remarkably clean, even cutting through parts of the fourth and fifth left ribs." Gerald looked closely. Sure enough, embedded in the dry gray muscle were segments of rib that had been sliced so cleanly through that they looked polished.

"Actually, I've been waiting for your arrival to finish. I decided to take a closer look at this sliced bone. It could be a centerpiece to this mystery." Voigt took up a scalpel in his small wrinkled hand and with deft, delicate strokes carefully sliced away at the muscle until he freed one of the rib slivers, wrapping it in gauze and placing it in a small plastic sample box. He handed the box to Gerald while he covered the arm and slid it back into the refrigerator.

Shortly, the sliver was under his microscope, where they saw a perfectly clean slice, with no discernible cut marks. After examining the sliver from all possible angles, Gerald sat on the old metal stool and stared at it.

"We need to see this with higher resolution. You know where we can use an electron microscope?"

Voigt smiled knowingly. "As a matter of fact, I happen to know this young lady who might help us."

After Voigt made a brief phone call, they drove in Gerald's van to the University of Missouri. Voigt sat in the seat that Gerald had swept clean of debris, holding the little box in his lap. As they negotiated the streets, Voigt described his interviews with the Zoners and everybody else involved with the limb from the sky. Gerald tried to drive with his notebook on the steering wheel, making scribbled notes at stoplights and sometimes, unfortunately, on wobbly turns. But Voigt, dressed in his herringbone sport coat and bow tie, didn't seem to notice, chattering happily on.

"They think it was a plane crash?" asked Gerald.

"Well, I heard on the radio that there is a small plane missing that filed a flight plan over the area. They found pieces of a plane. One piece hit a barn. But they don't think it's all there. They're still looking for more body parts. I hope they find them. I'd like to find out more about my gentleman and what happened to him."

Within half an hour, they stood inside the university's electron microscopy laboratory. His rheumy blue eyes twinkling, Voigt held up the box and worked his courtly charm on Gayle, the young, female microscopist who oversaw the laboratory. He had taught her pathology in graduate school, and she could never refuse Dr. George anything.

Within another hour, they had sliced the tip end off the rib, coated it in gold and inserted it into the sample chamber in the tall beige column that was the scanning electron microscope. The vacuum pump rattled busily as it evacuated the chamber and shortly the electron microscopic image of the rib tip appeared on the small green luminescent screen, looking like an immense plateau thrusting up from the middle of a broad desert. An *extremely smooth* plateau.

"This isn't possible," said Gayle, adjusting knobs to zoom in on the surface. Even at the highest magnitude there were no jagged edges, no slice marks. Only a glass-smooth slice through the bone, even beyond the highest polishing.

"But, dear, it *does* appear to be possible," said Dr. George.

"Is there anybody else around who could look at this?" asked Gerald. "Anybody who's looked at a lot of these things before?"

Voigt smiled, again knowingly. "Of course, I'll just give a call to some of my old students." Gerald wondered whether students might be appropriate judges of this exotic object, but said nothing.

Within another half an hour, the former "students" had arrived. Crowding into the room were the university hospital's chief of surgery, the chief of orthopedics, and the director of the biomaterials program.

All were brilliant men, with the extraordinary powers of observation afforded by dozens of years of medical education, and Dr. George's venerable pathology course. They peered at the sharp black-and-white image, and for half an hour requested different views, different angles, different electron beam parameters.

Finally, Gerald polled them. "Any of you know of any cutting tool, bone saw, energy beam . . . anything at all . . . that could slice something that smoothly?"

"Nope," said the chief of surgery.

"Got me," said the chief of orthopedics.

"I'll get back to you," promised the director of the biomaterials program. But Gerald knew that meant he was stumped, too. Voigt left the small troublesome piece of bone with Gayle, and he and Gerald walked out of the medical center down the broad sidewalk toward the parking lot.

"Son, I'm stumped here. I'm going to go back to my office and look at some references. You're welcome to stay, but I'm afraid that I couldn't help you much."

"Well, you did already," said Gerald as they passed by the large brick science buildings. "You found something incredibly important."

Voigt brightened. "Oh, indeed? That's very nice, but what could it possibly be?"

"That seemed to be an infinitely smooth surface. Down to the molecular level. An infinitely smooth surface means that it was cut by something infinitely smooth. I've seen this before." He told Voigt about Dacey Livingstone's smooth rock and the smooth slice through the bridge. Voigt's eyes widened. This was better than any simple murder mystery!

They returned to Voigt's small office, and he began to pull dog-eared criminal pathology texts off his shelf. In the process of setting them on his desk, he spied a pink phone message slip. It was for Gerald and it was the phone number of the Deus Foundation, which was the only place he had kept apprised of his travels. He called the foundation on his cell phone.

"A Brendan Cooper called," said the foundation secretary's efficient voice.

"Cooper? From Woods Hole?" Gerald had worked with Cooper on fluid dynamics calculations several times. He liked the no-nonsense oceanographer.

"Yes. He's got something for you to look at. Something he says is 'right up your alley.' He wants to send a plane to pick you up. Immediately, he said."

* * *

The face looming unsteadily at the rain-dappled window of the police car was snaggle-toothed and with a scraggly beard flecked with dried food. The dirty hand rapped sloppily on the glass, and the cop lowered the window, unfortunately allowing the wet breeze to carry the fetid body odor into the squad car. A truck rumbled past, its tires hissing on the wet pavement, but the Bronx street was otherwise quiet.

"Ah wanna repo ah messn pusn," mumbled the face, the alcohol-reeking breath rolling into the car.

"You what, pal? You wanna what?"

"Messn pusn. Frinna mine's gone. Jerry's gone. Down inna hole like."

"Missin' person?" interpreted the cop. "Go down to the precinct station. File a report." The New York cop had seen too many drunks not to know that most of them hallucinated most of the time. But this drunk would not be put off. He stood up to his full height, teetering and slapping the top of the car and shouting.

"He's jus' gone! He's a goo' guy, an' ya gotta come help him! Yeah! C'mon. Lemme show ya."

The cop looked over at his partner and shrugged.

"To protect and to serve, remember?" joked his partner.

"Shit. Well, by God, you gotta come, too."

"Wouldn't miss it!" The partner switched off the car's engine and they both got out, slid their nightsticks into their belt holders and followed the drunk. He wobbled his way into an alley lined with dumpsters and dirty cardboard boxes. A snore emanated from one of the dumpsters and pairs of suspicious eyes peered blearily from some of the boxes.

"'S gettin' cold," explained the drunk stopping and looking over his shoulder to make sure they were still following. "Jerry, he looked for somewhere warm, 'n he found this hole; 'n now he's gone."

"Just show us," said the cop, pulling his cap low over his eyes and plunging ahead. It was an odd sight, the weaving drunk leading the two tall crisply uniformed, fully equipped policemen through the grimy, garbage-strewn alleys.

They had gone about a block, when the derelict pushed hard against the rusty steel door of an abandoned building, scraping it open, and went in.

"Look buddy, this is far enough," said the cop, peering into the murk. "We're outta here."

"Nah, nah. Jus' a little farther here. Other side a' this buildin'."

The cops both flicked on their flashlights, scanning them about the inside of the building. They also both made sure their guns were loose in their holsters. The drunk lurched through the building, crunching over broken glass and kicking discarded cans. Muttered complaints floated from the darkness, emanating from beneath piles of dirty blankets in the corners. The drunk stumbled against a pillar, and cursing unintelligibly, staggered through the other doorway. The cops followed. The drunk stood triumphantly and pointed.

"Here. This here's where Jerry went." The cops followed his pointing to a dark place against the side of the building.

The first cop shined his flashlight into the gloom, revealing a perfectly round hole, about the size of a manhole. It was partly bored in the vertical side of the building and partly in the dirty asphalt of the alley.

"What's this? A drain hole? Your buddy get stuck in a drain hole?"

"Nah, nah," the drunk waved his hand. "We heard this damn noise and came out and this here hole was here. Right here, like this. Shit. Ain' no fuckin' drain hole."

The first cop squatted down and shined the flashlight directly into the hole. Warm air wafted from it. The hole slanted down absolutely straight as far as he could see. The hole's sides were as smooth as glass.

"Well, you guys did a damned good job of diggin', I gotta hand it to you."

"Nah, didn't dig it, man. Couldn'a dug it. Look!" The drunk got down on his hands and knees and felt around, coming up with a wine bottle. He confirmed the bottle's emptiness by tipping it up to his lips, then slid it into the hole, giving it a flick with his wrist. The clinking sound of the careening bottle reverberated from the hole, becoming fainter and fainter and fainter, until it faded completely. The drunk stood up and braced himself against the building. "'S too damn deep. Jerry's in there. He got his blanket and got in there and I could hear him slippin' away. He kept slippin' and hollerin'. Then I didn't hear 'im no more. I think maybe the devils got 'im."

"Devils? What the hell is this, pal?" The cop shined his flashlight directly into the drunk's face, revealing the scarred, dirt-stained geography of a ruined life. The drunk squinted and became indignant.

"Yeah, we seen devils come out. Damn right! Jerry had the mojo magic to put 'em back in there."

"Aw, shit, this is some rummy's nightmare," said the partner. "I'm not goin' down in some sewer after some drunk that may or may not be there."

"Tell ya what pal," said the cop loudly to the drunk, who was beginning to nod off. "You wait here for Jerry. Maybe pitch a rope down. If he doesn't show, you go down and see Sergeant Ryan. You file a report with him."

"Ryan's gonna be pissed at you, siccin' that drunk on him," said the partner.

"That'll teach him to screw me into holiday shifts," said the cop. The two cops turned, got their bearings and headed out of the alley, avoiding the building, to the street to find their car.

The drunk slumped to the ground beside the hole, moaned once, and was soon asleep.

CHAPTER 12

The four-ton Remotely Operated Vehicle settled onto the pitch-black ocean bottom like the most delicate of ballet dancers putting down a tentative toe onto a stage. The sediment stirred around the huge ungainly box, but not much, settling back quickly. The darkness was absolute two thousand feet below the Atlantic, but it yielded instantly to the SeaProbe's brilliant floodlights that switched on, piercing the frigid gloom in front of the machine out to a dozen yards. A faint fog of sediment swirled through the lights, but the cameras could see clearly as the two large mechanical arms stretched out and moved back and forth experimentally, then refolded themselves. Powerful streams of water spewed from the robot's cylindrical thrusters and it lifted itself, stirring the sediment once more and turned to its right, then its left, scanning the area. Then it settled quietly onto the bottom, waiting for further instructions.

Far above, however, was turmoil. Gerald paced back and forth inside the cramped shipping container that was the SeaProbe's control room. The robot's operator, diving expert K.C. Wang, sat tensely at the SeaProbe's thruster controls, his eyes glued to the three-D eyepieces that gave him a view of what SeaProbe's twin cameras saw. Wang was a stocky, round-faced Chinese man with a luxurious head of thick black hair and an enthusiasm for anything that involved underwater exploration. The cumbersome SeaProbe wasn't his favorite underwater machine, even though the three-D view its cameras afforded made him almost part of its liquid world. However, it did allow him to do underwater exploration and still remain dry.

Sitting beside Wang at the SeaProbe's manipulator controls, the Woods Hole oceanographer, Brendan Cooper, was just finishing an argument with the ship's captain. They only heard his side of the conversation over the ship's telephone, but they could imagine the captain's.

"I don't give a shit!" Cooper listened a bit, a scowl on his face. "Well, I still don't give a shit!" He listened some more. "Listen, I know this ocean better than you do. I know these storm systems. I've seen the radar. Storm's still way out there. You can damned well hold station for three more hours! So, do it!" He slammed down the receiver, especially frustrated because he knew that his bluster was hollow. The captain alone would decide where the ship would go, and he could only hope that bullying worked better than pleading. He turned his attention to Wang. "Let's get on with it." Wang said nothing, but tensed his jaw and went back to his eyepieces.

And Gerald continued to pace. A heave of the deck threw him off balance. He stumbled against Phillippe Togani, who was the only one who was quiet. The oil company structural engineer sat patiently behind Cooper and Wang, taking notes, watching the underwater robot's progress. He was planning what structural inspection he would ask for when they encountered the sunken tanker.

"Gerald, will you sit the hell down!" barked Cooper, putting his eyes to a companion pair of three-D eyepieces.

"Sorry. I'm thinking." Gerald was, indeed, immersed in his own storm of conjecture. So much mystery here! So much to take into account. The briefing he'd received had set him to trying to recall his knowledge of thermodynamics, heat flow equations, metal matrix structure. A supertanker had been sunk by something that violently heated the water for a mile around. They were about to see this devastated tanker, and he had to know what scientific questions to ask, what data to gather. His instinct told him this disaster would somehow fit with the other bizarre phenomena. But it was a puzzle in which he only had pieces, with no overall picture. In fact, he didn't even know the shape of the pieces. And he just couldn't figure it out sitting down. The deck lurched again as the Acorn crested a wave caused by the oncoming storm. But he compensated this time.

"Okay, where from here?" asked Wang. Cooper consulted the SeaProbe's sonar.

"Go ten degrees port, a hundred yards. Sonar shows a big blip."

K.C. unlimbered his fingers and nudged the small joystick forward on his control panel, his eyes glued to the eyepieces. The robot's cameras showed that it was easing forward. He looked up and watched the direction and distance register on the digital readouts, checking the view occasionally on one of two video monitors above the control panel. "I think we're there," he said, turning to Cooper. "I see some junk on the bottom."

"Scan the cameras."

Wang did so, and they each glued their eyes to their eyepieces, scrutinizing the murk for signs of their quarry.

"Look there," whispered Wang. "Damn!" The robot's cameras showed the faint outlines of an immense, shattered hulk reaching upward into the darkness. Gerald stopped pacing and sat in his chair, his gaze riveted on the video screen. The robot moved closer and the gigantic steel corpse became clearer. "That the bow?" he asked.

"Stern," said Togani.

"Let's do some exploring," said Wang, pushing the joystick forward.

Two thousand feet below, the boxy robot, topped by a large chunk of orange, buoyant plastic foam, eased toward the giant wall of steel. Its thrusters—whining high-speed propellers housed in protective cylinders—rotated, and it rose along the wall. Finally, the scorched twisted railing of the lifeless ship came into the lights.

"Can I please see the stern superstructure?" asked Togani.

Cooper nodded, and Wang touched the controls shifting the robot ponderously to the right around the stern until the large shattered windows of the master's cabin came into view. The curtains were singed. The bed linens flapped in slow motion from the wash of the thrusters. A wooden desk chair wavered back and forth trapped against the ceiling. It was the bedroom of a dead man. Togani bent and scribbled some notes.

"The stern section went down after it broke apart," said Togani.

"Let's just make sure we got the right ship," said Cooper.

Wang worked the controls and the robot obediently sank downward, below the chilling sight. The painted legend, "Castile," rose into view.

Above, Wang sat back in his chair. "As if there were any doubt."

"Okay, let's see what happened to her," said Cooper, just as the deck lurched violently, and at the same time the phone to the bridge beeped insistently. Cooper ignored the sound. The dull roaring of the storm had risen, so that they had to speak louder now to be heard.

"You going to pick it up?" asked Wang.

"Sure," said Cooper, picking up the receiver and laying it on a nearby desk. "Happy?"

"I'm pulling out," said Wang. "We'll come back next week."

"C'mon, K.C. Haggerty's on the warpath about this," said Cooper. "And this is the Atlantic. That wreck could shift God-knows-where or go over the shelf in a week."

"It's true," said Togani quietly. "Haggerty will be looking for the data or else."

"It's my robot," said Wang. "It's my ass. I'm hauling out."

"Look, just check topside," said Cooper. "Ask how the drum's behaving."

Wang radioed the technicians handling the robot's cable and the huge underwater spool that maintained the cable's tension. He got his answer over his headphones and looked at Cooper and Togani for a long time before answering. A faint sheen of perspiration rose on his forehead. The roaring rose and fell outside.

"I'll give you thirty more minutes on the bottom," said Wang. "Takes an hour to bring it up. That's it." Again, they felt the ship lift and fall, as a wave rolled under it.

Togani smiled. "Thanks. Let's go right to the shear point where the stern broke away."

Gerald remained quiet, his gaze intent on the screen. In his mind swirled the equations for the incredible pressures, the immense forces that ruled these depths.

Wang cranked up the robot's thrusters and flicked the joystick to begin moving toward the place where the ship had been torn in half.

"This ain't no damn hot rod, y'know. It'll take ten minutes to get there at full speed."

"C'mon, K.C., I know what you can make that thing do," said Cooper. All was silent in the room, except for the gentle whine of computer cooling fans. After a few minutes, Wang said quietly, "That's the break that killed the Castile."

In the three-D viewers and on the video screen, they saw the huge portside gash that had caused the stern of the ship to violently rip away from the rest of the ship. The thick steel plates had been melted away, looking like dark gray melted candlewax. Large globs of tar, looking like black coagulated blood had oozed from the open tanks onto the light gray ocean floor. Some of the globs were as large as cars. Cooper gave Togani a look through the three-D viewer.

"That steel plate was melted," breathed Togani, peering into the eyepieces.

"Three, maybe four thousand degrees at least . . ." said Gerald. He did some mental calculations. ". . . applied for maybe ten minutes over a surface of a hundred feet."

"Jesus," said Togani.

The room heaved violently. The steady roar was punctuated by a crash.

"Let's go," said Wang, flicking a switch on the control panel to connect him with the deck crew. "I'm pullin' out."

"We need samples of that metal," said Togani. Gerald nodded in agreement. Deep in the structure of that metal was a story beyond his experience.

"Screw the samples," said Wang.

"You gave us thirty minutes," said Cooper. "We've got ten left. You chicken?"

"I'm two point five million dollars worth of chicken! This is my machine and it's my ass!"

His eyes still riveted on the eyepieces, Cooper made a chicken-clucking sound.

"Shit," spat Wang. Cooper smiled, knowing that he had won. Wang directed the robot in toward the huge wall of torn steel. He set the thrusters to maintain station. Abruptly, the view on the video screen jerked. Wang spoke into his headphone mike and listened. "They're having trouble maintaining slack in the seas."

Cooper ignored the warning and inserted his fingers into the manipulator controls, which looked like thin plastic arms with fingerholds. He pushed his arms forward.

In the dark crushing depths below, the robot's sturdy metal arms obediently reached outward for an extended blob of the melted metal. The left arm, with a two-fingered clamp grasped the segment. The right arm ended in a welding torch, which erupted into an intense white flame. The torch lit up the depths of the ship, revealing the twisted wreckage of pipes, valves and ladders, like the snarled intestines of a corpse that filled the interior of the ruptured tank. The torch applied itself to the thick steel and slowly began to cut a semicircle around the segment held by the other hand.

An alarm beeped.

"Shit!" cursed Wang again. "I got torque on the arms from the cable being yanked."

"C'mon K.C., it's within design specs." Cooper's eyes were glued to the viewer, his fingers deftly operating the arms far below.

Their view of the bottom jerked again. Wang gritted his teeth and maintained position. Within three minutes, the chunk broke free and Cooper directed the arm to stow it in the robot's sample box, clamping the box shut with an expert flick of the manipulator.

"Okay, haul ass!" Cooper shouted into the microphone, drawing the manipulator controls toward him, which stowed the robot's arms safely away. Wang pulled on the control joysticks and backed the robot well clear of the mammoth wreck.

"No," said Gerald. "Not yet!"

"Hell, another member of the peanut gallery heard from," said Wang. "Listen, I'm out of here."

"No! no!" Gerald stood suddenly, marshaling his arguments. "Look, there's got to be evidence around that'll tell us where the heat source came from. It has to be nearby."

"Well, it'll just have to wait," said Wang.

"If we get it now, we're closer to a mechanism. Right now, all you've got is a destroyed ship. Just run a line out a hundred yards or so."

"Screw you," said Wang.

"Give him a hundred yards," said Togani. "We've still got a few minutes."

"You're outvoted, K.C.," said Cooper.

Wang cursed again, but he complied. The robot swerved away from the shattered hull and began a slow run across the bottom, which was littered with debris.

"I'm comin' to the end of the tether," complained Wang. "I can't go any further. You understand?"

"Just keep on," said Gerald. "Just a little farther. Wait! Aim the cameras down!"

In the darkness below, the robot paused in midwater, hovering off the bottom, its twin video cameras and floodlights angling downward. They revealed a segment of what appeared to be a massive scar of melted slag across the bottom.

"That's it. That's the track of what killed your ship."

The picture jerked again as the ship lurched violently.

"Okay, okay, you got your picture," said Wang. "We'll come back with Deep Flight. Just let me get the fuck off the bottom."

Gerald nodded and sat back, his gaze intense. The track had been about as wide as the holes. Where did that track lead? He had to know!

Wang threw the thrusters hard down and the robot rose rapidly away from the bottom, immersed once more in deep-ocean gloom. At the same time, he gave the order for the deck crew to begin reeling in the robot's tether.

"Hope you're all happy."

"Yeah, K.C., you were adequate," said Cooper.

"Well, then you three can go topside with me and help get my baby back on board."

"Sure." Cooper checked the video recorder and other instruments to make sure all the data were secure.

Wang shut down the robot's maneuvering systems and began to pull on rain gear, preparing to go topside. He handed gear to the other three. "Okay, so you got any theories?" he asked them.

"No," said Togani quietly. "That portside hull looked like it had been blast-furnaced like nothing I've seen."

"And that slag on the bottom looked volcanic, but I bet it wasn't," said Gerald.

"It's sure beyond anything to do with ocean currents," said Cooper.

"So, what're you saying, guys?" asked Wang.

"Well, we need to survey that area," said Gerald. "And we need a geologist onboard. I know somebody who's working on something that may be related." He smiled slightly as he put on the rain slicker. He'd soon see Dacey Livingstone again.

"Fine, great," said Wang. "But for now you're just going to get real wet." He pushed open the control-room door and led them lurching unsteadily along the heaving cargo hold deck toward the stairway.

CHAPTER 13

"So, where's this submersible?" Dacey stood on the broad deck of the Acorn in magnificently rolling seas, with the sunlit ocean highlighting each gleaming wave. She had just emerged from the oil company helicopter that had flown her from Tenerife in the Canary Islands to meet Gerald, oceanographer Brendan Cooper and the submersible pilot and diving expert K.C. Wang. She had met the oil company structural engineer, Philippe Togani, briefly, when he took the same helicopter out with a portable hard drive with the video data and the metal sample, off to Shell headquarters.

Squinting and windblown, she greeted Cooper and Wang as Gerald introduced them. She repeated her question louder to be heard over the departing helicopter and the wind and waves.

Wang laughed showing white teeth and said, "You're standing beside it, Doctor."

Dacey was undaunted. "This is an airplane," she insisted. Indeed, the thirty-foot-long streamlined, white craft did look like a jet airplane, except with stubby sawed-off wings and a v-shaped tail with small side fins. It even possessed what appeared to be jet engines built into the rear, their intakes a series of gill-like slits on top of and below the fuselage.

"It's called Deep Flight Six," said Wang. "It does fly, but underwater." He walked down the sleek body of the craft, patting it like a used car salesman. "The wings can be angled to give reverse lift to take us down, so we don't need ballast tanks. When we're finished with the dive, we just stand her on her tail, aim upward and she powers to the surface. Aluminum hull, fuel-cell power, electric motors. She can go to eleven thousand meters and withstand sixteen thousand pounds per square inch."

After the inspection, Cooper motioned them inside the Acorn's aft cabin and into the small wardroom. For the next two hours, they drank coffee and viewed videotapes of the SeaProbe robot's dive on the Castile and were briefed on the findings so far. Dacey examined the seismic records from the area, finding them similar to the ones taken near the holes in Oklahoma and San Francisco. She decided this adventure would likely be worth it, like the San Francisco trip, even though that episode had her hanging from a wire on the side of a bridge. She needed all the information she could get. She was certainly no closer to an answer in Gillard, so it was worth leaving the seismic profiling work there to her graduate students and flying off on another of Gerald's invitations. Gerald was right, bless him. Somehow all these strange events seemed to fit together. She looked over at him and smiled, and he smiled back.

Cooper also showed infrared satellite images of the ocean off Africa. The images from the National Oceanographic and Atmospheric Administration revealed a light blotch marking the region of heated water that they sat in the middle of now.

"The NOAA people said this wasn't the first time they'd gotten such an area of heated water, but they never could get off their butts and get out to the areas in time." He gave a wry smile. "Now we're going to do some of their work for them."

Finally, Cooper played for them the hydrophone recordings taken from the Navy's Sound Surveillance System in the area. For decades the extensive network of underwater listening posts had lain in the ocean depths listening for Soviet submarines and surface ships. What it recorded the day of the Castile's destruction was far stranger.

"I've been listening to hydrophone recordings for fifteen years and I've never heard anything like this," said Cooper, as the hissing, gurgling sounds filled the small room.

"Sounds like a cross between a boiling teakettle and a big hissing radiator," said Dacey.

"We've done frequency and trajectory analysis and that's about what it is. Water being boiled into steam, at immense depth and by a point source." He paused and looked at the other four. "A *moving* point source."

"Well, let's just go see where that point source started from," said Wang.

They filed out to the Deep Flight Six and crawled into the narrow cockpit through the nose, which was a large, clear acrylic bubble that swung open. Wang and Cooper settled into the two front seats, and Dacey and Gerald into the back seats. In front of them were binocular viewing ports for the three-D high-definition video cameras mounted in the craft's belly. For closer viewing of the bottom, the aluminum seats could be swung out of the way, and the rear observers could lie prone on the vessel's deck, peering through thick, acrylic windows in the belly.

Once they were settled, Wang spoke into his microphone to the crane operator, and with a gentle lurch, the sleek vessel became airborne, hoisted by the Acorn's huge crane off the deck.

Dacey and Gerald watched the ship fall away beneath them and the heaving ocean rise to slap the submarine's bottom. They rested on the surface, the waves tossing them up and down like a cork. Dacey found herself looking up at waves that would slam onto the top of the vessel, driving it down, only to see it pop up again, as if challenging the next wave.

"This is the worst," said Wang. "Just hold on for a few minutes and we'll be under, where it's calm." Sure enough, Dacey felt her stomach begin to churn from the jouncing. She glanced at Gerald, whose eyes were determinedly closed.

Wang peered out of the front bubble and once he was sure the vessel was clear of the crane cable, eased the throttle forward. A deep whine filled the compartment and the craft accelerated through the waves, which rolled smoothly over the craft. Clutching a joystick between his knees, Wang pushed it forward and the Deep Flight Six angled beneath the waves. The bobbing transitioned into smoothness, the surface receded and all became dead quiet, except for the hum of the electric motors.

Wang switched on the vessel's sonar, the video recorder and the powerful headlamps aimed to the front and below the craft. Peering down between her knees, Dacey could only see the vague glow of illuminated seawater. She breathed in and smelled the metallic tang of compressed air. She breathed out and saw vapor and realized that the cabin was growing cold as they descended. Wang switched on the heaters and the warmth returned.

"Sorry we can't offer any sights on the way down, but we'll be on the bottom in fifteen minutes," said Wang.

He spent the time studying the bright blotches on the green sonar display. His target, the remains of a thousand-foot supertanker, was easy to spot, but he took great care nevertheless.

Dacey was startled when the wreck abruptly emerged from the gloom below them, a gargantuan twisted steel corpse. They skimmed over the Castile like an airplane flying over a dark fog-shrouded island, its lights illuminating only the section beneath it. They flew the length of the bow and midship section, its deck covered with twisted, ruptured pipes and valves. Then they flew over a debris-strewn section of undisturbed sediment, a respite from the destruction until the stern section came into view, its windows shattered, its paint blackened by oily fire.

Cooper and Wang conferred briefly and Wang banked the submersible into a smooth humming turn.

"It's around here. You might look out the bottom ports." Cooper bent over to study the bottom through the bubble. Dacey and Gerald eased off their seats and folded them away, stretching out on the padded deck and peering through the portholes. Dacey became acutely aware of Gerald's body lying next to her. He glanced at her before looking down, his long dark mop of hair falling forward. She'd noticed him looking at her a lot.

When they rested their foreheads on the padded headrests and looked down through the ports, they could clearly see the silty bottom slide by beneath the gliding craft. Occasionally, a pale deep-sea fish would dash away as they passed over, or a white lobster would raise its spiny antenna, but the bottom was largely an undulating grayish plain of unrelieved monotony.

Then abruptly it appeared, a forty-foot-wide path of melted slag slashing across the bottom. With a triumphant "Hah!" Wang circled to find where the path dissipated and finally ended and ordinary sediment continued.

"Looks like it left the bottom here, whatever it was," said Cooper. "Let's see how it started."

Wang circled again and began to skim along the path of the slag. It narrowed and broadened as they went, but remained basically a furrow of melted rock and sediment material that looked like a mix of oatmeal, dirt and chunks of black glass.

Dacey shook her head. "You know, for some reason, this reminds me of the Gillard tunnel. It's long and a bit twisty, but the surface looks basically smooth."

"Well, we'll damned sure find how it started," said Cooper. "Maybe it was a torpedo or something and we'll find a disabled sub. Or maybe it's the fissure from an undersea volcano and we'll find a hole—"

"Or maybe we'll find this," Wang interrupted. "Nothing." They saw that the furrow abruptly ended, and the usual silty bottom material resumed.

"What? Go back," commanded Cooper. "We just missed the hole. We missed the fissure. Hell, we must've missed something."

Wang eased the control stick over and circled the craft back, banking it into a tight continuous turn over the end of the melted trench. Under the lights of the circling vessel, they could see that the trench began in a round depression of melted material, but showed no sign of any opening. "Old buddy, we didn't miss anything. It just started. It just started right here."

Gerald pulled back his hair and looked over at Dacey, his expression seeming to be a mixture of puzzlement and determination.

"Something appeared," he said quietly. "It just appeared." This was enough, he decided. He'd gathered enough pieces to this puzzle. It was time to start trying to construct the picture. He hoped Dacey would help.

●　●　●

Encircling the narrow valley in the Lang Shan district of Inner Mongolia, craggy mountains of light gray granite jutted far into the early morning sky. The valley's floor was a dry, cold grassland, where the herdsmen could profitably graze the shaggy sheep that produced a wool prized for its sturdiness. In the gray, icy dawn, the sheep stood scattered peacefully through the valley among the grassy meadows dotted by sparse scrub trees and shallow rocky washes. The herdsmen sleepily stoked the small campfires outside their hide-covered yurts, preparing their breakfasts of strong tea and fried meat, and smoking the potent tobacco in their clay pipes. A few had already left on early hikes into the mountains to tend their goats, or perhaps to kill one of the small antelope that would provide a relief from their diet of mutton.

The roaring sound burst into life so loudly that it shattered the eardrums of humans and sheep alike, sending blood trickling from their ear canals. The cataclysmic roar drowned out their screaming and bleating. And the blinding light brighter than the sun seared away the eyesight of any who looked at it. The roiling wall of fiery heat that followed instantly flamed into incandescence all living things in the valley. All trees, all grass, all humans, all animals burned into one cloud of ash swept up in the hurricane of boiling flame. Only the rock survived the initial onslaught and it began to glow and slump in defeat.

Those in the mountains saw an intense flare of light at the east end of the valley and the birth of a huge flaming ball that instantly produced a thick eruption of steam that rose to become a monstrous cloud in the sky. It seemed as if a new sun had determined to obscure the old, reserving for itself the honor of being the source of light and heat.

A herdsman far up in a mountain pass was instantly blinded by the light, but despite his searing pain, reached down and clasped his hand over his small son's eyes, refusing to let go. Together, they stumbled away from the heat that burned their exposed skin and singed their thick coats. Gagging from the sulfurous gases, they staggered blindly along the familiar trails up into the mountains to the pass that would lead to the cool plain beyond. By the time they reached the top, ten miles from the valley center, the roaring monster had completely shrouded itself in its obscuring cloud and was now a vague, brilliantly glowing shape prowling in the distance.

As the shape drifted, blindingly radiant within its vaporous covering, it melted rock into orange-red magma rivers that flowed thickly into glowing pools, covered by the gray ash that only minutes before had been humans, animals and vegetation.

Above the smoking hell, the great boiling cloud rose higher and higher, until its pure white top could be seen by the people far away over the mountains. They wondered at the strange, frightening sight and consulted their elders to understand whether there was any precedent for it.

The incandescent monster floated across the valley, transforming the small haven of life into a blasted melting wasteland. It reached one of the towering granite mountains, but did not stop, eating its way with fiery ease into the mountain's depths, creating thick streams of magma flowing out of the hole and great avalanches of heated rock that exploded from the slopes.

Then all suddenly stopped. All grew quiet except the crackle of cooling lava, and the periodic rattle of falling rock. The great enveloping cloud thinned and wafted away, and the intense heat yielded slowly to the cold wind blowing through the passes. The wind froze the melted rock into fantastic tortured sculptures and billowy forms that would remind the people for centuries of the evil "second sun" that had visited this day.

CHAPTER 14

Gerald switched on the light and Dacey found herself profoundly surprised. His house exhibited none of the mess she had expected after seeing his van. The wall of bookshelves held books that had been carefully arranged, it seemed by size and color. The large window by the front door of the stone house held some carefully tended house plants and a handsome bonsai tree of considerable age and beauty. From the hall she could see into a large living room with a stone fireplace and furniture that included a light gray overstuffed couch and a matching chair, as well as a large comfortable easy chair and ottoman. Beside the chair was a table with scientific journals fanned out neatly.

The walls held framed abstract prints that seemed to have been chosen with great care to complement one another. Dacey admired them; her practice was to hang stuff on her walls using whatever hooks the previous tenants had left behind. The floors were gently creaking polished oak, covered with what looked like expensive antique oriental rugs.

"I guess for some reason I thought this might look like the back of that van. This doesn't look like you."

Gerald smiled as he brought in his duffle bag and set it down.

"Well, it's not really. Mother has somebody come in when I leave and straighten up. She lives down the road."

A mama's boy? thought Dacey. He didn't seem it, but it might explain his diffident way with her. She set down her own bag, which he immediately grabbed and lugged along with his up the stairs. He invited her to look for some wine or beer. He guessed there was some in the house, since his mother restocked the place when he was gone, too.

"I'm always coming home and finding new kinds of food in the refrigerator," he shouted down. "The guest room's on the left here."

She had already begun to wander about and explore. She passed the living room and entered a formal dining room, which held a large antique oak table with carved chairs and an antique sideboard. Behind the dining room she found a large well-appointed kitchen with a pantry that had a fair selection of pastas, sauces, spices and high-quality canned goods. Dacey checked it, because she believed that pantries told much about a person—in this case probably Gerald's mother. Dacey's pantry was filled, too, but with makings for cornbread, chili, and barbecue.

The kitchen also included a small eating nook surrounded by large windows that looked out over a garden in the back, although it was too dark to tell what the garden was like.

She was surveying the kitchen utensils when he returned, his dark hair slicked back from washing up. He had on a fresh plaid sport shirt and jeans and white socks. He seemed far more relaxed in his own environment. He rummaged around looking for wine and glasses, and she excused herself to wash up. She found the guest bedroom as tidy as the rest of the house, with an old four-poster double bed covered with a down comforter. The bed made her remember how tired she was, and she thought she might make it an early night. But a shower perked her up, and she arrived back in the kitchen, padding in on stockinged feet, smiling and fresh, with her hair still damp and wearing blue jeans and a beige blouse. Gerald had filled two wine glasses with a red wine and offered her one.

"Listen, I'm a pretty fair cook," she said taking a sip and reviewing the larder in her mind. "How about I pay my rent by fixing dinner? I think you've got some good fixin's here."

"Sure, fine. I don't cook much. Mother usually sends something down and leaves it in the refrigerator. I sort of let her do these things; gives her something to do."

"Some mother you've got there. I'll have to meet her."

"Maybe tomorrow. She's just down the road."

"You said that already, Gerald." Dacey smiled.

"Oh, right, I did."

Gerald seemed a little nervous being alone with her. Well, she actually felt a little *something-or-other* being alone with him. Maybe she sensed an atmosphere of potentialities between them. But no, she finally decided, they'd have to remain friends. Just colleagues.

As she set about developing a menu from what she found frozen or canned, they talked.

"I forgot to ask. You rented a car at Logan. Where's the van?"

"Left it in Missouri. Well, actually I gave it to some kids."

"But that was your home, Gerald. Whatta nice guy!"

Gerald shrugged and smiled deprecatingly. "Well, they were kind of freaked. They'd seen an arm fall from the sky." He proceeded to tell her about his encounter with Voigt and the mystery of the arm. Voigt had emailed him with his final report, which found that the arm had, indeed, been sliced with an infinite smoothness.

"They identified the victim," said Gerald. "Turns out he was a pilot who was flying over the area at the time. The plane disappeared off radar after there was an incredibly loud noise in the sky. Searchers found parts of it scattered around the area. But only parts."

"Parts?" asked Dacey fetching pasta and the makings of spaghetti sauce from the pantry.

"No engine, no fuselage. Only parts of wings and tail. Sliced off. *Cleanly* sliced off. And no body. The National Transportation Safety Board has started an investigation."

Gerald began to set the table in the dining room, finding with some difficulty the necessary plates and utensils in his own kitchen.

"So, is this another of your disappearances?" asked Dacey.

"Both. Something appeared that made the noise. Then something disappeared. The plane and the pilot—or most of him."

It took considerable small talk and two glasses of wine each for them to recover from the vision of what must have taken place in the skies over the small Missouri town. He sat in the kitchen with her, as she produced a bowl of linguini with meat sauce and a dish of steamed frozen vegetables.

"Not bad for spur of the moment, eh?" she said as they returned to the dining room. "You got a candle? Let's do this right. I always like candles."

He stopped and seemed to lapse into deep thought. He wandered toward the kitchen and there were the sounds of rummaging. He arrived back with a white emergency candle.

"Matches?"

He disappeared into the kitchen again. More rummaging. He emerged and went into the living room, reappearing with fireplace matches. He lit the candle and dripped wax on a dessert plate, set the candle on it and set it on the table.

As they ate, they talked, and the sharing grew as the candle burned down.

He said, "I went to this high school in Chicago for science and math. I started doing physics, but I was finished with all the textbooks by the third week of class. So, they sent me off to the University of Chicago. I sort of went into a shell. Young kid with older people. Maybe if I'd had brothers or sisters, it wouldn't have been that way, but I'm an only child. Took me until I got to Harvard for graduate school to think about coming out of it."

She said, "I loved rocks. Always have. Used to stuff my jeans with rocks until the pockets tore and ask my dad about them. My sister hated it, because by the time she got my hand-me-downs they were wrecked. My dad joked that I was so interested in rocks because of our last name. He took me to the library, and we got all kinds of books. I've always wanted to find out how rocks got where I found them. What kinds of stories they'd tell. Y'know volcanoes, floods, winds. They almost seem like they're alive, but with a different kind of lifetime."

He said, "I felt the same way about physics. There always seemed to be these invisible forces that were almost magical. I just wanted to understand them. I had one girlfriend who kind of got me, but mostly they thought I was . . . well . . . sometimes imagining things, I guess."

She said, "I married my first year of college. I was basically this kid from the boonies of Oklahoma. He'd graduated already. The marriage was . . . well . . . not good. He didn't want me to finish college. He was . . ." She took a bite of linguini and didn't finish the sentence. "Anyway, the divorce went through eight years ago."

He said, "I almost got married. But deep down I didn't want to. I just had things I had to do. Like this thing with the things appearing and disappearing."

She said, "I guess if I used all my names, I would be Candace Kane Livingstone Schaumberg Robertson. Candace was Mom's idea, y'know *Candy* Kane. But as soon as I realized that, I changed my nickname to Dacey. My middle name's Kane after my grandmother's maiden name. My dad's name was Livingstone, but he died when I was twelve. He was sick for a long time with multiple sclerosis and I took care of him. My mother remarried my step-father, named Schaumberg. I married Robertson. How about your father?"

He said, "divorced" with such an utter finality, such a coldness and ensuing silence, that she knew the subject was permanently closed. They talked on for a bit, finishing their meal and doing the dishes, and went to the couch. He lit the fire and the flickering light and the wine seemed to soften the evening again, to lighten the mood. He sat down at the other end of the couch, propping his white-socked feet on the edge of the glass-topped coffee table.

She took the other end of the couch, stretching out her own legs on the coffee table. "Okay, so let's talk about this 'thing with the things appearing and disappearing' as you call it, that you haven't figured out."

"Well, I think really I'm getting there. I'll tell you my theory, but you can't laugh."

"Of course I can, but I'll make it just chuckles. How about that?"

"I think it has something to do with space-time dimensions."

"Go ahead. I'm not laughing yet."

"Well, all this matter and energy just totally appears and disappears . . . like the house that disappeared. And the hole in San Francisco.

And like the heat that melted the tanker. And the plane. Stuff had to go away into somewhere—or come from somewhere—beyond our ordinary environment. I think somehow it comes and goes through another dimension. That's the only way I can figure that stuff just totally disappears or appears."

"Okay, c'mon now, I'm getting ready to laugh. There aren't other dimensions. That's like *Star Trek* stuff."

"Well, there are. It's really solid, well-established physics. Every physicist knows there are other dimensions."

"Where?"

"Here?"

Dacey looked around the room doubtfully. "You mean like really here?"

"Yeah, like, think of the three dimensions in our space—length, height, width. Call 'em X, Y, and Z."

Dacey noticed that Gerald gestured eloquently with his hands to explain his concepts, holding them flat and cocking them at different angles to show the different dimensions. He was really into his work; really loved it. She understood that feeling. She poured herself another glass of wine and took a healthy sip. The wine was taking her into another dimension of mellow, so she guessed she was ready for some weird physics. "Yeah, I know about X, Y, and Z. I took geometry. Aced it."

"Okay, now what if another universe had dimensions in X, Y, and P? It would be just as real as ours, but we couldn't see it. It just wouldn't be available to us."

"How about all the other letters? Do they get to be used?" She pulled her legs up beneath her and leaned back on the couch, peering into her wine, trying to visualize other universes right next to this one.

"All the letters and more." Gerald smiled, pleased that she was interested in his ideas. He was a bit tipsy, too. "There could be universes with dimensions X, Y, and R. Or Y, Z, and G."

"A, B, C? D, O, G?"

"Yeah. Even with more than three dimensions. Like D, A, C, E, Y." Gerald squinted his eyes in slightly self-mocking seriousness. "I can visualize five dimensions . . . six on a good day. But the universes that don't share any dimensions with ours aren't next to us. It's like soap suds.

Our universe is like a bubble in soap suds. It's got lots of other universes next to us. Other bubbles. Maybe an infinite number." He wiggled his fingers to signify soap suds.

"Cool!" Dacey laughed, but then the memory of the Gillard hole intruded. This was serious. "So, you're saying that somehow one of our dimensions opened up to a dimension in another universe. How?"

Gerald's brow furrowed. He took a sip of wine and his slightly wavering gaze became distant. "Don't know, exactly. Only things that maybe could link dimensions are maybe black holes. But that couldn't be."

"And black holes are . . . ?"

"Well, when a big star, like ten times bigger than the sun, dies and collapses down, it squeezes all its mass into a point." Again, his expressive hands clasped together into a ball. "That's a black hole. It has such huge gravity that it makes a deep dent in the fabric of space-time. Like a dent in a rubber sheet if we were thinking in only two dimensions. Only we've got three. Some people think black holes actually poke a hole into another universe. But black holes are so powerful they tear matter apart when it falls in. If a black hole somehow appeared on earth, it would suck up earth in an instant. Whatever we're dealing with is something else entirely. Something that makes . . . not a hole . . . a sort of gate that matter and energy can go through intact."

He grew silent, his gaze distant, and a fatigue invaded the silence. They both had much to think about, and it had been a long day. Just before the silence became awkward, she stood and finished her wine, kissed him on the cheek, patted his shoulder and went to bed. Snuggled beneath the comforter on the soft bed, as she fell asleep she thought of the gentle man and his strange thoughts. And in the quiet darkness, she thought of ghosts; maybe the things that appeared were from other dimensions. Space-time ghosts. Who knew? She didn't.

CHAPTER 15

No sound awoke her. The house was still, its solid stone walls impervious to outside noises, and its size damping any stirrings within. Maybe the stillness was what woke her. She was used to the morning traffic, the slamming of car doors, the sounds of children outside her townhouse. She sat up on the soft bed, swept her hair out of her face, stretched deliciously, and padded barefoot out into the hall wearing the oversized Dallas Cowboys jersey that was her nightshirt. She considered going back and getting dressed before exploring further, but the house was so utterly quiet, she sensed she was alone.

She stepped carefully down the narrow creaking stairs, one hand on the old bannister, one rubbing the sleep from her eyes. The living room light was still on, and a slew of books had been pulled from the bookshelf, left lying open on the oak coffee table. A sheaf of scribbled-on papers spread across the table, spilling onto the floor, and the decorous fan of scientific journals had been scattered, as Gerald had no doubt been reading them. A pair of socks lay on the floor, along with a tape dispenser. She grinned. Yes, this was the real Gerald. Not the pin-neat person who kept house for him.

In the kitchen, an empty coffee cup and plate with crumbs on it told her he'd already been up and gone. The refrigerator door had a sheet of yellow paper taped to it.

"I've gone to my mother's house. Come on up when you're ready. It's the only house up the little road." A scrawled map would guide her.

She went back upstairs and showered in the meticulously kept old bathroom, drying off with the same thick towel she'd used last night. She combed her hair and dressed in fresh jeans and blouse and put on sneakers and the battered leather jacket that had seen so many adventures.

She stepped out into a cool, brisk, sunlit New England morning to find Gerald's rental car still in the driveway, so it must be a short walk. Looking forward to the exercise, she hiked down the narrow road that ran beside the house. On either side of the road ran low stone walls, and behind them a grove of large handsome oaks, their leaves touched with fall amber. As she walked, she drank in the crisp air redolent with the tangy organic fragrance of old forest. The land stretching away on either side of the woods seemed handsomely maintained with rolling meadow and tended shrubs, as if it were a park, she thought, and not some wild forest.

She'd walked about half a mile, enjoying the limbering of muscles that hadn't been used in the day of travel. But still the house had not appeared. She was beginning to think she'd somehow taken the wrong road, when she glimpsed through the trees a large stone building away from the road on the left. The road wound around to the left, bringing the structure into full view. She stopped, stunned.

Arrayed before her was a massive mansion fronted with a white-colonnaded portico. The center of the mansion rose three stories, and it was flanked by two massive wings with high leaded windows. The mansion was topped by a slate roof, with large stone chimneys jutting from several places in the structure, and a thin curl of smoke rising from one. She looked around for a house, thinking that perhaps this was some school or college, and that the mother's house was nearby. Then she realized that the road she had been walking wasn't a road. It was a driveway!

"Woof!" she said to herself, taking a deep breath and walking the final block to the house, passing graceful marble statuary of nymphs, lions, and a cherub-topped fountain that had been shut down for the coming winter. She reached the portico, climbed the stone steps and pondered whether to use the massive brass doorknocker shaped like a swan. Fortunately, there was also a doorbell and she pushed it, hearing no sound.

The door was opened by a pleasant, round-faced woman in a gray uniform. She smiled warmly.

"I'm looking for the Meier house."

"This is it, dear," said the woman. "Gerald said to expect you. Please come in." Still smiling, the woman led her toward the rear of the house. "Mrs. Meier is in the sun room. She said you should come in there and say hello and maybe have a little breakfast. You want some breakfast?" As the woman talked, they proceeded through a marble-floored, high-ceilinged hall with a large crystal chandelier and a broad carpeted staircase going up one side. The entry hall was spacious, as if meant to hold influxes of large numbers of people. French Impressionist paintings lined the hall, which was brightened by light streaming from open double doors at the rear of the mansion.

They went through those doors into a high-ceilinged sun room with large windows looking out over a lawn sloping down to a lake that lay still and gleaming in the morning sun. A trim, erect older woman sat primly at a glass-topped table, sipping coffee and writing in a leather notebook. She wore low heels and a conservative straight wool skirt and sweater that Dacey recognized as probably something like a Gloria Vanderbilt. Her gray hair was done in short, soft ringlets, carefully combed. She rose to greet Dacey, her fine features breaking into a smile. She approached, extending a small hand.

"You must be Gerald's friend. Is it Dacey? I'm sorry, but Gerald sometimes doesn't pay enough attention . . . doesn't give me names right, so I'm sometimes rather embarrassed."

"Yes, it's Dacey, and you're his mom?"

"Call me Katy. Gerald's been shut away in the library since I got up. He keeps most of his books and computers in here. I'll show you, but you must have breakfast first. Cook is marvelous, and she demands that we eat her breakfasts." Dacey gratefully accepted, realizing she had worked up an appetite. The round-faced maid took her request—eggs and toast—but she and Katy encouraged Dacey to expand it to a three-egg Denver omelet, bacon, croissants and fried potatoes. "Cook will be happier that way," said Katy Meier. Pleased at the successful order, the maid bustled off to the kitchen.

"This is a gorgeous house," said Dacey sipping from a glass of fresh-squeezed orange juice Katy had poured for her. "I don't know how to say this, but Gerald doesn't . . . well . . . act like he's—"

"Rich? Dear me, he certainly doesn't!" Katy Meier laughed and shook her head. "Well, I guess it is sort of irrelevant to him. Maybe it's that he was raised with it. I think he feels like it gets in his way, and he'd prefer a simpler life. I know he was driving quite a woebegone van for a while."

"Not any more. Gave it away." Dacey took her first sip from a cup of hot, perfect coffee.

"That's Gerald."

"So he lives in the house down the road?"

"Used to be the caretaker's house. I'm pleased he does. When you've only got one, it's nice to have him nearby. I guess he felt he wanted to stay near, too. I do sometimes need help running this place, although Gerald's contribution is in the area of advice. It made sense for him to stay here because he works at Harvard, anyway. It's only about forty-five minutes away. But he didn't want to live with Mom." Her voice dropped the slightest bit in pitch, assuming a tone of gentle mocking. "And he *does* have his own ways."

"I've noticed. Do you know what he's working on?"

"He's told me. I'm not sure I understand it all. But what I do know is that it sounds mighty peculiar to me. If anybody else had taken off on a wild hare chase like that, I'd have had the man with the net after them. But Gerald has always had a pretty good head on him. The director of his center tells me that his physics ideas have been invariably brilliant." She smiled as a mother smiles when discussing a precocious child.

They continued to chat amiably as breakfast arrived and Dacey ate heartily. But she didn't feel self-conscious. Katy showed an easy grace, thought Dacey, in how she formed the conversation into a warm, personal sharing designed to put Dacey at ease. She told how the house had been in the family for ninety years, so she didn't feel she should sell it, even though it was a bit much. Anyway, she liked to keep it for special occasions like Christmas, when all the Meier relatives visited.

She drew from Dacey the story of her involvement with the Deus Foundation and the adventures in San Francisco and in the Atlantic. Katy shook her head in genteel wonder, expressing hope that Gerald, with all his notions, hadn't gotten her involved in something too dangerous.

Finally Dacey folded the linen napkin and placed it on the table, thanking Katy for the fine breakfast. Katy showed her from the room and down a long side hall in the east wing to large mahogany doors at the end. She opened one and marched in, and Dacey followed. The library was a spacious room, awash in morning light from the leaded glass windows that occupied one wall. Beneath the windows sat overstuffed leather easy chairs with ottomans and sturdy side tables with carved legs. The other three walls were covered with bookshelves solidly populated with richly bound volumes of all sizes. A wheeled traveling ladder allowed access to the upper shelves. Dacey envisioned generations of bewhiskered, vest-wearing men climbing the creaking ladder to bring down a leather-covered volume, which they would take to the chair to read over an after-dinner brandy and cigar. Indeed, Dacey imagined she could smell the faintest aroma of tobacco amidst the mildly musty fragrance of books and leather.

She noticed that a section of one bookshelf wall was populated by an incongruously colorful collection of books that had obviously been shelved and reshelved in a jumble of horizontal and vertical modes, with hints of a rather intricate filing scheme that was probably perfectly clear to their owner. That wall was clearly Gerald's.

In the venerable library, Gerald sat behind a computer at a large table in the middle of the room. His hair tousled from an apparent night of toil, he stared owlishly at the glowing screen of a high-end sophisticated computer work station. Certainly more expensive than the geology department would buy her, thought Dacey. The table was covered with books and papers with a scattering of Coke cans.

He looked up as they entered and smiled, but the smile had a hint of mildly lunatic inspiration.

"Dear, here's Dacey," said Katy, crossing the room to hug him. He squeezed her hand and she patted his face and left, excusing herself for her "morning chores." Gerald motioned to Dacey to come look at the computer screen.

"Something's happened! Something's appeared!"

Dacey stepped across the oriental carpet to look over his shoulder at a satellite image showing a mountainous terrain with a thick pall of smoke swirling from one of the valleys.

"It's in China. There was a huge explosion! I just downloaded this from the satellite image service. And look at these!" Gerald spread out printouts of wire service reports.

"My God," said Dacey, scanning the reports. "This event was massive. It's almost certainly not volcanism. It's mid-plate. Volcanoes only happen where crustal plates collide."

"Yeah, I think a hole opened up. Maybe to a star on the other side. The temperature calculations are right for a star like the sun."

"So what are you saying?"

"Maybe it's the same thing that killed that ship. We should go there. Take Cooper and the oil company guys. This would go a long way toward proving my theory."

Dacey pulled up a chair and sat, as Gerald continued to call up satellite images, each showing the devastation in more detail.

"Well, I've got classes to teach," she said dutifully, but she was becoming more and more fascinated with the incredible images. A whole valley had been decimated. Then she shook her head, as if rattling her brain to change subjects, and stood up. "Wait a second! I've got to get something else straight here! Gerald, you're rich. What're you doing being rich?"

Gerald tore his gaze away from the computer screen and looked sheepish.

"Yeah, well, I'm sorry."

"What I don't understand is that if you're rich why do you need . . ." Dacey stopped herself, paused, and threw back her head in a sudden dawning of realization. "Ohhh! Waaaiiit a minute!" She paused again for a long time, putting puzzle pieces together in her head. She looked Gerald square in the eye, arching one eyebrow. "Gerald . . ." she said with her best low, accusatory voice ". . . are *you* the Deus Foundation?"

Now Gerald looked downright embarrassed. He shifted in his chair and tapped a few commands on the computer keyboard to give himself time. "Well . . . um . . . yeah."

"Why?"

"Um . . ." Gerald sat back in his chair, looking like a small boy who had been caught with contraband cookies. "Started four years ago. I decided the government was just too conventional. Wouldn't fund bleeding-edge scientific research. Stuff that was maybe only wild speculation. So, I started the Deus Foundation. Called it that because I wanted to help understand the ultimate scientific questions—all the way to what we think of as God." His brow knitted in puzzlement. "And when all these things came along . . ." He made a helpless gesture at the computer screen. ". . . I knew I needed to help people who wanted to find out about them. And I needed to investigate them myself, and when I told people I was from a foundation, I got more cooperation." He looked at her hopefully, gesturing to the satellite image. "But you'll stay with it, won't you? You'll go see what this thing was?"

Dacey tapped her fingers on the sheaf of wire reports. She thought of the incredible phenomenon represented by the Gillard hole. And of the tragedy of the mother and her children there. And of the catastrophe the satellite images revealed. She took a deep breath.

"Oh, hell, Gerald, all right!"

. . .

On Neptune the distant sun casts but a dim radiance on the pale blue methane clouds carried by supersonic winds that stream across a featureless rocky surface. The huge frozen planet has rotated slowly on its axis for billions of years, drifting around the sun in quiet obeyance of the laws of orbital dynamics.

A fiery, violent blast shatters that ancient serenity, erupting from beneath the thick ice mantle. Matter alien to the universe contacts the crystalline ice, unleashing a planet-shattering explosion of heat and light that bursts the core into razorlike shards for thousands of miles and explodes away much of the atmosphere, sending it careening into space. The vast hammering blow rolls outward from the lacerated planet, hurling the smallest moon from its grasp and launching the largest moon on a new, crazily looping circuit that triggers deep shuddering moonquakes.

The deformed planetary corpse reels drunkenly in its orbit, wobbling and casting great masses of the icy jagged rubble spinning into space. The remnants of the planet scatter the planet's moons and rings into a cloud of swirling particles. The immense turmoil produces flashes of cold lightning glittering across the atmosphere's wispy remains.

Roiling waves of radiation stream outward from the planetary holocaust in an expanding light-speed bubble. By the time the visible light reaches earth, however, it has waned into the faintest shimmer, which is automatically registered along with billions of other emanations from the heavens by the few optical telescopes that happen to be pointed in that direction. The heat radiation is similarly detected by an Earth-orbiting infrared telescope, which records the arriving infrared wave as a faint ember-like glow from the previously frozen planet.

But the real messenger of cosmic violence are the gamma rays, the highest-energy radiation from space. They are registered as an anonymous burst on the detectors of an orbiting gamma ray telescope. But since the huge satellite cannot pinpoint the direction of sources, the telltale signals will not carry the news of the planetary cataclysm.

All the telescopes and satellites dutifully transmit their raw data to be stored in their respective computers.

But the planet is such a routine citizen of the solar system, and the various pieces of data so subtle and disparate, that the information lies unanalyzed, uncorrelated.

The computers, thus, do not tell their human masters of the titanic cataclysm, that has all but torn apart the giant, frozen planet.

CHAPTER 16

The sleek Chinese Z-9 helicopter skimmed above the rugged Mongolian mountains touched with the first snows of winter and swooped down to roar across the valley below.

"Ah, yes," shouted Li Feng, the Chinese army interpreter, to the passengers. "Yes. This is it. Look!"

They craned their necks to see out the windows a blasted surface of tortured, blackened rock. They saw no movement that would indicate any surviving life. The helicopter sped down the valley for miles, with the same frozen violence passing beneath, then lifted upward, banked left and circled back, returning more slowly.

Swathed in a thick wool coat that limited her movement, Dacey recorded the scene with her video camera, stopping occasionally to marvel at the heat that had created such devastation. Beside her, Gerald Meier, Gordon Haggerty and Brendan Cooper crouched unsteadily in the metal and canvas seats. At the scientists' urging, Haggerty had reluctantly persuaded the Chinese government to lend the coats, the helicopter, and the interpreter. The government had gladly done so, since he was a top executive of a company they hoped would invest billions in their oil industry. The oceanographer, Cooper, was totally out of his element, but Dacey had encouraged him to come as a third set of scientifically trained eyes.

Staring grimly at the visitors from their seats were three nervous Chinese soldiers with their AK-47s and belts of ammunition. The northern province of Inner Mongolia was not a place they liked to go, even though things had been relatively peaceful there of late.

"Where to land?" asked the interpreter.

Dacey scanned the gray-black waste through the scarred window, searching for solid, smooth ground. She pointed to the left. "We've got a level-looking magma fan there."

Cooper got up from his seat on the other side of the helicopter, deftly negotiating the unpredictable undulations of the hovering craft, and joined her. "Yeah, yeah. That's as good as we're going to get, I think." He spoke to the interpreter who relayed the instructions. The helicopter eased forward, flared out and settled onto the rock. The Chinese soldiers pulled open the armored metal door and jumped out, scanning the area, their impassive expressions showing no hint of amazement at the alien terrain.

The others followed, standing beneath the lead-gray sky, each silently marveling at the landscape of blast-furnace-sculptured rock surrounding them.

Dacey set her large knapsack down and began video recording a full-circle pan of the valley for later study. She didn't notice Haggerty stride out across the great wrinkled fan of lava, which looked like a dull, black bedsheet that had been draped across the ground. The helicopter's engine died, leaving only the whisper of a cold breeze across a dead-quiet landscape.

"So this is what you brought me to see?" Haggerty called back to the group. "I've seen volcanoes. I know damned well—"

"STOP RIGHT THERE!" commanded Dacey, looking up from her camera.

Haggerty turned and cast a dark look at her. He turned away to walk farther.

"DAMNIT, I SAID STOP!"

"Better listen to her," said Cooper.

"What the hell for?" Haggerty demanded.

With an exasperated expression, Dacey handed Cooper the camera and found a large jagged chunk of lava, pried it up and hefted it in her hand. She walked out toward Haggerty and stood beside him. Her annoyed gaze still on him, she lofted the rock five feet beyond where he stood. With a light crunch, the rock broke through and disappeared, leaving a jagged hole.

"Many times in these formations, the skin of a lava flow will solidify, and the melt underneath will flow away leaving a thin crust over a deep hollow. That would've been a thirty-foot drop onto the sharpest rock you could imagine. Like that stuff." She gestured up the valley, where vapor bubbles had frothed the black rock into a vicious terrain of razor-sharp points and edges.

"All right. So, thanks." His life saved, Haggerty was more amenable. "Let's hear your story. Convince me this was some damned hole in the universe, same as killed my ship. Give me an act of God I can sell to the insurance company."

"First of all, this isn't a volcano." Dacey waved her hand around the landscape. "You see any caldera? Any volcanic cones? Any ash? You smell sulfur? This wasn't an eruption of magma. It was a melt of surface rock." Gerald stepped up with his backpack and unrolled a map and Dacey continued. "We're here, at the north end of the valley. Gerald has some satellite photos, so we could map the path of this surface melt. It's a lot wider than the ocean-floor melt under the Castile, but it's still a characteristic formation."

"Characteristic of what?"

"A stellar transdimensional aperture," said Gerald.

"A *what*?" asked Haggerty.

"That's what I call it. I calculated what would happen if a star's hundred-thousand-degree fusion furnace erupted through a hole, say, thirty feet in diameter. That temperature could do this."

"How the hell do you get from a volcano to this stellar whatever?"

"We've got something to show you." Gerald smiled, scratching his beard. He nodded to Dacey, who hefted her knapsack onto her back, attached her helmet camera, and led them down the center of the wide flow toward a distant ridge. She stopped occasionally to test the strength of the crust and to collect rock samples. She sealed the samples in plastic bags, marked them, recorded them in a small notebook and stuffed them into her knapsack. She had consulted a volcanologist at the US Geological Survey about the satellite images, and he had agreed with her initial interpretation. But the video recordings and rock samples would clinch it.

The others followed, picking their way among the rubble. They talked little during the ten-minute walk. They reached the ridge and climbed carefully up, keeping their footing on the slick lava flow. Several times they had to use their hands and found the rock still hot to the touch.

Dacey and Gerald reached the top first, and Dacey began to video their destination. Haggerty and Cooper pulled themselves up. Feng talked to the three soldiers, who stood guard at the bottom, looking out over the broad heat-blasted valley from where they had come. Feng trudged up the slope. "They said it is okay that we go up. They will watch."

He found the group standing together, staring up in amazement at a yawning cave entrance some five hundred feet in diameter melted into the side of the mountain. Looking back, they could see that the path into the cave was over a flow of solidified lava that looked like a gigantic black tongue extruding from a mouth. Dacey pointed out that the sides were smooth and glassy.

Gerald turned to Haggerty and Cooper. "What happened here was that something round and extremely hot, about a hundred thousand degrees, and floating above the ground melted its way into the side of this mountain. I did a computer simulation of that scenario, and this is exactly the formation you get." He reached into his knapsack and passed out large flashlights. "Now we'll see where this thing goes."

"Not just yet," said Dacey. "Let me see what's up there first." She hauled her climbing harness out of her knapsack and strapped it on. She switched on her camera and headlamp and donned climbing gloves. Paying out a rope behind her, she gingerly picked her way up the great corrugated tongue of lava and disappeared over the lip into the blackness of the cave. The rope wriggled slightly with her movement. After half an hour, the group heard the faint sound of hammering. Shortly afterward, Dacey reappeared, carefully letting herself down by the rope.

"The floor's slicker than snail snot," she proclaimed. "You'll be essentially walking on glass. I went as far as I could and belayed the rope. I've got to warn you. It slopes down, so if you let go, you'll slide away."

She turned and pulled herself hand-over-hand into the cave, and the others followed, clicking on their headlamps. The beams played about, reflecting off the black-mirror surface of the cave walls, revealing the absence of the usual rubble and rock formations. It was one great, smooth hole. The gray outside light waned as they made their way deeper into the hole, and soon only the headlamps illuminated the immense chamber.

A baking warmth from the cave's sides enveloped them, and they smelled the smoky tang of melted rock. Dacey had them stop periodically and hold their lights still, so she could video sections of the cave and take samples.

Haggerty abruptly slipped and slammed to the floor, cursing and beginning to slip away into the cavern. Dacey lunged for the flailing man, catching his leg, sliding along with him. She reached out her gloved hand and grabbed the rope, straining to hold them both. Gerald grabbed her, and together, they hauled Haggerty back and helped him to his feet.

They recovered and continued. After a few minutes of more carefully making their way down the shallow slope, they reached the point where Dacey had hammered a piton into the rock to fasten the rope. The cavern appeared to begin tapering away to a point. Dacey pulled out a chemical glow stick, cracked the glass ampoule inside and pitched it forward. It slid away, growing fainter until it was no longer visible.

"See. It just stops," said Dacey, her voice echoing in the chamber. "The hole started closing here. That's where you would have ended up, Gordon."

"Yeah, thanks again," said Haggerty. "Closed?" They let the question hang in the darkness and silence.

Gerald finally answered, "I say it closed because I didn't know what else to call it. 'Closed' will have to do for now."

Inspecting the walls with his headlamp, Cooper said, "Well, I'm not willing to conclude anything just yet, Gordon. But something like this could easily have taken out the Castile." Cooper pulled himself up toward the entrance and turned to peer back at the terminus. "But, hell, there's got to be a more down-to-earth explanation." His voice was amplified by the peculiar acoustics of the cavern's end.

"We're beyond 'down-to-earth,'" said Gerald, his voice rising to echo louder in the cavern. "'Down-to-earth' doesn't work, Brendan. Just look at the logic of this theory. A stellar . . ." He paused, realizing that the technical term seemed pompous. ". . . a sort of *gateway* into the interior of a star like the sun is what sank your ship, Mr. Haggerty."

"Tell you what," said Dacey, shining her headlamp in Cooper's direction and climbing up toward the faint light of the cave's mouth. "Nothing like a first-hand account. Let's interview somebody who was there. I was talking to Mr. Feng on the helicopter. He says he heard of a village that had some survivors. Let's go there."

"Look, this is pretty goddamned far from an ocean and my ship," grumped Haggerty.

"Hey, Gordon, you hired me for answers," said Cooper. "Let's just take a shot."

"Yeah, well, it's my nickel."

"It's also your ass if this doesn't get solved."

Haggerty's response was to vigorously pull himself away toward the cave entrance. Cooper grinned. It was Haggerty's way of agreeing and still maintaining his distance, should something go wrong. They followed him out of the cave and joined the soldiers to pick their way back down the treacherous lava flow toward the helicopter. They pulled themselves aboard and the helicopter roused itself from silence and spun its rotors up to a vicious whirling chop through the cold air. The helicopter hoisted itself into the sky and rose over the mountains to skim along over a vast grassy plain.

After half an hour, a small village of tents and mud huts came into view. The helicopter circled once and settled down nearby, drawing a crowd of curious people dressed in bulky woolens and heavy hide boots, with broad Mongol faces and eyes as black as obsidian. The children giggled and shouted, but the adults were wary, respectful. When the soldiers emerged, their rifles at the ready, the crowd shrank away, eyeing the guns and moving the children back in the crowd. The dogs barked and bared their teeth, and the children merrily whacked at them and sat on them to quiet them. Nearby, several mangy-looking fly-infested camels brayed their displeasure at the intruding helicopter.

Li Feng followed the soldiers out, moving among the crowd talking briefly to several, some of whom backed away, waving their hands in reluctance. Finally, Feng settled on an elderly man with a wispy white beard, wearing a large woolen cap and a thick frayed coat torn at both shoulders. The conversation was animated, with the old man jutting his chin forward, glaring at them with one open rheumy eye. He gestured angrily at the soldiers, who stood watching the increasingly sullen group with evident suspicion.

Feng turned back to Haggerty. "He says some people have, indeed, come here from the fire valley. He says there are two, a nephew of his and his son. The nephew was so close he was blinded. But the old man says he will not take you to them. He does not like the soldiers. There is great resentment of the central government here. He thinks you are from the government."

"Tell him we are Americans," said Haggerty.

Feng did so. The old man broke into a broad snaggle-toothed smile and began to chatter something to the other villagers. Smiles replaced the suspicious looks, and the crowd took up the phrase and became more animated, moving closer to the visitors. The words sounded at first like "Sian In In."

"What the hell are they saying?" asked Haggerty.

Feng laughed. "They think you are from CNN. I think they will want payment for their help."

Haggerty muttered an obscenity. "Negotiate with them. Tell them we're from PBS."

Feng did so, and the crowd grew less enthusiastic. The old man continued to smile, but perhaps less effusively. He made a curt gesture that they could not interpret.

"He says they will accept less, but they want to negotiate commercial rights, in case the film shows up on a network. He says they have a person in the village who acts as a sort of agent."

"Jesus!" said Haggerty. "I can't believe this. Just work it out."

Feng and the old man launched into a round of vigorous haggling, complete with animated gestures. Shortly, a slim young man dressed as the others, but with an earring and a moustache, arrived, and the bargaining became sharper.

"Neg myanga!" both the young man and the old man shouted. "In dollars! Twenties!" they added.

Feng shook his head and countered. "Zuu! Zuu!"

After several rounds of shouting, the young man abruptly turned and strode off through the crowd, toward a large, crude circular animal-hide yurt that sat beside an adobe hut. Feng followed and motioned for the others to follow him.

"We have reached agreement. They wanted a thousand dollars. I countered with a hundred. We settled on five hundred. The man will see us."

"Fine, fine," said Haggerty, fishing a wallet from the depths of his coat. He gave Feng the money and Feng paid the old man. As the old man counted the money and scrutinized the bills, the young man disappeared into the tent. After a moment he reappeared, holding open the embroidered felt flap. He exchanged a few words with Feng.

"We may go in. Remove your hats and do not step on the threshold. It is very bad manners." They crouched and filed in. The tent was dark, lit only by a single candle and the dim yellowish light filtering through some of the thinner hides. The air was warm from glowing coals in a center pit in the earthen floor. Its smoke curled through a hole in the roof. The yurt smelled of the smoke, human occupation, the grease of a recent meal, and a faint odor of burned fabric.

Once their eyes became used to the dim light, the visitors discerned a man lying on a rug at the end opposite the door. He lay on his side, a plastic bottle of water beside him, as well as a battered metal dish with a few scraps of fried mutton in congealed grease. Feng squatted near him and greeted him with a "Sain baina uu," and they exchanged words in Mongolian. Feng motioned the others to join him, and Haggerty, Cooper, Dacey, and Gerald crowded together in the small yurt, sitting across from him. The man's brown face was blistered, and the burned skin was beginning to peel away, revealing lighter new skin beneath. Patches of cloth covered his eyes, and bandages of similar material, stained with grease, covered his hands.

The tent flap opened again, and a boy entered the tent and moved to sit warily beside the older man. They exchanged a few brief phrases, and the older man felt for his son's shoulder and patted it. The boy moved to the fire and poured tea from a blackened kettle into small bowls for the guests.

"Bayarrila," said Feng, and indicated for the others to say the same. They managed an approximation of the Mongolian for "thank you."

Feng asked some questions, and the man answered in the affirmative. He turned to Haggerty.

"He is Damdi Choibalsan and this is his son." The man nodded. "He is agreeable to the payment of five hundred dollars and he will answer truthfully all that you ask."

Haggerty nodded curtly. "Looks like he'll need it. Ask him just to tell us what happened." Feng did so, and—with Dacey video-recording the interview—the man launched into a chatter of Mongolian in a strained voice. The memory apparently gave him pain, because of the way he stopped periodically and stiffened, trying not to show his anguish. Feng translated as the man spoke.

"He says he is camping with their flock just before begin shearing. Him and brother and wife and wife's brother. And son. He and son left early in morning to check the goats and go hunt in mountain. They get far up in the mountains and hear huge sound down in the valley. He look at sound and see light . . . bright light . . . all of a sudden on east side of valley. He went back where he could see into valley. He looked too much. His eyes began to hurt and he became blind. His son had just come down the path, and he grabbed him and would not let him look. The heat came then and . . . burned them. He guided his son by telling him how to get across the mountain to get here. He thought the thing that came was a piece of the sun."

The father said a few words to the boy, who also spoke, and Feng translated. "My father did not know that I saw. After the blinding light, there was great flame. Great clouds. The thing was mostly hidden by the clouds. That is what I saw."

Gerald leaned forward intently. "That's exactly what you'd expect. The gateway opens up, and the heat and light energy begin to come through. But then hydrogen is also pouring through, because that's what's in stars. The hydrogen catches fire in our atmosphere, making a fireball. And when you burn hydrogen, you get steam. That's where the clouds come from. It fits. It all fits!"

Through Feng, Haggerty and Cooper began to question the man and his son more intensively. They had moved closer, trying to glean from the man as much detail as possible about the sound they had heard, when another sound intruded. The distant dull pop of gunfire. One of the soldiers entered the tent and barked an order at Feng.

"There is a group coming that we should not encounter," said Feng, rising quickly to his feet and motioning for the others to do the same. "They are the local rebels and the soldiers say we should leave very quickly."

"Well, let's just do that, then," said Haggerty. They hurried out of the tent into a crowd that importuned them with various versions of "PBS! I got story! I got story!"

They sprinted for the helicopter, which had already started its engine and begun turning its huge rotor up to speed, raising a cloud of tan dust into the late afternoon sun. They climbed in as the shooting grew perilously close. The last of the soldiers slammed the door shut and the helicopter rose ponderously into the air accelerating into a roaring ascent. A bullet twanged off the fuselage. And another. But they were safely away.

Haggerty talked briefly to Cooper and Feng and then made his way forward to sit beside Dacey and Gerald in the darkness lit only by a dim light over the door to the cockpit.

"If you consider me a test case, you made a little headway," said Haggerty. "I still don't know how, or even whether, I'm going to try to sell this to the company. But in any case, I'm sure easier to convince because I've seen some of this stuff. You two have a bitch of a job ahead of you if you think you're going to get everybody else to believe this. I'm sure as hell not going to go public."

"Doesn't matter whether you do or not," shouted Dacey over the engine noise. "Like Gerald says, it all fits." She patted her knapsack containing the video camera and rock samples. "These'll show that."

Gerald said nothing, but his brow was knitted in a way that told her he was already immersed in plotting a strategy.

CHAPTER 17

Gerald had been driving his new battered van for two hours that morning, wandering back roads that went east toward the sun, aiming himself generally back toward Boston. He was glad he'd decided to take a week or so and drive from Los Angeles, where the China flight had landed. Anyway, Dacey and he separated there, with her going to Oklahoma and him to Boston. He'd bought the old van for the trip from an ad on Craigslist. He felt comfortable in them. Maybe he wouldn't give this one away. The camping trip had given him time to think on the road from California, seeing the scenery, walking in the high plateau country of Mesa Verde, eating a store-bought sandwich at a lonely rest stop.

He thought of his visit with George Voigt in Columbia, Missouri, the day before as he sipped a coffee from a McDonald's drive-through. The arm was still a big mystery, George had said in quiet, gentlemanly frustration. No other body parts and few of the plane parts had been recovered. The man was a businessman from Ohio, flying himself to a meeting in Kansas City. Nothing unusual, except that almost all of him disappeared from the face of the earth. As they sat in George's cluttered office going over the lab findings, Gerald had told George of his theory.

The old pathologist hadn't laughed, but he'd gotten a twinkle in his eye. George said he'd think about it.

Gerald was frustrated. A long trip usually gave him enough time to develop a new theory, see things from a new perspective. Maybe it was the other thoughts that intruded. About Dacey. Her wry smile, her terrific eyes, the sort of what-the-hell way she leaned her body against his desk, looking over his shoulder, the subtle fragrance of soap rising from her skin.

He brought himself back to the problem. The holes represented something totally alien from the usual physical theories. He had to come at the problem from an entirely different perspective. As he drove along the quiet road, the morning sun warming his face, he visualized the equations governing space-time, let them float in his conscious, rearranging themselves, the parameters altering, the multiple equations appearing and fading.

His mind wandered from the equations. He remembered that dream from the night before. How strange it was to dream of *Alice in Wonderland*, even though he'd loved the book as a kid. Maybe it was the rabbit hole. He remembered mainly the Cheshire cat, sitting beside him grinning. It had dark fur like the cat, Smokey, he'd had when he was a kid. The Cheshire cat ate a mouse. Then it faded, like the one in the cartoon sitting in a tree. And all that was left was its smile. And the cat yawned.

"DAMN!" he yelled, as the idea hit him like a physical object in the face. He swerved off the road, skidding on the long wet grass. A car honked angrily as it passed him. He took his hands off the steering wheel and sat staring straight ahead. "Wow . . . yeah!" he breathed to himself. His mind a tumult of ideas, he looked around. There was a store up ahead, a market with gas pumps. He gunned the van onto the road toward the store. Outside, a young man in a windbreaker and backward baseball cap was pumping gas into a small truck. Gerald pulled up and leaned out the window, his hair askew, his eyes wild.

"Uh . . . can you tell me what state this is?"

The young man looked at him strangely, then said. "It's Illinois. You lost?"

"Which way to Oklahoma?"

The young man thought a second, then pointed down the road. "Well, you wanna get forty-four, so you go down that way—"

But Gerald nodded, thanked him and was gone before he could finish.

•   •   •

Dacey's office was once more a mess, as it had been before the Deus Foundation man's visit. But it was a necessary mess. Multiple glowing display screens, paper charts and maps, photo prints, and rock samples covered every flat surface and festooned the walls, even taped to windows. She needed the sprawling mess. She needed to be able to grab a rock from China, or scrutinize a topo map of the Atlantic seafloor, or a photo of the San Francisco hole. She was sure that they were all somehow puzzle pieces, and maybe by having them splashed across her office, she would understand how they fit into a scientific picture.

She sat at the desk in her usual jeans, t-shirt and flannel long-sleeved shirt, sorting through the latest seismic sounding maps of the Gillard cavern.

After ten days back in the office, she'd finally gotten a chance to really concentrate on the maps, which revealed a giant undulating tunnel that suddenly opened then closed. Like the object in China.

She spent the first days back catching up with her teaching and her graduate students. Then she'd had to deal with the university bureaucracy over the Deus Foundation grant. She'd almost given it back, but finally decided to keep it. The chance to understand these phenomena was too important to let her qualms about accepting money from Gerald's foundation get in the way.

Besides holding classes and going over grad students' research progress, she'd been pestered by the university grants office about the bureaucratic process of taking the money. And a university fund raiser had shown up to ask pointedly whether more money might be squeezed out of the foundation. For forty million, they could name a building after the foundation, for example.

Through all this, she wondered what the hell had happened to Gerald. He'd been quiet during the whole return trip from China. At the airport in LA, where they parted, he promised he'd let her know what was going on. She had kissed him on the cheek again and given him a sisterly hug, which he returned—with a sort of subtle catch in the rhythm of letting go, hinting he wanted to make it more.

Then he'd evaporated. She phoned his mother, but she'd only heard that he'd bought another van in California and was driving back. She mentally shrugged and immersed herself once more in the data.

Then, Gerald suddenly materialized in her doorway, grinning and haggard. She'd never seen him grin before.

"I've got it!" he breathed excitedly, his expression glowing with triumph. She'd also never seen the usually placid Gerald so exorcised. "I've got it!"

"Well, take a pill and get rid of it." She stood up and gave him an exasperated grin, shaking her head. "Where the hell have you been? You look really grungy."

He ignored the insult. "Driving. Thinking. Talking to some people I know. Listen, I know what's going on!"

"The appearances and disappearances? The other . . ." She hesitated. It was weird to talk about these things. ". . . universes, dimensions?"

"Yeah, but I've still got a lot to work out. I wanted to tell you." He looked at his palms, on which something was written in ink.

"What's all that?" Dacey rose and took his hands, examining a series of equations penned in blue ink. Gerald peered at them slightly embarrassed.

"Uh, well, it's a bad habit. I sometimes forget paper, and I have ideas, and I have to write them somewhere."

"Well, here's a pen and paper." She found a scribbled-on yellow pad, tore off the used sheets and handed it to him with a pen. "Write them down, wash your hands and we'll go eat dinner and you can tell me." He did so and they walked downstairs to his van, parked at her building's loading dock. He said he would drive her to her Range Rover parked in the nearby faculty lot. At first she planned for them to have dinner at one of the restaurants on the main drag near campus. But as she watched him hunched over the wheel, bleary-eyed and haggard from his day of driving, she decided that a dinner at home was better. She had some hamburger in the refrigerator that was probably still good, and maybe some buns. She needed to get some food into him.

They reached her Range Rover, and he followed her through the surface streets to her townhouse. Gerald parked at the curb and followed her in with a sheaf of notes.

He began to tell her about his theory, but she admonished him that his seminar would have to wait; that he looked like he needed some food first. So she went into the small kitchen and opened two beers, handing him one and beginning to put together a dinner of hamburgers and fried potatoes. He sat at the bar between the kitchen and dining room, and they talked about what they had done since they saw each other last. He enjoyed watching her move about the kitchen, making patties, sprinkling on Lawry's salt, frying onions and potatoes, pausing occasionally to take a drink of beer.

The aroma of food was making him hungry, and he needed to stretch after the day of driving, so he wandered into her living room. Her brown corduroy overstuffed sofa and matching easy chair were made to be used, and they had been. The sofa was scattered with bright, print pillows, two of which had been piled at one end, under a large, brass reading lamp, where Dacey, no doubt lay in the evening and read from the pile of books, magazines and scientific journals on the light oak coffee table and end table. Bookshelves held a few travel books and a large collection of rocks and a few seashells, with some framed pictures of what Gerald took to be Dacey's sister and mother. On the walls were a couple of Gauguin prints, some posters of Yosemite, and near the door a collection of children's scrawled drawings taped in a jumble at child-height off the floor. Beside the door was a backpack and a pair of bedraggled hiking boots that had walked many miles.

He went up the narrow stairs to use the bathroom, whose shower curtain was imprinted with lyrics to rock 'n roll songs. He washed up in the sink, next to which was her hair brush with long light brown hairs in it, a small bottle of Charlie perfume, some silver earrings, and a used bar of Zest soap.

When he came downstairs, he heard her say, "Okay, old buddy, let's get you fed," as she brought out into the dining room two plates with hefty hamburgers and piles of fries.

He took a bite of the juicy hamburger and was glad she had insisted that he eat. They were halfway through the meal, when he said, "I've just got to tell you about this. It's really incredible." She smiled, rolled her eyes and made a face that indicated she had relented. He quickly spread out his notes on the dining table and she moved around beside him, bringing her plate. "I haven't figured it all out yet." He consulted the notes. "Now, remember about all these holes. The holes in China and at the ship. Those were holes into stars. And the vacuum holes in Gillard and San Francisco. Those opened up into outer space on the other side and sucked stuff out."

Dacey nodded and chewed a bite of potato.

"I knew these might be space-time holes opening up, but they couldn't be black holes, because they just suck everything in and it never comes back out. And black holes have incredible gravitational forces. They would rip everything around them apart. They couldn't be the reverse, so-called 'white' holes that just spew stuff out." He found the yellow pad with his latest scrawled equations.

"Then what?" asked Dacey.

He held up his equations in triumph. "They're wormholes!"

"And what are they?"

"They're wrinkles in space-time so extreme that they tear the fabric of space-time; they open up holes into other universes . . . or maybe to another part of our universe." He held up the yellow pad. "Like punching a hole through two pieces of paper that are next to each other. But theoretically, wormholes couldn't exist without huge masses of exotic stuff called negative-mass. We think that's the case here."

"So, why here, why now?"

"Well, I think the solar system is passing through a region of the galaxy where physical laws have glitched a little bit. The quantum foam—the stuff that makes up space-time at a subatomic level—is flawed. It provides negative-mass."

"But why do they open up in Oklahoma, or China, or under the Atlantic? Why not everywhere?"

"I think it has to do with the magnetic field. If there's a magnetic field like the magnetic field of earth, a dimension of space-time unravels, linking two universes . . . or maybe another part of ours. That explains why there are star-holes. The stars on the other side blast right through the holes. And the outer-space holes open into a vacuum!" Gerald smiled at his theoretical triumph.

Dacey was stunned. She sat back and tried to digest what she had heard. "Will we all die? Will we be swallowed up into another universe?"

Gerald's expression grew somber. "Well, I think . . . I hope I'm right . . . that there's a size limit. I think in this region of space, the flaws are such that the holes can only reach a maximum size. Like soap bubbles can only reach a maximum size. If the holes just kept growing, we would have seen other stars in the sky just disappear."

"Look, this just seems so . . . weird . . . exotic. It seems that things this strange just couldn't happen."

"Yeah, well, we wouldn't believe that tornadoes and volcanic eruptions and earthquakes could happen, unless we'd seen them happen. They're weird, too."

"Okay, so explain why they're so different. Y'know, Gillard just sucked stuff up, but in San Francisco it went through like a bullet."

He sat back and picked at the label on his beer. "They were both the same kind of vacuum hole . . . into the vacuum of outer space on the other side. But the San Francisco hole opened way outside Earth. It was carried along by Earth's magnetic field. It had this incredible velocity relative to Earth and so it zipped through like a bullet."

"So, we can expect some that just sort of move along slowly and some that come through like bats outta hell."

"I guess." He raised his eyebrows and took a drink of beer, leaving a few flecks of the amber liquid on his moustache. "Anyway, I'm going to call some of the people I work with and bounce it off them. There are a couple who won't let it out; who know enough about these theories to tell me whether I'm right." He took a bite of his own cold hamburger and chewed for a while. "But I am right."

They finished their food, put the dishes into the dishwasher and sat in the living room, still talking about his theory. She peppered him with questions. What made the holes disappear? Does the solar system eventually leave the affected region? Can we predict them?

He had some answers, but mostly, he had to think about it. After a while, he seemed to begin to sink into the sofa and his eyelids became heavy. She considered that he planned to sleep in the van and decreed that he would stay in her spare bedroom. She showed him upstairs to the room. Most of it was taken up with an office, but there was a foldaway couch that her sister or mother slept on when they visited. She supplied him with a pillow and blankets and showed him the trick of opening up the sofa. She patted him on the shoulder and bid him good night, leaving him standing tiredly beside the bed, shutting the door behind her.

She turned on the television set in the living room and sank onto the sofa to watch the evening news. At the end, there was a joking piece about a peculiar hole in the ground that had been discovered in New York. Dacey perked up. The hole had gone unnoticed for quite a while, because it was in a slum. But now, the city of New York was trying to figure out who'd dug this perfectly round, glass-smooth hole that was so deep, the city engineers hadn't figured out its true depth yet. They wanted to fill it up, but some scientists from Columbia thought it needed to be studied. That there was something strange about it.

"Maybe it's the famed rabbit hole from *Alice in Wonderland*, right here in the Big Apple," joked the TV reporter.

Dacey remembered Gerald's strange comment about the Cheshire cat. She went upstairs to go to bed, but stopped in the hall for a long moment beside the closed door to his bedroom. She thought about going in and telling him about the New York hole. She also knew she was thinking about going in there for another reason. Since he'd appeared at her office door, she'd felt a stirring beyond friendship. She knew how Gerald had looked at her; the growing chemistry between them. How odd it was, this chemistry. She knew she admired his spirit, his devotion to this idea, however oddball, that there was some alien phenomenon out there he had to know about. But it was more; she found herself attracted to his gentleness, wanting to nestle herself within it, and she knew why. Then a pang rose within her, one that she did not want to deal with. She was beginning to care about this man. She liked men. But she couldn't let herself care for one man. After what she had gone through, she had decided not to do that anymore.

CHAPTER 18

When she woke up the next morning, his door was still closed. She showered and washed her hair, but decided not to dry it. The hair dryer might wake him. She combed it out and pulled it back in a ponytail, put on jeans and a sweatshirt against the morning coolness and fixed herself coffee and a bagel. Hearing the kids noisily gathering at the bus stop nearby, she decided to go sit on her front stoop in the warm morning sun and watch them play. Next door, Nancy opened her screen door to let Sammy out, saw the van and gave Dacey a significant look that asked, "New boyfriend?" Dacey returned it with a dismissive shake of her head, and Nancy volleyed back another look that said, "Oh, yeah?" Sammy was much too busy to give her a hug, as he passed by on the way to the bus stop. Little Karen had engaged his attention, and they trundled off together with their kid-sized backpacks. Maybe Sammy would make up for it by making her another drawing that he would tape up in the gallery beside her door.

As she watched the bus arrive and the kids climb onboard, she decided the plan for the day. She didn't have any classes or appointments that morning, so she'd head for the store. If Gerald was going to stay a couple of days, she'd need supplies. She smiled at herself. Maybe if she bought lots of food, he'd stay longer and she could fatten him up.

She took a sip of the strong, black coffee and thought about his theory. Surely the terabytes of data on her computer and the papers festooning her walls must support or refute this idea of wormholes into other dimensions. These holes must have some properties that would be revealed in the seismograms, photos, satellite data, and chemical tests. She mentally rummaged through her computer files and her office papers, trying to picture all the data on all the events: the Gillard Hole, the supertanker disaster, the holes in San Francisco and China.

The Gillard hole data. The images of the underwater slag furrow on the bottom of the Atlantic, which was piled on the work table. The data on the hole in San Francisco also on the work table, and the stuff on the China solar hole on the desk.

Finally, she shrugged and went inside. Gerald's door was still closed, so she checked her wallet for funds and climbed into the Range Rover. As usual, she didn't have a list, so she'd wander up and down the aisles pulling things into the cart that looked good. That was how she came to own a jar of pickled pig's feet and one of jalapeno jelly. She resolved to be careful.

The supermarket wasn't crowded, with only a scattering of people buying morning orange juice, pastries, and cigarettes. She took a cart and started up and down the aisles. Visions of the data rolled through her mind. She absentmindedly walked up one aisle and found orange juice and started down another aisle to find bread. Eggs were at the end in the dairy case. She started up a third aisle, looking for jam. Three aisles. Parallel aisles. She stopped at the jam section before the shelved jars and stared, as a glimmering of realization dawned. All the maps of the events arrayed themselves before her in her mind. The maps. She arranged them side by side in her mind. The maps! Trajectories! Paths! Magnetic fields! She picked up a jar of something without even looking at it.

"Damn! Wow! Cool!" she exclaimed, making a middle-aged lady down the aisle eye her suspiciously, wondering how anybody could become so enthused over jelly.

She hurried to the checkout stand and paid for her purchases and burst from the store, jumping into the Range Rover, automatically negotiating the morning traffic, again mentally flipping through and examining the maps and charts, one by one. She was certain her idea was right! She parked illegally in front of her office and ran up the stairs. Nobody was in yet, so she didn't have to stop for greetings and morning banter. She tore through the office, pulling out maps and diagrams that her mental office tour had pinpointed. She rolled them and put a rubber band around them and was back in her Range Rover just as the thin, hawkfaced campus cop arrived in the little traffic shack, cocking his eye at her to remind her that he'd been lenient because he liked her. She waved as she left.

Back at her condo, she plopped the groceries onto the coffee table and went upstairs to bang on Gerald's door. "Get up! Gerald, I've got something to tell you!"

There was a loud thump and some rustling. The door opened and Gerald stood there, hair wild, eyes glassy, holding his jeans as if undecided about whether to put them on. He wore briefs, she noticed.

"Huh?"

"Gerald, get dressed. I've figured out something really cool about your wormholes!"

"Oh. . . . yeah. . . . okay." He tried to focus his eyes. Gerald was not a morning person. "Be right there," he mumbled. He closed the door, and she went downstairs to fix more coffee. After a while, she heard the toilet flush and the water run. He appeared at the bottom of the stairs, hesitating as if trying to remember where he was.

"I've got coffee. Come sit down." She sat down at the dining room table, and he obediently sat beside her, staring at the coffee blankly for a long moment before picking up the mug and taking a sip.

She unrolled and spread out maps and diagrams of the three events. "I just couldn't find any reason for how these events fit together. But you said they had to, so I kept looking. There was no pattern in their location . . . above ground, below ground, underwater. And none in their behavior. They were sucking matter in or blasting energy out. I just couldn't figure it out. Then I was in the grocery store and I was going up and down the aisles. They're all in the same direction."

"So?" His brow furrowed in puzzlement.

"So, look at the maps! All the trajectories of these things are in the same direction. Magnetic south to north!"

The puzzlement was replaced by his best skeptical scientist face, his lips pursed. "Hmmm, well . . ." He scrutnized the maps. "Maybe just coincidence." He took another sip of coffee, rubbed his beard and began to examine the diagrams, his gaze moving acutely from one to another, reading the notations on each.

"Couldn't be coincidence," she said. "They follow the magnetic field lines of earth. They're affected by magnetic fields! But not by gravity. This links them all together!"

He stood up and paced beside the table, beginning a nod. "Yeah! Yeah! It does!"

"Remember, you said the force of a magnetic field opens them? Like the magnetic field of earth. But gravity doesn't seem to affect them. They just float around like bubbles."

"Yeah, because they're not objects. They're *holes*."

"But holes that don't move randomly," she said. "Now we can predict their movement, and we can ask how they close. If they're opened by magnetic fields and they follow the field lines of earth, does this mean that maybe a glitch in the magnetic field closes them? Or maybe a weakened magnetic field? Or something like that?"

"I'm not sure," Gerald took another sip of his coffee. He was fully awake now. "Could be lots of things. But better figure it out." He stopped and sat down again, looking at her, now fully awake, dead serious. "I've just got another feeling. I've had it for a while. A huge disaster could happen from all this. More than just a solar hole. I just don't understand what." He leaned over and began to shuffle through the maps again, as if seeking the answer buried in one of the scribbled equations.

"So, what now?"

He looked at her with worry in his eyes. "I've thought about what to do. I guess it's time to present this thing. It's time to see whether it'll stand up in the scientific community. In December is the American Physical Society meeting in New York. That's when I have to present the theory." He fiddled with his coffee cup. "I just don't know if I can."

"What do you mean? Of course you can."

"Well, I've got to admit something. This whole business terrifies me. Jesus, standing up there in front of this crowd of physicists . . . and the reporters . . . and trying to convince all of them that I've found some radically different phenomenon that's going to change some basic paradigms about physics."

"Well, y'know, if paradigms are to be shifted, kiddo, you're just the guy who can shift them." She knew that, he must be feeling very close to her to be able to tell her these things. "You can do it. You just gotta have the confidence to get out there." She smiled and patted his arm and left her hand there for a moment. Then she caught herself, got up briskly and fetched the groceries from the coffee table. "You want eggs? I got eggs."

He didn't answer, but took another healthy sip of coffee and stared at the maps.

CHAPTER 19

Gerald answered the door to his hotel room, and Dacey stood there grinning. He was wearing a clean white shirt and an unaccustomed tie, neatly tied, although it was definitely out of style.

"You look official, Gerald." She looked beyond him to see the room's desk, low dresser, and bed strewn with maps, photographs, computer printouts and piles of notes on yellow legal pad paper. His laptop displayed a Powerpoint screen, with an array of slides. "I see you've been busy. You ready? You're gonna be the main event, y'know."

Nodding shyly, he backed up and opened the door wider to let her in. He raised his eyebrows slightly at her attire. She wore a beige linen pants suit that accentuated her hips, and a white silk blouse that showed off the emerald-green obsidianite crystal from Mount St. Helens that she wore around her smooth neck. Her hair was done up in a braid and she wore delicate, dangling silver earrings. She noted his appreciative look. She kissed him lightly on the cheek.

"This hobby of yours is making you famous," she said. "I saw the story in the *Times*. Who leaked it?"

"Don't know. I didn't talk to them. Somebody at the center, I guess. I'm inundated with email requests for copies of the paper." He swept the materials on the bed into a pile so she could sit down. Prominent among them was a page from *The New York Times* with a story headlined "Scientist to Reveal Holes into Other Universes."

"So, at the risk of spoiling the surprise of your talk, what's been going on for the last few weeks? You mentioned on the phone that you had a surprise."

"Well, one surprise is that I've just about decided not to do it."

"*What!*" She leaned forward searching his expression.

He sat down in the desk chair alternately rubbing his hands together and rubbing his face. "God, Dacey, I'd be getting up in front of a couple of hundred physicists and all those reporters, basically throwing my professional life away. I've got enough trouble . . . well . . . I'm just not up to it. Not up to facing this. Maybe it's why I'm a research associate not a faculty member."

She watched him for a moment. He really was in trouble. She made a decision. "You can. Look, I have."

"You? You've always had confidence in yourself. You've been the one who's made me get this far."

She took a deep breath. It was going to take all her courage to say what she had to say. But he needed her to say it. "Y'know, I haven't always had confidence. I'm going to tell you something only my mother and my sister know. It's about my marriage."

His attention moved from himself to her. He slid the chair closer. They were not touching, but they could feel an intimacy. "Your marriage to . . . Robertson?"

"Yeah . . . Bill. We didn't just have a falling out. He was . . . abusive." She stopped for a moment and stared down at her hands. "He first slapped me about a week after we were married. It was just a slap and he apologized, and he felt so bad that I sort of let it go. But then there were more slaps over the next year. Then punches. He told me it was because I kept talking back. I believed him."

"But you're so strong."

"Well, I was weak then." A long pause became a silent prelude to telling her secret. "I got pregnant."

Gerald's eyes widened. He saw in her drawn tense face a hint of what was coming and he didn't want to believe it.

"One night he wanted to go out and I didn't. We started to argue. We were standing at the top of the stairs to our apartment and he hit me. I fell and I swear he meant for it to happen. I went down the stairs. When I woke up, I was in the hospital and the baby was gone. All I really remember were sirens and blood." Dacey's lip trembled and tears filled her eyes. "The hospital called the cops. They talked to me and they decided to charge him and they arrested him." Gerald took her hand. She took a deep breath and composed herself. She wanted to finish. "Bill got out on bail and came to see me in the hospital. He was crying, but I saw through him. I told him we were done. He didn't accept it. After I left him, I got my own place, but he began to stalk me. I got a restraining order, but he was smart. I never really saw him, but I knew he was there. I decided I was going to be strong. A counselor helped me understand that I was worth something. So, I took lessons in how to protect myself. One night he caught me outside my apartment and he was drunk and he said he would end me." She paused again. "I put him in the hospital. The cops knew his history, so they said it was self-defense. Since then, I'm determined that I'm worth something." She looked at him, a tear rolling down her cheek, her voice breaking. "Gerald, you're worth something, too. You just have to understand that. You can do what you need to do."

"So that's why you whacked me when we met?"

She suddenly straightened and smiled, tears still running down her face. "Yeah, that's why I beat the hell out of you. Nothing personal, y'know."

Now *he* smiled and she knew her story had worked. "So, sweetie, I want you to go out there and gut it out. You should know deep down inside you can do it."

He stood up. "Only if you're out there in the audience."

"I wouldn't have it any other way."

They looked at each other appreciatively. Maybe this friendship might become something else. But the talk loomed.

"Besides, y'know, you've got one person who thinks you're a hero."

"Who?" asked Gerald gathering his notes and his laptop.

"Anita Lafferty. The woman whose husband disappeared in Gillard. I went out to see her. She feels like you've settled the mystery. Now, she and her kids can get on with their lives. Think about that, Gerald."

He smiled. "Well, that's a good thing. That's a really good thing." He'd regained his confidence. They walked down the carpeted hallway and took the elevator down to the hotel's ballroom level. His talk was part of a symposium on "Physics of Natural Phenomena." The abstract of his talk in the program only said that he would present a physical theory that sought to explain "recent natural disturbances." But the newspaper article had made it clear what his purpose was. He'd tried to stay clear of science reporters, not answering their emails, texts and phone messages, to avoid the appearance of being a publicity-seeker. He'd seen such men at other meetings, oddballs with absurd theories about perpetual motion machines or the origin of the universe. He'd watched them pass out DVDs to reporters and try to buttonhole prominent physicists. He didn't want to be lumped with them.

They reached the ballroom, and Gerald politely put off two television reporters who asked him for interviews. It was a harbinger of things to come. They entered the ballroom to find the cavernous hall, filled with hundreds of physicists, old and young, as well as a dozen or so reporters with laptops open and small digital audio recorders. His talk would be instantly Tweeted and blogged. Their low chatter seemed to have an expectant edge to it. He was to be the entertainment that night. Gerald stopped, but Dacey squeezed his arm encouragingly. He looked at her, took a deep breath and walked on, encountering a courtly-looking elderly man in a herringbone sport coat and bow tie. The man was someone he wanted to see.

"Dacey, this is George Voigt," said Gerald. "Dr. George Voigt. He's the pathologist who examined the arm that came out of the sky." Gerald explained who Dacey was, and George's eyes lit up.

"Dear, it's such a pleasure to meet you." He took her hand warmly. "We must talk about your experience."

The San Francisco pathologists Ralph Gaston and Jimmy Cameron emerged from the crowd milling at the back of the room, much to Gerald's relief.

"I'm glad you came."

"Hey, we wouldn't have missed this for anything, even if that foundation hadn't given us bucks," said Cameron. "Everybody in San

Francisco is all over our butts for not figuring those holes out. Of course, I blamed it on Ralph."

Gaston smiled. "Please get me off the hook, will you?"

Brendan Cooper entered the hall, making his way to them and being introduced around. "Well, you've certainly got a tough crowd," he said, scanning the audience. "Hope you've got your shit together, Gerald."

The six of them threaded their way down the center aisle toward the front row. Murmurs from the crowd accompanied them, as the people recognized him. Gerald decided he felt okay as he switched on his laptop to bring up the slide show. He thought of Dacey's revelations. He could be strong, too. He mounted the platform and took his place at the white-cloth-covered table. The table sat five, but he was alone. He was first on the morning program. He looked out over the crowd sitting beneath the massive, gleaming crystal chandelier of the ballroom, and his confidence evaporated.

Filing in to sit down were some of the leading lights in American physics, along with members of their research teams. Mitchell Cadey and Randall Klebbs of Harvard. Aaron Cohen of Caltech. Frank Loeb and Leo Washington of MIT. He knew why they'd come. They were members of an informal scientific hit squad. It was not organized, not scripted. But they'd read the *Times* story that some unknown physicist was going to try to foist a half-baked theory on the world, and they were there to stop it. They'd had to deal with the fallout from such theories in the past. They had let the climate change doubters go too far before they scotched their ignorant criticisms, but they planned to nip this theory in the bud.

Gerald was introduced by the moderator, a portly, elderly professor at the University of Chicago. As he stood to take the stage, waves of abject fear tore at every fiber of his being. He felt as if a cattle prod had been applied to the base of his skull. He plugged his laptop into the projection system, leaned against the large walnut lectern, shuffled his notes and coughed. The screen showed the simple title, "Evidence for Terrestrial and Solar System Transdimensional Apertures."

He looked out and saw Dacey. An eerie calm came over him. He realized that this information was critical for the world to know. The scientific bombshell he would drop would reveal that his theory was critical for its survival.

He began haltingly by outlining the many strange occurrences. He showed images of the phenomena—the holes in San Francisco and Oklahoma, the melted tanker far beneath the Atlantic and the violently erupting heat in China, the venting on the moon, and the New York hole. He showed images of the continuing multitude of inexplicable astronomical events. The glowing "asteroids" that appeared and disappeared. The strange whirlpool "storm" on Jupiter. But he would save the most shocking image for last. As he got into his presentation, his dread simply evaporated. His evidence fit together so well, it gave him confidence.

Then, Gerald began to outline his theory to explain the evidence. His confidence grew as he showed the intricate equations he had developed to support what would be a stunning conclusion.

"These equations predict that scattered through the universe are concentrations of negative mass," he said. "These deep wrinkles in the fabric of the universe could create weaknesses in its space-time. My theory also builds on existing theory that there could be a vast number of parallel universes, each occupying its own three dimensional space . . . what physicists call a membrane. Each of these universes is separated from others by yet another dimension that is curled into an infinitely small size. So, these weaknesses could allow other dimensions to uncurl, popping open passageways into universes that exist in other dimensions . . ."

He paused, both to add drama and because he knew the effect that uttering the next phrase would have.

". . . in other words, *wormholes*."

A collective dark murmur arose in the audience, with some members shaking their heads in exasperation. Others began to raise their hands, itching for the question and answer session. And the keyboards of the bloggers and reporters began quietly clicking, posting real-time reports of his outrageous assertion.

The murmuring and clicking only increased when Gerald asserted that, "My calculations show that matter and energy can pass unchanged through these wormholes. And the phenomena we are witnessing show that the earth is passing through a region of space peppered with the space-time wrinkles that are giving rise to wormholes."

Then he paused again. Now he presented the bombshell evidence for the incredible danger of the wormholes. He'd told no one. It hadn't been in the *Times*. He flashed a slide of Neptune taken through the Hubble Space Telescope. It was not the bright blue marble they had seen so many times before, but a shattered planet with bright chunks of debris orbiting above it.

"The Space Telescope Science Institute has provided these new images and spectra that, taken together, indicate that an intense burst of electromagnetic radiation emanated from Neptune." Before announcing his conclusion, he showed other Space Telescope images, as well as the graphs of gamma ray and infrared data. He carefully explained what they meant. Then came a second bombshell.

"I have concluded that these data show that Neptune experienced a violent gamma burster produced by the collision of matter and antimatter. This antimatter has come through one of these wormholes." Now gasps were added to the murmuring from the crowd. He continued.

"As you know, when matter and antimatter come in contact, immense energy is released. And as you also know, gamma bursters are incredibly huge, unexplained bursts of gamma rays, detected coming from somewhere in space. These gamma bursters reflect explosions large enough to obliterate entire solar systems. But there must also be smaller gamma bursters. I think this is what happened on Neptune. I think a wormhole opened on Neptune into an antimatter galaxy, and the resulting energy release devastated the planet." He paused again, looking around the room. If the physicists were eager for the question-and-answer session before, they would be almost rabid after what he said next. This was the statement that would echo around the world.

"If the theory I am proposing is correct, such a wormhole could open up into an antimatter universe near earth. If even a small amount of antimatter leaked through and touched matter, it could destroy the planet. A large amount of antimatter could create an explosion that would end the solar system."

The room erupted in chatter as the moderator called for quiet and asked questioners to line up at microphones in the aisles. There was a rush of people, and the line grew to the length of the room. The first question set the tone of what was to follow. It was from a graduate student of Loeb's. Gerald recognized that he was merely a stand-in for the famous physicist.

"Sir, frankly, I'm standing here wondering if you haven't got another theory that links the Loch Ness Monster, Elvis's death and the sinking of the Titanic."

A wave of laughter swept the room. It was a time-tested way to dismiss new theories. Ridicule them.

"Do you have a question?" asked Gerald evenly.

"Well, yeah, I guess it's about this huge variety of phenomena you've tried to fit under this one umbrella of some really exotic theory. I mean there's geological phenomena, astronomical phenomena—"

"They all fit," interrupted Gerald. "Look . . ." He walked to the front of the platform, staring down at the young man. He decided an attack was the best defense. ". . . if you just go over the data, you'll see that these phenomena are just too exotic to be explained by commonplace theories." He emphatically ticked off the points of his theory, touching a tip of each finger as he listed them.

But the graduate student was still in the hunt for a coup de grace. "Okay, then why don't one of these holes just expand and swallow the earth? Why are we even still here?"

"My calculations show they're self-limiting," Gerald shot back. "Like soap bubbles. Bubbles don't keep growing to the size of houses. They pop. And these holes collapse above a certain size."

The tone had been set. The battle joined. The questions continued to be argumentative, some sarcastically so. A few scientists respectfully asked him to explain technical points, but most of the questions showed overt derision, mocking. Gerald didn't care. His anger rose. He periodically glanced over at Dacey, sitting indignantly erect in her chair, and at Voigt, Cameron, Gaston, and Cooper. They all had similar annoyed expressions. They knew the truth. They had seen the stunning reality.

Gerald glanced over to the microphone in the right aisle and his nervousness rose again. Aaron Cohen stood patiently in line. He was among the best in theoretical physics, a perennial candidate for a Nobel Prize. Gerald continued to take questions, aware of Cohen, the short, intense older man, coming closer and closer to the front of the line. Finally, he was there and Gerald pointed to him.

"I'm having a bit of trouble reconciling your theory with the data," he began modestly, his hands casually stuffed in his pockets. It was the classic posture of a confident academic about to demolish a flawed piece of reasoning. "I mean, there are perhaps more parsimonious ways to explain these things." With that, Cohen launched into an elegant discourse, detailing how each of the strange occurrences could be explained by underground water, or volcanoes, or meteors. Cohen masterfully wielded his deep knowledge of geology, astrophysics, and a range of other fields. There was a smattering of applause as he ended his discourse with a sly insult. "Now, don't such explanations seem more reasonable than these magic gateways you postulate? These rabbit holes?" The now-cliched reference to *Alice in Wonderland* still brought a few chuckles.

Gerald decided to attempt the impossible. To lecture one of the world's greatest physicists.

"I'm very surprised at you, Dr. Cohen. I would have expected you above all others to be willing to go where the data led, no matter how strange the path seemed. I've just got to say that intellectually, you appear to be living complacently in a Newtonian universe. For Newtonians, the planets are all neat billiard balls that obey neat Newtonian laws of physics. They orbit neatly around one another and do all those nice things we're used to. But that's not the way the universe really is. As you should well appreciate, there really are black holes out there. Really are other dimensions, other universes. Really are gamma bursters. Now, this is a case of the real universe coming to our quiet little cosmic neighborhood. This real universe of phenomena that could cause our destruction. We'd better figure out what we're going to do! And we'd better keep our minds open!"

A stunned silence settled over the room except for a few people letting out low, amazed mutters. Cohen was unfazed, demanding an answer to his question. And Gerald once more listed the basics of his theory and how they fit the data.

He took three more questions after that, but they were anticlimactic. Gerald Meier was famous now, the audience members would agree later around dinner tables and in bars. Some would brand him an insolent crank, others as an extraordinarily courageous thinker willing to risk the establishment. The consensus was decidedly mixed.

The session over, people crowded around with more questions. He was exhilarated, as one who'd just made his first parachute jump or run a marathon. He gave interviews to the media, summarizing his theory for television cameras. After an hour, he extricated himself and made his way back toward the hotel bar, where he'd agreed to meet Dacey and the others. He began to deflate. He realized that the battle would be immensely difficult. Around a small table, amidst the chatter and clatter of a bar, they reviewed the event.

"I couldn't believe it," fumed Dacey. "They weren't even listening! They had their own preconceived notions!"

"You did okay," said Cooper, with a deadpan expression. "You almost had me convinced."

Gerald smiled as the other three repeated congratulations, but then quizzed him about his stunning revelation about Neptune and the possibility of antimatter galaxies. Dacey noticed that he had adopted that distracted expression she had seen before. It told her he was lapsing into the absent-minded musing when he was grappling with a theory.

"I don't know," he said quietly. "I just feel that this has to be settled quickly. So much needs to be done. So much. But they're just not going to believe, maybe, until it's too late." The others began to talk around him. Dacey tried to involve him.

"Jesus, it looks like the only way they're going to believe is if you catch one of the damned holes and present it to them. Right?" Gerald said nothing. "Right?" Dacey repeated with more emphasis. She bent down and looked directly into his face. "*Hello in there!*" He looked up. He seemed to stare right through her. She became worried, even more so when a strange smile bloomed over his face. He stood up and took her face in his hands and kissed her full on the lips. The others laughed at his daring act and her shocked expression.

"I love you," he whispered in her ear, grinning. Dacey jumped as if an electric spark had touched her ear. She stammered, perhaps for the first time in her life, and before she could recover, he turned on his heel and strode out the door without looking back.

"What the hell kind of answer was that?" she demanded after him. "What the hell kind of answer was that? I mean, somebody asks you a perfectly good rhetorical question and you give an answer like that! Come back here and say that again!"

But he was gone.

CHAPTER 20

The office phone rang while Dacey was in an advising session with an undergraduate, a girl who wanted to go into geology. The girl saw Dacey's brow furrow, her mouth purse in annoyance, as she heard the voice on the other end. It was a voice she hadn't heard in three weeks. Dacey politely—perhaps overly politely—asked the student to excuse her. But once the student closed the door behind her, the anger erupted.

"Where the hell are you and what the hell do you think you're doing! You go and walk out and disappear for weeks and leave me to deal with the reporters and everybody else who's looking for you! I called Norm Mankiewitz to find out where you were. Hell, even your mother called me to see if you were here!"

"Look, I'm sorry; I just had to do some thinking."

"Some thinking? Some thinking! Well, pal, screw you and anybody who looks like you!" She stopped herself, surprised at her vehemence. There was silence on the line. Then he laughed and she couldn't help but smile herself. "I mean, Jesus, what kind of weird guy am I dealing with here?"

"I still love you."

Again, a long pause. She decided to try to ignore it. "Yeah, well . . . you are peculiar. Let's just deal with what the hell you've been doing."

"I understand."

"You understand what?"

"That you have to come around at your own pace."

"Where were you? Answer the question, *Gerald*." She spiced his name with a large dollop of sarcasm.

"You gave me an idea. An incredible idea. I knew I could never work it out with all the confusion going on . . . the calls from reporters and everything. I needed to disappear."

"Okay, you disappeared. You're back. So did you work it out, whatever it is?"

"Can you come up to Boston? I want to show you."

"Not a chance, unless you tell me what idea I gave you. And maybe not even then."

"We're going to catch a wormhole."

•   •   •

Dacey felt a little foolish. Actually, she felt really foolish—on the ride to the Oklahoma City airport; on the flight to Boston; during the taxi ride to the address Gerald had given her. She felt dumb because she'd really stretched her rationale for coming, stitching together a couple of too-weak reasons. There was their possible relationship. Weak, because of her past history of avoiding relationships. There was his nutty idea. Weak, because of her scientific skepticism. But she somehow managed to make two semi-lousy reasons into one good one.

After the swerving ride from the airport over the maze of old freeways, the battered taxi rattled along the patched streets through a bleak industrial section outside Boston. Finally, it creaked to a stop before an old red brick building that had probably once been a factory. Its painted metal multi-paned translucent windows were propped open slightly, and the whine of machinery and the clank of metal on metal issued from them.

"Want me to wait, lady?" asked the cabbie, scanning the deserted street. Dacey nodded and went to the metal door and knocked on its surface, dislodging a few flakes of the peeling gray paint. The faded sign on the door said Megamag, Inc. After a moment, the door opened, and a round-faced man with a pug nose and a scruffy beard peeked out. He wore a thin, short-sleeved plaid shirt whose tightness suggested it had been purchased when he was many pounds lighter. His worn jeans also held onto his paunchy figure for dear life, hanging below the round belly and threatening to slip from the nonexistent hips altogether. He had on scruffy gray Nikes, spattered with stains and well broken-in to accommodate a wide, short foot.

"You Dacey Livingstone?"

"Yes. I'm looking for Gerald."

"Great! He's been waitin'. Good to see ya!" He grinned eagerly and opened the door, putting out a stubby-fingered hand. Dacey hesitated, until she saw Gerald striding lankily toward her across the gray-painted concrete floor from the back of the large machine shop. She waved the cabbie away and stepped in. They embraced only perfunctorily, in deference to the formality of the occasion and the fact that Dacey was still ticked at Gerald.

Gerald introduced the hefty ebullient little man as Andy Mullins. "He used to work for the Magnet Lab at MIT. Then he started his own company to make experimental magnets for research groups. This is his company."

"Yeah," said Andy, "C'mon. Show you the place. It's great! My toy store!" He trundled solidly and vigorously toward an office at one end of the shop, his baggy-butt jeans still threatening to yield to gravity. As he went, he jovially pointed out the machines, explained the projects, and introduced them to engineers dressed in the same uniform of old shirts and jeans. Dacey had seen the uniform before. These were hands-on engineers who got grimy building machines themselves. The huge room smelled of oil, metal and electricity, and echoed with the sounds of workers using drill presses and other machine tools to produce huge ovals of metal wound with wire and festooned with piping.

"We do superconducting magnets," said Mullins over the racket. "All kinds of configurations. Special experiments. Fusion, magneto-hydrodynamics, stuff like that. Got a contract with the University of Florida. One with MIT. Another with the Japanese. We're doin' pretty great. Gotta remember to send out the bills, though!" He laughed probably only half in jest.

"Andy figured out a more cost-efficient way to make the magnets and it made sense for him to start a company," said Gerald. "He's a genius."

"Awww," said Mullins modestly, as they entered the cluttered offices and turned left to go past a large computer room into a conference room. Dacey was surprised to see a seemingly odd couple—the sandy-haired young oceanographer/oil company consultant, Brendan Cooper, and the dapper elderly doctor, George Voigt—sitting around a large walnut table. Mullins closed the door and the sounds of the shop receded.

"Yes, he talked me into coming here, too," said Cooper, anticipating the question. "I just couldn't resist seeing this."

Voigt clasped her hand and bowed slightly. "I find this all just fascinating," he said. "A real challenge. At my age, I thought I'd seen about everything."

Gerald sat at the head of the table. "I asked Cameron and Gaston, but they couldn't get away. But they still want to be involved."

"Involved in what, exactly?" asked Dacey.

"Like I said, catching a wormhole." Gerald paid little mind when Cooper rolled his eyes. "I wanted us all to work together on this. We've all been involved with these holes. I thought everybody would like to be in on catching one. I mean *really* catching one. Imagine actually having a stable aperture into another universe!"

"Gerald, I've got to say this sounds just too far out," said Dacey.

"I don't want to be too dramatic, but it could be one of the greatest technical achievements in history," said Gerald.

"Gee that sounds too dramatic to me." Dacey smiled wryly and Cooper chuckled. Her sarcasm was only partly in jest. She didn't plan to make it easy on Gerald, given their relationship, whatever the hell that was.

"I know I've got to prove all this," Gerald admitted. "Well, first I'll say that my calculations show it is possible to form a stable magnetic field around these holes to secure them in place. That done, we can actually enclose them and transport them wherever we want."

"Show me," said Cooper, adjusting his glasses. "You said on the phone you had a demonstration."

Gerald nodded to a grinning Mullins, who opened the conference room door and led them back out onto the shop floor and toward a separate laboratory.

"Got it pretty much figured out," he said, as they struggled to keep up with his short, pumping legs and decipher his shorthand sentences. "Still some bugs. Few technical glitches. But pretty much. Nothin' major."

Entering the cluttered old laboratory, they passed through a wide aisle of electronic test equipment to a steel chamber with thick windows. Andy waved his stubby fingers to direct them to take up stations along the windows. They peered into the chamber to see a golf-ball-sized sphere suspended from an almost invisibly thin wire.

"Magnetically isolated chamber," said Mullins, cheerfully waving his hands. "Use it to test magnet designs. Julio, do it!" He nodded at a skinny, curly-haired technician, who sealed the chamber door and began typing commands into a computer terminal whose cable led into the chamber. A hum issued from the chamber and the ball began to swing upward, hanging from the wire at an angle.

"Okay," said Gerald. "Now, we've put a magnetic field in there that simulates the earth's and this magnetized ball is being attracted northward, just like one of the apertures. . . . the holes."

Julio pressed a few more computer keys and moved two joysticks, causing a pair of large, clear basketball-sized hemispheres to extend on long arms from either side of the chamber toward the ball. Covering the outside of each hemisphere was a complex arrangement of metal windings attached to electrical cable that ran down the arms. The hemispheres approached the ball, easing closer and closer.

"Okay, now we're gonna see somethin'!" said Mullins, his eyes gleaming. "Watch for it, guys."

The ball seemed to come under the influence of the spheres, wobbling and jittering, jerking back and forth. It slowly settled down, hanging vertically from the wire between the hemispheres. Mullins waved at Julio, who touched the joysticks, bringing the two hemispheres together, sealing the ball inside, with the wire sticking through the top. Although it was suspended most of the time, periodically the ball would jerk back and forth inside, clicking against the side of the sphere as if trying to escape.

"Okay, that's cute. What did we see?" asked Cooper.

"We saw a system of automatically controlled electromagnets," said Gerald. "They adjusted to the earth's field and the position of the ball to create a magnetic field shaped to trap the ball inside the sphere. And the field held it suspended inside. We just caught a wormhole."

"You mean almost," said Dacey. "That little ball was bouncing around pretty good in there. Y'know, I've seen what those holes do . . . the ones that have vacuums," said Dacey. "That happens with a real hole, you've got a disaster. It's one thing to catch a little metal ball; it's another to catch something that's pulling a hard vacuum . . . something that can eat a house!"

"Yeah, yeah," said Mullins, knitting his brow. "You're right. Got some work to do. But we can do it. We can."

Gerald nodded his head. "We improve the automatic controls. Then scale it up. We put one hemisphere on each of two mobile vehicles, say a couple of surplus tanks or bulldozers that're heavy enough not to get sucked in. Then we've got a hole-catcher."

"Excuse me," said George in his typically polite tone. "But those holes can cut through about anything. I saw the results and so did the two gentlemen from San Francisco. That control has to be absolutely perfect. What if a hole escapes when you're trying to persuade it to be captured?"

"It's risky. We've just got to reduce the risk as much as possible. Listen, I think it's important enough that I'm willing to be in one of the vehicles."

"Okay, so you've got two hole-grabbers. But there's another tiny problem," said Dacey. "These things don't come to you. I mean they pop up all over the place. You got some sort of hole-attractant?"

Gerald frowned. "I don't know. Only thing I can figure out is to go where we have the best shot of finding out about them the minute they pop up. In major cities." He looked expectantly at Mullins, who shrugged in resigned agreement. "So, we just build enough of these systems to place in some major cities, where we know we'll hear about them."

"Gotta be a better way," said Dacey. "You've got to have some kind of warning. I can just see a couple of tanks with these big dish doohickies on the front, trying to get through a bunch of downtown streets when there's some disaster like the one in Gillard."

Mullins folded his beefy arms and leaned against the window. "Well, maybe one of these holes pops up in some big city, they'll be happy to let us try to catch it. Give us right-of-way, like an ambulance or something."

"Next big question." Dacey looked through the window at the large sphere and the small metal ball visible inside. "How much money? Where do you get it?"

"That's two questions," said Gerald. "The answers are a couple hundred million dollars and a high-tech company that wants to control the most incredible phenomenon in the world. Deus can provide R&D funds, but nowhere near that amount. But I think some smart company would go for it. The holes might prove an unlimited energy source; maybe a way to dispose of hazardous waste, maybe a path to new physics. We can't even imagine the possibilities."

"Well, I'm afraid I can't imagine any company I've dealt with going for it," said Cooper. "The CEO would say 'here's this guy with this theory that was ridiculed by the best physicists in the business. And he wants millions of dollars to put tanks in the streets of American cities to catch something that probably doesn't exist.'"

Gerald's face took on an expression that Dacey had never seen before—an odd mixture of smoldering anger, determination, and reverie.

"We just can't let this go by. This is too big a chance. Too big a danger if we just let these holes appear with no controls."

CHAPTER 21

After some persuasion, Cooper agreed to pitch the Shell Oil vice president Gordon Haggerty to finance the project. Haggerty arrived at Boston Logan airport the next day, watched the spheres trap the little ball. He immediately launched into a Scottish-accented tirade about how he'd lost a tanker and his consultant hired some guy who'd come up with a theory that even the most daring underwriters at Lloyd's of London would laugh out of the office.

Haggerty turned his ire onto Gerald. "Do you know what the *Daily Mail* said about you and your theory of the accident? They bloody well said you had a wormhole in your head!" As he left, he threatened never to use Cooper again, to which Cooper responded by promising never to buy his gasoline again.

Over the next month a succession of potential investors visited the lab, saw the trapping of the little metal ball, and reacted more or less the same.

"Really quite fascinating," said a vice president from General Electric, who asked a few questions, then took his entourage to the Legal Seafood Harborside restaurant to make boozy fun of the demonstration over plates of lobsters.

"Extremely interesting," said a polite research director from Mitsubishi. "We thank you very much for your time. We will certainly consider your proposal." He flew out the following morning, leaving no message.

"I'm afraid our board finds it quite controversial," said a program officer from the National Science Foundation.

"The science adviser regrets that he will be unable to visit your company when he is in town, but he wishes you the best of luck with your venture," read the form letter from the White House.

The same brush-off came from IBM, Motorola, Standard Oil, Keck Foundation, Rockefeller Foundation, and the Department of Energy, all of whose scientists listened to the theory and witnessed the little ball being trapped. Actually, they came to enjoy the carnival. Word had gotten out that the presentation was an amusing way to spend a couple of hours between appointments or before catching a plane.

Even as the refusals mounted, strange, violent phenomena peppered the earth and the heavens. Gerald contended they lent support for his wormhole theory. Others asserted very publically that Mother Nature was simply displaying examples of well-known principles. Same old geology; same old astronomy; same old science, declared the most senior of physicists, with ill-concealed disdain.

A gargantuan blast in the Ural Mountains flattened the forest for fifty miles around, snapping trees like matchsticks. Caltech astronomers insisted it was a replay of the 1908 Tunguska incident—a simple meteor slamming into the atmosphere.

A large round hole appeared through Ayer's rock in Australia. The district constable there called it the work of religious fanatics, out to produce a fake miracle to promote their cult. He did not explain how they had transported a gigantic rock borer there, made the hole with no witnesses, and disappeared.

On Jupiter, a second swirling whirlpool-like structure disrupted the planets colored bands, briefly rivaling the Great Red Spot in prominence, only to disappear. MIT planetary scientists judged it a transient storm that was nothing unusual in the great planet's history.

A small village near Sussex, England, was almost totally demolished by some great roaring storm that came in the night. Entire buildings disappeared. British meteorologists called it an extremely unusual, but perfectly explicable, tornado.

"These things happen," Aaron Cohen was quoted as saying in a *New York Times* article on the Meier theory. "You just don't have to go and invent an exotic phenomenon to explain them. Just extend existing science a bit."

Science magazine also quoted Cohen and a coterie of other scientists on the theory. Some agreed that the theory might be worth considering, but most dismissed it. "It's the abominable snowman of science," quipped the president of the American Physical Society.

The *National Enquirer* published proof that space aliens had come through the holes and mated with earth women, and theorized that Gerald Meier was one of the offspring.

People magazine printed a profile on Gerald and Dacey entitled, "The Stargazer and the Rockhound." The story's subhead was, "An intense young physicist and a beautiful geologist buck the scientific system."

· · ·

"You need somebody who doesn't give a damn," said Dacey, sitting across from Gerald in the small Cambridge cafe. She sipped her wine and looked out at the thick curtain of snow falling on the sidewalk outside. She'd managed to take off some time during the Christmas holidays to come north to encourage him. He'd invited her, he said, to help him make a decision. She'd also come to help her make a decision herself. He had said he loved her, and she hadn't answered back.

"Somebody who doesn't give a damn about what?"

"Somebody who's willing to back a risky venture because he likes long-shots that could pay off big. Somebody who likes the thrill. Somebody who hates corporations."

"Well, turns out I do know somebody."

"Who?"

"Calvin Lambert."

Her eyes widened. "Jesus, you know Calvin Lambert? The oil guy? The multi-billionaire?"

"Yeah, from a long time ago. He used to live up here. He said he'd meet with me in Houston. He sent a jet."

Dacey's eyebrows raised at the prospect of a private jet trip. "So, why didn't you just go see him earlier?"

"Well, I didn't want to then. But now I have to. Will you go with me?"

"Sure, of course. If you think it'll help." Dacey looked at him, puzzled. There was an odd emotional tightening in Gerald's voice she didn't understand.

"It will help. You're a geologist. He knows about geologists. And he'll be tough to deal with."

"Well, I guess we're going to have to deal with this tough customer together, then." She raised her wine glass. He smiled slightly and raised his, and they clinked glasses.

.   .   .

They were admitted to Lambert's penthouse suite that afternoon. The elevator door opened onto a marble-floored foyer the size of a large living room, covered with an Esfahan rug. Flanking two large mahogany doors were antique sculptures of the Greek gods Hermes and Apollo. A clean-cut, blue-eyed young man in a vested suit met them. He nodded to the athletic dark-blazered guard who had escorted them up, and the man pushed the button to close the elevator doors behind them. In a quiet voice, with the precise diction of one educated to discretion, he introduced himself as Lambert's administrative assistant, Robert Van Alston. He showed them into the living room. It, too, was marble-floored with vast, richly hued oriental rugs and a floor-to-ceiling glass wall looking out over the hazy Houston skyline. A large semicircle of light gray sofas faced an electronics-covered wall, including an array of large video screens. The walls opposite the windows displayed several Frederick Remington paintings of roping cowboys, and of Indians posed nobly on their ponies.

Calvin Lambert strode in from another room, nodded at Gerald and smiled at Dacey. He was a big man in his sixties, but he moved lightly, as one who kept himself fit. His short hair was steel gray, as was his large moustache. He wore khaki pants and black loafers with no socks, and a dark brown velour pullover with the sleeves pulled up to reveal powerful forearms. He wore a Rolex watch and a large diamond wedding ring on his left hand.

"Gerald, it's been a while. What? Five years? Six?" He put out his hand and Gerald took it, but slowly. Gerald introduced Dacey and Lambert's interest returned to her. "A pleasure. A real pleasure," he said taking her hand. Gerald explained that Dacey was a geologist and Lambert raised his eyebrows in appreciation of the fact. "Very good. Very nice."

"I like to think so," said Dacey evenly.

Lambert turned back to Gerald. "So, I've been reading about you. You're still doing the physics stuff. And I see you've made quite a hoo-hah there with your theory."

"That's what I wanted to talk to you about."

"Yeah, well, I'm having lunch. Join me?"

They stepped into a formal dining room, which also enjoyed floor-to-ceiling views of Houston. The long rosewood table was set for four places at one end, with silver, plates and crystal water goblets. They sat, and a uniformed waiter brought in large segmented platters with tortillas, meat, beans and other components of tacos. The waiter also brought large chilled mugs of beer. Lambert proceeded to assemble soft tacos and they followed suit.

A young silky-haired blonde woman came in, wearing a sheath dress that showed long, slim, brown legs. She moved with the grace that came of self-confidence and wealth. She placed a manicured left hand on Lambert's broad shoulder, showing a large wedding ring, and bent to kiss him.

"Sandy, this is Gerald. And this is his friend, Dacey Livingstone. My wife, Sandy. I thought you were going to join us."

"A pleasure," she said to Dacey and Gerald, taking each of their hands softly in hers. "Calvin, I've got to go out to the ranch. The caterer will be there this afternoon. You do your business. Besides, you know I'm not as partial to Mexican food as you." Then to Dacey and Gerald. "My God, he's got a stomach like a steel boiler. If you'll excuse me."

"Take the small jet, hon," he said in the way of a goodbye. "I'll need the big one." She departed, leaving only the most delicate aroma of perfume, and they resumed eating.

"So, you want two hundred and fifty million dollars?" Lambert asked casually between bites. Dacey stopped chewing in surprise, but Gerald was apparently used to Lambert's blunt style.

"Yes," Gerald said, still chewing. "I've brought some background. I can explain the theory and what we plan to do. I think you'll find—"

"Oh, I don't look at that stuff," Lambert waved a taco in the air. "I've got people to do that. They've already thoroughly researched your theory . . ." He smiled and took a bite, chewing and letting the tension build. ". . . They say it stinks. They talked to a lot of scientists, and they all say that your idea about Neptune and antimatter galaxies is bunk."

Gerald put down his fork and leaned forward, his eyes narrowing. "Well, they don't know what they're talking about. This theory is the only way to explain what's been happening. And the best explanation for what happened to Neptune . . ." Gerald went on to explain his theory point by point.

Lambert sat back and sipped his beer, a faint smirk on his face letting Gerald argue. He was obviously enjoying the show that Gerald was putting on; the show that he'd incited. Finally, he waved his hand and burped lightly. "You didn't let me finish. They said it stinks and that's why I'm inclined toward the project. Every so often I tell my high-priced experts to go take a flying fuck."

"Then you'll give us the money?" asked Gerald coldly. Dacey had never seen him so tense, so resentful.

Lambert nodded at the waiter, who left the room. Van Alston appeared instantly with a notebook and pen, as if he had been listening to the conversation. Dacey had begun to think of the assistant almost as a minor trophy Lambert kept to remind him of his influence. But Lambert kept his eyes on Gerald and Dacey.

"I'm not just going to hand it to you, son. Here's the deal. I invest two hundred and fifty million dollars in a corporation we set up to catch these things. That is, if your theory really doesn't stink. We patent your technology and I get fifty-one percent of any royalties. I also get seventy-five percent of the stock and a guarantee that I control any applications for these things. Like for waste disposal or energy production . . . or whatever-the-hell else my people come up with." Van Alston bent over his notebooks, busily recording Lambert's proposal.

Gerald pitched his napkin onto the table. "Look, Calvin, these are perhaps the most important objects that we've ever encountered. Who knows where they will lead us? These holes could change the destiny of our species. Or maybe destroy us. We can't launch into applications immediately. We have to do research on them! We have to understand them! They're not simply garbage disposals or power sources to run electric shavers!"

"Hell, partner, you can do all the damned research you want. But I'm in this for profit. That's what I do." Lambert wiped his mouth and stood up, stretching his large frame. "That's it. Take it or leave it. By the way, I've also had my people research how likely you'll get funding somewhere else. My people are damned good, they are." He leaned his hands on the back of his chair. "They say your chances are piss poor. So, you take my offer, or you sit up there in Boston with a bunch of equations on paper and little balls and magnets that won't be worth a shit."

Dacey looked back and forth between Gerald and Lambert, who regarded each other with cold stares. She broke the ice. "I can tell right now, it'd be a real joy working with you two."

Finally, Gerald stood up and without expression stuck out his hand. Lambert grinned in triumph and took it. He waved at Van Alston to show them out, and picked up a phone, turning away from them. The meeting was over.

Back in the wide foyer, waiting for the elevator's polished brass doors to open, Dacey patted Gerald's shoulder.

"What was going on in there? What's your background with this guy? This was more than business. You two seemed to have a mutual animosity going on."

Gerald looked down at the floor, then over at her. He clenched his jaw. "I guess I should have told you. He's my *father*."

CHAPTER 22

The reporters sat on the folding metal chairs out of the desert sun under the large tent, drinking soft drinks, eating sandwiches from the buffet and grousing about having to drive all the way out into the Nevada desert. But they had still instantly agreed to come. What's more, they displayed that edgy eagerness for a juicy story that they could sell big to editors. Some of the science writers had already opened their laptop computers and typed in preliminary leads and boilerplate descriptions of the project. The *Newsday* writer had begun work on a commentary observing tartly that the only newsworthy hole here was the one in Calvin Lambert's head for spending two hundred and fifty million dollars to capture something that most reputable scientists didn't believe existed.

But it was a big story in any case, so they sat and squinted against the glare, watching sweating television crews recording establishing shots of the isolated complex of sandblasted hangars that had once been an Air Force test site for classified aircraft and rockets.

After four months of work, the complex was operational, complete with a freshly painted Deus, Inc. logo on the gate and refurbished hangars and blast-proof blockhouses. In the guard shack by the highway only a single unarmed guard stood where once squads of soldiers had patrolled with M-16s and dogs. Lambert's lawyers had negotiated shrewdly with the government to buy the site, as well as to equip it with the masses of instruments needed for the project.

Gerald and Dacey stood in the deep shade of one of the smaller hangars, talking with the San Francisco criminalists Jimmy Cameron and Ralph Gaston. They'd eagerly taken leaves of absence to join the project. After all, a hole that could penetrate any matter would be the biggest ballistics phenomenon in history.

The doctor George Voigt—clad in a suit and tie even in the heat—stood with them. They all peered into the hangars, fascinated as the rotund, sweating Andy Mullins and his Megamag engineers tinkered final adjustments on the huge machines to be activated today.

Although Gerald wore his customary t-shirt, jeans and sneakers, he seemed different. It wasn't just the desert sunburn, or the shagginess from being too busy to get a haircut. He was more intense than before, if that was possible. He was also more driven. Now he wasn't just chasing some vague hunch. He knew the promise and the profound danger of the exotic object they would soon attempt to harness. He also understood that it would take extraordinary luck, besides the meticulous planning and engineering, to bring a wormhole into their grasp—a creature such as humans had never seen. Knowing that challenge had changed Dacey, too. She hadn't minded the publicity, with the media trying to paint them as the "Bonnie and Clyde of Science" as one physicist had told *Science* magazine. Nor had she minded the warning her department chairman had given her about getting involved with such a dubious venture. She had tenure. She'd worked damned hard to get it. And now it gave her the freedom to take risks.

She took Gerald's arm and he patted her hand. He'd given her time to overcome her fear of commitment. And that fear was evaporating.

It was a good group, thought Dacey. They had gravitated to one another almost instinctively and it was natural for them to become a team. Not only did they share the common bond of having encountered the inexplicable holes, they all liked each other. The animated Mullins, scrambling around cheerily urging his men on to greater efforts, was eager for the technical challenge. Cameron and Gaston were itching to apply their investigative training to whatever the effort would yield.

George was, as usual, amiably determined to tease apart the strands of the mystery.

They heard the distant whoosh of a small jet and saw Lambert's plane swoop out of the cloudless blue sky and land on the nearby blinding-white runway.

Gerald set his jaw. Dacey knew he'd only seen Lambert a few times after the first meeting. The occasions had been cordial enough, but they had invariably come on the heels of brutal negotiations with Lambert's lawyers over commercial rights to the wormholes. Gerald knew that the friction had reflected the lawyers doing Lambert's bidding.

The jet rolled up beside the hangar and the door opened. Two large dark-suited men stepped out, clearly bodyguards. They were followed by three smaller dark-suited men, and then Lambert, dressed in a sport coat with no tie, a light blue shirt and wheat-colored slacks.

Lambert's public relations people had arrived the previous day, planning the news event to their boss's liking. They met him and briefed him on the procedure.

But Gerald forgot all the frustrations as he turned back to the results of their efforts thus far. He still got a thrill out of the machines. What amazing things they would do. Dacey moved up beside him, and they walked out of the hangar and over to the low platform holding the podium with its mass of microphones.

One of Lambert's suited assistants, his company's public relations man, called the news conference to order and introduced his boss. Dacey, Gerald and the others sat in the front row on metal folding chairs. Lambert stood easily behind the phalanx of microphones explaining how the Meier theory, as controversial as it was, had convinced him to invest in this project. He yielded the floor to Gerald, who described the facility and the strategy for capture. He finished and gestured to the massive building. "To your right is the hangar containing the first contingent of capture machines. After the questions and answers, we'll roll them out." Predictably, the questions came thick and fast, reporters shouting over one another. Lambert answered the questions with the smooth confidence of a billionaire, and Gerald with the sharply contrasting precision of a scientist.

From *The New York Times*: "What do you say to the vast majority of physicists who refuse to believe your theory?"

From Associated Press: "What are the chances of capturing one?"

From *Newsweek*: "What are the dangers?"

From CNN: "How do you all feel as this deployment is about to begin?"

From Reuters: "Are you aware that the Chinese Academy of Science has recommended a project to capture a hole?"

From *People*: "Now that you two are working together, do you still consider yourselves estranged from one another?"

Gerald pointedly ignored the last question, stepping down to stand beside Dacey. A last question was directed to Lambert from *Business Week*:

"Do you have plans to commercialize these things?"

"Good question," said Lambert. "These objects are perhaps the most important ever discovered. Nobody really knows what incredible benefits or dangers they represent to our species and our planet. Of course, there may be commercial applications, but I am interested first and foremost in a basic understanding of their properties. We will only consider applications if they will not compromise this critical basic research."

Dacey leaned over and whispered to Gerald. "He is an accomplished bullshit artist." Gerald just shook his head in amazement.

The group moved with their notebooks and cameras to the front of the hangar, and the massive doors began to slide open. From inside echoed the rumble of diesel engines starting up, the faint odor of diesel exhaust.

Rolling ponderously from the shadows into the sunlight emerged two massive armored vehicles, painted a light blue with Deus, Inc. logos on the side. On top of each vehicle, mounted on a boom of thick steel girders, was a thirty-foot-wide hemisphere of clear Lexan, each hemisphere covered with a complex lattice of thick, copper-wound steel bars. The dishes moved up and down, side to side on steel gimbals. Television cameras began to record the scene for live broadcast, and the rapid-fire clicking of cameras could be heard beneath the roar.

Cameron leaned across to Gerald, his grinning face mostly hidden behind sunglasses. "Damn, Gerald, they look like bra cups for the fifty-foot woman!" The remark drew smiles, even from Gerald. His smile also reflected the wry humor he saw in his father, the consummate showman, presuming to explain high-tech equipment.

"These are the basic capture units," shouted Lambert, standing easily beside the two vehicles. The video crews panned their cameras and the reporters scribbled notes and typed into their laptops. "They're Hurricane MAZ-543A Russian artillery carriers. They weigh seventeen tons each and can resist the pull of a hard vacuum without being drawn in. These were solid Soviet vehicles that the Russians sold us for cents on the dollar." His expression showing deep satisfaction, he patted the side of one of the huge vehicles. "The electromagnets on the hemispheres are powered by diesel generators installed in shielded compartments. The magnets are controlled by one central computer in a separate control van that communicates with the drivers."

"You sure the seals will hold?" came a voice from the knot of reporters.

"No doubts," Lambert said tersely. He was annoyed by the question in the middle of his spiel, just as he didn't like to be interrupted by bankers when he was pitching them on an oil project. "It's the same basic docking and sealing mechanism NASA uses to connect spacecraft." He turned quickly to a large van that had followed the carriers out. "Now, the control vans we're using were radar vehicles for the Russian missile batteries. Got them cheap, too." The van was also painted blue, its roof crowded with antennas. "The magnets around the hemispheres produce an intense, highly controllable magnetic field that can automatically manipulate the position of one of the magnetic holes. We plan to station units like these in Paris, Los Angeles, New York, Houston, Moscow, and San Francisco." He strolled toward a bare sandy area to the side of the hangars. "They are ideal for making a capture, as we will demonstrate." He nodded to the drivers, who gunned the two carriers out into the sand.

Followed by the control van, the two carriers took up positions about a hundred feet apart, facing one another. The reporters moved away from the hangar behind yellow ropes to witness the test.

Slowly, the two hemispheres rotated on the boom to aim themselves downward into the desert sand. A faint humming issued from them and the earth began to bulge upward. The ground erupted in a whooshing shower of sand as a seven-foot steel sphere tore itself from the ground, bobbing into the air between the two hemispheres. The camera crews moved back and forth behind the rope to get a better angle and photographers again triggered rapid-fire shots.

The hemispheres slowly angled upward, back to their horizontal aim, and the steel sphere rose to float between them, a faint rain of dust falling from its gleaming surface. Finally, the two carriers eased forward, the steel ball still floating between them, until the Lexan hemispheres met, enclosing the ball suspended within the sphere they formed.

"Okay, so you can do a scaled-up version of the lab experiment capturing those little balls," said the reporter from Associated Press. "What guarantee do you have that it will work in real life . . . if you ever get the chance?"

"We've done plenty of simulations," said Lambert. "And we've set off explosions whose outward blast duplicates in reverse the inward force of a vacuum. If we get the chance, this will work." Gerald smiled again. Lambert had never even seen the test. He would hardly have toiled away in the desert sun to set the charges, hunkering down in the blockhouse as they went off and climbing all over the dirt-covered test vehicles examining the results.

The carriers shut down their engines, and the reporters moved forward to examine them and the steel ball that now rested on the bottom of the hollow Lexan sphere.

The group boarded buses, which lumbered across the sun-baked desert floor to another hangar two miles away. There, the reporters filed out to tour the three cavernous vacuum chamber rooms, complete with door-sized airlocks, inside which the holes would be suspended.

"NASA used these to test spacecraft," said Lambert, standing beside the large doors, as television cameras recorded the huge blue-painted chambers with the Deus, Inc. logos. "We bought them and installed them here." After another hour of giving out quotes and doing standup television interviews, Lambert boarded his plane, and it rolled from beside the hangar and roared into the sky. He had to be back in Houston for the morning network talk shows the next day. The contract stipulated that he would be the spokesman for the project on national TV, even though the booking producers had requested Gerald be included.

Gerald squinted into the blue sky as the plane shrank to a dot and then was gone. Dacey came up beside him and took his arm. As the reporters trooped back onto the bus, they stood together, silently looking at the huge chambers. Without saying so, each knew the other was wondering whether the entire project wasn't some ridiculous fantasy.

"It's cooling off a bit. Let's take a ride," said Dacey, pointing at a nearby blue-painted jeep with the Deus, Inc. logo.

"Sure. Good idea," said Gerald. "You haven't really seen the area, yet."

"Nope," said Dacey, surveying the sunbaked rock formations. "And this is really my kind of place."

They got into the jeep and Gerald drove away from the huge, lone hangar out into the desert, where the low sun made the creosote bushes cast long shadows across the subtle tans of the sand and rock. They drove together for a long time, far beyond the complex and into a deep sandy arroyo where the sun had already set. They reached the end, and Dacey found a broad sandy area, where they could sit and watch the blue of the sky deepen and the first stars begin to come out.

"We haven't talked for a while. I thought this might be a good place to go."

"Yeah, thanks," said Gerald. "I needed to get away."

"I could tell." She took his ink-scribbled hand, turning it over in hers. "You've been working so hard there's layers of equations written here."

He laughed, as she gave him back his hand before the gesture turned into handholding. They sat for a while and enjoyed the desert quiet and the dry, gentle breeze.

"You pissed about all this?" she asked.

"At Lambert? No, not really. I knew what he was like. You know where they got the idea to paint those carriers blue? His publicity people said they'd be more photogenic that way. And he insisted we put a capture unit in Houston, so he could show it to his friends. Anyway, I expected to go through something like this. It's worth it."

"You never really said much about him and your mom. You mind if I ask?"

"No. She never really told me the whole story, but my aunt did. He was this hotshot young oilman. Went to Boston looking for backers and my grandfather was one of his targets. He met her when she was home from Smith. I think basically he swept her off her feet, but that's not what you can say these days. They were married for seven years. I think she was just a means to an end for him. A way to get with an old money crowd. Anyway, he messed around so much that she finally couldn't take it anymore. So, she divorced him and she never remarried."

"She loved him that much?"

"I think it sort of crushed her. She was this kind of sheltered person. Never knew somebody could be like him. Charming. Ruthless." He paused and looked over at her with a half-smile. "May I kiss you?"

"No."

He startled slightly "Why not?"

"Well, look, y'know, first . . . well, hell . . . I am not a demure person, y'know. It's just that, well—"

"You're afraid this is going to turn into something serious."

Trying to recover from her previous stammer, she blew out a sigh and didn't say anything. She was amazed at herself for being at a loss for words.

"Well, I'd be afraid it's not," he said. They looked at each other for a long moment without speaking, imagining each other's touch. But with mute gestures—a shrug, a sideways cast of the eye, a subtle arch of the eyebrow—they tacitly agreed that for a tangled knot of reasons that a certain line could not be crossed . . . for now. But they both remained acutely aware that something extraordinary could lie beyond that line.

●   ●   ●

Within two months, gigantic c-5m Super Galaxy cargo planes had flown pairs of capture vehicles to Paris, Los Angeles, New York, Houston, Moscow, and San Francisco. Except for the Houston unit, whose vehicles were prominently displayed on the plaza of the Lambert building, they sat in warehouses at strategic points calculated to give them the quickest access to any part of the city that experienced an appearance of the holes. For substantial contributions to the city treasuries, and some under-the-table contributions to officials, they were assured priority routing through the cities.

During the third month, a subterranean seismic disturbance of some kind collapsed a shopping mall on the outskirts of Philadelphia. Geologists said it was subsidence.

That same month, a violent cyclonic disturbance appeared above Beijing, China, obliterating almost a city block of the most crowded section. Meteorologists said it was a freak weather pattern.

"We're on the right trail," Gerald told an international conference call of the project directors. "Just as we thought, these things are being reported quickly in cities."

"Yeah, well, wrong goddamned cities," Lambert's voice growled over the speaker.

CHAPTER 23

The deafening shriek shattered the pastoral stillness of the French countryside, driving cows to panicky clumsy galloping back and forth across their pastures, trying to escape it. Sunday picnickers bolted for their cars, rolling up their windows, their fingers in their ears trying to lessen the searing pain. They peered through their windshields at the cloudy sky trying to see the source of the malevolent noise. It seemed to pass northward into the Paris suburbs, prompting a flood of alarmed calls to the gendarmes. Their ears beginning to bleed, people screamed and collapsed writhing to the floor. Dogs howled in pain, cats hissed and spat in fear and the glass in window panes in houses rattled and cracked. Along with the unearthly shrieking, a strange wind rose, seeming to rush toward the object in a rising gale.

The monster passed overhead toward the center of Paris and those who could stand to be outside witnessed its source descend from the tortured sky. They saw a round object, but only vaguely, for it was obscured by a roaring influx of vapor and dust sucked into its maw. Enveloped in the wind and hellish noise, the observers screamed to one another that a tornado was approaching. A strange aerial tornado. The object descended into the Montparnasse section of the city, eating its way with a great grinding sound into the narrow streets of stone houses. The wall of noise swallowed up the screams of dying people, their bodies shredded to unrecognizable red pulp. No dust, no smoke arose from the area, although the skyline seemed to disappear as whole buildings collapsed away into nothing.

Four miles away, a seismograph in a large stone warehouse registered a subterranean disturbance. The attached computer recognized the characteristic pattern and triggered a whooping alarm. Within a minute, three huge vehicles—a van and two Russian artillery carriers with giant hemispherical dishes on their fronts—accelerated out of the warehouse. They followed speeding police cars with sing-song sirens and flashing lights down the broad avenues of Paris into the narrow side streets and toward the scene of unimaginable devastation.

Inside the van, a young brown-haired technician studied a computer screen issuing orders to the police car and the two artillery carriers. A sheen of sweat rose on his forehead. He glanced nervously at the other technician monitoring the magnetic fields. At his signal the police cars veered away, their occupants glad to be relieved of the duty. The van stopped, and the young man continued to issue radio orders directing the mammoth carriers along separate routes to a rendezvous.

Inside the carriers, even with the roar of the engines and diesel generators, the drivers could hear, and even feel, the deep rumbling destruction ahead. The beast was moving underground, slicing through the dense, intricate jumble of sewers and power lines as if they were made of smoke.

In one carrier, the driver touched the medallion around his neck, the one his young wife had given him. He held up a thumb to his colleague, a round-faced red-headed man who would monitor the magnetic field and make sure the dish was aimed correctly.

In the other vehicle, the burly driver gripped the steering lever with white knuckles, removing a hand only to nervously brush back the mop of dark hair. This was his chance to show what he could do. Behind him a young woman monitored the magnetic fields. She was a very brilliant and somewhat intimidating engineer, whom he'd been trying to impress. Now, she would be impressed.

Both carriers maneuvered into place northeast and northwest of the beast, which was relentlessly tunneling its way toward them below the city streets. If they understood its past behavior correctly, it should move beneath and between them.

They waited. In thirty seconds, it would reach the target position. All was happening as planned. It grew closer. Now it created bone-rattling vibrations in the earth which grew powerful enough to heave even the immense machines up and down like toys. But they stayed on station and manipulated the controls to point the hemispheres down to attract the beast to the surface. They switched on the magnetic fields, and the computer automatically shaped, balanced and rebalanced the magnetism according to the beast's changing position as it came into range.

Suddenly the beast stopped. A tense silence fell. The controller in the van held his breath. Then with a roar, it rose from the earth, drawn from its hiding place by the fields. The technicians stared at their monitor screens in both anticipation and fear, following its approach.

It surfaced with a rumbling, crackling sound, eating away the pavement around it, tearing away at nearby buildings, as if raging against its captors. First came benches, signs, garbage cans and other miscellany of the street. Still the carriers held their positions, maintaining the fields.

But then the beast seemed to claw the very structures of the old stone buildings around it, rending their walls and sucking the stones toward it. The stones became its missiles, smashing into the carriers with a reverberating metallic clang, careening away, then arcing into the monster's embrace to disappear. The bombardment became even more terrifying because it was cloaked in impenetrable clouds of swirling dust and smoke.

Inside the carriers, the deafening cannonade unnerved the operators, distracted them and slowed their reflexes. A large granite stone dislodged from a disintegrating church steeple, slammed down into one of the hemispheres and tore away a crucial cable, causing the magnetic field to falter. Another stone followed hard on the first, compounding the damage.

The beast had freed itself from the magnetic cage. Before anyone could react, it skewed toward the intact carrier, drawn by a remnant magnetic field that was not shut down fast enough. It ate harmlessly through one side of the hemisphere and continued to skirt along the south side of the vehicle, which was successfully resisting the vicious pull of its vacuum. But now the field was off and it could resume the steady northerly path that had been its nature. It veered in a deadly drift into the vehicle, slicing through the metal plate and eviscerating the carrier as a predator draws the soft living substance from a broken egg.

The young man with the medallion and his red-headed friend lived only an instant before they were crushed and swallowed into another universe.

Over the radios came the static-laden sounds of screaming, shouting, and sobbing from the remaining carrier, as the creature continued its unhampered drift northward, consuming houses, offices, stores. After a while, it wafted into the sky, again resuming the shriek that was its call.

Abruptly, the hellish sound ceased, as if it were choked off. The abrupt disappearance left the faint wail of sirens, an immense, jagged smoking scar of destruction across the city and the shattered remains of what had been a confidently designed scientific plan.

· · ·

"Jesus, we can't even talk to the people who were in the surviving carrier!" Brendan Cooper's frustration spilled out of the phone line from Paris. In Nevada, Gerald and Andy Mullins sat huddled around the speakerphone in the small office just off the hangar. Outside the office, the engineers from Megamag and Deus crowded around the door, straining to hear the conference call. Cameron was linked from San Francisco, and Dacey was in Oklahoma. Cooper, who had sat agonized in the control room during the catastrophe, continued, "The doctors've got them sedated, and they're not even sure the guys are going to come out of this sane."

"Brendan, I know it was traumatic, but could they be rendered insane?" asked Gerald.

"Well, the way the docs told me, it's major post-traumatic stress disorder. These people encountered something that turned their whole world . . . well, their universe . . . literally inside out. They couldn't cope. Gerald, you've got to rethink this whole thing. You've got to rethink the equipment, but you've also got to rethink the people."

"God. My God, what have I done." Gerald whispered, resting his palms on the desk, staring down at the phone.

"C'mon, Gerald, it wasn't just you," said Mullins. "We all developed this thing . . . did the best we could with what we knew."

"Yes, but people died."

"Bullshit," came a third voice through the phone. "This happens. I've had people killed on my rigs, and it's a bad thing, but you just figure out what went wrong and you forge ahead." The voice rose and fell in volume as Lambert apparently moved about in his office.

"Calvin, don't you feel *anything* here?" asked Gerald.

"I feel like you people didn't take everything into account. Hell, didn't you ever expect these things to make crap fly around?"

"We thought the control system could handle it . . . shut down quick enough. We just didn't realize the holes have no inertia. They'll move instantly responding to the subtlest change in a magnetic field. We'll fix it next time."

"Fine, you do that," said Lambert. "You also call a news conference. My people will be there inside an hour to run it. Make sure you emphasize that this . . . event . . . proves that these things exist. No fucking way this could have been some tornado."

"Calvin, we will emphasize that it was a terrible tragedy that these people died," said Gerald. "We'll emphasize that we made mistakes, that—"

"For Christ's sake don't say *mistakes*. I've had my share of lawsuits. We'll have the families, the damned French government, everybody, on our asses. My pockets are deep, but I'm not going to open them for this."

"I *will* say that. I will tell what I think—"

"Gerald, you are an employee of Deus, Inc." His voice grew louder. Lambert had leaned right into his speakerphone. "You will say what you are told to say, or I will fucking cut this project off. I will pull out and say that I was hornswoggled, that your theory doesn't work worth a shit, do you hear me, Gerald? Your choice, Gerald?" There was a click. Lambert hadn't waited for an answer.

"What a shithead," said Cameron's voice over the phone.

"I think that's a reasonable assessment," came Dacey's voice. "Gerald, don't worry about him. Look, I'm flying out. Let's go over all the information; figure something out. There are answers here." They talked for a while and agreed that they would all gather the following day to go over all the data about all the occurrences again. When he hung up, Gerald found he was as determined as ever.

Reporters packed the news conference that afternoon in the cavernous hangar. Footage of the Paris disaster had run all morning on CNN and the morning talk shows, complete with hastily called experts. So, the reporters were primed with full details of what had happened. The trail of devastation had run for three miles through urban Paris, with 937 people known dead and billions of dollars in damage.

Flanked by suited PR men from Lambert's company, Gerald stood and delivered a statement on what was known about the failure of the Deus attempt to capture the hole. Then, he answered questions, choosing the questioners from the forest of insistent hands that would shoot up after each answer. He gave answers, some not his own:

Yes, it was a terrible tragedy.

Yes, it was reminiscent of the Challenger space shuttle disaster. The two people in the doomed capture vehicle, Roger Cavendish and Emily Corot, gave their lives for science, as well as to stop the hole in its destructive tracks.

Yes, it was obviously incontrovertible proof that the Meier theory was correct. Amateur video footage from the Eiffel Tower clearly showed the hole slice through its center.

No, Calvin Lambert was not pulling out. However, he was not available at this time for his reaction.

Yes, an enormous amount had been learned about the phenomenon to allow improvements in the system.

No, Deus, Inc. did not make any obvious mistakes. An act of God cannot be controlled, especially one as entirely new as this one.

Then, the question that Gerald expected:

Yes, he would somehow manage to be in one of the two capture vehicles that encountered the next hole. He wouldn't ask others to risk their lives if he wouldn't risk his.

· · ·

"Nothing comes from nothing." Ralph Gaston smiled inscrutably and leaned back in the chair, studying wall-sized screens full of maps and charts, and the incongruously ancient blackboard covered with equations. The others looked at him expectantly, waiting for him to say something else, but he didn't.

"Damn, Ralph, you doing your Confucius imitation again?" Cameron perched on a nearby work table drinking a Coke. But Gaston didn't reply, letting his proverb sink in.

They were all bleary from ten hours in the large briefing room in the former Air Force administration building. Besides the newly installed computer screens, it held several worn work tables, old metal arm chairs and a yellowing topographic area map on one wall.

Covering the tables were laptop computers, rock samples, photos, and anything else that pertained to the appearance of the holes. In particular, Dacey's sheared-off rock from beneath Gillard sat in the middle of the largest table, a singular object of contemplation surrounded by coffee cups, sandwich wrappers, and yellow pads with pages covered with scribbles.

"He's right, you know." The elderly doctor George Voigt stood apart in an easy slouch, his hands in his pockets, gazing at the screenfuls of maps. He wore his usual white shirt, slacks, and bow tie, but also a brand new pair of hiking boots that Dacey had helped him buy. "In my experience, there's never been a time when, say, a murderer didn't give clues beforehand about what he was going to do. I had these deaths once in this hospital. Thirteen. It was the killer's unlucky number. I had all the bodies exhumed and found traces of a muscle relaxant in most of them. The killer turned out to be an orderly. He wasn't supposed to be near a hypodermic. But we got onto him because before he had even begun his killing, somebody once saw him practicing giving shots on an orange."

"Okay, George, then you and Ralph are saying these things must give warning." Gerald sat at the chair by the large computer terminal, rubbing his beard tiredly. "Where do we go from there? We can get anything we want from the government computers. NASA, DOD, DOE . . . everybody's opened up to us. Sky's the limit."

"Yeah," said Dacey. "Sky's the limit, but we don't know where to start to get there." She took a sip of old coffee and seemed to shake herself awake. "Okay, then, let's start at the sky. If we're going to catch these things, we need a warning. That means we need surveillance that has to be from the sky. That only means satellites."

Gerald sat back and began to scribble a list of earth-scanning satellites. "All right. We got GOES, GPS, NOAA—"

"What's that alphabet mean?" asked Cameron.

"Uh. . . . satellites to study the atmosphere, global positioning satellites, weather satellites . . ."

Dacey went over behind Mullins, who sat in a chair off to one side. She slapped his beefy shoulders like a trainer would a boxer's. Andy was fresh, having just spent half an hour snoring away in the chair. "Andy, imagine we got something that makes a magnetic disturbance. What would we see?"

"Yeah, well—"

"Wait, I know!" exclaimed Dacey. "Maybe lights! Before an earthquake, there are sometimes lights in the sky. Seismologists think they come from magnetic fields affecting the atmosphere. Gimme some data, guys. Gimme some help here."

"Lights!" echoed Mullins helpfully. The engineer heaved his roly-poly bulk out of the chair with an oof and grabbed a yellow pad, flipping back the equation-covered pages and writing more of his own. "Let's see. Got earth's field. Got that. Then add field—"

"There *might* be a new field," said Gerald. "From the other . . . side. The other . . ." He hesitated to say "universe." It seemed so Star Trekky. "An added field that penetrates through to our side just like matter and energy can. Or, maybe a field generated by the hole itself when it warps space-time."

"Maybe! Maybe!" Andy held up his yellow pad, although nobody could possibly have deciphered the wild scrawl of equations. "There could be light flashes!"

"Could we see them?" Dacey looked from person to person.

"Military satellites could," said Gerald. "DOD has spy satellites that look for light flashes and infrared signatures of rockets being launched. And they've got the resolution to see even small flashes and pinpoint them immediately." He grabbed a laptop and began pecking away at the keys. He quickly displayed a list of satellites on one of the big screens. The group leaned in. "Okay, yeah . . . there are military satellites up there that look for light flashes from launches. And NASA's got satellites that detect lightning flashes. We've got to call the people who run them. Put in a request."

"Like hell 'put in a request'!" exclaimed Cameron, forcing a grin onto a face sagging with fatigue. He waved a cell phone. "We go right to the top. We get the damned President out of bed. I'd really like to do that."

After some persuasion, Gerald made the phone call and in an hour they had results. He had triggered a chain of calls from the President, to his science advisor, to the Chairman of the Joint Chiefs of Staff, to the Secretary of the Air Force. The Secretary called Gerald with a code word, hung up the phone, and issued a priority order that rattled down the Air Force chain of command to a coffee-primed captain on night duty at the Strategic Air Command in Colorado. The captain called them back, his voice betraying suspicion at the odd order. But after Gerald offered the code word, he gave them passwords to access the archived digital images from the Air Force's IKON spy satellites. Gerald and Mullins had already linked the computer to a secure DOD network connection. The captain also talked Gerald through the commands to analyze and compare the images for anomalous light flashes. He hung up and began the process.

The phone rang again shortly with another call from a NASA computer specialist who'd been rousted out of bed by another order that rattled down NASA's chain of command to him. He gave Gerald instructions for accessing the earth-resources satellite images.

"This'll take a couple of hours," said Gerald without looking up from the computer. "Go get some sleep." Suddenly, they all felt the weight of twenty-four hours awake, except for Mullins, who'd had the requisite periodic catnap that was his habit. Leaving Gerald typing and Mullins hovering over him like a cherubic vulture, they all wandered tiredly down the gray-painted hall to the dormitory wing where pilots had slept before missions. The wing consisted of rooms bare of decoration, save for double beds, worn dressers, mirrors and bedside lamps. Pairs of rooms had connecting doors, and Dacey and Gerald had earlier, without comment, taken a connecting pair, but had not opened the door between them. Dacey managed to remember her room number, as did the others, and they were soon all inert forms in their beds.

Dacey had lain for an hour in the deep sleep of dreams and soft paralysis, when a voice drew her awake. She felt a hand on her shoulder.

"We got 'em," whispered Gerald conspiratorially in her ear, and she came wide awake, only having to take a deep breath to clear her head for conversation.

"Got what?" She sat up, seeing his form illuminated by the light from the hallway, as he crouched by her bed.

"Flashes! We found *flashes*!"

She leaped up, smoothing down her t-shirt over the top of her jeans and followed him in stocking feet over the worn linoleum tiles down to the briefing room. She heard sleepy moans behind her, as Mullins' less-soothing commands rousted the others. Shortly, they all stood blearily before the large display screen, with Gerald at the laptop keyboard. He typed in a command. Two satellite images of a vast darkened landscape peppered with lights began alternately flashing on the large screen, one after the other.

"What are we seeing?" asked Gaston.

"Southern France," said Gerald. "One image was a month ago. Another last week, a few days before the . . . uh . . . event. Both are the same region. I superimposed them so we can go back and forth."

"Speed 'em up now! Speed 'em up!" demanded Mullins eagerly.

Gerald touched a key and the two dark images flashed one after the other on the screen. A few pinpoint lights blinked, indicating that the lights had been on during one image, off during the other.

It was George, used to studying subtle images of cells under a microscope, who saw it first. "I see a peculiar flash! It's faint, but it's there! That's not artificial lights!" He pointed to an area on the screen. The others leaned in. A soft reddish glow appeared on one image, disappeared on the other.

"Right. That's it," said Gerald. "We also found something like this before China and before Gillard."

"Damn, man!" exclaimed Cameron. "Damn! We got the suckers!"

"That we do," said Gerald, a bone-deep fatigue permeating his voice. "That we do."

CHAPTER 24

"You're going to thank him, aren't you?" asked Dacey. "Gerald, you should thank him." She and Gerald stood in the thickly carpeted outer office of the President's science advisor. They watched the advisor's gray-suited aide shuffle through a large blue folder containing briefing papers on their visit, to be taken into the advisor before they would be invited to enter.

"Sure, I'll thank him. He helped us now. But I don't know if I'll shake hands with him. He basically told us to screw off before the Paris incident."

"For once we agree on something." They turned to see Lambert striding into the Executive Office Building waiting room with all the confidence of his billions of dollars. Trailing behind him were his assistant, Van Alston, and another large dark-suited man. "But you will still shake hands with me, won't you?"

"Well, Calvin, I will say that although you are a son-of-a-bitch, at least you are open about it." Gerald shook hands with his father. Lambert registered only a subtle surprise at Gerald's new outspokenness.

"Thank you," he said, with no hint of irony. He turned to Van Alston. "Tell them we're all here and let's get on with it." Van Alston nodded and passed the information to the science advisor's assistant, practically his clone, and the assistant disappeared into the science advisor's office. While the large, dark-suited man stood in a corner facing the door, Lambert sat in one of the leather easy chairs and crossed his legs, ankle-on-knee. He looked up at Gerald. "So, my people say you're a big deal now. Accepted by those scientists."

"Yes, there was a colloquium today at the National Academy of Sciences. I was lead speaker."

"I had somebody there. He said all the big-shot physicists claimed they believed you all along, eh?"

"Something like that. But in any case they're all working on expanding the theory about these things. Doing some good science."

"Whatever. But they're with us?"

"Yes."

The door to the science advisor's office opened and the aide invited them in. They entered the large office, which included two wing chairs flanking a large fireplace and a large matching blue sofa directly across from the chairs.

The science advisor stepped forward from behind his walnut desk. He was a slightly plump middle-aged man with a fringe of white hair and a precise, confident way about him that marked one who had run a large aerospace corporation. He wore rimless glasses and a blue pinstripe suit with a maroon tie decorated with small, tasteful images of spacecraft.

"I'm Allen Randolph," he said shaking hands all around. "I'm so pleased that you could come."

Randolph and Lambert sat across from one another on the chairs and Dacey and Gerald took the sofa. Other various assistants, notebooks in hand, sat behind them around the room. They were brought coffee and made small talk about the trip and the colloquium. The science advisor took a few sips of his coffee, then set it aside and motioned to be given the blue folder, which he opened on his lap.

"Well, I see that there have been a considerable number of these . . . occurrences . . . in the month since the Paris disaster." He flipped through pages of photocopied clippings. "There was this two-mile section of the Amazonian jungle in Bolivia that disappeared within ten minutes. The explosion in Antarctica. Our people on McMurdo Sound said they could feel the heat and read a newspaper by the light. And there's that hole in the Bronx that's still drawing quite a crowd. And there are dozens of astronomical sightings to date. Mostly basic thermonuclear events. Wormholes, I guess you call them?" He held up an iPad and scrolled through headlines, chuckling. "I see the media have named the different kinds. Big suckers, screamers, starholes—"

"We've been following all of that, Dr. Randolph," said Gerald. "It's all consonant with the theory. We've still got a lot of uncertainties. Like Neptune."

"Yes, well I'm sure you'll make progress," Randolph smiled encouragingly. Gerald could tell he wanted to dismiss the Neptune business. His astronomer friends had no doubt declared that Gerald's theory about antimatter remained just too far out, even given the wormholes' existence. "Well, all these happenings just emphasize the need to understand what to do about all these things. There is a potential for more disaster."

"No shit," said Lambert, gesturing to his son. "That's what Gerald's been telling you for the last year."

The science advisor's cordial facade slipped for an instant. He knew Lambert as a heavy contributor to ultraconservative causes and a vocal opponent of the President's energy policy. "Mr. Lambert, may I say that at some point you might learn something about scientific process. Things have to be proven; there have to be data. In any case, I hope the colloquium today gave us some ideas about how to head off those disasters." The science advisor pointedly turned away from Lambert. "But I wanted your own assessment, Dr. Meier."

"Well, clearly, holes into antimatter galaxies, like the one on Neptune, are the most potentially cataclysmic. I know most people still doubt their existence. True, they seem rare, but they're real." The science advisor's stony expression signified his steadfast refusal to discuss the Neptune occurrence. So Gerald veered onto a track he knew would be acceptable. "Of course, now the most important thing is to catch an aperture that opens into a vacuum. That's really the only kind we can hope to handle. Then we can analyze it and figure out what our options are."

The science advisor closed the folder and leaned forward, smiling. "Ah, well, we'd like to help. We'd like to arrange for federal funds for you to do your work. We have the national labs at our disposal and we can help increase your technical capabilities."

"Well, one reason for this meeting was about the facilities you've made possible," said Gerald. "The planes and satellites. I wanted to thank you for all—"

"Wait a minute," interrupted Lambert. "About this federal funds thing. Now I've got your game. Look, when they were looking for money before, you were holed up somewhere incommunicado. Now that everybody believes them and you've had the thing blow up in your face, you're suddenly ready to be his buddy, to clean his fish for him. You government types want to come in and then claim credit for catching one of these things. Hell, even ownership. Now, if you want to license Deus's technology, maybe. The fee will be goddamned high."

Randolph again assumed a poker face. He turned to Gerald. "You agree with that? What do you want?"

"I want to isolate a hole. The important thing is to figure them out, so we can prevent other . . ." He paused, his jaw tightening. The Paris disaster ate at his conscience. He recovered. ". . . sure, I'd like all the help I can get, and I think we can work something out. But Calvin did put up money when it wasn't very popular to. He has controlling interest in the technology. It's his call."

"Yeah, you dance with them what brung ya," said Lambert. "And I'm not going to let some damned government—"

"Just hold it, Calvin," said Dacey. "I've sat here and watched you guys compare testosterone levels. Let's get settled on what our priorities are. Catch one, figure it out, learn enough to close it. Right?" She didn't wait for an answer. "Calvin, you can give up some of your precious technology rights, can't you? And Dr. Randolph, you can write special rules that give the company commercial and patent rights to anything that comes of this, can't you?"

Lambert and Randolph eyed each other warily, silent in their assent.

"Well, let's try to work together and get as many resources on this as we can, shall we . . . *gentlemen*?" Her tone indicated she didn't think either of the parties were, indeed gentlemen.

"I think we can work something out," said Randolph finally, nodding to his assistant. "But I have to say one thing up front. You've had a chance already and it was a disaster. What's to prevent it from happening again?"

"We've improved our methods." Now Gerald was in his element and he warmed to the subject. "I announced at the colloquium that we can see precursors . . . faint light flashes, sort of a small aurora . . . a couple of days before what we call 'breakthrough' . . . when a hole opens up. So, now, we've got these capture vehicles and support vans sitting in Air Force cargo planes in each major city. They can take off in minutes and be anywhere within a day. And we've got DOD and NASA satellites programmed to detect the flashes real-time."

"Tell them about the technical improvements," prompted Dacey, noticing the faint outlines of a penned equation on one of Gerald's palms as he gestured. He'd been making notes to himself again.

"We've made technical improvements, too. Each group has *three* carriers now, so one will be on the scene as a backup," said Gerald. "And the magnetic capture system instantaneously changes the fields. We've also done some reengineering of the capture dishes to make them more structurally solid."

"And we'll have drivers inside who can take combat conditions," said Lambert. "Ex-army tank drivers. Damned good nerves, fast reflexes. We're givin' 'em a hundred thousand a year, just to train. And I added a bounty of a hundred thousand for each man in the team that catches a hole." He sat back with a satisfied grin. "I firmly believe in a capitalistic approach to these kinds of things."

"Well, it's been weeks," said Randolph, a slight note of accusation entering his voice. "There have been events all over, including a couple in cities. But none that you've managed to get in ahead of."

Gerald took a breath to reply, but an aide deferentially interrupted them, a cell phone in his hand. He gave it to Gerald, who took it and listened a moment. He smiled slightly, looking at Dacey, then the others, his dark eyes intense.

"A flash," he said, his voice thick with tension. "They've seen a flash."

CHAPTER 25

"Alpha to Control. Target surfacing!" Gerald's voice echoed in his own helmet's headphones. He could also hear his own heavy breathing, as he crouched in the artillery carrier's cramped passenger compartment. A deep gut-shaking rumble rose outside, penetrating even the carrier's two inches of steel. The rumble rattled the twenty-two-ton vehicle like a toy, but the driver, Clark, sat imperviously in the driver's seat, his gloved hands firmly gripping the controls, scanning the instruments and peering out the front slit. Clark, the squat, solid ex-army officer, only cared about fulfilling his mission, and Gerald was thankful for that. He scanned his own instruments that told him of the dish's status. The electronics gave him a peculiar sense of security. He'd buried any fear under his excitement long ago. This was an encounter he'd never dreamed of. The paper theories about the wormholes were real, and one of them had roared to deafening life outside.

The magnetic capture display told him the dish was working, and the radar screen pinpointed the hole's location. Peering over Clark's shoulder through the slit, he could see the inward rush of debris marking the huge swirling disruption a thousand feet away. But a building partially blocked his view. Then the building disappeared.

"Bravo, look outside!" he shouted over the shriek of twisting metal. "Can you see it? It ate a building in front of me! That's a steel warehouse! Still can't see the thing clear, though. Lotta stuff flyin'!"

". . . see it a little bit," he heard Dacey say over the radio, above the thunderous noise.

"Alpha, you're twenty yards too far south." Mullins' voice from the control van was thick with excitement. "And you're too close. Avoid the crater it's making! MOVE! NOW!"

"Okay, Andy, I see on the display," shouted Gerald. Behind him, the five-hundred-horsepower diesel engine growled to life. Clark jammed the controls in reverse to back away. If they fell into the chasm the wormhole ripped in the earth, it would be all over. They had to catch it aboveground, or to attract it there. "In transit," said Gerald.

"We got slammed by an incoming," shouted Dacey. "Damned big chunk of steel! Rang our bell!" Gerald caught his breath. He was more afraid for Dacey than for himself. Somehow, he felt immune. He'd already trapped this hole into another universe in his web of equations. He knew this thing. He understood what it would do. But Dacey had only that incredible, brash self-confidence to protect her from utter panic. Fortunately, the driver of the other carrier, Herndon, was as rock-solid as Clark.

"Are you operational with that hit?" asked Mullins, who had joined Cooper to manage the capture. "You want vehicle Charlie to take over?"

"Negative, Control, my readouts look okay. Can you get a visual on me? From one of the helicopters?"

"Nobody can see zip, Bravo. We've gone totally to instruments. Dacey, can you see anything out the front slit?"

"I can see my capture dish. It's got some flutter, but it looks okay."

"Guys, I'm activating your capture dish fields. We're on computer now. I can't believe this luck . . . that the target surfaced. Watch your displays. Move like the computer tells you. And damned quick. And keep the hell away from that hole!"

"Okay," said Clark. "On track."

"Roger," said Herndon. "Come to mama!" Herndon was clearly exultant at the greatest adventure since his tank-driving days.

"Good . . . good . . . good." Mullins' voice rose in pitch with each word. "Radar says the target's right between you. It's just floatin' there maybe ten yards from each of you. Can you see it?"

"Hell, no!" Dacey spat.

Gerald smiled at the lilting sing-song way Dacey had answered. He knew it was something of a front. "Same here," he replied, trying to exude the same bravado.

"Gerald, if it looks like it's gonna come in and give you a kiss, just reverse out," she said.

"Bravo here. First kiss I ever backed out of."

Mullins' voice came on the radio. "Everything's stable. Fields are just real fine. Move forward."

"Damn! I'm hittin' turbulence! I can hardly breathe!" Dacey's voice was tinged with fear.

"Put on your mask, Dacey." Gerald felt the violent shaking, too, as if a giant fist had begun pounding the carrier. The atmosphere grew thin, as if the air was trying to escape the fury. He snapped on an oxygen mask. So did Clark.

"Am I stable? Am I stable?" It was Herndon's voice in his headphone. "I feel like I'm skiddin' forward! I'm blind out here!"

"Bravo, you've got it by the shorts!" Mullins answered. "Don't give up now!"

"Really appreciate the cheering section, Control," shouted Dacey.

"Forward ten yards. Both of you," shouted Mullins.

A screaming wail rose, as the hole rose into the clear atmosphere, its maw sucking in only air. An ear-splitting whistle rose as the tortured air streamed into the hole.

"Son-of-a-bitch! My ears!" yelled Clark. "I see it! I see it! Jesus!" It was the first time Gerald had detected emotion in Clark's voice. Out the front slit, Gerald saw a vague, round blackness floating ahead of the vehicle, chunks of concrete and earth leaping into it.

"Incoming!" shouted Herndon. "Shit! I—"

"Bravo, just keep going forward," said Mullins. "Alpha, go three degrees left!" After a long moment, Mullins asked, "Are your dishes in position? Are the docking probes in position?"

"Affirmative," said Clark. Gerald felt the vehicle suddenly lurch forward, sliding downhill into the crater the hole had excavated. "Whoa, mama!" exclaimed Clark. "I'm gonna need new tires!"

"Bravo, you copy?" asked Mullins.

Nothing but static.

"Bravo? *Bravo*!?" Now with more urgency.

Still no reply from Dacey or Herndon. Gerald peered intently out the slit. Through the tornado of swirling dust, he could barely see the other carrier. "I think Bravo's antenna got sheared off. She can't hear you. But she's still in position."

"Mag field's still okay," reported Mullins. "Move to close on target. Alpha! Do you hear? Move to close!"

"Roger, closing!" Gerald riveted his attention on the radar screen. He couldn't tell! He just couldn't tell what was happening! Clark jammed the carrier's gear controls back and forth and jerked the steering lever, trying to keep the bucking vehicle lined up. He leaned forward and looked through the slit at the huge capture dish. It was vibrating, but solid. The blinding dust abated for an instant and Gerald could see the other carrier, still sitting unmoving. Dear God, had they been killed? Suffocated? Killed by a piece of steel penetrating the armor? His heart pounded violently.

"Bravo's not moving! Dacey doesn't answer." He tried to calm himself. He wouldn't do her any good by panicking. "But we can compensate, I think." In front of him, Clark nodded his helmeted head and slammed the controls, to make the carrier back away so he could start another approach.

They eased forward in the blinding dust, the deafening shriek. The heat became stifling in the small space. The other carrier still sat immobile.

The dishes met and the debris became a circular ring of inrushing dust around the edges. Gerald held his breath. What if a chunk of debris lodged between the spheres? A chunk of rock did catch for a moment. Then it was gone and the dishes slammed together. His instruments registered the closure. "CAPTURE DISH CONTACT!" he shouted, feeling his vocal cords nearly snap. "WE'VE GOT INITIAL SEALING! IT'S STILL LEAKING VACUUM! JESUS, WHAT A NOISE!"

"Engage your capture latches!" Mullins shouted. Gerald could barely make out the words over the scream and the growing static in the headphones.

"Roger. Okay." Gerald flipped switches on a console and leaned forward to look out the slit. He could see nothing from his angle. He found himself holding his breath again and forced himself to inhale. If the latches didn't engage, they were trapped with the ultimate deadly tiger by the tail. Abruptly, Clark gave a gloved thumbs-up sign. "ENGAGED!" shouted Gerald into the microphone.

"Bravo, you copy?" Mullins didn't attempt to hide his alarm. "Alpha, what's happening with Bravo?"

"Her latches aren't engaged. Hasn't moved." The seal still had not been made and Gerald could still hear the high-pitched hiss of leakage.

"Shit, we're gonna be stuck here with a half-assed capture," said Clark, his low voice that of a soldier preparing to die.

"Can't you signal?" asked Mullins. "Clark, can't you signal?"

"How? You want me to go topside and fuckin' wave? Wait . . . wait . . . I can see his latches engaging! THEY ENGAGED! WE'RE DOCKED! LOOKS SOLID!"

Gerald reined in his excitement. He scanned his gauges. The magnetic fields were all stable. The hole was not moving inside the sphere.

"Okay, guys," Mullins gasped in relief. "Target looks stable in there. By God, it looks stable! Alpha, set your controls, climb out and go find out about Bravo. Then everybody run like bunnies!"

Gerald whipped off his seat belt and tore off his helmet. He slammed open the overhead hatch and scrambled out onto the top. Clark followed immediately. Before them rose the huge sphere formed from the two dish halves, a frozen vapor condensing on it. The sphere vibrated as if it caged a monster that struggled to escape, but it appeared to be holding . . . for now. Gerald peered beneath the sphere across to the other artillery carrier. No movement.

Then the hatch opened and he glimpsed Dacey pulling herself out, throwing off her helmet, and leaping lithely off the side. With a triumphant whoop, he jumped down from the carrier and they embraced as tightly as either of them ever had. Clark and Herndon followed, shaking hands and cursing jovially. The generators mounted on the vehicles hummed steadily, reassuringly. But they reminded the celebrants that one tiny glitch anywhere in the system and the beast would free itself and devour them and their vehicles. So, they quickly inspected the sphere, set up a monitoring video camera, checked the generators, and scrambled away over the wasteland that had once been Manitowoc, Wisconsin.

CHAPTER 26

Gerald picked his way among the rubble that was once a town, stepping over a twisted steel girder and across a shattered brick wall. He carefully aimed the video camera as he went, transmitting his progress. He breathed heavily, even though the exertion wasn't extreme. This was it. He would be the first to really see the hole. It seemed to draw him toward it as if he, too, were affected by magnetic fields. But he knew it was his curiosity that attracted him toward the deadly captive object.

He heard the drone of the diesel generators before he saw the two converted artillery carriers. He skirted a mound of shattered concrete bristling with rusted fingers of twisted steel rebar, and the carriers came into view. They sat amidst a broad, flat depression that had been scoured clean by the hellish gale created by the hole. The carriers held the Lexan sphere, its surface thick with a white crystalline frost. The ice sparkled in the sun, periodically sloughing off onto the ground, forming a rapidly melting pile of slush. It seemed almost a religious object, a shrine for some scientific pilgrims.

But the generators had only an hour's worth of fuel left. So, he increased his pace, jogging toward the frosted sphere, tripping once on the stub of a street sign that had vanished into another universe.

The monitoring video camera had still showed the sphere holding firm against the vacuum. But it was Gerald's job to decide whether the transfer could continue. He insisted on going in alone. Dacey had persuaded him that she would drive him in the army Humvee within a thousand yards, but he made her stop at a safe distance. If the hole escaped its magnetic trap and sliced through the sphere, no rescue was possible. Helicopters—military, police, and television network—circled in the distance like buzzing insects in the clear, blue sky. They could all see him well, so his death, if it happened would be carried live around the world. He didn't let himself think of that. His job came first.

As he approached the carriers, he perceived another sound beneath the generators' roar—the rich resonant hum of the confining magnetic fields. He brought up his camera, transmitting a second video picture of the capture sphere back to the control van, to be relayed to the world. He walked closer, setting the camera on the battered deck of one of the carriers and pointing it at the frosted sphere. He moved toward the sphere. He *had* to be the first to really see the wormhole.

He stepped close to the sphere and reached up. He smiled in amazement. His breathing grew more rapid. He felt its frost-covered surface vibrating fiercely beneath his hand—maybe from the magnetic coils, maybe some cosmic effect new to science. He figured that the sphere was so cold because heat was radiating through the hole into space on the other side.

The other side! Just feet away lay the cold vacuum of interstellar space, perhaps of another universe! Excitedly, he scraped away some of the frost and tried to see in. He could just make out a region of utter darkness wafting back and forth inside the sphere, but it was indistinct. Even the sphere's supertough Lexan had been abraded by the vicious bombardment of debris streaming into the hole. He was disappointed. He would have to wait for a clear view until the hole was transferred to the large vacuum chamber in the desert.

Inch by inch, he meticulously inspected the sphere's surface, its latches and seals, and the magnetic coils surrounding it. It was holding firm, he decided; the transfer could take place. As he worked, he couldn't resist touching the sphere again and again, feeling it shiver, feeling the numbing frigidity beneath his fingers.

He radioed the control van and within minutes, a bulldozer appeared, shoving its way through the rubble, clearing a path to the sphere. It departed and a flat-bed trailer truck appeared, fitted with a generator, a crane, and a steel-girder frame that would accept the sphere. The truck backed into the depression up to the sphere and Andy Mullins jumped down from the passenger side. Clark stayed in the driver's seat, his hands gripping the steering wheel, in case a quick escape was necessary. The wide-body Humvee, driven by Cooper, careened into sight and swerved up close to the tractor-trailer. Dacey leaped out of the passenger seat, stopping reluctantly and making a frustrated face when Gerald held up his hand pleadingly for her to stay a safe distance.

"Okay, let's set up for switchover." The short, round Mullins grinned like a kid who'd just been handed the keys to Disneyland. He plugged computer and power cables from the trailer into the sphere's magnets and tested them for a firm contact. Then Clark, Mullins, Gerald, and Dacey climbed into the Humvee.

"What's it like? What's it like?" Dacey demanded. Gerald shook his head and smiled at his inability to describe the sight. She smiled back in understanding as Cooper expertly gunned the vehicle through the cleared path a mile away to the control van. There, they crowded into the van and watched the swarthy, skinny Julio, who was Mullins' chief technician, run tests of the connections to the sphere, and type in a final command to the computer.

"Okay, let's see if we can switch over faster than this thing can react," said Julio. His finger poised over a red button on the control panel. "Countdown to switchover five, four, three, two, one, *zero!*" He hit the button. They stared at the computer screen, which displayed a diagram of the magnetic fields, the sphere, and the hole.

"STILL GOT 'ER!" shouted Mullins, clapping his pudgy hand on Julio's shoulder. Instantly, they clambered back into the Humvee and sped back to the site. As they neared, Cooper slowed the vehicle to give them a chance to make sure that the switchover had been complete.

"Sensors can lie," he declared. "Nothing like first-hand observation."

The sphere was intact.

Clark and Herndon arrived in a Humvee, and they all worked to attach the truck's crane to the sphere, ever-so carefully hoist it into the trailer's frame, and bolt it securely. Throughout, the sphere hummed like a huge hive of bees, vibrated fiercely, and shed clumps of white frost, as if it were struggling to free itself, seeking the smallest flaw in their trap.

After checking the status of the computers and power, Gerald gave Clark a thumbs up, and he revved the truck's engine and eased slowly away. Gerald stood quietly and watched it go, hearing sirens rise in the distance. The truck would have a clear road along the entire freeway leading to the nearby airport, with a phalanx of Wisconsin state trooper squad cars leading the way. It would roll onto a C5-A cargo plane for the trip to Nevada. There, they would perform one more field switchover into the huge vacuum chamber, and their captive would be secure. Then they could begin to fathom its mystery.

· · ·

"Damn, let's just go on up there and see the thing for ourselves," said Lambert, standing impatiently in the blockhouse in the Nevada desert, his arms folded, watching the wall-sized video screen. The sphere was being slowly lifted from the truck, which had backed up next to one of the giant vacuum chambers.

"No," said Gerald with absolute finality. For once Lambert said nothing. This was Gerald's show. Lambert knew that if it was successful, he could announce *his* triumph to the media. If not, it was Gerald's failure. Still intent on the monitor, Gerald continued. "I put that vacuum chamber two miles out in the desert for a reason. Until we know how these things react, only a few people are going near them. You can watch it from here."

Instead of replying, Lambert barked an order to his assistant, who sat in a rear observation gallery with four other Lambert men, to bring his plane around. "I'll be leaving after I get a look," he said. "If all I can do is watch television, I might as well be in Houston. Hell, I can see this on all the damned networks, anyway."

George Voigt sensed Gerald's frustration. "It's a wise move, putting the chamber out there . . . limiting access," he said reassuringly. The spare old doctor sat in a chair at the main data console, where he would monitor the vital signs of the first space-suited people who would enter the vacuum chamber to actually encounter the hole. "You have the firmest grasp of the theory," George had told him. "You'll be more effective watching the data come in; figuring out what's happening. Let Brendan and K.C. do the reconnoitering. They can handle this sort of thing." He'd also persuaded Gerald to keep Dacey, and the criminalists Cameron and Gaston, in the control room, much to their frustration.

Brendan Cooper and K.C. Wang had campaigned mightily to be the first ones to enter the chamber and attempt to traverse the hole.

"Whoever goes in there had goddamned better well have experience operating under pressure inside an isolation suit," declared Cooper. "And there's no bigger pucker factor than being inside an aluminum deep-dive Hardsuit at two thousand feet. Both K.C. and me have done that. You also better have a situational awareness from being inside a suit or you'll be not only merely dead, but really most sincerely dead," he said puckishly quoting from the *Wizard of Oz*.

Gerald had reluctantly agreed, and as Cooper and Wang prepared, Julio and the Deus technicians performed the perilous maneuver of moving the wormhole-containing sphere into the vacuum chamber. They had swung the massive steel doors shut, and evacuated to a safe distance. From the blockhouse, Mullins threw the switches to evacuate the chamber and open the sphere, unleashing the hole to float free inside, suspended only by the chamber's magnetic fields.

"Oh, my God!" Dacey exclaimed at the first sight over the video monitors of the hole, floating free.

"Goodness," said George. "Are those stars?"

"Yes," said Gerald. His heart pounding, he steadied his hands by placing them on the console, as a wave of emotion swept over him. He felt tears welling in his eyes and glanced up to see lines of wetness on Dacey's face. When he had begun this obsession, all had been cool mathematical theory. But then came the excitement and utter fear of the hunt and the capture. But throughout, even after its capture, the holes had been only vague shapes, whether devastating a city or trapped inside the sphere.

Now, floating before them on the screen was a wormhole in astonishing crystal-clarity. A shimmering sphere ten feet in diameter, it hovered in the middle of the chamber, with faint swirling auroras of glowing light playing about its edges. It drifted slowly back and forth, like some predator seeking an opening to attack.

From inside the sphere shone stars. Not the faint, twinkling stars seen from earth, but icy points of intense light set against absolute blackness. Gerald broke the stunned silence that had blanketed the room. He spoke softly, reverently. His words were pragmatic, but those who heard him knew that they marked a portentous beginning for humans, perhaps of destruction, perhaps of a new millennium.

"Let's give it some time. Check the parameters. Then go in."

CHAPTER 27

“You got a good seal, Brendan?” Mullins spoke into the microphone, watching the bulky space-suited figure on the large video screen. It was bigger than life, the high-definition picture showing every detail. The wall of the control room held four such screens—one showing a distant view of the vacuum chamber hangar, and another the men in space suits outside the vacuum chamber airlock. The third screen, however, showed the most mesmerizing scene—the inside of the chamber, with the star-filled hole floating almost seductively in the middle. The fourth screen was dark, soon to display an image from Cooper’s hand-held camera.

“I’m okay,” said Cooper, checking a reading on his wrist. Mullins looked expectantly at George, who peered through the bottom of his bifocals at the instruments monitoring the men’s vital signs.

George shook his head slowly, a worried look on his face. “They’re frightened,” he said. “Heart rate’s up, blood pressure’s up, body temperature’s high, too.”

“Make sure they’re okay,” said Gerald, who sat between Mullins and George, his eyes scanning intently back and forth from one set of instruments to the other. “If they’re not okay, take them out.”

"C'mon guys, we know it's tough in there," said Mullins into the microphone. "Brendan? K.C.? Can you guys make it okay?"

Cooper put his gloved thumb up, his face barely visible behind the helmet faceplate. "Yeah. We're jazzed. It's like a deep ocean dive, except in space. Instead of starfish, we got stars, right K.C.?"

K.C. nodded as best he could and took a few tentative steps. "We've got a little balance problem, here, though."

"Yeah," said Mullins. "It's different than floating around underwater. Just you be careful, okay?" Fortunately, the prototype suits loaned from NASA for planetary exploration were slimmer and more maneuverable than the suits made for EVAs in orbit. But still Mullins worried about the two oceanographers' ability to precisely maneuver in a vacuum chamber with a lethal portal to outer space.

"Switch on my camera," said Cooper, holding up his video camera.

Mullins touched a button and the fourth screen glowed to life, showing the camera's bobbing view of the metal hangar. "You're okay. Get ready to go in."

Lambert paced behind them, watching the process and talking on his cell phone. He'd been unable to sit all morning. The sight of the hole had made him forget his plans to leave. George more than made up for Lambert's edginess, sitting serenely, watching the instruments.

Mullins ran through checks of the magnetic field and the vacuum chamber. "Everything's optimal," he said.

"Okay, guys. You can enter the chamber," said Gerald.

Cooper threw a switch, and the chamber's airlock door opened. Both men stepped through and closed it behind them. The hand-held camera showed random, skewing views of helmets, gloves, airlock doors, and ceilings, as the men concentrated on operating the airlock controls.

"We got vacuum," said Cooper finally. "We're opening the inner door."

Gerald touched a button to zoom back the view of the chamber's fixed camera to a wide-angle. The screen showed the two men clumping awkwardly into the large vacuum chamber. Cooper aimed his camera at the hole. The control room fell dead silent. Lambert forgot his cell phone and stood transfixed.

Close-up, the wormhole was even more stunning. Its edges were absolutely sharp, and feathery curls of colored light swirled about its periphery. The hole maintained a perfect, elegant roundness. The stars showing through it were diamond-bright, glowing in subtly different colors of reddish, blue, and yellow. The space between the stars was of an utter blackness, but with small patches of pearly opalescence.

"Their heart rates are high," said George, breaking the silence.

"Ain't everybody's," said Dacey.

"Jesus!" breathed Cooper. "This is totally unbelievable!"

"We agree," said Gerald. "Walk around it."

The fixed camera showed Cooper begin to circle the hole with the camera. His camera showed the view through the hole shift as well. Multitudes of new stars rotated into view.

"Jesus, it's like walking around a crystal ball," said Cameron. "You can see in all directions."

"It's a sphere! Why is it a sphere?" asked Gaston.

"If you had universes in two dimensions . . . like sheets of paper . . . a hole punched from one to the other would be a circle, right?" said Gerald, his gaze still fixed on the screen.

"Yeah."

"Well, this is a hole between three-dimensional universes. So it's a three-dimensional circle . . . a sphere."

"Gotcha," said Cameron.

"Brendan, K.C., you okay to proceed?" asked Mullins.

"Fine," said Cooper.

"Your body temperature's down," said George.

"It's colder'n hell in here. But the suit heaters are compensating," said Wang.

"Then let's try the bar," instructed Mullins.

"Roger," said Wang.

With Cooper holding the camera on him, Wang stepped to the side of the chamber and bent with effort in the bulky suit to pick up a seven-foot steel bar. He hefted it under his arm like the jousting lance of a knight, holding it with both hands. He settled his grip.

"Ready," he said.

"Okay, then, see what happens." Gerald glanced at the others. "Let's see if we can put matter into another universe and keep it in control."

The hand-held camera bobbled a bit but steadied, showing a closeup of the steel bar advancing toward the hole. The bar's end reached the hole and crossed an invisible membrane, faint swirls of light playing about it.

"We're through! We're through!" shouted Wang.

There was a collective sigh in the control room, as many of them realized they had been holding their breath yet again.

"Damn," Mullins said quietly. "It's still intact!"

Through the hole, they could see the bar's other end extending into the darkened realm of the other universe.

"It's lighter!" exclaimed Wang. "I can feel that it's lighter in there!"

"It's in the other universe's gravitational domain," said Gerald. "You've crossed the dimensional threshold."

The change in the bar's balance caused Wang to overcompensate in controlling it, and it drifted upward against the hole's edge. The edge sliced the bar neatly in half, and the other end floated lazily away in the gravity-free space on the other side, receding into darkness.

"It just sliced away!" exclaimed Gaston.

"I thought it would," said Gerald. "The hole's edge is a dimensional discontinuity. It's the sharpest edge in the universe. Infinitely sharp."

Dacey leaned forward in her chair. "So that's why it could go through a house, or a building—"

"Or any other substance," said Gerald. "Passing through these things is going to be really dicey. You slip too far toward an edge and you're sliced in two pieces." He spoke into the microphone. "Let's do a three-sixty survey of the view from the hole. I want to see where this thing is in the other universe."

"Roger that," said Wang, setting the sliced bar down. "I'll get the frame." He stepped to the side and with exquisite care slid an aluminum scaffolding from the side of the chamber to encompass the hole. The scaffolding consisted of broad steps up either side and a platform bridging over the top of the hole. At the same time, Cooper brought the camera in close to the hole, crouching down as best he could to up shoot through the bottom. Again, the hand-held camera showed a rich panoply of stars against the blackness.

"This is going to be incredible once we can go through," said Cooper. He finished the low-angle survey and with Wang steadying the frame, carefully made his way up one set of steps to the top. He stood with one hand on the platform's railing and slowly brought the camera pointing down to shoot through the top of the hole.

Cooper suddenly screamed and fell backward dropping the camera. The camera disappeared into the hole, the video image it transmitted showing a confusing swirl of tan and suddenly going black.

"What?" shouted Gerald, Mullins and Wang simultaneously.

"IT'S . . . IT'S . . ." but the rest was garbled as Cooper tumbled down the stairs, trying to recover himself at the bottom.

Wang had just bent to help him when the hole erupted from all sides with an explosive burst of seething brown liquid. The fixed camera lasted only long enough to record the wave slamming the two men against the walls of the chamber, then it went black, too.

"My God, their body temperature's gone to zero!" shouted George.

"Chamber temperature's minus a couple of hundred!" exclaimed Mullins. "They're frozen solid!"

They all stared helplessly at the screen showing the view outside the chamber. The metal of the chamber abruptly grew a thick shroud of white frost and began to crack. The camera recorded the brown liquid spewing, then bursting through the cracks, washing out of the chamber and inundating the inside of the hangar. Then that image went dark. The remaining monitor trained on the outside of the hangar showed a thick cloud of vapor expanding outward.

The control room filled with shouts of "WHAT IS IT?" "WHAT THE HELL IS HAPPENING?"

Gerald frantically scanned the instruments and the monitor screens, trying to glean something from their wildly fluctuating data. "It looks like . . ." He gave Mullins a shocked look.

"Methane," said Lambert. They all turned to look at him, puzzled. "I saw a field test where they cracked open a tank of liquid methane . . . natural gas. To test a transporter. It looked like that."

"Where the hell would liquid methane come from?" asked Cameron.

"Oh, my God! A planet!" breathed Gerald watching the growing cloud. "The hole must have been near a planet that had an ocean of liquid methane. Like Titan . . . Jupiter's moon."

"What's going to happen?" asked Dacey.

"I'll tell you what," said Lambert. "The methane will evaporate into a gas. If this keeps up, it'll make a damned big cloud. The first spark that it meets, sets it off. Basically a fuel-air bomb."

"You mean like in the bomb where they explode a bunch of gasoline, then ignite the vapor?" asked Gaston.

"Yeah. They call it a poor man's nuke. The concussion'll take this place out like a nuclear bomb."

"Jesus, Calvin, what can we do?" Dacey looked at him with terror, her mouth agape, her eyes wide. They all fell silent.

"Die."

CHAPTER 28

"That's not quite true, Calvin." They turned to Gerald, who had been sitting quietly, watching the swirling vaporous shroud grow around the distant hangar.

"You got an answer?" Lambert had begun the mental process of bargaining with death and the quiet statement unnerved him.

"Yes. Use the missile countermeasure system I know you've got installed on your plane. It releases flares to decoy heat-seeking missiles."

"What do you mean?"

"You use the flares to ignite the cloud before it grows too big. It's like an old gas stove. When you first turn on the burner, you hold a match to it, first you get a whoosh, but then it just burns. But you wait a while and light that match and the house blows up."

"He's right! He's right!" exclaimed Mullins. "Just fly over and release the flares!"

"So just a few people die," said Lambert. "Anybody want to draw straws?"

"Nobody's likely to die," Gerald stood up and paced before the control panel, his eyes casting about, as if searching for the pieces to a solution. He stopped. "You'd have to fly low because the flares are short-burning. But you should have time to get to a safe altitude by the time they hit the cloud."

"*Should* have time? Bullshit!" spat Lambert. "Our best hope is to hunker down here and hope this blockhouse holds. I'm not about to go on some half-assed bombing run—"

"Excuse me, Mr. Lambert, sir." Cameron raised his hand in mocking irony. "I don't want to seem disrespectful or nothin', but it looks to me like you've traded your balls in on a bunch of money. Maybe you could use all your money to buy some back somewhere, you damn coward."

"YOU LITTLE BASTARD!" Lambert lunged at Cameron, managing to grab his shirt before the others wrestled him away. From the viewing gallery, Lambert's bodyguard burst into the room, pulling a pistol.

"HOLD IT! DAMNIT, JUST HOLD IT!" Dacey shouted. She turned to Lambert, her withering stare challenging him. "Calvin?" she queried tartly.

There was silence. Lambert glared fiercely at Cameron. Then with a curt flip of his hand, waved his bodyguard back.

"Start the plane," he growled. The bodyguard didn't realize the order was aimed at him "CALL THE PILOT, TELL HIM TO START THE FUCKING PLANE!" The bodyguard took out a cell phone and did so.

"Just make sure you don't just fly your rich white ass away, motherfucker!" Cameron hissed.

Lambert gave them all a final scowling look, then without a word spun on his heel and left.

"Think he'll do it?" asked Mullins.

Cameron suddenly grinned. "Sure he'll do it. Chumps like that, you question their manhood, you can con 'em into doin' about anything."

"Jimmy, for once I'm glad you're a bullshit artist," said Gaston.

By now the icy swirling white cloud of methane had expanded far beyond the distant hangar, and Mullins transmitted a warning to the Nevada state police to attempt to evacuate the crowds of tourists lining the distant perimeter of the base.

Gerald switched one of the darkened screens to a camera on the blockhouse roof, panning it toward the airstrip. They sat in breathless silence, watching Lambert's jet, gleaming white in the sun, speed to the end of the runway, swerve sharply and vault into the sky.

"Jesus, if he gets near that cloud with that jet, it'll blow. It'll take him out," said Mullins.

"He knows that," said Gerald. "He also knows that methane is heavier than air. And this stuff is colder. It'll tend to hug the ground." Indeed, the camera trained on the hangar showed the vapor rolling toward them, reaching icy fingers of fog across the desert. On the other screen, the jet grew more distant, shrinking to a mere speck.

"Damn! He's flyin' away!" Cameron slammed his hand on the back of a chair in disgust.

"No," said George. "He's circling to gain altitude. You did your job well, son."

The speck grew once more into a jet, now higher in the sky. Gerald zoomed in the camera view and tried to manipulate the controls to follow the jet's path. At the higher magnification, the image of the small craft bounced and jerked in the camera's frame. A string of brightly burning objects sailed away behind the jet, floating downward. The jet banked sharply away and climbed.

"He's done it! Get down!" Gerald grabbed Dacey and they flattened themselves against the floor, as did the others. They craned their necks upward to see the screens.

The hangar disappeared in a roaring flash, and the small armored-glass slits in the blockhouse blazed with a blinding yellow light.

The walls shuddered and cracked under the thundering blow of the explosion, as from the impact of a wrecker's ball. Light fixtures tore from the ceiling, clattering onto the floor, their fluorescent tubes shattering. The instrument consoles pitched forward slamming onto the floor. Thick choking dust erupted from the buckling concrete walls. The ceiling slumped downward, large steel rebars knifing out from the smooth gray surface.

Then the hellish blast subsided and a blanket of silence settled in, interrupted after a stunned moment by groaning and coughing. Dacey opened her eyes, brushing away the concrete dust coating her face. She coughed to bring out the choking dust in her lungs. The glow of the battery-powered emergency lights dimly lit the room through the cloud.

She reached over to touch Gerald's back, which was covered with small chunks of concrete. Thankfully, she felt the rise and fall of breathing beneath her hand. He rolled over, pushing away a chair that had fallen on him, and laid his hand gently on her face. They were both alive. They got up, debris falling from their bodies, to the sound of the slow stirring of dazed people. Again, they heard a groan and made their way toward it. Mullins lay half beneath a huge console, with George already bending over him. Gaston and Cameron bent to try to lift the console, Cameron's forehead showing a bloody gash, red against his gray-dusted brown skin.

"His signs are all right." George leaned down to Mullins. "My boy, if you don't mind, I'd prefer you as a live patient, not as an autopsy subject."

Mullins managed a small laugh and then winced, his round face screwed up in a pain that he tried desperately to hide beneath a brave mask.

"Jimmy, you're cut," said Dacey, and Cameron put his hand to the gash on his forehead, dully examining the blood on his fingers.

"I've had worse. Let's just worry about Andy for now." Gaston found a wad of napkins, and Cameron pressed those to his head, waving away any further help. George directed as they joined to lift the control console off Mullins, taking care to protect him from the shards of glass falling from shattered monitors.

George had crouched to examine Mullins' legs when the sound of a telephone beeping arose somewhere in the room. It came from the pocket of the bodyguard Lambert had left behind in the observation room. The muscular man was still dazed from a strike by a chunk of concrete, but he managed to haul himself up, slowly wipe off his dark suit, and pull the phone from his pocket. He pressed its button and mumbled a dazed hello. He stiffened slightly, coming to attention. After a moment listening, he came into the control room, stepped across the shattered remains of a fluorescent light fixture and handed the phone to Gerald.

"Looks like you fucked up," said the voice on the phone over the throaty hiss of a jet engine. It was Lambert.

"Yes," said Gerald, and let the thick silence hang between them.

"Well, listen, I'm heading back to Houston. I'm having my people put out the story about what happened. How you didn't figure on something like this happening. How I saved your ass. How I'm reassessing the project, and so forth." He hung up and Gerald stood mutely with the phone in his hand before absentmindedly handing it back to the bodyguard.

"Who was that?" asked Dacey, who cradled Mullins' head in her lap, brushing his hair back, while George checked his legs.

"It was Calvin," Gerald sat down heavily beside Mullins, placing a reassuring hand on his shoulder. "He wanted to make sure we were all right."

After a while, they managed to pull themselves together and wrench open the steel door to the blockhouse. They emerged into an enveloping blowtorch of heat and the distant roar of an inferno. Even two miles away, the heat from the burning hole beat in blistering waves against their bodies. Squinting their eyes, they could make out the billowing ball of fire, fed by the methane that continued to erupt through the hole. Now they had no control over the beast. It was drifting slowly northward for the moment, out into open desert.

They ducked around into the protection of the ruined blockhouse, with the men carrying a grimacing Mullins. Dacey started one of the Humvees and they carefully laid him inside. She accelerated across the desert, the breeze cooling their overheated bodies, aiming toward the distant complex of hangars.

. . .

"God," Gerald whispered, sitting on the side of the bed, staring blankly ahead. "Again. More dead . . . Brendan . . . K.C. . . . Why? What did I do wrong?"

"Nothing. You couldn't have known." Dacey closed the door of her room and sat down beside him. After George had checked them both out, she had gotten him to the dormitory. Physically, he might have been fine, but she had seen the psychological trauma in Gerald's desperate look, and brought him to her room so he could recover. The whine of a departing ambulance siren reassured them that Mullins was being looked after. But Dacey knew no physician could treat his wound. "Gerald, nobody's seen these things before. Never. Nobody can predict what they can do."

"But I'm supposed to. That's what all these theories . . ." He didn't finish. The theories had obviously not worked. "It's my own stupidity.

My own stupid damned *arrogance.*" He stood up. "Well, I'm just going out there and tell them that."

"No you're not." She stood facing him and rested her arms on his shoulders. "Wait a while. Think. Get cleaned up." She patted away a spot of dust that remained on one shoulder. "Go shower. Think about the real facts, Gerald . . . the facts that these are totally unknown things. That you've started something incredibly important. That you have to finish it. You can pick yourself up."

He smiled appreciatively. "Yeah. You know about that . . . how to pick yourself up." She patted him on the shoulder and put her arm around him, leading to the door between their rooms. He fumbled with the doorknob, but it wouldn't open.

"Guess it's locked from the other side. You have to unlock it from both sides to open it between rooms."

He held the knob for a long moment, staring down at it. A faintly perplexed look passed across his face, as if he were trying to figure something out. Then he turned, opened the door to the hallway and left.

After a moment, the lock on the door between the rooms rattled, the door opened, and he appeared, mumbling something about "Figuring it out." Saying goodbye, he shut it slowly. The door that separated them again made her think of the barriers and whether they could ever be overcome. Could she help him recover from this catastrophe, from the deaths of two men he had allowed to confront the monster? Could he help her overcome the traumatic memory of her brutal marriage? It had left her fearful of allowing anyone to touch her deeply; left her settling for safe, casual relationships with safe men, to maintain a distance.

This was not the time to think about that, she finally decided. She realized how tired she was and how grimy, and she stripped off her clothes and showered, letting the hot water run down her face, washing away the smell of concrete dust and scorched desert. She washed her hair and stepped out, toweling herself off. She emerged into the room, combing out her hair, letting the desert air finish drying her body before she dressed. It brought memories of how pleasant it had been on field trips to scrub away trail dirt in a desert stream and lie on a rock in the warm sun to dry. If only this were one of those idyllic times.

As she dressed, she became aware of an abrupt silence that had replaced the rumbling hiss of the distant flame. Gerald would know what the silence meant. She knocked on the door between their rooms and peeked in. He stood at the window, the amber light of the fading day illuminating his face. He wore fresh jeans and a shirt, but it had been haphazardly buttoned. Water droplets still glistened in his dark hair.

"The fire's gone. The hole has closed," he said quietly. "Don't know why. Don't know anything." He shook his head in frustration.

She joined him, and by looking out the window at an angle, they could see in the direction of the fire. The fiery glow they had seen on the horizon when they first got to the rooms was now gone. His gaze was distant, seeing beyond the fire to the ordeal to come. He would soon face a mob of shouting reporters demanding that he explain the disaster; and a denigrating crowd of scientists demanding that he explain his theory's failure. And he would have to visit the families of the dead men, explaining that failure and expressing his sorrow. He took a deep, tired, trembling breath.

"I guess it's time. I guess I've got to face them." She put her arm around him, and they went out the door together.

CHAPTER 29

"Are we there yet, Mommy?" Cameron slogged his way up the steep trail behind Gaston, who peered resolutely ahead. Cameron's sunglasses were slightly askew and despite the crispness of the thin mountain air, a silver sheen of sweat had formed around the bandage on his dark forehead. He continually looked left and right, viewing every bush suspiciously.

"Don't know," said Gaston, his energy ebbing. He abruptly collapsed onto a boulder, bending over, head down.

"You shouldn't have come," scolded Cameron, sitting down beside him. "You could have rested down below."

"I'm not doing that," said Gaston, his voice catching with the pain in his stomach. "I'll be resting a lot soon enough."

"Hell," spat Cameron. "You need another pill. Take another pain pill."

"No, goddamnit! And you keep your yap shut about my condition!"

"*Yap*? Nobody says yap anymore, old man," teased Cameron.

"Okay, then, button your lip, shut your pie hole, and keep it on the down low. Does that do it?"

"Yeah, that's better." Cameron was pleased that Gaston wasn't hurting too much to still have a little humor left.

Gaston, heaved himself up, taking a pained breath, and peering into the brilliant blue cloudless sky of the Sierra Nevadas. He hiked on, placing his feet solidly on the loose rock of the rising trail. After a dozen steps, he stopped again, steadying himself by holding a juniper branch. The sun was well into its afternoon descent, but they had time to reach the camp if it was only a couple of miles, as the ranger had said.

Cameron followed, eyeing him with annoyance. "Well, we've come as far as the ranger guy told us. Maybe it's the wrong trail. There's no signs. They oughta put up street signs."

"It's the right trail. We saw his van in the parking lot. He's up here."

Cameron grunted, unconvinced. "The ranger guy said there were bears out here," he reminded Gaston, who merely nodded. "Mountain lions, too. Remember they told us about that lady who got eaten?"

"She didn't get eaten," Gaston panted, understanding Cameron's game, to get him to abandon the hike, to rest.

"Well, a big chunk of her did." He peered dubiously up the trail. "Nature sucks. This city boy's startin' down in a few minutes. Phyllis'll have dinner ready at the cabin. We could try again tomorrow with the ranger guy. You remember Phyllis's barbecue?"

Gaston smiled back over his shoulder. "You can't tempt me, Jimmy. We told Dacey we'd find him."

"Y'know, Ralph, your problem is you don't have a family to go home to. It's just you and Wayne. You should start a family."

"Now that would be a real miracle." Gaston smiled grimly. It was Cameron's way of expressing optimism.

"Naw, man, I mean adopt."

"Right, Jimmy."

"Well, you could do a trial run. You could take my kids for a while. They're easy. All they do is play video games. What do you say?"

"I say I see smoke." Gaston pointed to the left toward a forested outcropping. A faint curl of smoke rose from behind the trees.

"'Bout damned time."

They reached the flat plateau on the side of the mountain and made their way among the thick fragrant evergreens, reaching a clearing below a steep cliff. A small red tent nestled near the cliff face, and nearby a ring of stones encircled a small crackling fire that had just been fed new sticks. A pot and a frying pan sat beside the fire. They stood for a moment scanning around, their city eyes unused to searching the forms and shadows of the forest. They heard a noise in the bushes, and Cameron tried to look nonchalant as he stepped closer to Gaston. Gerald pushed his way through the brush on the other side of the clearing, carrying an armload of wood. He stopped when he saw them, and his faint smile told them they were welcome.

They greeted each other, and Gerald showed them the view out the edge of a nearby cliff that looked out over the quiet valley, dotted with occasional houses, basking in the afternoon sun. To Cameron's question about whether he'd seen any mountain lion, he answered a terse "nope."

"So, Dacey told you where I was." Gerald sat down on the ground, leaning against a flat rock, gazing out over the expanse below.

"Yes," said Gaston, sitting down heavily beside him, as Cameron continued a nervous lookout. "She thinks you should try to get beyond the tragedies. I know the funerals devastated you. But you've been out here about long enough. Since we were nearest, she asked us to come up. There are things happening you need to know about. Things you need to do. She had to go back to the university. They're not too happy about her involvement with all this."

"The assholes are taking over," said Cameron peering dubiously over the precipice. "And there's a whole bunch of them. A herd of assholes. Or is it a flock?"

"Lambert is talking to Cohen about taking over the project." Gaston took off his glasses and rubbed his eyes. "Cohen says he wants to bring his own team in, to straighten things out.

"Well, you know I had to leave for a while, to do some thinking."

"Sure, of course. I've been in one of those shit storms. The media won't leave you alone. You handled it well, you know. I never got to tell you that."

"Thanks," was all Gerald said, but Gaston knew he was remembering the massive, accusing press conferences and the pointed public criticisms by the scientists. The physicist, Aaron Cohen of Caltech, had been perhaps the most vociferous, denouncing Gerald for sloppy planning and bad science. He publically blamed Gerald for the deaths.

"You've missed the coverage," said Gaston. "All the morning shows got experts who think they know what's going on. And there was an eruption of liquid nitrogen in the ocean two days ago. It made a big iceberg. A bunch of Cooper's friends from Woods Hole flew over it. They say it seems to be a hole from a frozen planet like Jupiter or Saturn. And did you hear about the Chinese?"

Gerald shook his head, not taking his eyes from the view.

"They're building a capture apparatus. They called Andy to ask him to engineer it, but he said no. So, they're going ahead themselves. And Iran, too."

"Iran? Jesus, that's scary," said Gerald. He tried to imagine how the holes could be used as weapons. He brought up his knees and rested his forearms on them, and said quietly, "I've figured out what happened."

At this news, Cameron stopped pacing and plopped himself down beside them. "I'm all ears. Ralph's all ears, too."

"I did some calculations. I know why the holes open up. I know why so many open up near planets on the other side, and not in deep space."

"Given the law of averages, they should almost all open up in deep space on the other side, shouldn't they?" asked Gaston. "Because most of any universe is space?"

"I realized it takes a magnetic field on *both* sides to open a hole. It's like one of those doors between hotel rooms. Until both sides are unlatched, it stays locked."

Gaston paused a moment, then as the realization sank in opened his mouth and let out a quiet, revelatory, "Ohhhh."

"No shit!" said an amazed Cameron. "It takes both sides being near a planet or something."

"It's both a blessing and a curse," said Gerald. "It means the other side is almost automatically in a solar system, near interesting things like planets. But it also means we're always in imminent danger of running into the planet or the star that made the hole open up. Like the planet that caused the methane."

"So, we're basically screwed, trying to catch one of these things," said Cameron, pitching a rock over the edge of the cliff.

"No, there's more. We can *navigate* these holes. And we can impose a magnetic field on the other side to keep them open." He paused and looked at them, smiling faintly. Both looked back with puzzled expressions. "I've just about figured the whole thing out. Let me show you something." Gerald stood up and motioned for them to follow, walking back to the clearing and crawling into the tent to fetch a tattered blue spiral notebook. He sat down cross-legged by the fire, which radiated a welcome warmth against the cooling mountain dusk. They sat beside him, and he opened the notebook, its pages mostly covered with scribbled equations. He flipped to a diagram showing an oval with arcing lines swooping through it. On either side of the oval were large solid circles, one labeled earth, encircled by its own lines.

"What do you mean navigate?" asked Gaston.

Gerald traced the arcing lines through the oval with his finger. "If we put an array of electromagnets up near a hole, we can extend magnetic field lines through to the other side. We can adjust the field to move the hole around in the other universe. To steer it. And the projected field will be enough to hold it open."

"We can *fly* the son-of-a-bitch?" asked Cameron.

"We can fly the son-of-a-bitch in the other universe," confirmed Gerald, his smile broadening. "Like a spaceship that has no mass. One that isn't affected by gravity. I haven't worked out the exact geometry of the magnets. I'll need Andy to help me do that."

"So, we can avoid planets?" But as Gaston asked the question, his face registered a dawning. "Jesus, wait a minute! We can do more!"

"Much more. We can explore the other side. We can fly a hole down to a planet surface. We can fly anywhere."

"These aren't just holes then."

Gerald placed his fingertips on the paper, almost caressing the lines. "No. They could be the ultimate spaceships. They could be starships."

221

CHAPTER 30

Gerald's faded blue van passed a motley collection of cars, trucks, tents, and campers lining the sunbaked highway for two miles before he, Cameron and Gaston reached the base. The makeshift city sprawled out into the surrounding desert, creating dusty avenues where people walked and greeted each other as they would on any city street. Dressed in shorts, baseball caps and sunglasses, they milled about, some lofting hand-painted signs proclaiming that the wormholes represented eternal salvation or damnation . . . or signs offering t-shirts for sale. Gerald slowed the van behind a car with Florida license plates, and they could read the t-shirts hanging in stalls shaded by portable awnings: "I Plugged the Hole," or "Watch those Suckers," or "Oops!" The last shirt, which made Gerald wince, had a large black hole in the chest, with bloody tatters as if it had punched through flesh.

One gaunt, bearded hawker held up two t-shirts, offering buyers opposite sentiments. In one hand was "Gateway to Heaven"; in the other "Gateway to Hell." The slow line of vehicles eased past one tent selling beer, and another with a wooden cross staked out front, the vigorous singing of gospel songs emanating from within.

"It's just been growin' and growin'," said Cameron, poking his head up from the back of the van between Gerald in the driver's seat and Gaston in the passenger's seat. "It's lucky we're not in Deus vans, or they would be cheering us or throwing stuff."

A limping man with a shopping cart held up a booklet to their window. It said, "The Hole-y Gospel." Gaston waved him away, as Gerald eased the van up to the chain-link gate with the Deus, Inc. sign. There were more guards than before, and they carried sidearms. Two Humvees were parked next to the gate and another had just left carrying armed guards along the fence line. A guard sauntered out of the air-conditioned shack, recognized Gerald, and hurried back in. Next, a beefy older man, clearly the supervisor, came out. He wore his guard's cap low over his brow, his sunglasses reflecting the scene around him. His face was red with sunburn. He wasn't a guard who had been there before.

"Dr. Meier?" He spoke with a raw Texas accent.

"Yes. We need to get back to work." Gerald heard murmurs of recognition sweep through the crowd of reporters that had camped up next to the gate in television satellite vans, motor homes and tents. They called out questions, to a rising chorus of the staccato clicking of cameras, like so many insects.

The guard pushed his cap back on his head and looked confused behind his sunglasses. "Well, I tell ya. I got orders you're not supposed to get in any more."

"Whose orders?"

"Well . . . Mr. Lambert. He's runnin' the show."

"He brought you in? He brought these new people in?" Gerald gestured at the other guards. "Look, I've got work to do in there. You know me."

"I got my orders."

Gerald climbed out of the van, and television cameras began to appear. He faced the guard, his hands open. "Look, two people died in there. It's my fault they died. And you know many more could die. Don't you?"

"Look, pal, just turn around—" They heard the roar of an approaching vehicle and turned toward the base to see one of the massive artillery carriers careening wildly across the desert, swerving left, then right, throwing up rooster tails of sand, then doing a series of tight loops that brought it progressively closer to the fence line. A Humvee appeared behind it, racing across the sand, attempting to catch it. A person riding the back of the bucking Humvee waved desperately toward the guardhouse and held a radio to his mouth. Unintelligible shouts erupted from the head guard's portable radio, and he clicked it on and listened a moment. "Jesus H. Christ, the damn idiots let one of them damn things get away from them!"

The carrier veered abruptly, heading right for the gate, slamming into it and knocking it flat with a loud clang. The reporters scattered, taking care to keep their cameras trained on the sight. This would be great footage for the nightly news.

The guards scattered, too, when they realized that the armored carrier was headed for their guard shack, which at this moment seemed quite fragile.

Only Gerald stood his ground, looking impassively at the roaring, lurching, twenty-two-ton, sky-blue mass of steel.

"Gerald, get the hell out of there!" shouted Cameron. "The damned thing's gonna run over your ass!" He sprinted a few steps down the road, but stopped and came back, waving his arms. He glanced over at Gaston, who'd emerged from the van and was standing as quietly as Gerald. Gaston was smiling. The carrier skidded to a stop before them.

"What the . . ." Cameron looked up to see a familiar head pop out of the carrier. It was Mullins, grinning a grin so wide that it enlisted his whole round face.

"Hi! How's it goin'? Follow me!" He disappeared back into the carrier and the vehicle wheeled about and accelerated away down the road. By this time Gerald was back in the van's driver's seat, and Gaston and Cameron had leaped into the other side. The guards could only shout futilely as the van clattered over the fallen gate and sped away toward the research complex.

"How'd you know?" asked Cameron, turning to peer through the back window of the van.

"Those things don't go out of control." Gerald kept his eyes fixed on the road, glancing occasionally through the rear-view mirrors. "I figured something funny was going on. Andy must have seen us on the remote cameras. I've known him a long time, and he'd cook something up like that."

"I figured as much," said Gaston. "They're not following. Their orders must've been just to keep us from getting in. Now, they'll have to call Lambert for other instructions."

They sped along the straight blacktop road for the three miles across the desert, reaching the hangar complex. The artillery carrier entered the huge main door of one hangar, and Gerald parked in its shade. They let themselves in the smaller metal side door. A Megamag engineer welcomed them heartily and guided them past half-opened crates containing electronic gear and huge Lexan spheres studded with magnets. Mullins cut the carrier's engine and hauled his portly body out of the driver's seat. He pulled out his crutches, accepted a slap on the back from one of his engineers, and hobbled toward them, hefting himself along with vigorous hops.

"Pretty good progress, huh? Glad you're back! Lots going on here, y'know!"

"Andy, you do know how to put on a welcome," said Gerald, shaking his hand. Cameron and Gaston followed suit.

"You know about Cohen?" Mullins scowled when he said the name.

"I know he's coming in soon," said Gerald. "To take over."

"Well, yeah. Lambert told us. Gerald, we don't want this to happen. But what do we do? We're stuck. We're rebuilding the vacuum chambers, but beyond that . . ." He shrugged as best he could, balanced on the crutches.

"Listen, I know what went wrong," Gerald said. "I know why the eruption happened. And I know how to stop it."

Mullins grinned and executed a semblance of a jig on his crutches. He waved at two of his engineers to join them, and they took the van and a Humvee over to the administration building.

Pacing before them in the briefing room, Gerald explained his new theory, showing the equations on the large display screen. Mullins sat at a table with his engineers, furiously executing diagrams of new magnets on one of the computers. Soon, rotating before them on the large screen were three-dimensional renderings of capture dishes with newly designed magnets. Sheaves of magnetic field lines swirled around the magnets, altering shape as the engineers fed in new parameters. With Mullins waving a half-eaten sandwich in the air for emphasis, the engineers created plans for the new capture and guidance system. Gerald suggested refinements, and Cameron and Gaston looked on, lost amidst the technical talk, asking for explanations as the work progressed.

"We've got a ways to go, that's for sure," said Mullins, picking up his cell phone. "But it's a start. It's sure a start." He called his workshop in Cambridge, informing them that he was transmitting a plan for a design of a system to capture and steer a hole. "Tell the guys, we want it *now*. Tell 'em we're depending on them," he said, nodding happily at the answer. He ended the call and waved the phone at Gerald. "They said they'd go 'round the clock." He chuckled. "Asked if they could take apart my car for parts. They're good boys, y'know, but a little nuts."

As they refined their plan, the base phone rang.

"It's the front gate," said Andy, looking questioningly at Gerald. "Aaron Cohen's there. He says Lambert has asked him to take over."

"Tell them he's not to be allowed in," said Gerald.

"Hey, tell him we're not at home," said Cameron, sipping a Coke nonchalantly.

Mullins did so and hung up the phone. They had worked for another half an hour, when the phone rang again. This time Cameron answered it. He listened for a moment.

"Say, Cal, how they hangin', shithead?" The others scrambled to wrest the phone from him. "Are you pissed, Calvin? I'm real damn sorry, Calvin."

Gaston was the first to reach him. "Jesus, Jimmy!" he scolded grabbing the receiver and punching the speakerphone button. The angry voice of Calvin Lambert filled the room.

"—let Cohen the goddamned hell in there, or I'll bring in people to take the place by force if I have to." The transmission was faint, crackling with static, but Lambert's fury was crystal clear.

"Calvin, it's Gerald—"

"And, look you little prick, I'll have your—"

"Calvin, listen a minute—"

"What . . . Gerald? You're not supposed to be there. I hired Cohen. He knows what the hell he's doing."

"Just listen Calvin, let me explain."

"I don't want explanations. Apparently . . ." There was a brief crackle of static. ". . . you fucked up. There's nothing to explain."

"But I know why."

"Cohen's coming in. He's going to honcho this."

"Calvin, give me some time. I can fix things." Gerald explained his new theory, including the ability to steer the holes. There was another moment of crackling silence on the line.

Then, Lambert's faint voice away from the phone. "Where the fuck am I?" They heard a muffled answer. Then Lambert came back.

"Look, I'm off the coast of Sumatra right now. I'm coming back in a week. You've got a week to convince me and Cohen. And get rid of that little prick, Cameron." The line went dead.

They all breathed a sigh of relief, then returned to refining the new capture system. Gerald felt the old exhilaration of obsession rise in him once again. His weeks of solitude on the mountain had recharged him.

But as they worked, he knew there was a place he had to go, a place he couldn't bring himself to visit until now. When they took a break in their planning, he excused himself and climbed into his van, driving out along the road past the airstrip and out into the desert. The sun was lowering behind the mountains, and the gentle desert breeze wafted through the van. He passed the battered blockhouse, with its cracked concrete walls, and continued on. He passed twisted chunks of metal scattered in the desert where the explosion had blown them. Then much farther on, he came to the crumbled, blackened wreckage of the huge hangar. He pulled the van up to the ruin and got out, standing for a moment in the dead stillness of a desert twilight. He stared at the crumbled, torn metal sheeting of the hangar walls and the jagged remains of the ruptured vacuum chamber. Weeks of desert wind and sun had already cleansed the site of smoke and vapor, but he thought he could smell death there.

He could hear his own breathing in the silence, feel his heartbeat. The hearts of the two dead men would never beat again. He felt his throat constrict in sorrow, and tears well in his eyes. He remembered the families of the men, how brave they had been. He had been so selfish. He had surrounded himself with theories—carefully woven, precisely constructed, but sterile and devoid of life. So inadequate.

He stepped over the pieces of metal debris, his shoes crunching in the burned grit, working his way toward the very center of the wreckage. He felt the two men's presence. He reached the vacuum chamber, its thick steel plate torturously shredded from the blast.

What violence had struck here, he thought, forces more extreme than any he could imagine. And he had the arrogance to think he could easily contain those forces. Now he had been humbled. But he had not been beaten.

He had never been religious, but he bowed his head. He made a silent promise to the two dead men. He would push himself as far as he had to, do whatever was necessary to master these unearthly objects.

The breeze brought the faint sound of an approaching car. It pulled up and Dacey climbed out. She wore jeans and a t-shirt and her hair was in a ponytail that stuck out the back of her "Schist Happens" baseball cap. She smiled at him, her eyes participating happily in that smile. She picked her way deftly through the wreckage, stepping over the sharp slivers of metal in her small hiking boots, and reached his side. She said nothing, but put her arm around him, as he did around her. They stood there for a long time, drawing strength from one another's embrace.

CHAPTER 31

Enveloped in the thrumming roar of the C5A cargo plane, Gerald bent bleary eyed over the control panel. He stared obsessively at its instruments as if diverting his gaze for an instant would allow the wormhole to escape—or disastrously, to careen toward a planet in the other universe, attracted by its magnetic field.

For seven hours he had crouched on the metal stool, watching the glowing instrument console mounted near the furiously humming frost-shrouded sphere. Bolted on the back of the flatbed truck, it looked like a massive snowball, reflecting in glittering white the interior lights of the plane. It contributed its own alien coldness to the icy temperatures inside the huge cargo bay.

As when they had captured the first hole, he had touched it, feeling its resonant vibration. Again, he had brushed away the frost, glimpsing the hovering blackness within, obscured by the translucence of the marred surface.

Now he sat watching and listening for any hint of a change, poised to grasp the joysticks that controlled the sphere's course through the other universe. The rattling overtones of the twin diesel generators added their reassuring sounds to the mix. Mullins had temporarily left his post beside Gerald to check their fuel levels.

Two months they had waited. Two months of round-the-clock building the new blockhouse and installing the new vacuum chamber. Two months of perfecting their new capture system. Two months of poring minutely over satellite data, seeking the telltale light flashes that would warn of the opening of a new hole. They had forecast several, but none was ideally positioned. They'd predicted two in the Pacific Ocean and one near the Arctic Circle.

A hole that opened in the ocean off the Marshal Islands had been a "sucker," as the media had dubbed those that connected into the hard vacuum of outer space. That hole generated an immense whirlpool, drawing a cubic mile of water into its maw before closing.

The other north of the Galapagos had been a solar hole, erupting hundred-thousand-degree hydrogen that boiled the ocean for miles around, proving that the supertanker Castile had been destroyed by such a beast.

The Arctic Circle hole began as a vacuum, then abruptly exploded in a volcano of rock and lava. Dacey had flown there immediately, joining the expedition of planetologists and geologists to help collect the first pieces of a planet from another star system ever to arrive on earth.

Now she lay curled under a blanket sleeping, in the small passenger compartment at the front of the cargo bay. Soon she would be up, no doubt insisting that he get some sleep to prepare himself for the arrival in the desert of the new sphere.

For Calvin Lambert, two months was far too long. He had constantly harangued them in phone calls, demanding to know when the next hole would be captured. Alternately, he was declaring that they couldn't possibly finish the new facility on time. He'd reluctantly delayed installing Aaron Cohen as project head, when even Cohen had agreed that Gerald's new theory seemed sound. In fact, he'd publically distanced himself from the project, apparently wanting to give himself room to deny involvement should it fail.

But Gerald was determined that it wouldn't! Shivering in the borrowed army jacket, clutching a styrofoam cup of cold coffee in his hand, he remembered with haggard triumph the hole they had captured. He remembered the faint flashes in satellite images of the Argentinean pampas; the launching of the cargo planes into the sky carrying the capture vehicles; their precarious landing on the buckling asphalt road that crossed the vast, lonely grassland.

And he remembered the same incredible violence of the hole's birth, this time shrieking and tearing at the dry, tan earth, witnessed only by frightened cattle and the small capture team. Conditions were perfect, and they had made a good capture, but the moments after had been gut-wrenching. The new television cameras inside the sphere had revealed a looming planet on the other side, with an intricately swirling frigid atmosphere of red and yellow gases. The huge planet had grown closer by the moment, and it would have drawn the hole inexorably into it, erupting a monstrous gush of ultracold liquid methane through the hole.

But this time they had been prepared. They had designed the new sphere with electromagnetic steering probes sprouting from the inside— large metal fingers extending to the very edge of the hole. Immediately after capture, they had sent precise surges of electricity through the probes and into the magnetic coils at their tips, creating a carefully sculpted field that reached through the hole. With intense relief, they had found they could pilot the hole to reverse course, sailing smoothly away from the planet whose magnetic field had brought it to life in the first place.

And thus they had maintained the hole, holding its ferocity in magnetic stasis far from any planet, until they could install it safely in the new vacuum chamber.

Then they would enter it and even fly it!

The stunning prospect, as well as the six cups of coffee he'd con-sumed, had kept Gerald doggedly scanning the instruments, scrutinizing the monitor screens for any sign of the returning planet.

His life had become immersed in cameras. Besides the cameras trained on the sphere, there were cameras in the cargo bay and mounted on the truck. Their unblinking red lights reminded him that the entire world was watching. Lambert had sold television rights to the project for three hundred million dollars. The networks had complained bitterly, but had readily signed on, and billions of viewers had avidly watched the capture live. Now, they were glued to television sets around the world, staring at him as he stared at the instrument panel.

He had given them a good show, only allowing himself bathroom breaks. And even then, he had circled the truck, making sure it was still chained securely into the cargo bay of the huge transport. He had accepted sandwiches from Andy and chewed them absentmindedly at his post.

Mullins returned, climbing awkwardly onto the back of the flatbed, still favoring the injured leg, even though the cast was off, and plopping into the chair next to him. Dacey appeared at his side, clasping a hand commandingly on his shoulder. She handed him a cell phone. He looked up at her in hazy puzzlement, but held it to his ear.

"This is George," said the distant voice of the old doctor. "I'm watching you on TV. Go to bed. Now!" He managed a sheepish smile as he handed back the phone and surrendered to fatigue, climbing slowly down from the trailer. He stumbled forward to the small cabin and lay down across two seats, not bothering to move the seat belts from beneath him, to fall instantly into a dead-solid sleep. The only fleeting thought that managed to find its way into his waning conscious was that the sphere would be well monitored by Dacey and Mullins. They had all trained intensively on the new capture system.

He plunged through a cycle of deep slumber lasting four hours before he surfaced far enough toward consciousness to remember where he was. He forced himself awake, unfolded himself creakily from the hard seats and went into the small lavatory to splash water on his face and with gulps of the cold water to wash away the brown morning taste. He made his way forward to the cockpit, where the crew sat vigilantly in a darkness festooned with the glowing lights from the instrument panels. Out the windshield lay a sky giving way to the first light of dawn.

The captain crisply informed him that they were two hours from landing. The information sparked him fully awake. He hurried back to the main cargo bay to find Mullins and Dacey still intent on the instrument panel.

"The sphere's flyin' good," said Mullins, patting the instrument panel. "We passed near a moon or somethin'. The hole was being sucked in. Dacey piloted her free, though."

Dacey sat with her hands resting lightly on the joysticks controlling the steering fields. She placed a finger on a video monitor showing a small, round white dot in a field of absolute black. "We'll show you the recording. We didn't get a close look at the moon, but it was big." She looked up at Gerald, her eyes wide with excitement. "Jesus, the places we're going to go! The things we're going to see!"

The next hours allowed no such eager speculation. The massive gray-green air transport landed smoothly on the runway in the clear desert dawn and taxied ponderously across the concrete to the hangar holding the new vacuum chambers. At Gerald's insistence, the pilots evacuated during the transfer for their safety. They sped away across the desert in a Humvee, passing Gaston and Cameron coming just as fast in the opposite direction. Gerald had learned not to argue with any of them. They had been with him before, and they were determined to be with him now. But he would be the only one to take the ultimate risk.

With Dacey video-streaming the process for the world to watch, Gerald lowered the massive rear gate to the transport. They all stood by, tension tightening their faces, as Mullins carefully backed the truck holding the vibrating, frost-covered sphere out of the transport and eased it into the hangar.

Months of practice made the next steps almost automatic. The engineers hoisted the capture sphere into the vacuum chamber, switched over the magnetic field, and sealed the chamber.

Back in the new blockhouse, Mullins flipped switches to pump the chamber down to a hard vacuum, unlatch the two hemispheres and pull them apart. As before, the hole floated in the chamber, suspended in the embrace of the chamber's magnetic fields.

"It's *beautiful!*" exclaimed Dacey, watching the screen. "So incredible."

Even though they had seen it before, they remained awestruck at the void's utter blackness, the shining points of light beyond, stars like gleaming diamonds scattered on black velvet. And as before, the glowing, undulating halo played delicately about the hole's edge. Its luminous fingers seemed to invite them, to challenge them, and to taunt them all at the same time.

They all sat at consoles in the new blockhouse, its massive concrete walls offering more protection against disaster. Its two tiers of monitoring stations were also filled with Megamag engineers, and included every possible kind of sensor that could be trained on the hole—magnetic, thermal, chemical, radiation. Even the most subtle change in its status would be recorded. All in the room watched their instruments and the six wall-mounted video screens showing the outside and inside of the chamber.

Lambert, ever the entrepreneur, had filled the blockhouse's glass-walled observation room with potential commercial clients. There was a nervous-looking man from the Nuclear Regulatory Commission, whom Lambert had persuaded of the holes' potential to dispose of nuclear wastes. And there was the colonel representing the Joint Chiefs of Staff. He would report back on the weapons potential of the holes.

In fact, they would all report back to somebody. They were all second-tier people, as Dacey had noted, chosen because they were expendable, in case something should go wrong again.

Indeed, Lambert was not there, either. Aaron Cohen sat on the front row, observing all. He would report back to Lambert. Lambert had designated Cohen as his representative, and the slight old man with the eyes like obsidian had applied his penetrating intellect to every aspect of the project. He'd peppered Gerald with questions about his plans, his measurements and his theories.

And there were Lambert's lawyer and public relations man, distinctive in their expensive dark suits, ready to install Cohen as head in a moment should there be problems.

Mullins decided that the time was right, and after checking with his technicians, flipped switches and placed his hands gently on two joysticks, easing them forward. The large-screen view inside the chamber showed a large cylinder, suspended on a jointed arm, moving up to the hole. Gerald switched on his microphone to explain the process.

"You're seeing one of the propulsion units moving into place. Each cylinder has an array of electromagnets mounted on its end, which we can activate to drive the hole in the other universe." He activated a camera at the end of the cylinder.

Stars filled one of the video screens, and the engineers scrutinized the image for any sign of a nearby planet or moon that would lure the hole into its magnetic grip. The propulsion unit circled the hole like some wary mechanical dragon.

Mullins activated another set of joysticks and two other propulsion units eased up to the hole, to give full maneuvering control. Two other video screens showed views from those cylinders.

"Ohhh, shit!" exclaimed Mullins, as gasps rose in the room. One of the screens showed a rapidly looming moon, the dappling of craters visible on its surface.

"It's that moon! The hole reversed course!"

"Remember, the hole has no inertia," Gerald said, his voice strained. "It's going to move like nothing we've ever encountered. Take care of it, Andy."

"Computer can handle it," said Mullins, his stubby fingers dancing across the keyboard, feeding in navigation coordinates. The sulfur-yellow sphere grew to fill the screen, its crater-pocked surface showing a tracery of rifts.

"Jesus, it's gonna hit!" exclaimed Dacey.

Mullins stabbed the key activating the computer control, and the three arms came smoothly to life, moving about the hole like cobras circling prey. They locked themselves into positions dictated by the computer and switched on their magnets.

For an excruciating moment, nothing seemed to happen. Then, almost imperceptibly, the moon began to shrink.

"Nah," said Mullins, smacking his lips and adjusting his round frame happily in his chair. "Ain't gonna hit. Got it licked!"

"Jimmy," said Gerald quietly, a smile on his face. "We're flyin' the son-of-a-bitch!"

Cameron laughed, but Gerald grew immediately somber, aware that what he was about to say had been said before.

"Let's go in."

CHAPTER 32

"How fast are we going?" Dacey leaned over Mullins, who fiddled with the computer keys, stuck the tip of his tongue reflectively out the side of his mouth, and peered critically at the result on the computer screen.

"Real damn fast," he concluded with authority.

"Okay, how fast is real damn fast?"

Mullins drummed a tattoo of strokes on the keyboard and rechecked his results.

"You ain't gonna believe it."

"Try us," said Cameron.

"Oh, 'round seventy thousand miles an hour, it says here."

"You're right. Real damn fast," said Dacey.

Beyond speed, Mullins had reported that the wormhole appeared stable. And, he confirmed, with no mass or inertia, the merest tickle of a magnetic field could accelerate it instantly away from any planets or moons into the distant reaches of space, where it would remain so.

But Gerald was distracted, feeling the confusing mix of fear and exhilaration that a man must feel on the eve of his first parachute jump. Or perhaps his first suicide attempt. Tomorrow he would take himself into a realm so totally alien that he could not fathom the experience, much less its meaning. Gaston asked if they could take a walk, offering some relief.

They left the blockhouse and hiked out across the broad, flat desert surrounded by the quiet darkness, and he scanned the vast, black bowl of the night sky with its great swaths of stars. How strange, he thought, that tonight the vast desert seemed almost too small to contain his agitation.

"I know you mean to go alone," said Gaston, peering up at the sky. He smiled and looked over at Gerald, but it was a smile that seemed almost of sad resignation.

"Yes. I just can't let anybody else risk their life."

"You need somebody else, you know. It's not wise to go alone." Gaston took off his glasses and rubbed his eyes. Gerald realized how haggard his face looked without their distracting glimmer.

"Everybody's already tried to talk me out of it." Gerald took a deep breath, remembering the blunt argument by Dacey, the warnings by Mullins and all the others.

"I want to go with you."

Gerald was gently exasperated. "Why are you asking now? We've been all over it. The plans are all made."

"Gerald . . ." Gaston put his glasses back on, put his hands in his pockets and looked down, then somberly back up at Gerald. "I've got pancreatic cancer. Stage four. It's spread." Gerald opened his mouth to speak, but Gaston continued, knowing that Gerald would need time to really figure out how to respond. He'd seen people react before. "I've been HIV positive for many years, so I expected something like this. It's a complication. I've known about the cancer for about a year. Nobody else knows except Jimmy and Wayne. I know what's coming. I want to do something. I want to do this."

"God, I am sorry, Ralph." Gerald felt profoundly the inadequacy of anything he could say. "I know it must be terrible. I don't know what to say. But, you know, I still can't let you—"

"I know what's coming," Gaston said again, with more emphasis. "It'll be soon. And I've decided that this will give my life meaning."

"Your life already has meaning. Look, you're an expert criminalist. You've solved terrible crimes. You've done so much good. You've helped this project enormously."

"I know. I don't minimize that. But it would mean so much if I could do this. And no matter what you say, you are going to need somebody out there with you. Let me help. Please."

Gerald looked away out into the desert, to the distant shimmering lights on the hangar containing the vacuum chamber. He pondered how Gaston had kept this secret; how disciplined he must be; how much courage it must take. He finally knew he couldn't refuse the request. The distant, waiting lights also helped him realize that, to some extent, Ralph had given him an excuse.

"Ralph, I do need help. I'm sorry this was what it took for me to admit it. But I do."

"Fine, then. That's fine." Gaston extended his hand and Gerald shook it. He sensed a steadiness in Gaston from facing death, one that calmed him, made him almost serene. They walked back toward the blockhouse, whose slit-windows glowed brightly, looking like half-closed eyes in the impassive gray concrete face, splashing a pale light out along the desert floor. Maybe now he could hope for some sleep.

• • •

Gerald flipped on the light in his small room, thankful at the room's simplicity. A bed, a dresser, a desk and a feeble attempt at decoration: a framed print of jets against a cloudy sky. He would have little to distract him from trying to sleep, or at least make it to dawn. He had just begun to take off his shirt when there was a knock at the door between his room and Dacey's. He opened it and she stood there tentatively in her jeans, t-shirt and stocking feet.

"You've got to shave," she said. "Remember what George said?"

"Oh, right." He smiled slightly and rubbed his beard. George had insisted on a smooth face. If he had to put on a gas mask or use an oxygen mask, there could be no leakage. "I've had it for years. I'm not sure I'll remember how. I don't have a razor."

She took his arm, guiding him with mock authority. "C'mon, sport. I've got one I use on my legs. And I would shave my dad when Mom was working." She steered him into her bathroom and sat him on the closed toilet lid, tipping his head back. She filled the sink with hot water, the moisture curling into the dry air and fogging the mirror.

"Okay, let's start by doing some pruning." She fumbled in a black zipper bag on the sink and came up with a pair of small scissors, beginning to carefully snip away at his beard.

He became keenly aware of the closeness of her body, her touch on his face, the aroma of her skin.

"You okay?" she asked quietly as she trimmed. There was a timbre in her voice he hadn't heard before.

"You mean right now?"

"Jeez, you *are* thick. I mean about tomorrow."

"Scared silly."

She didn't answer, but stood back, judging the ragged stubble that was left "Okay, we've got wolf man here, let's keep going." She soaked a towel under the hot water and gingerly wrung it out, wrapping the steaming cloth gently around his face.

"You'll be fine," she said, patting the towel so the moist heat would soften his beard. "You hear? You'll be fine."

"Sure," he said. His voice muffled.

"I heard you're taking Ralph with you. I'd have been better."

"I know you'd have been great. There were reasons."

"In any case, I'm glad you're taking somebody."

He noticed that she hadn't asked about his reasons. Maybe she knew about Ralph's cancer. Maybe she wasn't being her usual quick-witted analytical self at this particular moment.

She removed the towel and the cool on his face felt as good as the warmth had. She took up a bar of soap, dipped it in the hot water and vigorously worked up a lather between her hands. She applied it carefully to his face and began to scrape gently and meticulously at the beard. Periodically, she wet the razor, reapplied soap and continued. He lay back with his head against the wall and let her do her job, feeling her gentle way with the razor. He'd never felt so relaxed, especially with a woman, and never with a woman wielding sharp steel on his neck. After a while, he felt a hot wet towel rubbing over his face. She was done.

He opened his eyes. "So what do you think?" He watched her face for a clue. He saw tears in her eyes.

"Wow," she said softly, a tear rolling down her face, her lower lip trembling. "We've got a little bit of Robert Downey, Junior. Maybe a touch of Joaquin Phoenix." Then her facade crumbled completely. "Oh, hell!" She cried, pitching the razor into the sink and sinking to her knees, throwing her arms around him. She buried her face in his shoulder and he felt her body shudder in a sob. He stroked her hair and hugged her in return.

"What?" he asked, already knowing the answer. "What?"

"God, Gerald I am scared for you. I love you. I am so sorry I've not been able to . . ."

"I know. I know."

"You were so patient. I was this damned coward and you were so patient." She looked up at him, her face wet.

"I was scared, too. I didn't know . . ." He shrugged and wiped away her tears and brought her face to his and they kissed. They embraced, and the kisses that followed made it obvious to both of them that they would fully commit to one another that night.

"I shouldn't have waited. This could be . . ." She didn't let herself finish.

Each began to unclothe the other, seeking the reassurance of skin on skin. They moved out of the bathroom and into the dark bedroom, where they made love in the most consuming way each had ever experienced. Afterward, they shared whispered confidences with a combination of urgency and intimacy, clinging to each other, each remorseful for the time they had allowed to be lost, each needing the other for support.

Finally, he drew away enough so he could see her face. "This wasn't . . . ?"

She took a moment to bring herself to focus. She knew what he was going to ask. She impatiently pursed her lips, one eyebrow raised in mock scolding.

"A sympathy screw? I assure you, Gerald, I'm not just after your mind." She stroked his newly shaved cheek. That night, she would further demonstrate that fact, as they created an intimacy that would be a defense against tomorrow.

•　•　•

The phone rang three times before Dacey emerged from sleep and from beneath the covers, fumbling the receiver to her ear. The touch of plastic coolness against her face helped her wake up. She mumbled a hoarse hello.

"Is he all right?" tersely asked a distant voice.

"What? Who?" She turned over. The bed next to her was empty. She remembered a hand gently stroking her hair as she floated in half-sleep, a kiss on her cheek, then a vague sense that he had gone. The aroma of the night lingered.

The voice on the phone brought her back. "Is Gerald all right? Is he competent? Is he ready to go in there?"

As her head cleared, Dacey realized it was the voice of Calvin Lambert.

"Why are you calling me? Why don't you ask him?" But with the question, she began to realize the answer.

"Because I'm asking you."

She rolled over on her back and smiled sleepily at the dark ceiling. "Calvin, you're worried about your son, aren't you?"

There was a single beat of pause. "I'm worried about my investment."

"Bullshit."

"Is he going to blow it?"

"'Course not. He even finally decided to take somebody with him. Ralph Gaston."

"Is Gaston a good man?"

"Yeah, absolutely. He's trained. I think I would have been better. But it's his decision. In any case, it relieved the hell out of me."

"Cohen tells me the plan's solid. The hardware's solid."

The words brought Dacey's mind to crystal clarity, even though the little glowing electric clock beside the bed said 4:21. "Calvin, you're a damned faker. You never intended Cohen to take over this project. You intended for him to watch over Gerald."

The answer was a click, as the line went dead. Dacey hmphed to herself at her new knowledge and threw back the covers to challenge the day.

CHAPTER 33

Gerald snapped his helmet down onto the collar ring and gave it the locking twist. He'd done it so many times in practice, but now the click that signaled a firm seal had a sharp, definitive sense of commitment to it. Now all his abilities, determination and fears were hermetically sealed inside this suit. He didn't know whether they would produce courage or cowardice, brilliance or stupidity.

Neither he nor Ralph were military pilots or astronauts. They were just two regular people who were about to enter another universe. And so they found themselves periodically fighting surges of anxiety.

He turned his suit to look over at Ralph donning his. Gaston seemed steady. Perhaps he'd already come to terms with the prospect of his own death. In any case, his calm inspired Gerald.

The portable air pump kept a flow of fresh air through the suit to save the tanks, but Gerald felt stifled nevertheless. He breathed in hard for reassurance. Soon, though, it would seem puny protection against the absolute vacuum he was to encounter. He tried to imagine the vastness on the other side. As the technicians examined his suit, he wondered whether it was possible to experience claustrophobia and agoraphobia at the same time. The sound of his breathing in the helmet became a steady, whispering reassurance that he was all right.

Dacey and George had been fussing over them all morning, directing two other doctors in monitoring their vital signs, giving each of them one last, long hug. Dacey's touch had been subtle, a pat on the back, a squeeze of the arm, but it had communicated clearly the feeling that had grown between them.

George took a headset from one of the technicians and held the microphone to his mouth.

"You're just fine," he said with the usual sunny encouragement. Even through the helmet radio, the voice still had that resonance of experience that had carried them through so much. George brought his parchment-wrinkled face up near the faceplate and peered through his glasses at Gerald. His eyes seemed a bit more shiny than usual. "I'm going to the control room to start monitoring. Godspeed, son."

Then Dacey brought her face up to Gerald's faceplate and looked him in the eyes. She smiled and it brought a reassurance beyond words. She took up the microphone.

"I waited to tell you this. Calvin called last night. He was worried about you."

The news had the desired effect. Gerald laughed wryly and forgot his nerves for a moment. He hefted himself to his feet, leaning forward to counterbalance the weight of the oxygen pack. He turned ponderously to Gaston, now also fully suited.

Without a word, they switched over to the tanks and stepped to the airlock, turning back to the small crowd of technicians. He looked at Dacey a last time. Her jaw was clenched, with just the slightest shine of moisture in her eyes. Cameron, holding the door, nodded and mouthed a single silent word. "Thanks." He knew about Gaston. Gerald nodded back as best he could and they opened the airlock and stepped clumsily in, feeling elephantine inside the bulky, heavy suits. Gaston shut the door and turned the metal latch, and they peered through the window one last time, as the people outside hurried to their trucks and Humvees to head back to the blockhouse.

Now they were alone. Soon they would be in another universe.

The indicator on the airlock wall signaled a vacuum, and Gerald unlatched the inner door and swung it open.

Waiting for them was a pitch-black maw floating in the middle of the room, weaving slightly back and forth, the stars shining through with a majestic, perhaps malevolent, indifference. He'd never seen a hole exposed first-hand before, in all its stunning cosmic power. He was transfixed, staring first into the floating blackness beyond, and then at the faint colorful swirling evanescence around the edges. The deadly edges. One touch of the infinite razor sharpness would slice through the suit and his body.

But the lure of the star-filled center overcame any fear. Gerald felt with every fiber of his being that he had to see what was in there. He felt his suit heater come on, sending a wave of warmth into his hands and feet. The hole was a voracious devourer of heat, drawing it from the chamber into the two-hundred-degree-below-zero cold of space.

The three clunky mechanical serpents with their long jointed necks and cylindrical heads, were still poised almost comically around the hole, seeming to peer curiously into it at odd angles. The magnetic head aimed upward from below the hole came to life and withdrew itself obligingly out of the way, still looking into the hole from the side. They would climb up into the hole from the bottom.

They attached the cables that would serve both as tether and communication line and began a steady exchange with the control room over their radios, George's and Mullins' voices filling their helmets. They described the hole carefully, noting its behavior in the captive magnetic field. A glitch in that field and the hole would move. Even a shift of a few feet would cause the hole to slice through them. Satisfied that the hole was stable, they rolled a laddered cylindrical framework into place beneath it, and ensured that it was firmly set on the metal floor. Because of the rigid helmet, Gerald had to lean back to see up, and the surrounding blackness overhead made him almost forget to breathe.

They turned to one another and shook hands, holding the handshake for a long time. Gaston smiled, his face inside the darkened helmet seeming to glow with excitement. He turned and flipped a switch on the framework, it began to extend itself like a telescope up through the center of the hole. Gerald leaned backward, bracing himself against the framework and tried to see the result. The framework seemed to extend smoothly through—a good sign. He turned to the ladder, grasped the handrails, and with effort bent his knee and pulled himself up onto the first rung. Gaston gave a steady series of positioning instructions so he would avoid the deadly edge.

The effort was hard, given the weight and bulk of the suit. He made another rung, then another, then another. He looked beyond the ladder and realized that his eyes were at the edge of the hole. He almost didn't go on, so incredible was the sight. A faint, swirling colored glow danced around his helmet. Below an infinitely thin line was the familiar, lighted chamber; above the line, the star-filled vastness of another universe.

"You okay?" It was George. "Your heart rate just shot up."

"Yes. It's . . ." He couldn't describe it. Wouldn't even try. His helmet camera would at least show some semblance of what it was like. He forced himself to continue on and felt a strange lightheadedness. His breathing grew more rapid, shallower. Then he realized and laughed at himself. Some astrophysicist! Of course he was feeling lightheaded! His head had entered gravity-free space! His breathing steadied.

The stars again! The incredible gleaming swath of diamonds, rubies and sapphires so clear he felt he could touch them. They were large and small, silver-white, pale red, and delicate blue. The black vault of the heavens all around him made him want to shout, scream, shriek, bellow, howl in a roiling mixture of wonder, fear, joy and panic. But all he heard in his helmet was a kind of awed inadequate whisper to himself. "Incredible . . . incredible."

He panted with excitement and took another step. The effort was far easier. He felt dizzy. He stopped to give himself a chance to reorient, but realized it was impossible. Too much was happening. Again instructions from Gaston guided him to avoid the edge.

He stepped up again and his whole body was through, its weight vanished. He felt the shift of flesh on his body, the slight puffiness in his face and hands, the change in blood distribution that came with freedom from weight. Now he clung to the ladder for security not support. With a gentle tug, he pulled himself to the end and bent to look back. Confusion overcame him for a moment, before he managed to restore his retreating intellect. The ladder to which he held fast extended itself from a perfect glowing sphere floating in space, visible within, the ladder, Gaston, and the vacuum chamber. But he knew he had gone into a sphere on the other side. It was a real-life Escher painting, a real dimensional paradox. Of course, he had expected the alien geometry. After all, the hole had to be a sphere on this side as well as the other.

"I'm behind you," he heard Gaston say in his helmet radio. He decided it was time. He pushed off from the ladder and floated free.

"Oh my God," he heard himself say. "Oh my God!" He spread his arms to the new universe and lost himself in its magnificent immensity. He spun very slowly, watching with moist eyes as the stars passed before him in stately procession. His mind told him they were inanimate objects, immense globes of roiling thermonuclear fire, but his imagination heard them whisper of possibilities beyond his experience. They whispered to him of the amazing worlds that they harbored, and they promised him that now he and his kind would see them.

He caught his breath as a spiral galaxy slid into view, an opalescent whirlpool of a hundred billion stars. The spiral's center glowed with the heat of a cosmic firestorm of colliding suns. Its wispy starry arms curved away far into space, shining crystalline necklaces on celestial display against black velvet.

There were stars in his helmet now, faintly shimmering points of light floating across his vision. He realized they were his tears, drifting away from his eyes to become tiny perfect droplets floating in weightless space.

He felt the tug of the tether and knew he had floated far from the hole. The tether's pull rotated him around so he could look back toward his origin. He gathered his wits and gave Gaston the same guidance to avoid the edge.

Then, Gaston was through, too, holding onto the end of the ladder. A realization struck him like a physical blow. They were so alone! No comforting earth loomed nearby; no massive white spaceship hovered to take him onboard. Only a small hole in the indifferent vastness that could collapse away at any second.

"We're going to be different now," a voice said.

"What?" asked Gaston. The voice penetrated his vision, bringing back reality.

Gerald realized he had said the words. "I . . . guess I said we're going to be different now."

"Yes." The single word told him Gaston had experienced something, too.

"Get back in! Now!" Mullins's voice pierced the moment.

"What's wrong?" As Gerald asked the question, he sensed some change in the hole, something besides the glow of the light from his universe. The ladder swayed back and forth, the framework almost touching the edge of the hole. Gaston held on, his grip revealing the precariousness of his situation.

"The vacuum chamber! We've got a leak!" said Mullins.

Gerald suddenly realized that floating free at the end of the tether, he had no way to get himself back quickly and accurately to the hole. The ladder lurched to one side, one rail grazing the edge of the hole. It sliced cleanly away, the ladder crumpling slightly. Gaston held on, leaning to one side to compensate. If the ladder went, if the frame broke, their reentry would be suicidal, given the lethal edges.

"We don't know what happened," said Mullins. "We're sending a team to patch the chamber. You have to get back . . . *now!*"

Gerald felt a tug. Gaston was hauling him back by his tether, slowly, carefully, so that he wouldn't veer into the edge.

"Just hold still," Gaston said. "I think I can . . ." The ladder abruptly lurched again, slicing a shallow tear in the leg of Gaston's suit. But the suit held, for now. Gaston stepped down two rungs, half his body now in the hole. If the framework gave any more, he would be sliced in half, but he remained in place, pulling Gerald in hand-over-hand.

Gerald touched the ladder, grabbed the top rung, and swung himself ponderously around in the weightlessness. He couldn't see down now, because of the helmet. He didn't know whether Gaston was alive, or whether he would have a way back.

"Ralph?" he asked.

There was no answer.

"Ralph!"

Then Gaston answered "I'm almost down. I'm going to hold . . ." The ladder tilted sideways and Gerald held on. "I'm going to hold onto the ladder. Step down."

Gerald did so and felt the ladder swaying violently beneath him. Something flew upward past his face; something white. The vacuum chamber was leaking, spewing air into the hole, along with whatever debris was caught up in the maelstrom. His breathing grew ragged and he felt sweat trickle down his temple, joining the wetness already inside his helmet. A panic clutched his gut like a vice.

"Step again." Gaston's voice was calm, reassuring. Gerald did so. "And again. And again. Stop." The ladder canted to one side, then righted itself.

Gaston continued to guide Gerald down. He felt the weight return to his legs, his waist, his chest. Finally, his helmet was at the edge. The ladder lurched again and his helmet listed over close to the edge and he jerked back to avoid having it cut through.

But finally, the welcome tug of gravity had returned to his entire body. He was through! He realized how hard Gaston had worked to steady the ladder beneath him, hauling back and forth to compensate for the swaying from his weight and the whirling gush of air out of the hole.

Gaston stumbled back against the wall and leaned against it. Gerald backed away in time to see the framework lurch so badly, the ladder sliced clean away and float into the darkness of space. He leaned against the wall, too, feeling the vicious winds buffeting their suited bodies.

"Get into the airlock! Get out of there!" shouted Mullins. They hauled themselves across the chamber against the hellish wind of the leak, and entered the airlock, shutting the door. Gaston operated the controls and after a minute they stumbled out of the chamber and into the arms of Megamag technicians. The technicians hustled them far away from the chamber, fighting a gale-force wind flowing toward the huge metal structure. Once they were a safe distance from the chamber inside the huge hangar, the technicians helped them to sit down and remove their helmets. Gerald relished the delicious, sweet desert air drying the sweat from his head, cooling him. Gaston's helmet came off and he opened his mouth in relief, his eyes closed, his long brown hair plastered to his skull, the sheen of sweat on his thin face testifying to his exertion.

With the helmets removed, they became more aware of a vicious high-pitched hissing sound, like a hundred steam valves going off at once. Gerald laboriously turned in his suit to see two technicians wearing harnesses approaching the chamber. They were tethered by steel cable to a girder on the hangar wall, which were being payed out by a motorized winch operated by other technicians, who were also tethered on shorter cables. The two carried a metal plate in front of them like a shield. They aimed the plate at a spot on the chamber just above their heads. The cables zinged taut and they were both dragged toward the chamber. A wooden crate tumbled past them and leaped into the air at the spot on the chamber wall, slamming into it, crumpling into splinters and being sucked away through the small hole. The men fought to keep their balance and to keep the plate in front of them. Abruptly the plate, too, slammed against the side of the chamber. The hissing grew fainter, then stopped.

"Jesus fucking Christ," muttered the young frizzy-haired technician standing by Gerald. "We never ever thought that would happen!"

Gerald and Gaston looked at each other. They smiled knowingly. Then, the smiles blossomed into exultant laughter. The technicians looked on puzzled, as they stood and slapped each other on the padded shoulders and shouted in utter, glorious triumph.

●　●　●

"Best we can figure, it was about the size of a grain of sand," said Mullins, gesturing at the projected image of a tiny round rupture in a gray-painted steel surface. He bobbed restlessly about the room full of scientists and engineers crowding around the long conference table and sitting in chairs lining the wall. At the table's head were a haggard Gerald and Gaston, still wearing the blue coveralls they'd donned after taking off the space suits.

"Any sense of where it came from?" asked Gerald.

"Well, it almost certainly came out of the hole, traveling maybe a thousand miles an hour. You guys were really lucky it didn't go right through either of you!"

Gerald and Gaston shared a glance that combined shock and relief. They had been so close to death.

"There's more," said Mullins. He screwed up his face and peered nearsightedly at the keyboard of his laptop, located the key to advance the image and tapped it decisively with his pudgy finger. Other, similar images, one by one appeared on the screen. They also showed close-ups of the chamber's metal plate, with a welter of dents, furrows and mars in the smooth surface. Mullins punctuated them with "Here. Here. Here." He stopped at an especially dramatic image. "Inside of the chamber is pitted. Took a number of other hits, but none of the others penetrated."

"Lotta space crap out there, eh?" asked Cameron. "You guys better figure out how to stop it."

"Yeah, well, we've already started." Mullins tapped a few keys and brought up a three-D diagram of the hole, the magnetic field lines and the steering apparatus. "Particles are coming through, usually from the direction we're traveling, relative to the local flow of stuff. Say, stuff orbiting a star. The particle that made the hole may have been going around the star where we were." He stopped, grinning, realizing that he had dropped a bombshell. "Oh yeah, we're doing computer enhancement of the helmet video. Didn't want to say anything till it was done. Guess the cat's out of the bag. The video picked up a nearby star and planets. Now we know our hole is in the outer reaches of a star system, with planets, moons, stuff like that. We're, like, out where Uranus would be if we were in our solar system."

"Whoa! Wait a minute!" Dacey leaned forward over the table. "We've got *planets*? Let's look at that data!" Mullins nodded his head vigorously and waved at the screen.

"Yeah, first let me tell you how we figured to protect ourselves. We'll deflect particles by directing energy through the hole in the direction of travel. Head 'em off." He clicked to an animation of arrows streaming through the oval. "We'll use lasers. Light exerts a pressure, like water from a hose. We figure we'll use a combination of high-powered lasers, different colors, shining through the hole. It'll deflect particles before they get to the hole."

"Headlights," said Cameron. "You're installing headlights on the thing."

"Yeah! Exactly!" said Mullins happily. "We called Lawrence Berkeley Labs. They do big lasers for fusion research. They said they could gin up a combination of lasers that could fit inside the vacuum chamber. Expensive. But it's better than getting pinged at all the time. It'll be a really intense white light."

"You got low beams and high beams?" cracked Cameron. Mullins laughed along with the others in the room, shrugged, hitched up his pants and continued. "Okay, about those planets. Dr. Cohen has been looking at the images." He nodded to the Caltech physicist, Aaron Cohen, who stood up, as Mullins brought up images that looked very familiar.

"It's a yellow dwarf like the sun, a bit younger from what we can tell." More images of dots floating in space. "The cameras picked up four or five planets, but the images were fuzzy."

Dacey scribbled furiously on a yellow pad. She stopped Cohen and efficiently ticked off the next steps. They would need to train telescopes through the hole to get better images. Her planetologist friends would go absolutely bonkers. They would have to find out as much as possible about the alien planets.

Then they would visit them! They would sail down to their surfaces, riding their magnetically propelled "transdimensional aperture." And they would step out onto the surface of another world!

CHAPTER 34

The debriefing ended when Mullins realized that they had subjected a sagging Gerald and Gaston to four hours of questions, and the rest of the world was waiting eagerly to see the two. They walked out into the bright sun to a nearby hangar and the ebullient crowd of engineers and technicians, who were already polishing off their second case of champagne. There were toasts and congratulations and deeply felt thanks.

Gerald seemed to gather a second wind as he sipped champagne with Dacey and a raucous group of Megamag engineers. But then his brow knitted and he grew quiet. He abruptly got up and whispered something to Mullins and they retired to a small office in the hangar. Dacey could see them through the window bent over a desk, Gerald drawing something and Mullins nodding vigorously. The little man held up his hands, palms open, fashioning an imaginary large globular object in the air. They emerged and Mullins beckoned to one of his engineers and hurried off with him.

Gerald returned to Dacey and Gaston, but he wouldn't answer when Dacey persistently quizzed him about the meeting. He couldn't talk; it was time for the news conference, he said.

They drove to the news conference site, a hangar near the entrance gate that had been turned into a media center. Lambert's Boeing 767 was already parked nearby, and he stood at the bottom of the stairway giving interviews to reporters.

The news conference went as before, except the attendance now was massive, a restless, aggressive gang of some three thousand reporters aiming their professional attention at Lambert, Gerald and Gaston. Standing before the forest of microphones, Lambert offered congratulations and explained how he had faithfully supported the project from the beginning. Gerald and Gaston stood to a rattling chorus of clicking cameras and patiently answered questions ranging from the magnetic parameters of the propulsive system (*Physics Today*) to why Gerald had shaved his beard (*People*).

A question from the *Los Angeles Times*, stopped him: "Do you think these holes represent an opportunity or a threat to humanity?"

For a long moment, he stared at the questioner, a tall, dapper man with a salt-and-pepper beard.

"Both," he finally said, his dark eyes glancing around the group, as if searching for answers. "I'm not a philosopher. Talk to some philosophers for a good answer. But I know that these are incredibly powerful things. The wormholes could represent a way out for our species. I think we're in danger on this planet. From ourselves. We're trapped in our own foolishness. This is a way out of the trap. But they also represent a way *in* for things we just don't understand." He shrugged at the inadequacy of his answer and shifted uneasily.

The reporters continued their questioning, thrusting their hands in the air, shouting for attention. After Lambert's public relations man stepped forward to call a halt there was a mass exodus to file their stories.

Lambert, showing a hearty good cheer from the press conference, invited Gerald, Gaston and Dacey onboard his jet. They entered to find four slickly groomed men in dark, expensively tailored suits and two generals in military uniforms festooned with ribbons. They sat at a confident ease in the leather chairs of the main lounge, sipping champagne or more substantial glasses of scotch.

Lambert introduced the men, naming the conglomerates or military branches they represented. He did not give titles. It was understood that they were the heads. They offered perfunctory handshakes and coolly cordial greetings.

"We've been talking about the commercial possibilities," said Lambert, with the barely concealed relish of a bargainer with the upper hand. "There's nuclear waste disposal. We could assure that the wastes we put through would be completely disposed of. It would open up the nuclear industry; make it possible to start building reactors again."

"But there's so much we don't know yet," said Gerald, quietly, glancing over at Lambert's assistant, Van Alston, sitting quietly to the side, an open leather notebook on his lap, taking notes. "This is only the beginning. There's the physics of these holes, the astronomy of the other universe. First, we have—"

"Sure. Right. Of course," interrupted Lambert. "But to do all that, we need support. We need income. We'll charge the scientists."

"There's government support," said Dacey, who like Gerald, remained standing, leaning against the bulkhead, watching the proceedings with evident suspicion. "The government will fund the basic research."

A flicker of disdain crossed the faces of some of the men.

"Nah, I already nixed that, remember? No dice," Lambert sat down in his chair and took up his scotch. "If the university types want to get money from the government, that's fine. But we'll charge an entrance fee. We're contractors like any other contractors." He nodded smiling at the two generals. "And there may well be military uses." The pointed reference seemed designed to emphasize some discussion that Gerald suspected had been going on before he arrived. He understood from the generals' stoic non-response that pressures were being brought to bear. He also realized that the military might well invoke national security to commandeer the holes.

"Look," he said tersely, moving toward the exit. "I'm sure we can all talk about the possibilities. You can, anyway. But all this will have to wait. First we have to understand these holes, how they work. Most of all, we have to know how to close them once they open. Do you want another Paris?" Without waiting for an answer, he turned and ducked out the door and down the stairs. Gaston and Dacey followed. They stood at the bottom of the stairs taking in the vista across the desert to the distant mountains, finding it refreshing after the close confines of the airplane and its powerful men.

"I'll tell the others what happened in there," Gaston said shaking his head. "They'll have to be prepared."

Gaston started off, but Gerald stopped him. "Ralph . . . thanks . . . thanks for *everything*."

Gaston nodded, managing a half-smile and started off across the runway to a Humvee.

"Gerald," came Lambert's stern voice from the top of the stairs, his husky frame filling the doorway. Lambert peered down at him for a moment, then descended.

But before he could speak, Gerald struck. "Okay, you provided the funding, but this is my project. All these plans you're hatching, the possible military involvement, you could be endangering not just the project but huge numbers of lives. You just—"

"But there's something you don't know," interrupted Lambert. "The fruit salads in there told me their satellites intercepted some transmissions, but it'll be public soon."

"What's that?"

"China's captured a hole. Two days ago in the Gobi desert. We don't know what it means."

"Well, it means we can find out more about them."

"It also means we've got to figure out *now* whether these things can be used as weapons."

"I'm sure we'll know soon enough, thanks to you and them." Gerald, squinted up at the plane's doorway. He turned and strode away.

Dacey remained long enough to catch a certain twinkle in Lambert's eyes, a faint smile. "I've got your number, y'know," she said conspiratorially.

"What the hell's that mean?"

"You know damned well, Pop." She grinned, made a tongue-click out of the side of her mouth and set off after Gerald.

.   .   .

Gerald turned on the shower, stripped off his jumpsuit and underwear, and stepped in. The shower was hot and powerful, and it felt good. He had soaped his face, when he heard the shower curtain rustle and felt warm skin on his, arms encircling him. He cleared his eyes to look down at Dacey's face, her clear blue-gray eyes, her slightly bent nose, the lovely mouth smiling puckishly, gently up at him.

"Hi," he breathed, kissing her deeply.

They took turns using the soap to wash away each other's stresses. And they stayed together in the shower much, much longer than they needed to, deeply enjoying each other's bodies.

Finally, they gently dried each other and slid between the sheets of the bed, as the last vestiges of dampness evaporated from their bodies, leaving a dry softness.

"So, you going to tell me?" She shifted her body against his, so she could see his face.

"What?" he asked woozily, sinking slowly toward sleep. But his tone revealed that he knew exactly what she was asking about.

"You were excited about something at that party. You talked to Andy and he got excited. C'mon, tell me."

He stroked her back gently and smiled, his eyes closed. "Okay. You know how you can fly the holes from this side. Fly them around in the other universe?"

"Yeah."

"Well, I figured, you could go into the other side. Into the other universe. Take magnets, apply a controlled magnetic field from there, and fly a hole through *this* universe. Andy's gonna build the system."

"Wow!" She disentangled herself and propped herself up on one elbow, wide awake. "Wow!" she said again as the idea sank in. "We could go anywhere! This universe or another one! We could land on any planet; we could . . ." She looked down. His eyes were closed, his face in repose, his breathing regular. He was asleep.

She couldn't tell him about *her* plan!

CHAPTER 35

Dacey hauled herself up the ladder, feeling the alien planet's winds gust through the hole, buffeting her suit despite its weight. The winds whipping around the helmet created a low roaring sound in her ears. Her head reached the razor-sharp boundary between one universe and the other, and she felt suddenly disoriented. Below the infinitely fine line, she saw the familiar gray steel vacuum chamber, now no longer holding a vacuum, but containing the swirling hot atmosphere of the planet. Above the line lay the planet, a sprawling, bright vista that made her gasp, uttering a wondering "Whoa!"

Stretching away as far as she could see lay a mass of verdant green—a sea of ground-hugging foliage that followed the low rolling landscape like a rich covering of the lushest carpeting. A luminous diffuse gray light bathed all. Patches of bare red rock showed through in places, but the green had covered all that it possibly could. Life was as tenacious here as it was on Earth. Above, she saw thick rolling clouds whipping across the sky in streaming clumps, now and then parting to reveal a pale blue sky, and blinding glimpses of a sun that seemed more brilliant than their own.

"You okay?" She heard in her helmet radio. Gerald's voice carried the weight of an abiding anxiety for her. "You can back out if you're not okay. We don't have to do this."

"We do. You know we do." Dacey remembered their argument as she continued to scan the landscape. Three days ago, the optical telescope installed in the chamber had revealed the planet—a tantalizing blue and white ball hanging in space. The fourth planet from the alien star, large swaths covered in liquid water, could harbor life. Of course, logic suggested that they approach the planet cautiously and before venturing onto it, do months of observation, recording volumes of images and taking careful measurements to understand its exotic whims.

But Dacey had argued that it was simply not possible to wait. They had little idea how much time they would have until the hole closed. One glitch in the magnetic field could be the end.

"Exactly," said Gerald. "The end. And if you're on the other side? It's suicidal."

"This is too important," she had said, gesturing at the video image of the gleaming planet, its skin of atmosphere swirling with clouds. "The data, the samples, standing on the surface of another planet that has life. I'm going! That's it!"

Bolstering her argument was Lambert, who informed them via a phone call from somewhere over Kuwait that he'd negotiated worldwide television rights for five billion dollars. The money would pay for a massive increase in their research. Maybe it would even mean they could capture enough holes to understand them, to learn how to shut them down. Maybe they could learn enough to avoid the undefined catastrophe that Gerald's well-educated theoretical gut feeling told him was coming.

Cameron had announced that "Suicidal" was his middle name and that he'd been damned patient while everybody else had fun. After all, Gerald and Gaston had made three more space walks to gather data. Three passages into another universe that had brought them back with awed tales of other star systems.

Now it was his turn, insisted Cameron. Besides, he'd argued to Gerald that, as a forensics expert he knew how to take valid biological samples, complementing Dacey's skills as a geologist.

What's more, he proclaimed, he'd be about the safest person to go with Dacey, since he'd make damned sure they both got their asses out fast if there was any sign of trouble. Left unsaid was that Brendan Cooper would have otherwise been the other astronaut. Cameron understood that this expedition would be a tribute to their fallen comrade.

So Cameron had won the spot, and after a stunningly fast trip to the planet, the hole's laser beams clearing its path of space dust, the spherical orb had settled gently toward the planet's surface.

Scanning the planet for a final moment before preparing to enter it, Dacey remembered how they had all watched, wide-eyed and slack-jawed, as the hole skimmed over vistas of wind-blown deserts, violently rolling oceans, and most promising, sprawling regions of living green.

And now this incredible planet was hers! She pulled herself up the last few rungs and into the grip of the planet.

Gerald had warned her about the geometric anomaly of the hole. She had climbed *up* from Earth into the hole. Now, she climbed *sideways* out onto the other planet, feeling its gravity pull her down. The ladder sagged under her weight toward the hole's edge. She felt a knot of fear rise in her stomach. She steadied her breathing, listening to its rhythm inside her helmet. She moved with utmost care, watching the ladder come within inches of the edge, but steadying.

"She's out," said Cameron's voice in her helmet radio, reporting her progress. Then, to Dacey: "Okay, now you wanna move your ass, so I can get out too?"

"Jimmy!" she scolded.

"Oops, sorry." He remembered that nearly the entire population of his home planet was listening to him. "I *meant* to say, please translate your current position into one that is more amenable to my egress."

"Better," she allowed, pulling herself over the end of the ladder. She reached down and unlatched a hinged extension to the ladder that was made just for such exigencies. It swung down, hanging vertically beyond the sphere of the hole. She swung her legs out and managed to roll herself over so she could put her feet on the ladder, letting herself down to the ground. Trickles of sweat rolled down her temples, despite the suit's cooling system. The small refrigeration unit could barely keep up. The temperature measurements they made as they approached the planet read over a hundred and twenty degrees in the temperate zone, with a hundred percent humidity. Mullins warned that it would feel like taking a steam bath in a hurricane.

She made sure the fiber optic communication cable and tether leading back through the hole was unsnarled. The cable made her feel like little more than a walking space probe, feeding data to earth. She tried her footing in the knee-high tangle of plants with their leathery cylindrical leaves. She stumbled drunkenly before finding her balance. Hidden beneath the short, dense forest was a tangle of ankle-twisting roots that held tenaciously to the soil below. Despite the planet's lower gravity, she had to brace herself against winds that battered her suit so viciously she could barely stand. She held a brief conversation with Gerald, as they went over the exit checklist.

And now, keeping her feet wide apart for balance, she turned away from the hole, once more to the planet's vista. She tried to hold down her excitement, analyzing the landscape with her geologists' eyes.

They had chosen their landing spot well. While large swaths of the planet were reddish desert, they had landed in one of the large regions of living green nestled between seashore and mountains. There, life had flourished, protected from the most violent of the planet's constant winds, and watered by the evaporated moisture of the oceans captured as rain by the mountains. The sheltering mountains were not high, no doubt worn down by eons of wind erosion. But they offered shelter enough, and the thick green mass climbed partway up their gullied red slopes, as if entreating them to remain and give life.

"Whoa! Fantastic!" she heard Cameron exclaim. He'd come through the hole now. She looked up to see him reach the end of the ladder and drag the cylindrical case through behind him. He let himself down and pulled the case after. She helped him lower it to the ground. A howling gust of wind caught him and he staggered back, falling into the mass of vegetation. "Damn, these are vicious."

"The planetologists were dead right," said Dacey as she helped him up and they held on to one another while the gust died. "The planet had no moon to slow it down over its formation, so it kept spinning fast. That means these winds never let up."

"Also means the days are short," said Gerald's worried voice in her headset. "You've only got about five hours of daylight. Remember, only eight hours in a day. And you've only got three hours of air left."

Dacey smiled at Gerald's mothering, checked Cameron's cable and they both stepped away from the hovering, glimmering sphere, pulling cable out along with them. Cameron dragged along the black cylindrical case with their instruments and sampling equipment.

"What was that?" Cameron stopped, gripping her arm, steadying himself against the winds with the case.

"What?"

"Saw something out of the corner of my eye. Over there." He pointed to a small plant-encrusted rise. "Stand real still."

Abruptly, a leathery brown stalk popped up from the vegetation, then just as rapidly withdrew back into its depths.

"See it?"

"Yeah. Stay still."

"What do you see?" It was Gerald's voice.

"Something moving."

"Then get out. Get out now!"

"No. We're all right," said Dacey.

Another leathery stalk popped up nearby, then withdrew. Dacey could see now that it was forked at the top, with each branch ending in a large sphere.

"Animals!" She shouted. "Damn! Animals!"

"Like snakes?" asked Cameron. "I hate snakes."

The stalks *were* snakelike, but there was something about them that didn't suggest snakes.

"It's like they're part of something else," said Dacey. "Attached to something. Let's go see. Move slow."

By now the stalks were popping up all around them, dozens nearby and fewer farther out in the thick mass of green. Most withdrew, but a few remained extended, waving slightly in the blasts of wind. Dacey suddenly recognized the spherical appendages on the end.

"Jimmy, those are eyes on the end! *Whoops!*" She tripped and fell face forward. Cameron helped her up. Most of the nearby stalks had disappeared, accompanied by tumultuous rustling in the foliage as objects barreled away from them. Dacey found that she had tripped into a shallow trench of clear red dirt that cut through the foliage.

Cameron stepped down into the trench with her. "We got pathways here. These are pathways. Should we be in pathways?"

"Yeah, they're trenches made by the animals coming through. They allow the animals to move around without going through the vegetation and stay out of the—"

A dark round shape appeared in the trench about thirty feet away scrambling toward them. It stopped suddenly, dead still, its leathery skin making it look like an old, scuffed medicine ball come to life. After a moment, a branched stalk about four feet long unfolded from its front. The stalk was muscular and prehensile, like an elephant's trunk. On the end of each branch, large dark eyes blinked in tandem. And at the fork, two small, wrinkled holes opened wide, sniffing the air. Above each eye jutted a kind of large silvery structure that looked something like a bicycle reflector. No sound could be heard over the steady roar of the wind.

"It's a proboscis," said Dacey into her microphone. "It's the animal's nose and eyes."

The creature tentatively shuffled closer, needing to come down the trail, but unsure of the tall creatures' intentions. As it advanced, they could see long taloned claws reach out from its low humplike body to pull it forward. It opened a wide mouth, perhaps in threat, perhaps in fear, to show large teeth and a thick rough black tongue.

"It doesn't look too damned friendly," said Cameron.

"See the teeth? Flat. For chewing vegetation. It's a browser. Not a predator. I think we're okay."

"Think? Think? Seriously? Not *know*?"

The animal folded back its proboscis into a protective slit along its back, leaving only the eyes peeking out. Its shyness winning over its need, it turned and bulled its way into the undergrowth, scrabbling with its large claws, and was gone. But then immediately, something else, something smaller and brown came scurrying along the trail. But before they could tell what it was, it turned and leaped into the thick bush itself.

"There's a regular zoo here," said Cameron.

"Yeah, well, I'd love to trap some of these things, but we should get about our business." Keeping watch for other creatures, they opened the black case and took out plastic bags and bottles, and began to gather samples of the plants and soil.

Periodically, they stopped, trying to catch sight of the source of a rustling in the brush or the flash of an animal scampering along the trail. Most of the varied creatures were a dull brown, although they showed glimpses of white, gray and reddish. Once Dacey glimpsed what could have been a small monkeylike creature, with bright eyes, long limbs and grasping fingers, but it pulled itself into the thicket of plants before she got a clear look at it.

During the gathering, they kept up a steady exchange with Gerald and Mullins, who pointedly announced their remaining air. George also cut in to comment on their elevated heart rate. Periodically, they would glance back for reassurance at the hovering sphere with the ladder extending from it.

They worked their way along the trail, dragging the umbilical, discovering an amazing variety in the vegetation. Green stalks of plants thrust upward, intertwined with the curled tendrils of vines that sought a way to penetrate the tangle. Almost all the plants had characteristic vertical cylindrical leaves. Dacey remembered enough college botany to theorize that the leaves would allow the plant to get the most energy from the rapidly moving sun, as well as extend themselves up sturdily into the wind without being beaten to tatters.

They tore their way beneath the covering of leaves to find the thick intertwined trunks of the vines with tough roots that searched for a hold in any fissure in the rock. They unearthed small passages burrowed in the thick undergrowth, no doubt the animals' tunneled side paths leading off the main open trail on which they stood.

As they worked, occasional breaks in the scudding clouds brought the intense sun, with a different angle of shadow each time, reminding them how rapidly the sun was inscribing its arc across the sky. They cursed those moments of sunlight, because the sun's relentless assault made their profusely sweating bodies even hotter.

Next, they pulled themselves out of the depression of the trail to stumble out across the tangled mass of vegetation to gather more samples. Now, the leathery stalks were popping up curiously everywhere, their goggle-eyes scrutinizing the strange vertical creatures in white suits, the animal's reflectors gleaming in the light. But the animals didn't as quickly withdraw now. The grazers were becoming more used to the humans' lumbering presence.

Cameron felt the yank on his cable first, because he was the farthest from the hole.

"What the hell was that?"

"We've got a problem," came Gerald's voice. "Get back immediately!"

"What?" asked Dacey, but as she turned toward Cameron, she was dragged off her feet bumping and sliding along the tops of the vegetation.

"The hole's shifting!" Cameron had grabbed his cable and was trying to pull himself hand over hand toward the sphere. Dacey twisted her body around to see the sphere drifting inexorably away across the landscape. It abruptly dipped into the planet's surface, gouging out a large chunk of green vegetation and red soil. Dacey and Cameron slammed into one another as they were dragged, trying to grab each other for support. They tumbled into the depression and through the red dirt and were dragged back out again by the moving hole.

"We've got a magnetic storm!" shouted Gerald in their helmet radios. "We should've known! The planet's spin! It's core is unstable, so the magnetic fields change. We can't—"

But the rest was lost as the sphere swooped upward, wobbling and spiraling, its infinitely sharp edge slicing away the framework and the ladder, which tumbled down onto the mat of vegetation. The severed ends of their cables fell like two long, black, undulating snakes onto the green mass.

Dacey managed to pull herself up, bracing herself against the punishing wind. Cameron followed and they peered through sweat-clouded eyes into the darkening sky for some sign of the hole. They tore away the vines and plants that had tangled themselves around the suits. They looked at each other frightened, their faces in deepening shadow. Each saw in the other's eyes the realization.

They were marooned.

CHAPTER 36

Gerald didn't look at Mullins as he asked the engineer. "Can you get back to the planet?" He was afraid that to remove his gaze from the computer screens would somehow allow the hole to close. He simply put away any thought of the consequences. He wanted so badly to run out of the blockhouse, leap into a vehicle, race to the distant chamber and try with some force of will to make the hole return to the planet.

"Got to profile the natural magnetic fields," said Mullins resolutely. "We get a measure, we can goose the propulsion fields on the hole and fight 'em. It's like we're on a sailboat and we hit our first hurricane. We got to learn how to sail in a hurricane." Mullins tapped out commands on his keyboard and mumbled instructions into his microphone.

Behind him, Megamag engineers crowded together, urgently working out magnetic vectors, power densities, coil strengths. They knew that their calculations would determine whether two people would live or die.

Two of the large video screens were blank where once had been scenes from Dacey's and Cameron's helmets. Another showed the inside of the vacuum chamber littered with chunks of alien dirt and vegetation that hadn't been sucked out when the hole was flung into space by the swirling magnetic storm.

The three metal serpents hovered around the hole, but this time their cylindrical heads were clustered together, the fields they emitted combined to force the hole back toward the planet. The three screens showing the views from their cameras all revealed the same frustrating picture of the small planet, as it continued to recede.

"Do it, Andy," said Gerald, almost to himself. "Do it."

●　●　●

"Night's gonna be a bitch," said Cameron, pawing through the contents of the case in the growing gloom. They had dragged it down into the gouge in the earth left by the sphere, to give themselves some shelter from the wind. Several plastic bags caught the wind and sailed away across the low vegetation. "Can't see shit. There's no moon."

"Yeah, it'll be dark as a wolf's throat," said Dacey. "But that'll be good. We've got lights. They'll be able to find us with no problem. C'mere." Cameron groped his way over to her and she reached out to his sleeve and clicked on a switch. A small red light on a box strapped to his arm began to blink. "Now we've both got our radio beacons on. They'll be back."

She set her jaw and intently scanned the alien landscape, memorizing it for later recall when they needed food, water or shelter. Just this kind of possibility was a big reason she'd insisted that she be the one who made this exploration. She'd been in field situations before where her life was on the line. Certainly she'd encountered nothing so deeply frightening as this alien jungle, and she could feel herself on the edge of panic. But she was certain she had enough courage in her to get through this. She knew Cameron did, too. He was irreverent, but she knew that the attitude was protective. He'd grown up where toughness was necessary and it was necessary here.

"Yeah, they'll be back," was all Cameron said, as he dug the two flashlights out of the case and handed one to Dacey.

Both decided privately that they would avoid any thought that the hole would not return; that they would be stuck here until they died or went mad. They busily tried out the flashlights, but decided to save the batteries until it was really dark.

The darkness came, falling like some immense black weight, and they sat in the depression, holding onto one another in the gale. They heard a vaguely familiar low rumble; then a flash of light from the sky. For an instant, Dacey thought it might be the hole returning, but a jagged brilliant lightning bolt slashed across the sky.

"Might as well save the lights now, too," said Cameron. "Looks like rain."

Another blinding flash of lightning was followed by a massive, shuddering jolt of thunder, and sheets of rain pummeled them, blown by the unrelenting winds. They huddled together, peering at the sky as a lightning bolt struck a nearby peak, dancing around it like an incandescent demon.

A beeping rose in Dacey's helmet. At first, its meaning didn't register, she was so overwhelmed by the tumult around her. Then she realized.

"We're out of oxygen!" In the flash of a lightning bolt, she saw Cameron's helmet nod in agreement. "We gotta take these helmets off."

"Oh, hell no!" exclaimed Cameron. "We don't know about viruses, bacteria—"

"AHHH SCREW IT!" shouted Dacey over the howling wind and crash of thunder. In the silver-white light from another lightning flash, Cameron saw her unlatch her helmet, twist it a quarter-turn and yank it off. He switched on his flashlight and aimed it at her face, to detect any reaction to toxic air. As the blinding rain pelted her skin, she registered nothing at first. She took a deep breath, and tried to clear her eyes of water. Cameron stared at her. Was this a last breath? For him, too?

Finally, she gave a thumbs-up. "Wind's taking my breath away. Rain's a killer. But I can breathe!" she shouted, rainwater spewing off her lips as she talked. "I figured as much. We knew there was oxygen. The animals can breathe."

Cameron jerked off his own helmet and immediately suffered the painful sting of the wind-driven rain. He could barely see through the gush of warm water cascading down his face. He breathed in a wet, rich, organic smell.

They sat for a while blinded, gasping for breath. The rain made them realize that they were dehydrated from the hours in the suits. So they turned their faces into the wind and opened their mouths, blindly trying to gulp in as much of it as they could.

"Know what?" Cameron managed to shout over the deluge, between drinks.

"What?"

"Nature sucks, don't matter what universe you're in!"

She took his arm and managed a smile. The rain let up after a while, only occasional drops striking their skin like liquid bullets. Then the storm was gone and only the wind remained tearing at them. But now the steamy, smothering heat reasserted itself, and they realized that, even with the gulps of water from the rain, their bodies were still badly dehydrated and becoming more so with the heat. They shone the lights into the bottom of the depression, but the rainwater there was scummy and full of vegetation. Dacey waved her hand in rejection.

"Let's go find a stream," she shouted. "Gotta be streams here. We just follow the trail. They'll see us by our lights and trace the beacons, no matter where we go." Her field experience told her, whether it was Earth or an alien planet, to listen to her body and to take in the information from the terrain. They both stood up out of the depression, squinting into the distance.

"Well, shit!" said Cameron in amazement. "So much for the flashlights."

They looked out across a landscape of glimmering, weaving points of incandescent color that reached as far as they could see. The lights cast a pale glow that lit the foliage of the low alien jungle.

"What do you think it is?" panted Cameron in the wind. "Christmas?"

Despite the suffocating heat enwrapping them, Dacey forgot their plight for a moment, mesmerized by the stunning otherworldly beauty.

"Bioluminescence."

"Like fireflies?"

"Yeah, only these aren't insects."

"They're signaling."

"Right. Like mating calls, territorial calls, whatever. I guess sound won't work for communicating because of the winds. Smell won't work either because of the winds. So they evolved this." After a while, she could distinguish two different kinds of light. One seemed to be elaborately blinking lights coming from the stalks of the grazing animals, specifically from the silvery structures above their eyes. The other source was the centers of the cylindrical leaves, which emitted a steady colored glow that seemed to be the equivalent of colored pigments in flowers.

"The plant lights maybe attract the equivalent of bees," said Cameron. He paused and pointed out across the landscape. "Like them." Sure enough, even in the high winds, dark flickers of wings hovered around the glowing plants, clinging to them, entering them to feed.

Dacey suddenly slumped down on a mat of vegetation, keeling forward. "We've got to get these suits off," she gasped. "We'll die from the heat."

She recovered and helped Cameron unfasten his space suit and shed it. Then he turned and did the same for her, and they sat panting in the lashing winds, in shorts, t-shirts and socks, the pale light revealing their exhausted faces. They removed the suits' homing beacons and strapped them around their wrists.

"Hell, I figured this would be a nice little walk, a couple of hours in the suit," said Cameron. "We'd pick up dirt samples, never have to deal with the outside."

"Guess you figured wrong, Jimmy. Think of it as something you'll tell your grandchildren."

"I'd rather tell them about a good meal in a nice restaurant."

"Now, we need water," Dacey managed to whisper hoarsely over the roar. The hot steamy blast of the wind was so unrelenting, so mind-numbing. It tore at her will.

But she took a deep breath and hauled herself up, helping Cameron. Holding hands, they picked their way over the thicket, which caught at their legs and gave only precarious, ankle-twisting footing. They reached one of the sunken animal paths and stumbled down into it.

Seeking a stream, they started along the path, lit by the surrounding glow of the plants and animals. The path skirted a low hill and seemed to head downward toward one of the gullies. Periodically, a gust of wind would tear at them, throwing them off balance, but it offered no relief. Dacey felt the dry mouth of heat prostration overcoming her. Dark shapes would suddenly appear out of the bush, only to skitter away at their approach. They rounded a bend to see one of the grazers holding its proboscis high, the structures above its eyes glowing with light, waving the appendage back and forth in some semaphore of its species.

Abruptly, the lights all extinguished, leaving them in total darkness.

"Jesus, now what?" asked Cameron.

"Let's put the lights on," said Dacey.

"Wait a second. Something don't feel right."

Even over the deafening hiss of the winds through the foliage, they could hear the high-pitched squeaking ahead. A roiling mass of dark forms cascaded toward them, and suddenly they were covered in small, wiry creatures with sharp claws digging into their skin, tearing at their faces, drawing blood.

Dacey screamed and flailed at them, but they clung fast, wrapping themselves around her neck and clinging to her arms. They burrowed beneath her clothes and she could feel them pulling themselves up between her legs and into her armpits. They were like spiders or insects, but they had small dark eyes that seemed like those of a rat. She smelled a kind of musky odor from their fetid little bodies.

"MOTHERFUCKER!" she heard Cameron yell and glimpsed him flailing at the creatures.

A light appeared, like a spotlight, bathing them in radiance. She frantically pulled one of the creatures away from her face, to try and see. The beam came from some animal, large and hulking and low to the ground, that had appeared on the trail advancing toward them. It swung its light beam back and forth on the ground.

"JESUS!" Cameron was still tearing at the creatures. His body now a writhing mass of the dark leathery animals. He staggered back, trying to hold his balance, not wanting to go down. "PULL THEM OFF! PULL THE GODDAMNED THINGS OFF!"

"No! Wait a minute! Lay down!" shouted Dacey.

"What? We do that, we're dead!"

"No. Lay down! Watch!" With some difficulty because of the welter of clinging animals, she knelt, then lay down across the trail. The creatures abruptly began to disengage themselves and skitter away. The predator pinpointed one with its light, snatching it up in powerful jaws and tearing its body apart with its claws, devouring it. Dark blood ran down the mouth, which it licked with a long curling tongue.

Cameron quickly lay down himself, and the animals began to desert his body, bolting down the trail and into the underbrush.

The predator approached Dacey's prone body, playing its light over her scratched and bleeding skin. Turning her head to peer up at the animal, she could see that the creature's light was mounted on the end of a stubby appendage right behind the one that supported its large eyes. She remained absolutely still. It sniffed her and backed away snorting, as if it had smelled something repulsive. It swung its light toward the bush, where one of the small creatures was searching frantically for an entrance into the safe undergrowth. It lunged, and there was a frightened squeal. Chewing away at the struggling prey, the predator scuttled away after the others.

"What was that . . ." Cameron couldn't finish. He tried again. ". . . what the hell was *that* about?"

"They didn't want to hurt us. They wanted to get away. We were like a big tall tree. That thing was after them. We were just convenient."

"And the light. The thing had a natural searchlight."

"Yeah, that's what made me realize what was happening. When I was doing field work in Louisiana, we went out frog gigging along a bayou. We used a searchlight. Just like it did."

They rested for a moment, then their extreme thirst re-exerting itself, staggered to their feet and continued down the trail. The scalding wind brought the sounds of animals all about them, but the lights came back on, so they felt safe. Soon they heard rushing water and came upon a stream. Without thought of what else might be at the water hole, they waded in. It was like a warm bath, but it cooled their overheated bodies. They gulped the water, tasting the tang of iron and other minerals. They sat down in the rushing stream, allowing it to bring them back to life.

It was darker here, so once he had recovered, Cameron switched on his light, playing it around. They were in a wide spot in the stream, which came gushing out of a canyon in the mountain above. It was swollen, no doubt by the nightly downpours.

"Y'know, I just figured it out," he shouted back over the low whistling sound the wind made through the canyon. "This whole thing isn't much more dangerous than walkin' through Watts on Saturday night. I grew up there, and some of the low-lifes there are worse than these low-slung motherfuckers with the eyeballs."

Dacey lay back in the warm water, taking another drink. She could feel stinging all over her body from the cuts.

Cameron waded upstream and shone his light around. His white shorts and undershirt seemed to float in mid air, because his dark body was invisible in the blackness.

A high-pitched shriek rose above them, and he shone his light upward. His beam was immediately answered by another larger one that lit his entire glistening body and a circle of rushing brown water around him. For an instant, Dacey thought it might be a helicopter; the light was the same. But she saw a huge dark animate form descend toward Cameron.

Cameron shouted in alarm and struck out with his flashlight as the shape hovered over him, spreading leviathan wings. Dacey leaped up and waded toward him, but a large leathery wing knocked her over, and she was underwater being carried downstream. She struggled back to her feet, her head breaking the surface to hear Cameron screaming.

"NO!" she bellowed. "NO!" She struggled forward to the flailing dark forms and found a hold on the creature's back and swung the flashlight with all her might, finding bone. She swung again and again. The huge flying creature was rising, its massive wings beating, its lungs making deep whooshing sounds, and she knew it was powerful enough to carry Cameron away. The animal's broad wings caught the wind and she felt it lifting him.

A blinding light struck them all, more brilliant than she could imagine. She shut her eyes against it, her hand losing its grip on the creature, which kicked her with a powerful hind limb. She sprawled back onto the shore. There was a roar of animal pain from directly above and she felt a hot sticky liquid covering her. She was aware of the hole hovering overhead. Its lethal edge had worked in their favor!

A chunk of what felt like internal organ struck her shoulder and slithered off. She heard a splash nearby and a moan, but still she could not open her eyes to the blinding light.

"Dacey!" The voice from above was Gerald's. She felt a gloved hand on her bare arm.

"Jimmy," she panted. "Where's Jimmy?"

"We're getting him. Just come on." She felt the rung of a ladder and drew from the last reserves of her strength to pull herself up. She felt the framework around her, and hands pulling her into a stillness she had forgotten was possible. She was in the chamber, her ears still roaring from the wind. She opened her eyes and saw two space suited figures taking her arms and helping her toward the airlock. She resisted, turning to make sure Cameron had made it, too. Sure enough, a third suited figure was helping him climb down the ladder and through the hole. The suited figure clasped his glove tightly on Cameron's shoulder, blood dripping from it. Dacey wriggled free and directed the two with her to take Cameron into the airlock first. They did, and one returned for her.

"We've got you, Dacey. You're back."

She saw Gerald's smiling face through the faceplate. She allowed herself to sink into the enfolding arms.

CHAPTER 37

In the void beyond the Earth's moon, there was at first absolute stillness. Then a swirl of faint luminescence signaled a change in the fabric of space-time. Starlight shimmered and warped as it passed through the small region. The magnetic field of Earth encouraged the weakness to blossom into a tiny passage. The passage opened, became a spherical hole. But a profound strangeness existed on the other side.

No stars showed through, but anti-stars. No planets, but anti-planets. No galaxies, but anti-galaxies. A tiny mote of the anti-matter found its way through the hole and touched a minute speck of its counterpart matter. A massive explosion launched waves of intense radiation streaming into space, heralding the arrival of the new, deadly visitor.

· · ·

Although the isolation mask covered Gerald's mouth, Dacey could tell his expression from the eyes. She'd become used to reading his eyes when he'd had his beard. He was grinning like an idiot, which told her that she was going to be fine. She had just opened her eyes from a deep sleep, thanks to the tranquilizer. The intravenous tube was still in her arm, dripping in a saline solution to hydrate her and antibiotics for any possible infections. The bandages were still on her arms where the animals had torn her skin. She could feel the tug of the tape elsewhere on her body when she shifted, but the painkillers had done their work well.

George, also masked and gowned in isolation garb, held her left hand gently, checking the status of the IV needle. She knew it was just an excuse to hold her hand. The old dear had been fussing over her since she was brought in. He'd called in some old favors, and she and Cameron had been examined by some of the best infectious disease specialists in the country.

"You look like a happy camper," she said woozily to Gerald, smiling up at him from the bed. She brushed a stray hair from her forehead. "Too bad you can't take that mask off and give us a kiss."

He took her other hand in his, and without looking, she could tell it was rubber-gloved, as was George's.

George finished his check, patted her hand and laid it on the sheet. "The people from the Centers for Disease Control said thirty days' isolation. No arguments or they shut us down. There's a gentleman here now checking us out."

"Yeah, but is he listening to the exobiologists?" She turned to Gerald. "They've said the chances of some alien bug infecting a human are essentially zero. Different evolution; different biochemistry."

"I'm working on them to get you time off for good behavior," said George. He patted her hand one more time and then ambled out of the room.

"Hey, I just got good news," she pressed the button to bring the motorized bed up more to a sitting position. "My chairman at the university called. I've been made a full professor."

"So, the trip was worth it?" asked Gerald

Her face grew sober with the memory. "How's Jimmy?"

"He's awake. Lost a lot of blood, but George says he's okay. Want to see him?"

She nodded and swung her legs over the side of the bed, revealing more bandages. She stood, feeling slightly dizzy from the effort, and Gerald held her arm. He helped her with her robe and she rolled her IV stand into the connecting room of the base infirmary. The two rooms had been sealed from the outside world by an army biowarfare team and certified by the CDC. But since Dacey and Cameron shared whatever germs they'd picked up on the planet, they were allowed to see each other without isolation garb.

Cameron lay on the bed, his thin dark arms resting limply on the white sheet that covered him. A large bandage enwrapped his shoulder and another obscured half his face. George and another doctor, a tall balding man with an easy manner, had just finished an examination of him and were stepping into a plastic chamber outside the room to be disinfected.

Beside Cameron's bed sat a slim black woman wearing the same blue isolation cap, gown and gloves as Gerald. She had dark almond eyes that were puffy from weeping. She looked up, but didn't leave his side.

"Phyllis, how's he doing?"

Cameron opened his eyes and answered. "I figured out my revenge," he mumbled. "I'm going to eat chicken every day for the rest of my life." Dacey laughed, which only spurred him on. "I guess we showed that bird, or whatever the hell it was, not to try dark meat."

Phyllis tossed her head and rolled her eyes in mock exasperation. "God, Jimmy, you just never give up, do you?"

"No, he doesn't, thank God," Dacey moved her IV stand up near him and sat down tiredly in the chair on the other side of the bed.

"Only thing I wish is that we brought back those samples," said Cameron.

"I was waiting for you to wake up and tell you," Dacey straightened up, color returning to her cheeks. "We got bunches of samples."

"How's that?"

"Well, remember when the hole scooped up that dirt? Then we got some good soil and vegetation samples."

"Outstanding!"

"And remember when the hole sliced the bird . . . or whatever it was? They found body parts in the chamber. Tissue samples, parts of organs, stomach contents. It's all a little mixed up, but it'll keep zoologists busy for a long damned time."

"Excellent! We'll go back. We can go back. How's the hole?" The news was having the desired effect. Cameron was returning to his old self.

"Stable," said Gerald. "I just came from the control room. The fields are holding it open. When they're steady, it's fine. It almost . . ."

he stopped. No use bringing up the fact that the hole had almost closed. They could see Cameron's eyelids beginning to grow heavy, so Dacey kissed him and hugged Phyllis, and they prepared to leave.

"Say . . ." Cameron opened one eye. "If you see Calvin, give him the bad news. Tell him I'm gonna be okay. That'll make his day."

Dacey gave him a brow-knitted, scolding smile and shook her head. Back in her room, Gerald helped her into bed, but stood there for a moment without saying anything. Again, she could read his eyes, the awkward stance of his body.

"What's up? What's happened?"

"I guess I should tell you. Yesterday, just after we got you back, we got a report from NASA. They've detected another gamma ray burst. Intense and close."

"What from?"

"An antimatter hole."

"In the solar system?"

"Worse. Near earth. They also got an optical flash that gave them a location. It appears to have been spawned by earth's magnetic tail. It's being drawn toward earth, coming up along the field lines."

"Jesus. Oh God." She lay back in the bed, feeling a shudder run through her. "You were right. They wouldn't listen."

"I shouldn't have told you now."

"What are you going to do?"

"We don't know. We know magnetic fields open these holes up. We know energy or magnetic fluctuations somehow close them. But we don't know enough. We're inviting everybody here to talk." He sat down on her bed, his body slumping with fatigue. "We just don't know enough."

* * *

Dacey spent the next few days watching television, frustrated at not being able to help with the massive mobilization of scientific talent the news reported. All the networks had preempted programming to cover the approach of the "anti-hole." They followed every detail of the events. She saw aerial shots of dozens of planes with markings from as many countries lining the sprawling runway of the Deus base. She watched the live coverage of the hastily-called symposium in one of the hangars. After a greeting by satellite from a somber president, the world's leading physicists spoke of the immense danger from the anti-hole and their attempts to devise some way to stop it. On large video screens in the hangar, Chinese scientists also conferred via satellite, in halting English revealing the data on their captured hole, hoping that the combined information would yield some insight.

And in the middle of it all was Gerald, whose warnings were now seen as tragically accurate. In the news conferences, his grim, drawn face revealed that he had conceived of no possible way to avert the approaching hole.

The words that the scientists used horrified the world. They warned of cataclysm, Armageddon, the end of life, the end of Earth.

The cameras roamed the globe capturing the effects of the news. They panned across vast crowds of Muslims gathered in Mecca, of Catholics at the Vatican, of Jews in Jerusalem, of congregations gathered in football stadiums across America. All raised their voices in prayer for deliverance from the approaching celestial monster. Still others claimed the anti-hole was divine retribution for mankind's sins, or the final triumph of Satan.

The cameras showed the riots, bloody desperate acts by people who had no outlet for their fear other than violence against those around them. They showed people sprawled in the street, dead of bullet wounds, rifles clutched in their hands.

Others took action against the hole, however irrational. In India, troops killed dozens of people storming a missile base, trying against all logic to commandeer a missile to launch at the anti-hole. In Russia, mobs ransacked the archives of the Soviet Academy of Sciences, when a rumor spread that secret data stored there revealed the hole to be an old Soviet weapon.

At the Deus base, cameras showed the arrival of army troops and tanks to guard against the possibility of riots by the crowds in the sprawling encampment that had grown outside the base perimeter. The television reporters interviewed the desperate people, who lined the fence in hopes that somehow being near the scientists would save them. Some demanded that they be allowed to enter the other universe to safety. Others charged that one hole had attracted the other, and that the whole thing was some sinister plot among the scientists.

And most frightening of all, the cameras showed telescope images of the brilliant flashes in the night sky that marked anti-matter emerging from the hole to meet matter in an explosive embrace. The blasts emitted a vicious cascade of gamma rays, fortunately stopped by the earth's upper atmosphere.

The flashes were growing brighter as the hole approached. Now they were as bright as Venus. Soon they would be as bright as the moon, then blinding. Then deadly.

Throughout, the cameras showed the scientists debating, sometimes angrily, over how to stop the anti-hole. But they were in bleak agreement about its future. Unless by some miracle the anti-hole closed, they grimly concluded, it would catch up to Earth. And almost inevitably, the hole would encounter the anti-world or anti-star that had opened it on the other side. The lethal anti-matter would spew through into this universe, meeting matter; and the titanic explosion would at the very least devastate Earth, but most likely would vaporize it.

As the data grew to a mountainous confirmation of the menace, Gerald tortured himself with the belief that there existed an answer somewhere in the mass of information. If only he were smart enough; if only he worked hard enough, he would find it. He visited Dacey in the hospital as often as he could. She needed the visits, but he needed them more, as if merely holding her hand gave him a resolve to continue.

Then on the fourth night, he appeared at her bedside in the darkness. She was immersed in a deep sleep, but since she had begun refusing her sleeping pills, she came instantly awake at the touch of his hand on her shoulder. He wore no mask when he leaned down and whispered into her ear.

"I need you."

She knew immediately it was not the whisper of a man needing a woman. It was the urgent whisper of a man in the grip of an idea.

"Why? What's going on?"

"I've had an idea! Andy thinks it'll work. We'll need everybody to convince Calvin, though. You seem to have some pull with him. Are you okay?"

"Hell, I've been okay! I want to get out of here." She rolled out of bed, found the clothes that had been brought for her, slipped off her hospital gown and began putting them on. "There's a problem, though. There's a guard outside, just in case Jimmy or I get antsy."

Gerald stopped, pondering about what to do next. The guard had readily allowed him in as a visitor, but in his excitement, he hadn't even considered the problem of getting Dacey out. But she needed only the time it required to finish buttoning her shirt and fastening her jeans to come up with a solution. She slipped on her sneakers and quickly tied them, then gestured for Gerald to remain in her room. She slipped through the connecting door to Cameron's room. Within a minute she was back. She quickly rolled up spare blankets and stuffed them under the bedsheet to give a semblance of a sleeping form. She motioned for him to follow her to the door leading to the hall. She stood there in silence, bobbing her head in a rhythmic counting of seconds, her long hair swaying with each count. Then she stopped.

A blood-curdling scream erupted from the next room shattering the nighttime quiet. Dacey listened at the hall door for a response. She smiled at the sound of the guard and the nurses rushing into Cameron's room.

"Jimmy's a great actor," she whispered.

They slipped into the hallway of the old infirmary and hurried away to the rusty metal staircase down to the wooden door and out into the desert night. Dacey felt the remaining bandages on her legs pull as she ran, but otherwise, she felt fine.

They had jogged about a quarter mile, and the lights of the infirmary had receded far enough so that they could stop. They stood in the still desert, the breeze playing about them, the glow of the massive public encampment in the distance.

But they were far from alone. The scientists, engineers and technicians from the base were scattered across the desert in shadowy groups beyond the lights of the buildings, as a three-quarter-moon rose in the sky. But they ignored the moon. Like billions of other humans who stood in the darkness each night watching the heavens and praying, they saw only the moon's savage new rival.

She had only seen the anti-hole on television before, because she was isolated in the infirmary.

It was like a malevolent gleaming eye floating in the black sky. She hadn't realized the gut-level fear that it could arouse.

"My God," was all she could say, and Gerald put his arm around her in answer.

The huge sphere was the antithesis of the constant moon. Its light was tauntingly capricious. When a bit of antimatter from the hole touched matter, the sphere would erupt a flaming burst of swirling colored light that surged into space. A moment later, the Earth would answer with a curtain of undulating colored auroral light, as the subatomic particles from the eruption streamed down the Earth's magnetic field lines onto the planet's poles.

But then the sphere would settle into an almost cunning quiet, like a lurking animal giving its prey a false sense of security. Then it would burst forth with another eruption, as if to reassert its domination.

"We've got maybe a few days," said Gerald quietly. "The gamma rays are getting powerful enough to begin to penetrate the atmosphere. And the eruptions are more frequent."

"You think its approaching something on the other side?"

"Yes. Maybe a planet. We don't know. But there's more matter coming through now." He gestured at the anti-hole. "And this is small stuff, the size of dust particles. When the big stuff starts coming through . . . well, that's it."

After a few moments, she remembered that he had gotten her out of the infirmary for a reason.

"Okay, tell me. What do you need me for?"

"You can talk to Calvin. We need you to help persuade him."

"About what?"

"We're going through to the other side with equipment so we can fly the hole from there. From the other universe. We're going to fly it to the anti-hole. We're going to collide them."

CHAPTER 38

"Hell no!" Lambert stood up to leave the briefing room, as did Van Alston, who carefully smoothed his suit coat and stowed his laptop in a briefcase full of papers. "I'm not even gonna listen to this bullshit."

"Calvin, it's the only way," said Gerald, his voice calm in an attempt to evolve the discussion from anger to reason.

"Maybe the damned hole will close. Maybe we make the Chinese use their hole. If you even think about doing this, I'll get the generals to commandeer the vacuum chamber; you won't have a chance." In response, Van Alston had pulled out his phone, preparing to call the appropriate numbers.

"Look, the Chinese have only made one entry into the universe on the other side of their hole. They don't have the equipment or the expertise. They're not even sure they can steer theirs precisely enough. And the anti-hole is getting too close. It doesn't show any sign of closing."

Gerald pressed a key to bring up on the display screen the latest telescope image of Neptune—or rather the shattered pieces of what once had been a whole planet. The image showed only a few separate points of reflected light, but it portrayed a planetary disaster well enough.

"This is the best-case scenario of what's going to happen," Gerald said. "The worst is that the whole solar system goes."

"Fuck the solar system," growled Lambert, but he did not leave. Van Alston wavered between opening the door and sitting back down.

"Calvin, it's something we've got to try."

"And the missiles? What about the missiles?"

"Everybody's ruled that out. A nuclear missile might close the hole, but if it touched anti-matter . . ." Gerald shrugged his shoulders.

"Calvin," Dacey leaned forward at the table, looking him in the eyes. But she said nothing else for a long moment. Calvin glared at her, but he seemed to understand some unspoken communication between them. "Just listen to the full plan. Just listen to it, okay?"

Calvin sat back down, and Van Alston unpacked his laptop and also sat down against the wall. Gerald nodded to Mullins, who typed commands into his laptop bringing up an image on the display screen. It was of the familiar oval depicting a wormhole.

"Okay, here's the deal. We go through to the other side with an electromagnet array attached to a computer and steer the thing around in this universe." He drew a set of radiating lines around the oval. "We've figured out how to surround the hole with electromagnetic steering probes. We're working on how to seal off the hole on the other side . . . like with some kind of cover . . . so when it leaves the vacuum chamber here it doesn't suck everything up."

Mullins turned to gauge the effect of his talk on Lambert. He saw only the same glower as before. He turned around and sketched a larger circle around the smaller one.

"We're pretty sure we can assemble a big spherical chamber surrounding the hole on the other side. Like thirty feet across. It'll have the steering probes sticking down toward the hole from the inside. We make it from two hemispheres of Vectran. Twice as tough as Kevlar. Fold it up, put it through the hole."

"But the damn thing's not rigid."

Mullins grinned and drew another slightly larger circle around the other two. "Yeah, well, doesn't need to be. We let pressure into the vacuum chamber, it'll be stiff like a balloon."

"Balloons pop."

Gerald stepped forward. "Not this one. And it won't need to be fully rigid in outer space. We'll include carbon-fiber ribs, so the shell will hold its shape when there's vacuum on both sides. Like an umbrella. The steering probes are mounted on the inside of the ribs. So, we attached a control unit with a power pack and a computer, and I can control the magnetic field to fly it from there. I'll be outside the chamber on the other side, guiding it toward the anti-hole in this universe."

"What about the lasers? Don't you need the lasers to keep the junk out there from putting a hole in your little balloon?"

Mullins paused, his round face showing frustration. Lambert had astutely revealed a critical flaw in their plan.

"Yeah, we can't haul the lasers through. We'll just have to hope we don't hit anything."

"*Hope. Jesus,*" said Lambert disgustedly. "And you're telling me when these two things . . . these holes . . . come together . . ."

"We get a sort of dimensional short-circuit. At least I think so."

"You *think* so," spat Lambert. "What bullshit!"

"When the two holes meet, it'll be like a couple of soap bubbles merging, but they'll connect the other two universes to one another and bypass ours."

"And so you're out there—"

"*We're* out there," said Gaston, who had remained silent until now. "It'll take two people to assemble all this equipment. Two experienced people." Gaston looked steadily at Gerald, who smiled slightly and nodded in thanks.

Lambert shrugged and waved his hands dismissively. "So you two are out there stuck in the other universe going to this anti-hole where this anti-matter crap is coming through. And even if you get back you're about a hundred thousand miles from Earth." The last words were uttered with a subtle catch in Lambert's throat, but only Dacey seemed to notice. She shot a knowing glance at him that he returned as a warning sideways glare.

"We have a lifeboat," Gerald continued. "Andy's people have made a cylindrical chamber that we can both climb into. It'll have oxygen for two for twelve hours. It'll have a small booster engine and a computer to aim and fire it to bring us back into low earth orbit. Just before the holes collide, we enter the shell and pull the lifeboat through to this universe. We get into the lifeboat, seal it up, and let the computer fire off the engine, and we're safely away from the holes before they collide. And there's a NASA Soyuz spacecraft on the launch pad right now. They've agreed to alter its mission and pick us up."

"Well, you don't have the stuff built, anyway."

"We do . . . mostly," said Andy, leaning back in his chair. "We started when Gerald first came up with the idea of flying a hole from the other side. Got a couple of sets of the equipment built already. All off-the-shelf. The company that makes inflatable space modules had leakproof seals and clamps. The lifeboats are missile casings. The retro engines are spare steering jets from an old Space Shuttle."

"But it's not tested."

Mullins' expression grew somber, the animated excitement disappearing from his face. "No, it's not tested."

"Sounds like a plan with lots more ways to fail and die than to succeed and live."

"Calvin, look, it's the only way," said Dacey. "You know that."

"Has Cohen seen this plan?"

"We presented it to all the scientists this afternoon," said Gerald.

"What did Cohen say?"

"He said he didn't have any better ideas."

Lambert stared at Gerald, then at Dacey, then at the display screen. He stood up, his face an impassive mask. "Fine, then. Then do it." But before anybody could answer, he was out the door, leaving Van Alston still sitting in the corner, his briefcase on his lap.

CHAPTER 39

The feel of her soft touch on his cheek, of the last quick but meaningful kiss, lingered after Gerald put on the helmet. It was a gratifying memory to carry with him. Gaston stood outside the hangar door in his suit, holding his helmet at his side, watching the Humvee speed away. His husband, Wayne, had come to be with him, but the slim, bearded, middle-aged man couldn't bear to watch his partner of twenty years step into the airlock.

Gaston came back into the cooler shade of the hangar out of the desert sun, his face serene, as it had been since their first entry through the hole. He strode across the broad concrete floor of the hangar to the dressing area and allowed the Deus engineer to help him put on his helmet.

The engineers examined the suits more meticulously than ever before. And they had Gerald and Gaston press buttons on small control panels on their chest to test-fire maneuvering jets on new backpacks. It was an unpracticed act. They'd used the maneuvering backpacks on only a single other foray through the hole. They needed to maneuver this time, because now they would have to float free in space. They couldn't risk tangling themselves in a tether among the complex collection of equipment that would be floating with them. Now, however, they would risk the danger of a wrong kick or a jet misfire sending them careening away into the alien space of the other universe.

The engineers finally finished their checkout, and the comforting hiss of flowing oxygen filled Gerald's ears. They both stood for a moment and looked through their faceplates at the huge metal vacuum chamber, its surface patched here and there from the impact of space debris.

With a last hug, Dacey was gone, sliding into the Humvee and following the last vanload of engineers across the desert into the distance. She didn't look back, but that was her way. He knew that her prayers were with him.

They almost automatically went through the ritual of stepping clumsily into the small airlock, manipulating its controls, hearing the faint hiss as it evacuated, and opening the heavy steel door within. The hole floated as usual in the middle of the chamber, still trapped by magnetic fields. How incredible, thought Gerald, that this object had become usual to him.

He felt little fear. He had locked it away long ago, making it a prisoner of his will. In its place, he felt a profound sorrow rise within him. Soon, the incredible universe visible through the hole would be lost forever to them. When this hole melded with the anti-hole, the dimensional short-circuit would bring a gush of anti-matter erupting into the other universe. And into the other solar system that was a tiny part of it. Perhaps the anti-hole would close before too much damage was done. But perhaps it would destroy the bright young sun they had orbited and the beautiful wind-whipped planet with its strange, hardy animals. In either case, he would never know.

But it had to be. There was no other way. Soon the giant main doors of the vacuum chamber would open and they would pilot to its destruction the shimmering spherical hole that they had worked so hard to capture and hold.

As usual, they moved clumsily in the suits, checking the two large cylinders and two bundled fabric hemispheres that would be passed through the hole. Each package was ten feet long, four feet wide, and designed to pass through the protective framework and into the other universe.

The framework waited beneath the large star-filled black round-ness of the hole, its ladder jutting into the sphere, a faint luminescence playing about it.

Gerald checked with Mullins in the control room. The hole was stable and had been flown far out in the solar system of the other universe. There would be no nearby planets, moons or asteroids to endanger them during their mission. The long-necked magnetic serpents had done their job of propelling the hole, and then withdrawn to the corners of the vacuum chamber. Now, long poles had been mounted on their heads, like the tusks on a unicorn, that would come into use later.

Gerald placed one boot heavily on the ladder, pulling himself up. Then another and another, until he began to feel once more the lightness begin at his head and pass down his body, until he perched weightless on the end of the ladder in the other universe, holding himself with one hand. He pushed off and once more floated alone and infinitesimal in the immense void of the companion universe. He tried to avoid paying attention to the gleaming stars and incandescent whirlpool galaxies. Before, they would be mesmerizing. Now, they were only distractions. He pressed the buttons on his chest to produce tiny bursts of the jets to maneuver himself around to the other side of the hole. He felt a twinge of space sickness from the weightlessness, and a rising panic from being unsecured by the tether, but he determinedly fought both off.

He reached the other side of the sphere and saw Gaston standing above him now on the catwalk overlooking the hole. The sight was disconcerting. He still couldn't get used to the strange geometry of the holes. Gaston had the first cylinder suspended from a pulley over the hole. It swayed slightly, but he steadied it with a touch of his gloved hand.

"Ready?" It was Gaston's voice in his headset.

"Yes."

The cylinder began its journey downward, sliding through the hole. Gaston was obsessively careful. To nick this cylinder would end the mission immediately. It was their lifeboat, the titanium cylinder with the gimbaled rocket engine on one end.

The cylinder passed easily through as it became weightless. Gerald grabbed a handhold on its hull, detached the line and guided it away from the hole. The cylinder felt comfortingly solid in his hands. With a puff of propellant from his jet, he returned to the framework and guided another cylinder through—this one containing the computer and batteries that would power the electromagnetic probes. Then came the two bundles that would form the hemispheres. He felt his movements becoming more deft as he gained experience. He kept his breathing steady, controlled.

Gaston appeared through the other side of the hole, pulling himself up the ladder. They floated free together, holding onto one another in the black vastness, floating among the four white objects that would all have to work perfectly for their world to survive.

Gerald confirmed the successful passage to Mullins, and the three metal serpents came obediently to life, like jousting knights inserting the long poles mounted on their heads through the holes at widely divergent angles. The poles would prevent the shell from contacting the hole as they assembled it around the hole.

Gerald propelled himself over to one of the bundles and yanked a cord on it. It sprang open like an umbrella, forming a thirty-foot white hemisphere with metal probes studding its interior.

"Yes!" he whispered with satisfaction. He signaled to Gaston who did the same with the other bundle. It, too, blossomed instantly, and they drifted amidst the two huge white fabric hemispheres, examining them. The fabric was undamaged, as were the long electromagnetic propulsion probes sprouting from the carbon fiber ribs running along the inside.

"Okay, hold a second," they heard Mullins say in their headsets. "Hold there." He was studying the images from the cameras on the serpents' heads. "Yeah, good . . . good." He pronounced the structures sound. With delicate bursts from their jets, they brought the two hemispheres together, first attaching them at one point like a huge open clamshell. Now they were ready to close the shell over the hole, to seal it for its flight.

"You look like a couple of ballet dancers. Fat ones. But graceful." It was Dacey's voice, and Gerald allowed himself a smile.

It was brief. Once they closed the clamshell, there would be no more visual contact from the control room. The serpents' cameras would see only the inside of the shell. And Gerald and Gaston would have only radio contact through an antenna that they would plug into from outside.

A few puffs of propellant drifted them into position, each taking hold of one side of the clamshell and carefully closing it. The heat and light that had shone from the other side disappeared, and a merciless cold enveloped them. Now there was only pale starlight and a yellow gleam from a distant sun. The suit heaters came to life, but instantly lost ground to the hundred-degree-below-zero cold. Gerald felt his fingers growing numb, and flexed them vigorously to maintain circulation

The cold only emphasized the overwhelming loneliness. He paused, looking at Gaston for reassurance. Gaston put his hand on Gerald's shoulder. They were going to be all right.

They went to work switching on their helmet lights and circling the closed edges of the shell, latching the edges with cold fingers, forming an airtight seal. Occasionally, they could feel the gentle, saving bump of the shell drifting into one of the probes held by the serpents.

Finally, they checked the hatch in the side of the shell. This would be their escape route, through which they'd pass the lifeboat back into their universe. As they worked, Gerald could see the firm-jawed determination on Gaston's gaunt face. He'd managed to stow his fear as had Gerald. But perhaps there was a difference. Gaston was under a death sentence as Gerald was not. Gerald brought himself back to his work and plugged his helmet radio into the antenna port on the side of the shell.

"Put a little pressure on and let's see how it holds," he said.

"Okay . . . tenth of an atmosphere," he heard Mullins reply.

Even through his gloved hand, Gerald could feel the fabric skin tighten, as air was let into the vacuum chamber on the other side.

Gaston began to pull himself over every square inch of the thirty-foot sphere shell using hand straps on the surface, his helmet close to the fabric, examining it for leaks. Meanwhile, Gerald drifted over to the tethered cylinder containing the computer and batteries, shepherding it back and strapping it to the side of the sphere. The penetrating cold had become an implacable enemy, sucking the strength from his body, but he fought it with thoughts of his mission.

Gaston returned, giving him a thumbs-up. They opened a panel in the cylinder's side to pull out electrical plugs, which they inserted into sockets in the side of the shell. Each went over the other's work, double-checking every connection. Gerald opened another panel on the cylinder, revealing the computer controls—an array of buttons, joysticks and computer screen designed to be operated by a space-suited man strapped down in front of them, floating in the vacuum of space.

Gerald strapped himself to the side of the control unit, as did Gaston. He took a deep, shivering breath. His mouth was dry, perhaps from nerves, perhaps from the dry oxygen he had been breathing. He flipped a switch and the computer came to life, one screen showing views from video cameras mounted inside the shell. The other screen showed the status of the electromagnetic probes and the hole's position coordinates. Gerald looked over at Gaston, who nodded in agreement at the silent question. They agreed that all was working properly. And they agreed that it was time.

"Go to one atmosphere." He heard his own voice quavering with the cold. "Open the vacuum chamber doors."

The shell tightened to become as hard as metal, as air was let into the vacuum chamber. Once more, Gaston made a quick, skimming hand-over-hand trip around the sphere. With the air came some faint warmth emanating from the sphere, but they knew it would disappear once they entered space on the other side. But it was enough to keep them going.

"It's holding," he said, as he arrived back and strapped himself in.

They watched the video screens, as the large chamber doors opened. They could see the familiar desert outside the hangar and the blue sky that was their destination.

"Power on," Gerald recited, his voice recovering its steadiness. He adeptly pressed the large buttons with his gloved hands. "Vector entered. Propulsive field activated."

"God be with you. I love you," he heard in his radio, as static rose to cover the voice. It was Dacey's voice.

He pushed one of the joysticks forward.

. . .

Everybody but Mullins deserted the control room, flinging open the metal doors and rushing into the bright sun to glimpse the departing hole. Their hands shading their eyes, they peered toward the distant hangar, straining to see it emerge.

"I see it! It's there!" shouted one of the engineers who had brought binoculars.

The hole drifted out of the hangar, catching the morning sun reflected off the white fabric of the shell enveloping it from the other side. It floated slowly along the ground for a few seconds. Then it vaulted into the cloudless blue sky, effortlessly accelerating to an astonishing speed as it went.

From the small crowd came cheers and a few sobs. In the distance, they heard car horns and sirens as the crowds surrounding the base marked the departure.

Calvin Lambert squinted into the sky, watching the hole shrink into the distance, until it became a faint shining point, and finally disappeared.

Beside him, Dacey took his arm. The big man did not pull away and he did not look down, keeping his gaze fastened on the point where the hole had disappeared. She saw for the first time in the bright sun how haggard he looked beneath his tan.

"Your son will be all right," she said quietly. "He'll come back to you."

Chapter 40

"We've got an anomalous magnetosphere!" Gerald listened for a reply, but there was only static. He repeated the radio message, more urgency in his voice. Still nothing. His breathing was more rapid now, the shivering worse in the enemy cold of space. He pressed three buttons, to check the hole's heading and speed on the computer screen.

He uttered an epithet through chattering teeth. The data showed that the hole was careening wildly through space on the other side, jerked about convulsively by the vicious magnetic storms spawned by the anti-hole. The screen revealed it veering off wildly in one direction caught in an invisible magnetic vortex, then skewing suddenly away in another. How strange, thought Gerald, to watch such vicious turbulence in his universe, while floating so quietly in this one.

"We knew we wouldn't be able to communicate," said Gaston, floating beside him in the enveloping gloom, the glow from the screens reflecting off his faceplate. "We can handle this," he said through chattering teeth.

"We've got to. We've got to figure something out. We've got to. Maybe if we had access to the ground computers."

"You're sure this'll continue, that the hole won't hold course?"

"Yes, we figured . . ." He stopped to work the joystick to battle the effect of another magnetic burst . . . "that there'd be some variation in the earth's fields. But not this . . . not this much. I thought we could just set the hole on a course toward the anti-hole and bail out. But not now. Not now."

Silence was their shadowy companion for a long moment. Again, Gerald reacted quickly to move one of the joysticks, bringing the errant hole back on course. The video screen showed their target, the anti-hole hanging in space, a burst of blinding flame erupting away from it in a fiery expanding bubble. The explosion yielded no sound, but their minds echoed agonizingly with the horrific prospect it presented; the death of billions, the end of their planet and all its life. The anti-hole's burst of energy also forced Gerald to a decision.

"There's only one thing to do," he said, reaching down with numbing fingers to tighten the straps that held him to the side of the cylinder and putting both hands on the joysticks. "Ralph, I want you to go back through. Take the lifeboat."

"And leave you here?"

"Yes." It was a statement weighted with finality.

"*No*," answered Gaston. He took Gerald by the arm of his suit and turned him so that their faceplates were toward one another. They looked at each other through the thick plastic, across the several inches of icy, airless space. "You're the one who goes."

Gerald shook his head. "This is my responsibility. This is my—"

"You're a logical man, aren't you?"

"Yes, and it's logical that I stay. I know this system better than you."

"Gerald, I've got maybe a year left." He let the statement sink in. "You've got a lifetime. And you've got to help cope with whatever these things do next. You know that."

Gerald twisted his body away, back to the control panel. He grabbed the joystick again as the hole deflected violently off course. "I'm staying. That's it. I've got to make sure the collision happens."

"You know I can do that. And Gerald, there's another important thing, too."

"What?"

"You've got Dacey. You can't leave her."

"She's strong. She'll be fine." But the thought of abandoning Dacey left him as empty as the space around them.

"Besides, I'm going to stay here in any case." Gaston reached down and cinched his own harness tighter. "And there's nothing you can do about that. So, no use this costing two lives. How about that for a logical reason for you to go?"

Gerald twisted back around toward Gaston. He stared hard at him, reading his pale face, memorizing the features. After a long moment, he unsnapped his harness with cold-stiffened fingers and floated free, reaching out to Gaston and putting his arms around him and embracing him. The damned suit, he thought. To leave a man to die alone and isolated in a suit, not able to feel anything.

"Ralph, I will never forget you. I . . ." But he couldn't finish.

"Go on. Now."

Gerald waited for a long time, desperate to figure a way for them both to be safe. He could not. He simply could not. Finally, he pulled himself away over the surface of the shell, which now was soft because of the vacuum on both sides. He grabbed the tether attached to the lifeboat and pulled it over to the hatch. He unfastened the hatch, opening a large circular hole in the side of the shell. A hellish red-orange glow greeted him. It was the anti-hole streaming its infernal energy into the silent vacuum. But with it came warmth and he could feel the temperature rise in his suit. He was grateful. He would need all the dexterity he could muster for the next steps.

He turned back to Gaston. They both raised their hands in a silent gesture of goodbye. Tears floated away from Gerald's face.

Gerald unsnapped the lifeboat from its tether and guided it carefully through the hatch and through the hole. With a precise shove of his booted foot he followed it through, avoiding the edge, and back into his universe.

The anti-hole cast a baleful glow across the darkness, washing out the stars and moon. When he turned, he could see the small, beautiful Earth that was its target. Like a bubble in a gale, the hole sped away on a jagged course, Gaston guiding it unerringly toward the anti-hole.

Gerald realized he had only seconds. He pulled himself quickly along the length of the cylinder, finding the hatch and unfastening its latches. He slipped inside and closed it behind him, grunting as he slammed down the latches as tight as he could. The warmth. The blessed warmth. Feeling began to return to his hands and feet.

He strapped himself into one of two webbed cocoons in the craft, pausing to contemplate the tragic meaning of the empty one. He flipped the switches that brought a flood of oxygen into the lifeboat and when the meters told him the interior was pressurized, unlatched his helmet and twisted it off.

His first breath was a sob of thankfulness and regret and mourning for his friend. He almost put his helmet on and went back, but he remembered the logic. He remembered the cold, efficient equation that told him it would be useless. He found the engine control panel and clicked on the guidance system, hearing its gyroscope hum to life. He took a deep breath of the cool, clean air with the tang of warming electronics and pressed the firing button. A breathy roar filled the capsule and he felt the kick of acceleration. He donned the capsule's headphones and switched on the radio, wondering how he would tell the Earth that only one person was returning. But static filled his ears. The massive energy flux from the anti-hole overwhelmed any transmissions. There would be time later, after the anti-hole was gone.

He lay there, suspended in the cocoon, waiting. As the roar continued unabated, he wondered: Was this a lifeboat? Or was it a coffin?

• • •

Ralph Gaston floated alone, the only human in this immense, silent universe. He had known loneliness before and he had coped with it. He would cope with this loneliness in the time he had left. He checked the air gauge on his wrist. He had forty-five minutes of air. He smiled at the useless gesture. It was a good joke; one that Jimmy Cameron would appreciate. He thought of Jimmy and of Wayne, and of his parents, and of his sister. And he thought of all his friends and the good things he had done and the foolish things. This would be a good thing.

He turned back to the control panel. The monster was close now, burning and fierce. How ironic that its growing, welcome heat radiating through the shell also heralded his death.

Time to meet it. He pressed the buttons increasing the magnetic fields to their maximum. He reached down, took a last breath and pushed the joystick as far forward as it would go.

And the shimmering bubble reacted instantly, sweeping like a bright, silent comet into the alien throat. For an instant came a burning, consuming strangeness that caused a sensation beyond pain. Then nothing.

•   •   •

The masses of people standing in the darkness of Earth's night, watching the sky with desperate hope, saw an ethereal swirling light suddenly erupt from the demon. Undulating, luminous wings spread out from its hellish center to embrace the night sky. The wings seemed to fold upon themselves, enwrapping the violence, dragging it away. Then all collapsed suddenly into blackness, leaving the constant, bright moon and the shimmering stars. On earth, a precious darkness descended.

If answered prayers created light, that night the thankful planet would have been flooded with radiance of a thousand suns.

•   •   •

Now, the Soyuz space capsule rests on the 321-foot rocket pointed at the cloudy night sky, its frosted external tanks burdened with millions of pounds of liquid oxygen. The rocket's solid-fuel boosters wait silently, ready for the electric flash that will ignite them like immense skyrockets. Millions of computer instructions course through the ship's labyrinth of wiring, as the five computers coordinate the massive machine. The streams of data mark a steady progression toward its launch on a vapor-shrouded mountain of orange-red flame.

The one crewman settles into his seat, strapping himself in, lying on his back, methodically going over final checklists with launch control. He anticipates a glorious launch, a gratifying mission. He will capture the small white cylinder speeding toward earth, carrying history's two greatest heroes. The men had rescued the entire planet, and this spacecraft will have the honor of bringing them home.

Preparations for the flight have been meticulous as usual, and the prospect of the rescue adds a certain excited tension. But the time line is comfortable. The two men in the lifeboat have twelve hours of oxygen. Launch will take place in ten minutes, then fifteen minutes to orbit, two hours to rendezvous and another thirty minutes to attach the lifeboat to the spacecraft hatch and bring the men in. Then the heroes will return safely to a celebrating world.

Five minutes to launch. The pilot carefully checks and then rechecks the myriad of softly glowing lights, dials and buttons surrounding them in the small capsule. He calls up data on the three small glowing screens between them. The pilot checks the squat, black joystick between his knees that controls the maneuvering engines, and the square black knob on the instrument panel that governs the small reaction control jets that will bring him inch-by-inch to meet the lifeboat. All is well.

Nine minutes. The Baikonaur launch control computer assumes command, running final light-speed checks of the immense system. The computers all work in precise nanosecond-by-nanosecond synchrony. They agree that the thousands of valves, relays and microswitches are operating optimally, and that the Soyuz is ready.

Three minutes. The pilot stows his ring-bound notebooks and readies himself for the bone-tingling roar and the thundering ride into space.

Thirty seconds. The massive pumps whine to spinning life, sending a cascade of liquid oxygen toward the main engines.

Seven seconds. Thousands of gallons of the cryogenic liquid courses into the combustion chamber. It meets the liquid fuel and ignites. The gargantuan craft, flame erupting from its giant nozzles, shudders in anticipation of vaulting from the Earth.

Three seconds. A sliver of metal shears off a turbine blade deep within a pump and slams into a fist-sized valve buried inside the booster's jungle of machinery. At first it clogs the opening, but an instant later it escapes to slash a hole in a fuel line.

The ground-control computer reacts instantly, shutting down the valve, halting the launch.

A flurry of frantic communication takes place between the crew and ground controllers. The ground controllers tell the engineers. The engineers tell the managers. Then, the managers tell the hopeful world of the damage and its tragic consequences.

The fuel tanks must be emptied of their explosive fuel; the giant spacecraft returned to the Baikonaur complex hangar; the intertwined tangle of machinery disassembled to reach the damaged pump and the torn fuel line, and replace it.

The world learns to its horror that four days will pass, before the Soyuz can reach the small white cylinder, now orbiting earth, containing the two heroes. Four days until their suffocated bodies can be brought home.

CHAPTER 41

"**N**o!" Dacey bellowed the word, her jaw set, her eyes gleaming with frustrated anger. "GOD-DAMNIT, NO!"

"It's done, Dacey," said George, gently placing his hand on her shoulder.

Her eyes darted accusingly around the briefing room, taking in the crowd of Deus engineers, the long table piled with papers, the glowing computer screens, the telephones, the lists of options covering the blackboard. "No, it's not. We will not give up."

"Look at the list," said Mullins, his round face pale and somber. "No other spacecraft up there. No way to get the space station into position. No way to resupply with an unmanned rocket. No way for them to reenter the atmosphere."

"Dacey, the whole world's trying," said George. "Everybody wants to bring them down. They just don't see a way. We've just got to prepare ourselves for the worst."

"There's a way! Do you remember how Gerald always found a way? Now you've got to find a way! *Think!*" She paced the room, turning to declare, "There's the Chinese hole! A hole got them out there; a hole can bring them back. You already got the equipment."

"Dacey, we've ruled it out," said Mullins. "We've got seven hours left. It'll take twelve just to get the equipment to China."

"Well, then get it the hell on the airplane and get it going."

"Then there's the fact that the Chinese don't give a damn who's up there," continued Mullins. "They won't let their hole be used. Last time we checked, negotiations between the governments were stalled. Chinese government just ruled it out."

"Well, then, I'll take care of the fucking Chinese government," growled Lambert, waving his hand at Van Alston. "Who's the guy in charge of this Chinese hole?"

"Li Chang," said Mullins. "He's head of the People's Army Nuclear Research Lab. They've got it."

"Get him," Lambert instructed Van Alston, who began punching numbers into the cell phone. "Get the ambassador to put you in direct touch."

"But there's the time," said Mullins. "There's still the time. We'll just be bringing them back—"

"*Dead*?" asked Dacey, her voice breaking. "Well, maybe, but if we don't try, there's no chance. At least we've got a chance if we try."

They argued on for ten minutes, when Van Alston handed the phone to Lambert. Lambert stood, staring at the group as he talked. His face assumed an intense expression.

"Doctor Chang, this is Calvin Lambert. Do you speak English? . . . Good. Do you have authority over your country's wormhole? . . . Sure, I know there's a chain of command. But this is between us. This is business, Doctor Chang . . . Fine, then." Lambert looked over at Van Alston, signaling him with a glance that he was to carry out what would come next.

"Doctor Chang, I will give the People's Army one billion dollars for the use of your wormhole . . . Yes, one billion. And the hole will be returned." Van Alston coughed and went pale, and there was a collective gasp throughout the room.

"And Doctor Chang, there is an agent's fee involved in this deal," said Lambert. "If you can give immediate access, I will give you personally one hundred million dollars. Between you and me. Check with the embassy. They know me. I want your answer now. When I hang up this phone, the deal is off." He paused, his gray eyebrows knit in concentration. Then, his expression relaxed in a faint smile. "Fine, Doctor Chang. Our equipment will arrive in twelve hours. I expect immediate assistance from your people." He handed the phone to Van Alston who began a quiet conversation in Chinese.

"Well, that takes care of the Chinese government," said Lambert.

* * *

"I'm going after them and that's final," said Dacey. She sat back in the leather chair in Lambert's 767, but her body had remained as tense as a coiled spring since they had taken off from the Deus base three hours ago.

"Dacey, we've got other people with us who—" Mullins started to say, but Dacey turned away from him to Lambert, who sat next to her.

"Calvin, who would you rather have go after Gerald and Ralph? An engineer who may just bail out if something happens? Or, somebody who would give her life for your son."

Lambert regarded her with cool calculation. He knew sincerity when he saw it. He'd seen little enough of it in his years. "All right," Lambert said. "You're the one. But there has to be two going out there."

"And the second one is me," said Mullins. "I know the system better than anybody." He hoisted himself out of the chair and knelt beside Dacey. "We'll do it, Dacey. We'll do it together. I know I've been negative. I was just trying to be realistic. But I'll be with you, no matter what." He put his hand on hers and she smiled and patted it. "I'll go call George and the others." He rose and made his way to the office area in the front of the plane to contact the Deus base, where George and a team of physicians and engineers waited to support the mission. He would also check on the cargo plane that preceded them with the equipment.

They were still nine hours from Zhengzhou and the sprawling Chinese physics laboratory that harbored the wormhole. That would be five hours too late. They were acutely aware, as was the rest of the world, that in four hours, the lifeboat's oxygen would be depleted. Not until a minimum of six hours too late could Dacey and Mullins capture the small craft.

The scientists had unanimously agreed that it would be wiser to wait for the Soyuz spacecraft to recover the bodies. Lambert's advisors had told him spending more than a billion dollars was a useless investment. The President had asked the world to prepare for a time of mourning.

But Dacey would not give up. Her own utter tenacity drove her on. And she knew that Gerald possessed that same tenacity. Her instinct told her Gerald was alive and would somehow find a way to survive. She didn't dare voice this sense of a connection with him. She would only be accused of drawing on women's intuition.

Dacey saw that Lambert's face was haggard. He sat hunched over, stroking his moustache and staring into space. But he was just as stubborn, never hesitating to give most of his wealth to save his son.

"Calvin, I'm risking my life, even though . . . he may be gone. Maybe it's time you tell me what happened between you two. And with his mother."

Lambert took a deep breath and looked appraisingly at her, deciding whether to tell her. "Well, you've figured some of it out, I suspect. See, I was just this kid when I met Katy. Just this Texas redneck kid with big dreams. I fell in love with her harder than I ever knew possible. I courted her. Her daddy thought I was after her money, but God how I loved that girl! And she loved me, bless her foolish heart!"

"And so you married her?"

"Yes, I married her. Her daddy—who by the way wasn't exactly the kindest old man in the world—hated me. But we were happy. We had Gerald right off, and God did I love that little boy, too! Well, my oil deals were falling through left and right. Just couldn't get a good well to come in. I was broker than ever. Finally, her daddy called me into the library at that big old house and told me if I stayed with her, he'd cut her off. He'd cut Gerald off. In the damned *library*, no less!"

"What was so significant about the library?"

Lambert peered down the length of the cabin to see if anybody else was near. "He found out something about me I thought I hid pretty well. It was kind of a wedge he used, proof of why I wasn't good enough for his daughter."

"Proof?"

Lambert looked her in the eye, as if to judge her reaction. "He found out I couldn't read or write."

Dacey started slightly. "But you're—"

"Rich? Oh, yeah, I'm richer than six foot up a bull's ass. I'm damned good at what I do. But I never learned to read and write, at least not well. I had to work the oil fields as a kid. I kept it secret from most everybody. I don't think even the kid over there knows it," he gestured at Van Alston, who was laboring over a laptop computer.

"So, you left them?"

"Well it was either that, or Katy and the boy would've had to live poor and cut off from their family. I didn't have much of a family . . . my daddy was a drunk and died early . . . and I didn't want them in the same situation. I figured I had to become a son-of-a-bitch. Otherwise, she'd turn against her mama and daddy. And Gerald would keep trying to contact me. So, I became a first-class son-of-a-bitch."

"You cheated on her."

"Yeah, well, I'd taken to drink, so I just added women to my repertoire."

"You think you did the right thing?"

"Hell, don't know. I did what a poor redneck kid thought was right at the time. I wanted them to be as happy as they could be. Now, I'm not even sure my boy . . ."

Dacey saw tears well in Lambert's eyes. He turned away and fumbled for a handkerchief, wiping them away. He sat with his head bowed, one hand on his forehead.

"Calvin, we're just going to do what we can. We're just going to go ahead. Even if we can't . . . save him."

CHAPTER 42

The Chinese military research complex at Zhengzhou was a jumbled mass of weathered brick buildings nestled against a green hillside, ringed with razor-wire-topped fences. Passengers in both the planes flew over the drab factory-like complex about the same time. Lambert's 767 had caught up with the slower cargo plane, and the two touched down within minutes of each other on the long, stained concrete landing strip that ran down the center of the small valley.

A dank, cold drizzle fell as they emerged from the 767 to meet a line of six People's Army trucks and three black, boxy Chinese Red Flag limousines. Soldiers trundled a rattling gray metal staircase up to the 767, and Mullins pounded down the steps and away to the cargo plane to supervise unloading of the equipment. He gestured urgently at Megamag engineers emerging from the plane, directing equipment to the various trucks.

Lambert, Dacey and Van Alston descended the stairs to find a short, round-faced Chinese man waiting for them at the bottom. He smiled, bowed and introduced himself as Li Chang, and extended a hand, at the same time motioning his lieutenants forward for introductions. Lambert took the hand, but ignored the other scientists, immediately asking to be taken to the laboratory complex. But before they could enter the cars, Mullins returned, out of breath, satisfied that unloading would proceed rapidly. He, too, wanted to see the hole as soon as possible.

Lambert looked at his watch as one would regard an enemy. Their faces all revealed the grim knowledge that time had run out more than five hours ago.

The motorcade sped along narrow potholed roads cleared of traffic by army troops, who stood beside their trucks and impassively watched the limousines pass.

But an altogether different reception awaited the cars as they rounded a sharp curve and arrived at the compound entrance. A battered army truck blocked the road, with a dozen troops arrayed menacingly on either side, their assault rifles held at the ready. A squat middle-aged man in a uniform festooned with colorful ribbons stood like a chunk of granite in front of the soldiers. He extended a commanding open hand, bellowing at the approaching cars in guttural Chinese, his jaw jutting forward in anger.

"What the hell is this?" Lambert leaned forward and looked across Dacey at Chang, whose expression revealed a growing worry.

"It's . . . it's." He coughed nervously. "It's the colonel in charge of the laboratory. I had to issue orders quickly and he was out of the province."

"I thought you had control here! Well, settle things! Now!" Lambert looked at his watch again.

Chang opened the door and pulled himself out. He made his way forward through the gray drizzle to the colonel, his posture hinting at a vulnerability to the colonel's whims. Dacey noticed that none of the other Chinese scientists followed Chang, remaining in the cars behind them.

The colonel jabbed a pudgy finger accusingly at Chang, his dark eyes narrowed, and began to shout and gesture, as two soldiers grabbed Chang by the arms.

Van Alston sat next to the driver, and Lambert leaned forward and tapped him on the shoulder. Van Alston knew without being asked that he was to translate: "The colonel accuses Chang of treason. Chang has endangered a national resource, he says. He will have Chang shot. He will hold the Americans." Van Alston stiffened at the next torrent of words from the colonel. He turned around and looked at Lambert, alarmed. "He says he has impounded the equipment at the airport. He will order it disassembled to detect any weapons."

"Jesus!" Lambert turned to Dacey. "Look, you and Mullins stay out of sight. I don't want you hurt in any of this. We need you for the rescue." He flung open the door and launched himself out, striding toward the colonel. The rain increased and soaked Lambert, streaming off his head and shoulders, but he paid it no mind. The soldiers leveled their weapons at him. Van Alston, taken by surprise at Lambert's exit, scrambled after him, hesitating when a soldier pointed a weapon at him. But he stepped up next to his boss.

Lambert towered over the colonel. He bowed and smiled, and the colonel looked slightly quizzical for a moment. He began to talk, with Van Alston translating. The colonel stared fiercely at him. Lambert continued, making placating gestures. The colonel looked over at Chang, then paced back and forth several times.

The colonel made an imperious sweep with his hand, and guns were leveled at Lambert and Van Alston. The soldiers forced Chang, Lambert and Van Alston into the truck, which roared to life and swerved off the road into the compound.

A soldier sprinted up to the driver's side of the limousine and shouted something to the driver. The car accelerated behind the truck. Dacey twisted to see if she could make out Mullins, who sat in the next car back. She couldn't see him. She looked at her watch and felt an ache in her chest, a profound tearing pain of loss.

•   •   •

"My God. Twenty-one hours. It's been twenty-one hours since they went into the lifeboat." Mullins paced back and forth in the large storage room where the soldiers had imprisoned the Americans. Except for Van Alston and Lambert.

"Where is he? Damn!" Dacey stood at the door, debating whether to pound on it again. She'd done it three times, and three times a guard had appeared to brandish his rifle and utter what she took to be curses in Chinese. The rest of the engineers huddled in a tight, fearful group. At the same time, they stood ready to leap through the door when released, to do the work they'd determined to do.

The latch clicked, the door opened, and Lambert stepped through, an angry look on his face.

"What happened?" Dacey demanded. "What the hell happened."

"Cost me another hundred million for the fruit salad. Son-of-a-bitch made me wait until it was in his bank account in Switzerland. Let's go."

They spilled out of the room to see Chang waiting, a chastened look on his face. They ran across a rainy courtyard and into a cavernous old brick laboratory.

Two lab-coated Chinese engineers met the group at the door, but Lambert and Dacey continued inside with Chang, while Mullins began to pepper the engineers with questions, as Van Alston interpreted.

In the far corner of the huge, musty building sat a massive cylindrical steel vessel, three stories high and fifty feet across. From the unused pipes and valves festooning it, the vessel seemed to have once held liquid, but to have been renovated as a vacuum chamber. Arrayed around the chamber were clusters of control consoles and computer monitors that were less technically advanced versions of the ones at the Deus base.

Mullins, Van Alston and the Chinese engineers moved quickly to the chamber. Mullins continued his rapid-fire questions, the Chinese answering succinctly.

Lambert and Dacey remained with Chang, back far enough so that they could see the entire laboratory.

"Doctor Chang, your equipment is sound?"

"Yes, of course." Chang nodded. "We don't have as much money as you Americans. Not as advanced in some ways. But we have contained the hole and maintained its stability."

Mullins came up to them as the rumble of trucks could be heard outside. "Thank God, they didn't screw with our equipment. We've got a few technical problems. We'll solve them. Dacey, let's get ready. The suits are in the first truck."

Within ten minutes, they had stripped down in a corner beside a pile of metal parts and begun to don two space suits. For Dacey, the suit brought memories of the terrors of an alien planet, but she used the memory to steel her determination. She had survived then; she would survive now. Mullins struggled into his suit, which had been made for a slimmer person. But once in, he moved swiftly to the large airlock welded into the side of the tank. Fortunately, the Chinese had installed only one huge airlock with twenty-foot doors, so they could wrestle all their equipment in at the same time. The other trucks arrived, and the engineers hefted the three large packages to the chamber.

The time! thought Dacey. Almost twenty-two hours now. She determined to ignore the tragic reality, to push as hard as she could. She persuaded herself that each minute lost could mean the difference between life or death. She comforted herself with the thought that if there was a way to survive up there Gerald would figure it out.

They donned their helmets and breathed in the dry oxygen, moving to the airlock. Technicians swung the giant airlock door open and helped them fill it with the three packages—the cylinder with the guidance computer and battery and the two folded hemispheres. The doors slammed with a reverberating clank, and Dacey and Mullins watched the technicians through thick ports as they hand-cranked the large wheel that sealed the door. Their turn would come with the balky airlock, a mechanical arrangement of latches, unlike the Deus system of servomechanisms.

A hiss of air and a loud rattle of a vacuum pump told them the airlock was being evacuated. The rattle faded into nothingness as the air that conducted sound waves disappeared from the airlock. Now they had no radio communication, except between each other. But they didn't need any. Their desperation drove them to fierce self-reliance.

Dacey waved her hand impatiently indicating that she thought vacuum had been reached. Mullins held his hand up in caution.

"We go too early, we get sucked in there right through the hole." Dacey waited but a moment, then grasped the large steel wheel of the inside door and began to yank at it. Mullins relented and joined her. Together, they wrenched it around three times until the door unlatched and clanged inward, driven by residual air in the airlock. They caught themselves on the door edge to keep from being drawn in.

The hole floated before them, a shimmering star-filled blackness into another universe, bobbing slightly in the middle of a forest of magnetic probes aimed at it.

"Don't like that bouncin' around," said Mullins over the radio. "Hole's damned small, too."

"We've got no choice," said Dacey clumping determinedly toward it.

"Yeah." Mullins followed. "Seems stable in size at least."

A large wooden scaffolding surrounded the hole, and a wooden ladder inserted into it from the bottom, encircled by wooden hoops to prevent people and equipment from contacting the hole's edge when they went through.

"There's no way to lower the equipment into it," said Mullins over the radio. "We'll have to push it up through."

"Fine," said Dacey, and with a powerful yank, lifted the computer cylinder and hefted it toward the hole. Mullins jumped forward and helped, and they quickly positioned it in place.

"I'm bigger," said Mullins. "I can lift it up to you. You go first."

Dacey tested the ladder with a foot, then hoisted herself up and in a quick sequence of steps pulled herself up through the hole. She forgot about the weightlessness and almost floated away before she caught the last rung and stopped herself. The last rung held several ropes that floated in space like lazy snakes. She tied one around her waist.

She turned to the alien universe, gasping at a gigantic globular cluster of stars lighting the entire sky almost to daylight. She willed herself not to be overwhelmed. She cursed loudly to bring herself back. She could not let herself see any of this. She could not let herself be sidetracked.

She waved down to Mullins, who with a grunt that sounded in her headset, heaved the computer cylinder through. She grabbed it, and floated it away from the hole, tethering it with another line.

Then came the two folded sections of the shell, and then Mullins. Finally, they both floated free, using an enormous effort of will to hold at bay their fear and awe, concentrating on the task ahead.

• • •

Lambert paced outside the chamber, trying to peer through the door, but seeing nothing. The single television camera in the chamber now showed only the inside of the enveloping shell. At least they'd successfully assembled that device around the hole. He couldn't contact them by radio to learn anything else. The engineers hadn't even had time to set up the communications.

"God," he whispered. He'd not used that word much before. Never needed to. Now he did.

"Chang, don't you have any way of knowing what's going on in there? Any way at all?"

Doctor Chang sat with three other technicians at the console, his hands gripping its surface. "We will know by the light. The light they will signal."

A flash lit the screen. They had shown a light through the hatch of the shell. They were ready!

Chang shouted a rapid-fire burst of Chinese to a crew of technicians next to the giant chamber door. He turned and shouted to another crew at the large doors of the laboratory. Chang flipped several switches on the main console.

"He said to open the chamber," Van Alston translated. "He said to open the outer doors."

A loud hiss filled the cavernous old building as air bled into the vacuum chamber. At the same time, the rattle of old wooden doors sliding on rusty tracks marked the opening of the other end of the laboratory. A cold wet breeze swept through the building.

The crew of Chinese and Deus technicians ran forward, cranking the wheel to unlatch the outer chamber door and swing it open, then moving to unlatch the inner door.

"Stand back!" Chang shouted. "All stand back!"

The Deus and Chinese engineers all leaped out of the path between the chamber and the building's open doors.

"Christ!" said one. "This thing goes nuts, we're all dead!"

A deep reverberating hum filled the building, rattling the old windows and sending tea cups skittering off the console. It vibrated the very skulls of the people, and several grabbed their heads.

A sudden, deep chill seemed to suck all the warmth from the room. The engineers backed away as far as they could, gasping, teeth chattering.

The hole appeared in a cloud of icy vapor, floating majestically out through the chamber doors. It stopped and bobbled slightly, then continued. They could see through it to the metal probes jutting from the inside of the shell. A blue arcing light played between the probes.

The shimmering hole gathered speed, sweeping toward the door. It sailed into the gray twilight, and forgetting all caution, the people all ran to follow it. They almost missed the sight of the white sphere vaulting into the sky, bringing frightened screams and shouts from people passing by the laboratory. It accelerated into the gray overhanging clouds and disappeared instantly.

CHAPTER 43

The cold seemed a marauding predator invading their space suits and trying to take their consciousness away in its icy jaws. Dacey shivered uncontrollably and held onto the controls, and Mullins studied the video screens with determined intensity.

"Where are they, Andy?" She whispered it over and over, as if the mantra would draw Gerald and Gaston to them. "Where are they? Where are they? *Where are they?*"

"Computers say orbit is about here," said Mullins through clenched teeth. "No damned beacon. It must have gotten fried by the pulse, like the radio."

"I'll sweep again." She jammed the joystick over, instantly swerving the hole around and speeding northward across the vast mottled face of Earth below. If not for the emergency, she would have marveled at the stunning freedom of movement with the hole, with its total lack of inertia. Mullins checked the readouts to make sure that the magnetic fields were controlling the hole precisely enough to prevent it colliding with the enveloping fabric shell. One wayward movement would slice the sphere open, preventing them from returning to earth.

"All the damned orbits. We've tried all of them. Dacey, can we stand this much longer?"

"Yes! Yes, we *will* stand it!"

Mullins checked his wrist gauge. "Forty-three minutes of oxygen. It takes us thirty minutes to get down, get out of the chamber. Oh, God." He stopped. He brought his faceplate closer to the glowing screen.

"You see something?"

"A dot. Just a dot."

Dacey shifted over to look at the screen, waiting for the faint reflection of sunlight that would mark a small cylinder rotating in space. She saw the dot. She figured its direction.

"Got the vector. I'm there!" With a shove of both joysticks, she sent the hole whipping about, accelerating toward the dot. It grew into a blob, then into a cylinder.

"It's them! By God, it's them!" Dacey shivered, this time from exhilaration as well as cold. The cylinder grew, and they slowed the hole, easing it the last yards toward the cylinder until they were within capture range. Dacey turned the controls over to Mullins, who held station with deft flicks of his gloved, trembling fingers. Dacey, who was slimmer and more agile, would perform the capture.

She opened the hatch and was bathed in warming sunlight. She took a deep breath and propelled herself through the middle of the hole, trailing a line attached to the shell. She reached the cylinder and grabbed it, hoping against hope that she could feel some life stirring within it. But she could detect no movement. Her heart pounded in fear for the two men, but she continued. She attached the line and pulled herself back toward the shimmering sphere and the blackness of the hatchway in the white fabric shell.

With enormous care, she guided the weightless cylinder through, and as quickly as she could, she closed the hatchway and slapped Mullins on the shoulder. He shoved the joysticks forward and the hole plummeted earthward like a shimmering meteor. Heat radiated from the fabric shell and it swelled to tautness as the atmospheric pressure increased.

Dacey ignored the reentry, pounding on the cylinder's hull, trying to detect movement inside. Her mind screamed at her to be realistic;

to prepare for the sight of the lifeless bodies of her lover and her friend. But she rejected her mind; clung to irrational hope.

In stunningly rapid succession, the video camera showed the sprawling Nevada desert, then the Deus complex, then the chamber, then its door, then its interior. They were home!

"NOW!" Shouted Mullins.

"We're here!" they heard in their helmet radios. "You're captured and stable!" They shouted with relief. It was George! Dacey moved to open the hatch, as she felt the shell going limper from the growing vacuum on the other side.

As the hatch flapped open, they saw the familiar black ladder poking through from one side, a hoist cable hanging down from the other.

Dacey swung the weightless cylinder around and guided it through the hatchway. The hand of a space-suited engineer reached in to attach it to the cable linked to a small crane.

The cylinder slid away into their universe, suspended by the crane. Dacey and Mullins pushed themselves through, too, grabbing the ladder and scrambling down it. Three space-suited engineers strained to haul the cylinder into the airlock. They stood back, allowing Dacey and Mullins to crowd in with the cylinder. Dacey pounded on the cylinder and shouted, but still could hear no sign of life inside.

A violent hiss, heard even through their helmets, told them the airlock had filled with air.

Not even bothering to remove her helmet, Dacey knelt over the cylinder as hands jutted into the view through her faceplate, unlocking its hatch.

It swung open. Gerald lay wrapped in the webbing, his eyes closed, his face pale. Dacey sobbed. She glanced farther down into the cylinder. The other berth was empty!

Gerald took a breath and groaned, half-opened his eyes and formed silent words with his lips. Dacey tore off her helmet, ignoring the delicious relief of fresh air.

"You're alive! What happened? Where's Ralph?"

Gerald tried to remove the webbing, but failed from weakness and the clumsiness of the space suit. The hands unstrapped him and he managed to sit up.

"He stayed," said Gerald, coughing hoarsely. "He guided the hole. He saved us. He saved me."

Dacey embraced him and they crouched there for a long time, their faces together, overcome by the profound, warring emotions of happiness and sorrow.

EPILOGUE

The young shepherd herded his animals into a ravine that held a small stream and enough graze for the night. He tapped at them with his herding staff, loudly scolding the laggards, which sent them scrambling away on their stubby legs, bleating in complaint.

The sun had just set, and a full moon would soon rise above the low, grassy hills. It was a good night to be watching the sheep. The moon would shed a welcoming light that made it easier to keep a lookout for lions.

He really needed the light. He had heard the distant roars of hunting lions. And he'd seen vultures circling on the horizon, waiting for scraps of carcass from a kill. He stopped and listened intently. No sound of lions came with the soft, dry breeze.

He shuddered. He remembered once seeing a lion attack a full grown ram from his flock. He'd cowered behind a rock watching the beast's silent stalk, its soaring leap and its clamping of a death grip on the ram's throat with its powerful jaws. The ram had jerked and fought, but it had died. The pride had gathered quickly to rip open its belly and devour its body, chunk by chunk. No other animals dared come near during a lion feed, but the night had grown shining eyes all around revealing the presence of waiting scavengers.

That time he'd vomited in fear, trying to remain quiet behind the rock. And when the animals had dragged off the carcass, he'd fled home to tell his father of losing the ram. At first his father had been angry at his cowardice. He should have flung rocks! He should've shouted! But then his father forgave him, telling of the lion that had ripped the flesh from his back with its claw as he fled an attack as a young boy.

But tonight the sheep rested peacefully, with no sign of alarm, so the shepherd curled his blanket about him and squatted beneath a scraggly tree, opening his meal pouch. He unwrapped his dinner, a chunk of mutton that his mother had cooked when she made his breakfast. He chewed it with relish. His mother had bought salt, pepper and other seasonings from the market that week, and she was expert at cooking mutton to make it tasty.

After he was done, he bent and cupped up water from the stream with his hands. The stream was nearly dry. The drought had been severe and game had left the area, causing the poor hunting that made the lions bolder. He listened once more for the sounds of lions, although he knew that the stealthy hunters seldom gave themselves away. He had a good defensive position, so he settled back against the tree, scratching his back luxuriously to relieve an itch from a bug bite. That task done, he pulled out the half-finished wooden spoon he was making for his mother and his small wood-carving knife. His older brother had made her a beautiful, ornate spoon, and he was determined to surpass it.

As he carved, his thoughts turned to the pretty, young Leah, on whom he'd had a crush ever since he could remember. Her long brown hair, her big dark eyes, her lovely dimpled cheeks—all made him stammer bashfully each time they met. But she had smiled at him the day before! He pondered its meaning, wondering whether it was just a casual gesture or a sign of something more.

A sound! He brought himself back from his reverie and listened intently. Was that a rustle in the nearby bushes? He made a nervous whimper, held up the puny knife and his staff, and stood peering into the twilight. He held them both straight out toward a clump of bushes that he thought had rustled.

He cursed himself. He should have dragged in chunks of wood and made a fire. But he knew even that wouldn't stop a hungry lion.

The brush shifted again! Close by! Silently it parted, and he could see the faint gleam of cat eyes. The lioness emerged, flicking its long tail in anticipation of an attack. It held its great head low, its predator gaze intent, its lips curling back to reveal its fangs. The moonlight revealed its smooth coat with rippling muscles beneath.

He knew he was trapped, the dead-end ravine at his back. He shouted at the beast and crouched, holding the puny staff forward, waving his small knife. He realized with desperate fear that he had made a fatal mistake not allowing for the shifting evening breeze that now made his camp upwind of a hunting lion. How easy it had been for the lioness to find him and his flock!

The beast slinked toward him, preparing for a deadly leap, unsheathing its claws as it came. He could see that it was gaunt, had not fed recently. It was ravenous, vicious. It would not merely circle him to get at the sheep, which were now bleating in fright, scrambling against the wall of the ravine. It would attack *him*!

The animal advanced with predatory confidence that it could evade his puny weapons and rip into his throat to feed on him. He sobbed and prepared for death.

A brilliant light as bright as the sun blinded him. With it came an intense resonant hum pulsating so powerfully that it made his skull vibrate. He screamed and threw himself to the ground, believing that this was somehow the sign of his death. But when he dared to look up, the lion was crouching in fear, too, snarling and slashing at the air with its claws. He managed to peer up through the branches of the tree to see a brilliant sphere floating toward them from the sky.

Roaring furiously, the lion paced back and forth, trying to understand what was happening. The sphere wafted closer to the ground.

"Oh, God! Dear God!" he cried. A white figure emerged from the sphere! A beautiful white figure with a shining face and wings on its back! He cried with joy, standing and forgetting the lion. The beast backed away, confused, tossing its massive head, baring its fangs in impotent defiance.

And then it was gone, loping away into the night.

He prostrated himself in worship, as the shining figure approached and gave him its benediction. He cried in thanks as it stood over him in blessed silence amidst the heavenly singing of the sphere. Oh, God! Two more figures appeared behind it!

After a moment, all three turned and moved back toward the radiant sphere, climbing up into its celestial luminance, disappearing. The sphere floated skyward, joining the full moon as a heavenly consort.

And then it was gone.

He stood and shouted with exultant joy, celebrating the golden light and his savior! An Angel! He had seen a holy Angel! He had seen three! They had come from God to save him!

Now his life would be blessed. He would spend the night saying fervent prayers of thanks for his deliverance. Then as the sun rose, he would herd the animals home and tell his village the wondrous news!

So much was happening! His grandfather had told him of the time long before he was born, when the new star had heralded the birth of the infant who had become their Messiah. And now the Angels!

•　•　•

Dacey emerged from the vacuum chamber, followed by the two armed security men, and removed her helmet. As she expected, George waited to examine them. She shrugged out of the suit, and sat in her shorts and T-shirt, putting on her sneakers.

"My dear Mrs. Livingstone-Meier, I thought you were only supposed to gather samples," he scolded as he checked her vital signs.

Dacey shrugged. "That's what we were doing, doctor. But we happened to intrude on an attack by a lion. Luckily, it didn't prefer to stick around, and the potential dinner was rescued. Besides, he was such a young boy."

"Okay, but remember the old *Star Trek* Prime Directive we decided to observe. We are not supposed to interfere."

Dacey nodded in embarrassed agreement and asked, "Where's my own little one?"

"Your son is with his dad and grandpa in the control room. Gerald's teaching him astrophysics, Calvin, high finance."

"Well, as long as he learns geology, too."

She and George strode out across the floor to the open hangar door. They stopped to enjoy the panorama before them. Arrayed across the sprawling desert stood four other hangars, gleaming in the low morning sun. Each harbored a chamber, and each chamber held a hole. The steel skeletons of three more hangars under construction broke the smooth line of the distant horizon, rising against the clear desert sky.

George gestured back toward the vacuum chamber with a deeply puzzled expression. "Y'know, we thought this star system looked so much like ours. Same number of planets. Same positions. And now this planet. Dacey, that was another Earth!"

Dacey Livingstone-Meier looked back into the hangar, pondering the massive steel chamber, a quizzical smile rising on her face.

"Well, George, maybe that was *the* Earth. Maybe *we're* on the *other* Earth."

George chuckled. "And he thought you were an angel."

"I guess I am. I guess we all are now."

Read on for an exciting sneak preview
of Dennis Meredith's new novel,

Solomon's Freedom.

Visit *www.DennisMeredith.com*
for more information

CHAPTER 1

Solomon knuckle-walked his hulking body back and forth across the cage, the chimpanzee's coarse black hair raised with anxiety. This would be the day, he was certain. Abby had explained everything and told him it would be all right, but this morning the dread still haunted him. To shake it off, he stretched and yawned, peeling back lips to reveal the formidable ivory canines that helped make him the group's alpha male. His joints ached with the usual collection of twinges, and his muscles suffered their usual morning kinks. His great skull throbbed with its usual leaden headache from hard slumber. But all these would recede with the day; they weren't the cause of his unease.

With his body hair puffed out, Solomon presented a formidable sight, but he was an imposing animal even when relaxed, hair flat. His broad, mature face with its sparse, grey stubble marked him as middle-aged. But his knowing amber eyes, set beneath a prominent brow, glistened with an intelligence that had taken advantage of those years to achieve both wisdom and shrewdness. Although his body had grown distinctly rotund, his thick arms and legs were packed with muscle capable of hefting his weight with practiced agility.

1

The others went about their morning routines with just a little more grunting and activity than usual, no doubt feeling the tension emanating from their leader. Occasionally, they stole furtive glances through the cage bars at the pacing Solomon, also watching Jonathan for any clues of the status of the ongoing power struggle between the two big males.

But the younger, muscular, aggressive Jonathan gave no hint of his plans, if he had any, for the day. He sat stolidly in the corner of his cage placidly nibbling with prehensile lips on the yam that was part of the chimpanzees' usual breakfast. He stuck out his legs and stretched easily, grasping the cage mesh with his feet, giving no sign that only days earlier for the first time he had overtly challenged Solomon's authority in the yard. Abruptly, the ape had refused to pay the normal obeisance by grunting softly, hair flat, bowing down and covering his head so Solomon could tower over him, hair erect, as an alpha ape should. Instead, Jonathan had stalked up near to Solomon, stiff-legged, his own hair on end, notching up his challenge to Solomon's leadership.

As Solomon sat in the corner of his own cage, forearms on knees, he contemplated the ongoing struggle with Jonathan—one reason Abby had given for his departure. He examined the healing slash on his hand from Jonathan's own impressive canines, inflicted during the fight that had resulted from the young ape's challenge. Despite the wound, he'd clearly won by enlisting his ally, the fierce Bruno, to eventually chase Jonathan away.

Surely, the volatile Jonathan plotted to challenge him again today when they met in the grassy open compound. Perhaps he would give Solomon a bump or an insolent look, or issue a defiant hooting. And just as surely, there would be more fights, perhaps even bloody ones.

Solomon grasped the heavy steel mesh of the cage wall with thick, leathery coal-black fingers, hauling his mass adroitly up the side, nimbly swinging across the ceiling mesh into the high transfer tunnel connecting all the cages. The sliding door to the next cage remained shut, separating him from the others as the keepers arranged the night before, when the chimpanzees entered their sleeping cages. Today was surely the day he would leave, but there was no sound, no movement where the people stayed. He grunted uneasily to himself, as he crouched in the wire tunnel peering into the other cages at the animals moving sleepily about. Besides Jonathan and Bruno, the group included young Earle, the handsome female Sandy, old Caliban, the young mother Wendy and her infant, Wombat.

He could see Sandy best, which was good, because he found her deeply attractive. She turned so he could see her face, with her wide eyes and softly contoured jaw. He remembered their last coupling in the yard during her estrous. Despite their deep attraction to one another, though, they had their quarrels, too; as had happened yesterday when he had crankily meted out a slap at her. But later they'd made peace; he'd offered a hand as a peace gesture, which she took in her mouth as acceptance, and they'd shared a make-up kiss.

A metallic click interrupted Solomon's reverie. He instantly recognized the sound of the door to their wing unlocking, and he swung out of the tunnel and over to the cage front. He clutched the wire and pressed his large face against the thick mesh trying to peer down the row of cages to the open door. A low babble of unfamiliar human voices filtered through the open door. Solomon sensed that the whispered commands contained an urgency, a tension. The others began to grunt in jittery curiosity at the strangers invading their home. Jonathan, trying to advance his status as alpha male, began a low pant-hooting that grew into a furious scream, slamming his body with a massive boom into the metal door to the outside. The others leaped and swung about their cages in anxious reaction to the visitors.

But Solomon remained quiet, focusing his senses. Now was the time, he knew. He stared suspiciously at a shadowy figure in the doorway. It was joined by another, and perhaps a third. At first he wasn't sure, but one of them appeared to be Abby striding toward him down the row.

It *was* Abby! Their leader, their protector, the most trusted human in their lives. The apes danced and swung about with gleeful hoots of greeting or raucous lip-razzes to attract her cherished attention. But she merely greeted the others, stopping in front of his cage. Solomon pressed himself as close to the mesh as he could, studying her face for clues to the decision he still did not understand. The slump of her shoulders told him it bothered her. He wanted to communicate with her, to go to the machine room to make more talking with the touch screen.

But the long-barreled tranquilizer gun she brought up meant there would be no more talking about this. Now would come the needle-sleep. He retreated, whimpering, dancing back and forth across the cage in anxiety, the hair on his body rising. The others saw the gun, and their raucous hooting and screaming rose in volume to thicken the atmosphere with fear.

"Okay, Solly, we've got to dart you," said Abby. "Just put you to sleep for a while. Turn around, big guy. Let me get a good shot." Despite her nonchalant words Solomon discerned the strain in her voice, not a difficult task after decades of paying rapt attention to her every mood.

He hooted softly, in a question. Why was she so nervous? From beyond the door, the strangers' voices rose again, one calling, "We need to get this operation underway, Dr. Philips."

"C'mon, turn around," said Abby softly. "We have to do this. We have to. It's a good thing for you, Solly."

Still whimpering in anxiety and puzzlement, Solomon obediently turned his rump to her, knowing the needle-sleep would come with the shot, but also trusting that Abby would be with him. Abby raised the gun, trembling slightly. The gun fired with a faint explosive poof, and the sting in his calf told Solomon the dart had entered. A wisp of sleep fog began to curl through his brain.

Abby asked for the dart, and he obligingly plucked it out and shuffled forward to give it to her. His vision blurring, he turned to see the strangers walking along the row, their appearance producing a new round of frightened, raucous eruptions from the others. Jonathan pant-hooted his way up to another piercing scream, and Bruno let loose an alarm whoop, as Earle skittered about in panic, hair raised. Others cowered, barked or flung their large plastic barrels against the wall with clattering crashes.

But for Solomon, the sounds faded as the fog thickened, brought darkness. The last thing he heard was Abby saying in the distance of receding consciousness, "It's okay, Solly. We just have to do this."

www.ingramcontent.com/pod-product-compliance
Lightning Source LLC
Chambersburg PA
CBHW020216260626
47156CB00002B/414